also by michael drinkard

Green Bananas

disobedience

a novel

w • w • norton & company • new york • london

disobedience

michael drinkard

Thanks to:
The Ingram Merrill Foundation
Yaddo

The author gratefully acknowledges *Oranges* by John McPhee
(Farrar, Straus & Giroux) as the source of the orange factoids
on pages 17, 44, 119, 129, and 323

The text of this book is composed in Monotype Walbaum
with the display set in Kabel Bold
Composition and Manufacturing by The Haddon Craftsmen, Inc.
Book design by Antonina Krass

Library of Congress Cataloging-in-Publication Data
Drinkard, Michael.
Disobedience : a novel | by Michael Drinkard.
p.   cm.
I. Title
PS3554.R495D57   1993
813'.54—dc20   *92-36920*

ISBN 0-393-03478-X
W. W. Norton & Company, Inc., 500 Fifth Avenue, New York, N.Y. 10110
W. W. Norton & Company Ltd., 10 Coptic Street, London WC1A 1PU
1 2 3 4 5 6 7 8 9 0

For Jill

disobedience

a novel

"Here there will at last be a *happy* American-born race."

—Bayard Taylor
1825–1878

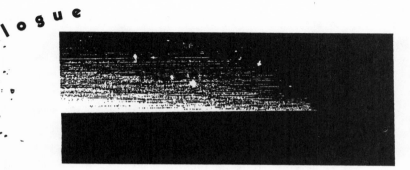

The mudslide crashed downhill towards the Wellses' split-level. Lightning flashed, catching in stop action the tumble of its boulders. There were orange trees in it, and marble headstones, and caskets.

"Dad," Aaron Wells said, turning from the rain-slicked window.

"Dad," said little Billybones.

"Copycat," Aaron said.

"Copycat," said Billybones.

In the backyard, one of the caskets crunched against the diving board and popped open. Though the boys couldn't have known, it was their great-great-grandmother's—Eliza Tibbets. Nothing remained inside but dust, ribbon, and a handful of mummified orange peels.

Franklin Wells, the boys' father, shouted, "Mom! 911! Mom!"

Grandma Goretex had Alzheimer's. She looked regal

with her gold lamé eyepatch and her telephone headset, which she wore like a crown. But she ignored her son's command. "Fraidy cat." Her good eye focused on Franklin's girlfriend, Caroline, who was dressed in a Lakers tank top. "I'd have given anything for nipples like yours," she sighed. Grandma Goretex used to be a Las Vegas showgirl.

"Nine-one-one, Mom," Franklin tried overenunciating.

"*Everyone* knows she never uses that phone," Billybones said. Grandma Goretex had implanted in her chest an Automatic Intermittent Cardiac Defibrillator Pacemaker that could be programmed over the telephone. "The Sony's only for heart attacks, and, like, talking to UFOs."

"Shut up, Midget," Aaron said.

"Shut up, Midget," said Billybones.

"Boys!" Dad barked. "Not now!"

The windows fractured, then imploded with a loud suck. Rocks and soil and an uprooted orange tree crashed into the house.

"Quick!" Franklin led his family to the master bedroom, the safest because it faced downslope. He shut the door and pushed a chest of drawers in front of it. Mud seeped under the jamb.

Caroline, Billybones, and Grandma Goretex sat on the wrought-iron bed, while Aaron helped his dad push an entire workstation up against the door.

But the frame split, giving way to a cascade of slush that rose fast.

It was cold and wet and horrifying. A hip-high wave swept Aaron to the bed. He climbed on, joining the others, except for Franklin, who clung to the TV arm mounted on the wall.

Grandma Goretex giggled at the sludge spurting from the central air vents as the landslide passed over the roof.

The electricity blew out. Amazonas, media goddess, popped to life on the television, like a misguided miracle. But it was only the VCR's self-operating battery function. Backlit by the screen, Franklin was attempting to wriggle free of the steel arm, but his sweatshirt got all hooked up in back.

"What's happening?" Caroline screamed.

Franklin had a vague idea: what geologists call debris flow. Anyone in construction, like himself, had to meet codes regarding just such "timetable disasters." The house was built in a floodpath. Lots of rain had destabilized the canyonlands and cemetery up behind the house. Landslides resulted.

But what Franklin had no way of knowing was this: Out back, the tombstone of his late wife—Mavy Tibbets Wells—bashed into the satellite dish.

He did know that her cemetery plot had no corpse to yield. She disappeared while hiking in the San Bernardino Mountains; her body was never found. After seven years, she had been declared legally dead, giving Franklin—who was never suspected of foul play—complete control of her inherited estate.

"Help!" Caroline screamed. The bed lurched and bobbed like a barge into a small dressing room, where the spear posts punctured the sheetrock ceiling. The decorative cast iron imprisoned everyone but Franklin. He was still attached to the TV arm. The more he struggled to unhook himself, the more caught up he got.

Onscreen, Amazonas was singing to dolphins; they sang back, but only one of them in English.

Suddenly, the house gave a giant groan, and the mud stopped. But inside, scum began to lather up.

"All your fault!" Aaron wanted to scream at his father. "See what you caused?" But he kept his mouth shut, kept his eyes fixed on the greasy foam, which continued to loft higher, inch by disturbing inch, up to Dad's neck.

Botanically considered, the orange is a berry, divided into 10−13 locules.

Aaron Wells couldn't resist watching himself being born. "Again," he said, sticking a hand out toward his little brother, Billybones. "Give me the control."

Today Billybones was Wolfspider, wearing a spandex suit depicting body segments, extra eyeballs, and a huge set of mouth pincers on his head mask. He scuttled away, holding the remocon out of reach. "I'm in charge."

"It's *my* birth." Aaron himself was barechested, his baggy surf jams crumpling at his knees.

It was the Fourth of July, the annual block party. All the neighbors' kids were gathered in the Wellses' living room. Their parents outside sat at the pool in styrene chairs and talked about taxes and recipes and the infrastructure.

"Come *on,*" the neighbors' kids said, staring at static, which was stylized by Atashakita to look like shooting stars, then commas, then stick figures, then static. "Come *on.*"

Aaron wanted them all gone. It was too weird, too public, this. Even so, he knew he couldn't stop himself. The temptation to watch was so great it was like something else.

Thumper, the big white dog, raised up his head sideways, barked once, cooled his tongue at the air conditioner, then lay back down. The dog had blue eyes and three testicles, the extra one——much speculated about and discussed among friends and family——an ironic guarantee, to Aaron, of realness. Anything normal was always suspect, or something you bought.

"I don't even have a birth," Billybones said, wobbly-voiced, angry. This was a sore spot. Billybones's birth was not videoed. In fact, his birth was one long iffy moment, and left him defective.

"Sure you do, Bones." Since Mom was gone, Aaron had to baby him; Dad never did. "Just look at yourself."

Billybones looked at his knees, then hands, and for a moment it was easy to imagine all eight eyeballs working.

"Come on!" the neighbors' kids yelled. "Don't bogart the god box."

Pretending the device transmitted some kind of beam, Billybones gunned down the whole room. Then he pointed it at Aaron and said, "Target annihilated."

Aaron absorbed the ray painlessly, wondering if perhaps some of his cells were being molecularly scrambled, and for a second, thought he felt it happening.

On screen several million red, blue, and yellow dots

consolidated: Mom in bed, naked, on all fours. She was rocking. Voices came from off camera: "Push." "There you go, Sweetheart." "Easy." You couldn't see her face, just her backside. It was kind of obscene.

"Dude, your mom was flip city," said Jimbo from next door. He lifted his sunglasses with one hand, and with the other fed himself a candied skull that bled red goo when chewed. "No wonder your dad iced her."

"Did not," Billybones cried.

"Shut up, Jimbo," Aaron said.

"I'll murder you if you say that again," Billybones threatened.

"That's so funny I forgot to laugh," Jimbo drawled.

On screen, a fire was going in the fireplace, and a globe hung suspended between polar electromagnets set on a bedstand. Attraction, repulsion, single electrons seeking bonds. It added tension to an already charged moment.

"I'm going to get mine surgically removed," Prudey sneered. She was fourteen. Each fingernail was Magic-Markered a different color, and the one on her left pinkie was so long it curled back like a miniature ram's horn.

On screen, Aaron's mother moaned and tried to get her breathing into some kind of rhythm. She continued rocking on all fours, gently, along with some music, a twelve-tone composition; eerie, like noise made from rubbing the rim of a steel bowl of water, no beginning, no ending, just an endless sort of wah-wah that you had to find your own melody in.

"She made up that song herself," Aaron said, suddenly remembering. He used to have the cassette, "Happy Birthday," written in Mom's slashy handwriting on the paper foldout; but he had lost it a long time ago.

"It's stupid," Billybones said.

"It's nice, I like the music," said Linda Delgado, the politest of the neighbors' kids. "It's nice." Face propped up in her hands, she lay on her stomach, flat out on the Navajo. Her ponytail was still wet from swimming, and her two-piece had soaked through her oversized T-shirt. "It reminds me of something."

"Ssshhh," said Brainy, twitching, squinting. Brainy was Aaron's best friend. Pale lips, a black bowlcut, and stringy neck cords. Brainy always stared, it seemed, concentrating. Permanently concentrating. He also always wore camouflage. Tree Stand, Mossy Oak, Branch Bark, Horizon, Spring Brush, Cattail, Full Foliage, Woodland, Tiger Vietnam, Snow, Blaze, Universal—he had many styles. Brainard was pathologically shy, but his desire to blend in made him stand out. Today he wore a Chocolate Chip Desert Storm Camel Flakvest. "Ssshhh," he said. His interest in the birth was frightening, but that was basically 'cause he was from a test tube, then cesareaned.

Suddenly Aaron's mother was screaming. It was painful to hear, but in another way it was not unpleasant.

Billybones boosted the volume.

The baby's head, squeezing out, looked unnaturally tubular, eyes shut tight, face clenched fistlike. That was me, Aaron thought; there I am. A confusion of tense, eternity, right here in the living room on the Fourth of July, and for some reason, the pleasantness went away, and Aaron's curiosity turned scary.

"Turn it off!" he said. But Billybones ignored him.

"You were so blue!" Prudey giggled, twirling a lock of hair with her pinkie nail. Seven years from now she would be famous, but not for reasons anybody who knew her could possibly imagine. "And what's all that gunk?"

"It's natural," said Linda Delgado in a way that began

to calm Aaron down. He took his eyes off the screen and let them rest on her. She was nice. She was pretty. And something else that was a good thing, peaceful maybe. She was ordinary without being normal.

Baby Aaron, coated in white mucus, was delivered into a pair of hands. Not into those of his father—a fact which Aaron completely understood, fathers weren't really hands-on about the birth experience back then—but into those of Josefina, the midwife. At the first human contact, he sucked in a lungful, turned crimson, and cried.

"It sounds like you're crying 'why,'" Brainy said. " 'Why? Why?' "

"Why?" all of them cried.

"Why?"

"Why?"

"Kids!" Dad called from the other room. "Kids!"

"Uh-oh," Aaron panicked. Earlier, he had lifted the laser disk from its hiding spot—the maple chest locked in his father's off-limits library—cracking the combination with Magneto Fingers. The ultimate crime. The chest was from Mom's side of the family, and contained important documents, old photos, and even a gun, as well as the birth disk.

It was against the rules to watch the home birth till Aaron was eighteen, four years from now. For as long as he could remember his father had spoken about it in mysterious tones. Sometimes winking: "Triple X-rated." Sometimes sadly: "What a woman, your mother." Sometimes as if it were the single most important reward for growing up: "You'll see, a miracle, you'll see."

Aaron's punishment would be severe. A grounding. Washing the cars all summer. Writing an essay with a paradoxical moral. Dad always made you plan your own punishments, which was bad, because if you were Aaron, you planned hard ones, then tried to live up to them.

But there was an even worse danger in being caught. It was hard to explain, but somehow, if his father knew Aaron knew, *life* itself would change. You can't watch yourself being born and pretend you're still innocent.

When the door swung open, Billybones hit STOP and the screen image dissipated, replaced by a show profiling celebrities.

"Kids," Dad said. His shaved head was covered with water droplets, and he held a bag of seaweed-and-carrot chips. He didn't look like the kind of man who would kill his wife, Aaron thought, then braced himself for the wave of guilt that usually followed imagining such a thing, but for some reason the guilt didn't come this time.

"What are you watching?" Dad asked.

No one answered, no one even looked at him; they all had on their TV faces.

"I thought I heard screaming."

Amazonas, almost life-size on the TV, was floating in a lagoon on an inflatable endangered giraffe and singing about drought and space weapons.

"The fire's ready, anybody for a hot dog?"

Thumper opened his blue eyes, wagged his tail twice, and began licking his third testicle.

"Do me next, Thump," whispered Jimbo, grabbing his crotch.

"Gross," said Prudey.

"Language," Dad said. "Come on now, that's language you're using."

"Sorry, sir," Jimbo said. *His* father always made him say "sir," and now he was in the habit.

"It's the Fourth of July, for chrissakes!" Dad said,

angry, but trying to sound upbeat. "What do you say, Spiderman!"

"I'm not Spiderman," Billybones said. "I'm *Wolf*-spider. Spiderman's *old* now, really really old." He was crouching on a chair and seemed to have all eight eyes on the television. "Anyway, HDTV is better than outdoors," he said. "Everything about it is better."

"Yeah," Brainy agreed, flexing his neck cords. "Machines edit out the stuff you don't need."

"I love her," Prudey said, gazing at Amazonas, who wore neoprene and lace, a crown of pearls, the antecedently curled pinkie fingernail. She was so popular, the show said, that she had the largest FNRQ, face and name recognition quotient, of anybody in history, ever, Elvis, Mao, Ghandi, JFK, Marilyn, Jesus. The *L.A. Times* ran a poll that showed more Americans believed they had a closer relationship to her than to God.

"Sweetheart?" Dad said.

Aaron hated when his dad called him Sweetheart. So did Billybones, who was pissed, about to cry as usual. Dad would only call Billybones Sport, or Kid, or sometimes, though with affection, Runt. Aaron wanted Billybones to be the son Dad loved best. See how *he* liked it.

"We'll be out right after the show is over."

"Good man."

After Dad left, Billybones hit PLAY.

"Give me the control, or I'll rip your face off," Aaron said, getting to his feet.

Billybones squeezed under the coffee table, popping up safely on the other side.

Aaron looked at the screen and was paralyzed. The placenta followed the umbilical. Dad had told him that Mom actually ate the placenta, like animals do. At least had a few bites. Dad exaggerates—but it was probably true. Aaron knew that Mom used to brew teas made from plants she grew in the backyard, comfrey, blackberry, burdock, and she never in her life shaved any part of her body. She drank only spring water, never took aspirin or anything in a bottle with a tamper-resistant cap, never ate fruits and vegetables at the same time, but plenty of each separately.

Blood and other fluids soaked the sheets.

Then a jump cut to Dad, young looking, gangly, wearing a designer sweatsuit and an old-fashioned medic's mask as he tried to caress the infant. Clowning, he shook the baby's hand, arm-wrestled, high-fived, made the baby flip the bird.

"Ahhhh," Jimbo groaned, as newborn Aaron groped for his mother's breast. "Gives you a warm feeling, doesn't it?"

"Sarcasm is, like, so Communist," Prudey said.

Aaron caught a quick profile of his mother's face, backlit, no real detail, as she ran a finger along a lock of blond hair, tucking it behind an ear.

The image turned him watery.

Billybones froze the frame. Made it go forward, backward, a step at a time, fidgeting, like a cat with a mouse.

Aaron's heart beat so hard his face hurt.

The whole home video had not one clear shot of her eyes. Another thing Aaron could forgive his father for— Steadicams weren't that common yet—but that just now seemed Billybones's fault.

Aaron grabbed him by the ankle, gave him a monkey bump, grinding a knuckle into his scalp. Bones looked so much like Aaron himself, the same droopy blue eyes, same way of talking, same yellow crewcut, chubbed-out knees, everything except the collarbone—Billy's so pronounced they called it the wishbone. Even their breaths smelled alike. Aaron knew exactly how to hurt him, and doing it felt good.

He wrenched away the unit, and held it just out of reach as Billybones began jumping for it.

After a few moments of this, Billybones turned and walked calmly to the TV, ejected the disk, and held it aloft. "I'll erase you."

You wouldn't dare, Aaron thought. There are some things you just don't do. He took a step forward.

Billybones Frisbeed the laser disk.

It caught the air and sailed, beautifully, aerodynamically, turning rainbow as it flew by the window, then silver again, a streak across the living room, until it hit the far wall and shattered.

"Fuck, dude. Wasted that disk," Jimbo said. "A fucking family of murderers."

Aaron stared at the pieces on the floor. The laser disk, he knew, multiplied, like a hologram, which, if broken into a dozen fragments, becomes a dozen complete holograms.

There are some things you just don't do. Aaron wanted to make Billybones understand this. Taking his little brother's throat in his hands, Aaron began to squeeze. Just don't do. Just don't.

"I told you I would," Billybones choked. Tears were running out of his real eyes.

Aaron let go. He punched his own fists together, hard. Clasping them at his forehead, thumbs digging in, he sort of prayed. The feeling was bigger than he was.

The concrete patio burned with the heat of two straight weeks over a hundred. It might go on like this for another month. Aaron took a sharp breath and dove into the pool, the crash of the splash outviolencing the shock of the cold.

Chlorine stung his eyes, but got up into his sinuses the way he liked. Pool water evaporated off his arms; thousands of tiny hairs there stood up and broke the sunlight into primary colors.

Aaron lost his virginity to the swimming pool, in the deep end, and so he was sort of in love with it. He had been resting at the side while under the surface the jet of just-filtered water gave him a boner. In the stream his dick felt hotter than usual, zingier, dangerous. He stayed until he couldn't stand it. Then a little longer. It was better than anything.

"What are you doing?" Linda Delgado asked. She was paddling around on a vinyl raft.

"Wanna see something?" he asked.

"Yeah," she said. "No. I don't know, do I?"

"Sweetheart, want to give me a hand?" Dad said, calling Aaron out of the pool.

Franklin Wells and Manny Delgado sipped their Amstel Mediums, watching the kids take turns off the diving board. Aaron watched too, while he husked the corn.

Linda Delgado, streaming wet in her bikini, stood tiptoe at the end of the board, getting ready to jump. She had only recently gotten breasts.

Aaron himself was just turning. It was true he was later than Brainy, than Jimbo, than most fourteen-year-olds. Twice last year, he rubbed dirt in his hair to get rid of that childish shine, to spur on the adult look, not greasy exactly, but not this baby shampoo sheen that signaled he was still a child.

"I didn't realize you have become so . . . potent," Dad

had said recently, wrinkling his nose at one of Aaron's tennis shirts. Then, on seeing his son's embarrassment, added, "Nothing to be ashamed of, Sweetheart."

But puberty *was* shaming, Aaron felt. His testicles were getting heavier. He craved red meat, the rarest, bloodiest cuts, root vegetables, chocolate milk. But eating only made him hungrier. At night he could feel his bones elongating. He woke up in the morning exhausted. Small painful lumps had appeared under his nipples. Kinky amber hairs had begun to grow in his underarm, in his pubic area, but only on the right side. The left half of his body was still kind of peach fuzzy, fine-pored. It was like something inside himself was hatching, something born voracious. Even his spit tasted different.

But the changes were explainable. He had read books, talked with Dad, watched PBS. Testosterone was rainbow crystals under the microscope.

Linda sprang into a swan dive. Aaron tried not to stare. Then he noticed his father was kind of staring, too, which should have sickened him but didn't. It just made him realize Dad had a private life.

Steaks, dogs, burgers, chicken, corn, and potatoes hissed and spattered on the grill. They were all hormone- and chemical-free.

In addition, Aaron's father sprayed the meat with Freehealth, a carcinogen blocker. It prevented the formation of heterocyclic aromatic amines (they had been proven to cause cancer in every organ in every species of animal), which formed whenever muscle meats came into contact with very hot metal, and of benzopyrenes, which formed when the fat in meat dripped onto hot coals. Freehealth did not change the taste of food, and, though it was itself suspected to cause cancer of the tongue in rats, it was less of a danger than the heterocyclic aromatic amines and the benzopyrenes.

With a two-pronged fork, Franklin served the guests.

"Mmm, four-star flesh," said Jimbo's father, Dr. Talkington. He was a cowboy plastic surgeon. He wore a Stetson and cutoffs. His wife was absentmindedly running an index finger through the hair on his back. "I haven't eaten a Q'ed steak in a steer's age."

"I'm with you on that one," said Uncle Brainy. Brainy's dad was not really Aaron's uncle; "uncle" was just a nickname. Dick Brainard held the patent for plastic pallets. His factory manufactured them twenty-four hours a day, three hundred sixty-four days a year. With his profits, he made fat campaign contributions to one senator or another. But, in the smaller, personalized world of the neighborhood, Uncle Brainy was sort of a kiss-ass. Balancing a plate on his knees, he licked each fingertip. The steak was thick, black, and still sizzling. "How'd you achieve the permit, Frank?"

"Don't rub it in," Franklin Wells smiled enigmatically. "I used a briquette chimney. And this *is* a special occasion, am I right?"

"Fourth of July and all," said Dr. Talkington, tipping the brim of his Stetson. "You're talking a two-year waitlist."

"Serious abracadabra, am I right?" asked Uncle Brainy, talking and chewing at the same time. "Am I right?"

Franklin Wells didn't answer, but put sunscreen on his forehead and felt good about people in general. He went to pains for friends. The pleasure in life was pleasing others.

"Hi Grandma, I just watched myself being born," Aaron said.

The only one Aaron could really talk to, Grandma had a Goretex aorta, a Teflon hip, a reprogrammable pacemaker, a glass eye, and Alzheimer's. You could tell her anything, even the truth. And, as fate would have it, Grandma was probably the only one who knew the true family history. Aaron was forever trying to coax it out of her.

"I filed a police report," said Grandma Goretex. She wore a long-sleeve silk blouse with hibiscus flowers printed on, and black silk pants with elastic ankles. A wide-brimmed straw hat kept her face shielded from the sun. Just to be sure, Dad made her apply sunscreen with an SPF of 124. She carried a palm-sized cordless phone with her always, in case she had to activate her transtelephonic defibrillator.

Though she was the only reliable source of information, there were lots of things unreliable about Grandma. Besides the imported glass eye, and the Goretex patch holding her aorta together, and a Teflon ball-and-socket joint in her hip, and stainless-steel pins keeping her wristbones attached, and saline breast implants, and synthetic hormones, and bottled oxygen for smoggy days, there was the latest addition: the PCD, pacemaker cardiac defibrillator. When her heartbeat went flippy, the defibrillator turned on, "like a mule kick to the chest," she said. "Whammo!"

Sometimes it didn't work, though. Aaron knew what to do in that case. There was a phone number to Redlands Community Hospital, where she (or someone with greater *presence of mind*) had to punch in her code. Then she (or someone with greater *presence of mind*) held the earpiece to her heart while the connection reprogrammed her by playing a series of tones.

The PCD was powered by plutonium. Grandma was registered with the EPA, a federal number and classification; it was illegal to cremate her. Dangerous radioactive particles would be released in the smoke. Greenpeace had petitioned to pass the legislation; Grandma had added hers to the list of names.

She put a dab of the coconut-smelling sunscreen on the tip of her tongue. The taste made her smile, and she sampled some more. "I don't count cards." After twenty years as a dancer, she used to work in Las Vegas as a pit boss, and later in public relations. "I look at faces."

"You're the only one who knows the truth," Aaron said.

"Not the only one."

"Besides Dad," Aaron said. "Whether he——"

"Van was not your father." Grandma sometimes mistook Aaron for Franklin, her own son. Van Galona, the casino owner, was her longtime gentleman companion.

"Now he wants to rip up the grove," Aaron said. "It just pisses me off so much."

"The calling game is a losing game. Raise to drive out other players. Raise to build the pot."

"Dad, you're not really going to plow up the orange grove, are you?" Aaron asked.

"Not this again," Franklin said, rolling his eyes. Then he turned up the music, opera, and said, "Hey, Runt." He led Billybones in a boxstep.

"Put that camera down," Franklin told Dr. Talkington. "I don't like videocameras."

"Oh, come on bud," Dr. Talkington said.

"No, I've had bad experiences."

"Haven't we all," Dr. Talkington said, rolling.

"I mean it."

Dr. Talkington stopped grinning, and put his camera down. "Okay," he said. "You don't have to get so . . . Hitler about it."

Dad continued dancing with Billybones.

"Do-on't," Billybones whined, limp spider legs dangling, swinging together in puppet-like choreography.

Linda Delgado sat cross-legged and began scratching the soles of her feet.

"Does it hurt?" Aaron asked, looking at Linda Delgado's peeling toes and chapped heels. In his heart, he'd always associated athlete's foot with athletes who had shoes named after them.

"No," said Linda. "Just itches."

Though the skin under her toes was chapped and peely, the tops of her feet were smooth and brown. Aaron's own were pale, veiny.

"It's a fungus," she said.

He suddenly wanted it.

"Bad air today," Dad said, red-faced, out of breath. He put Billybones down and clutched his own ribs.

Aaron liked smog. The brewer's yeast smell of it. How it made his lungs feel sharp and delineated, so he knew their exact proportions. The way it flattened perspective, replaced panoramas with views just like in a fairy tale, but grittier. In a couple of hours the sun would set, hot, pink, spherical, like a fingerpainting, unsubtle, heavy smudges of too many same-spectrum tints.

The opera climaxed.

Franklin gave Billybones one last twirl.

"I loathe you!" Billybones said.

Franklin kissed the top of his head and said, "I love you, too." Billybones ran away. Franklin turned toward Aaron. "Kid's having a hard day."

"Kid's being a fuckhead," Aaron muttered.

"Don't use that kind of talk with family."

"I only use it with family."

The joke about Billybones was that he was born during the San Bernardino earthquake. The second Big One in the series of Big Ones. But the quake itself didn't screw him up, the post-disaster Information Tsunami did.

Mom was driving herself to the midwife in Forest Falls when Highway 38 started whipping like a snapped rope. The asphalt cracked and the road ahead split. Mom put the car in reverse and, between contractions, backed her way down the Mill Creek valley until she came to a mobile home park where some of the aluminum trailers had been knocked off their cinderblock foundations and then rolled helter-skelter, crashing into each other. When the shaking stopped, retirees stood outside talking and laughing. Three hours later, Mom gave birth in the game room, on a carom board.

The trailer park was located under an artery of high-tension cables going through the desert pass, and between two mountain passes whose crests each supported an earthquake-safe Eiffel Tower—like structure. There was also a microwave satellite television relay tower.

The place already had a bad history: Brought back from the brink of extinction, California condors, hatched in captivity and hand-fed by puppets, used to perch there, but their radio collars got fried, after which they no longer turned up on monitoring screens.

The Information Tsunami hit hard. Aaron had seen

the AT&T map in his history text. Lines from Los Angeles streaked to Chicago, New York, Miami, Dallas–Ft. Worth, Philadelphia, St. Louis, Phoenix, Montreal, San Jose, all the major cities, through this geologic corridor. Charged electrons, radio waves, light pulses conveying bits of digitized info, image flows and soundtracks crackled through the cables and bounced off parabolas, generating so much friction and heat that glass and copper strands began melting down, dishes throbbed and warped. Scientists whom politicians branded as hysterics claimed evidence of certain high-altitude succulents actually having cooked in their own water content.

The *Redlands Daily Facts* labeled the event the "Information Tsunami," the first in history. Now they were fairly common, and protective measures had been installed to prevent them.

Billybones, the story goes, came out feet first, kicking to get back in. The umbilical cord was wrapped around his neck, and every time Mom pushed, his breathing stopped, heartbeat slowing treacherously. It was as if he were holding himself hostage, as if the condition of saving his life was not being born.

In the end, Mom won the battle of wills, but Billybones's collarbone got bent severely, and his nervous system, responding to the surging energies, sort of shorted out, reflecting a whole population's frenzied need to communicate. You could see it in his personality.

"They won't be ordinary houses," Franklin Wells told Manny Delgado. "It'll be a gated community."

Delgado sipped his beer. You are a white man and a polluter, his face seemed to say. You are a slick, money-grubbing, orange grove killer. A controller of nature. You are the devil. Even more horrible, you murdered your wife. "Sounds like you got a vision."

"An orange grove is a quaint thing, hell, my stockbroker's daughter is getting married in that one just off I-10 next week, but, Manny, and I think you'll agree, the past is the past."

Franklin Wells built this neighborhood himself. When they—Mavy and he—first inherited it, years ago, it was scrub and grove. Now it was a thing of beauty. None of the houses was older than ten, and each was constructed in a different style. Brainard's castle, Delgado's rancho stucco, Franklin's own split-level built on the site of the original Tibbets mansion, which burned down years ago. Each property on the block worth more than two million and change.

It wasn't just a neighborhood. It was practically utopia. Because there was grove involved, and a wildlife habitat—the olivaceous kangaroo rat, an obscure burrowing rodent—Franklin had to do an Impact Study.

So he paid for one. Paid for the campaign that got the judge elected, the judge who accepted the testimony certified by the lawyers he paid to certify the experts he paid to testify. There was a book in it, a book he paid the *Redlands Daily Facts* reporter not to write.

Then he paid a public relations firm to depict him as the environmentalist he was.

Only then could he cut and pour a concrete channel to help the arroyo drain the sure-as-clockwork flashflood, one every fifteen years, history showed. For added measure, each house had, on its north slope, a triangular retaining wall—like a ship's prow—made of recomposite high-magnesium Concreate TM, to moderate (or was it modulate? he'd have to reread the prospectus) the inexorable force of erosion. All this with a minimum of visual impairment of the canyon itself. The cemetery's land-mark status was, if anything, enhanced by the planting of fully mature palm trees around its perimeter. Leaving the fifty-acre orange grove had been his gift to Heritage. Heritage, like any worthy god, he supposed, demanded a sacrifice.

Now, however, Franklin was looking for a way to make getting rid of the grove appear to be a public gift. But the judge was going down in a parking-tickets-for-sex scandal, and city hall was a bunch of backwater reactionaries. And his son, his own son, was crying over a few goddamn orange trees.

"Manny," he said, pausing for effect, "I got an investment to protect."

Both of them looked at the terraces of orange trees that rose up the hill behind them.

"I am," said Delgado, "a sentimental man."

The music stopped and on the news it was reported that the Pentagon launched the first in a new wave of satellites, Operation Mosaic. "The satellites will combine surveillance capabilities with neutron lasers. Not only will this give us peace of mind," said the Pentagon's computer-chip, peroxide blond voice, "but Operation Mosaic should help stabilize the Lunar Situation."

Everyone looked up in the sky where a wedge of moon was barely visible through the smog beyond the tops of the palm trees.

"Fourth of July and here we are, just another country in decline. Never should have signed that treaty," Dad said. "What an embarrassment. Now Japan's got us by the *huevos.*"

"Japan and every other goddamn . . . ," Dr. Talkington said, *"civilized* country."

"The moon still belongs to all of us," Mr. Delgado said.

Richard Brainard hated himself, but loved his solitude. He hid out in the orange grove, rendered almost invisible by his camo. Even though it was desert style, it still worked. Crouching under a tree, he spied through a filched copy of Jimbo's dad's *Plastic Surgeon's Monthly.*

There were before pictures of faces hanging off skulls, teeth in neat rows showing through badly ripped flesh. Then after pictures of those same faces repaired. Not bad, though usually slightly funhouse.

Brainy scanned the party from his perch. He saw his father bowing his head and laughing, sucking ass to Aaron's dad. And his mother, constantly looking right and left, Where's Richard? Is Richard okay?

She worried because Richard gave her reason to worry.

Automobiles caused the most damage. A single eyeball, blue iris with a hazel ring around it, peering out of, well, hamburger. Richard studied it, tried to get a reading on the expression. There was none.

Splashing and music. Why didn't Richard like those sounds? He wasn't the same as other people. Happy people. What did happy even mean? Happy, happy, we're oh so happy.

Richard saw Aaron bouncing up and down on the diving board. That home-birth vid was almost as good as *Plastic Surgeon's Monthly.*

Richard slipped out of his pants. The air felt wonderful. He watched Aaron dive in, the splash going sideways, a bar of opera floating by on the breeze, and began to masturbate.

A little boy whose ear got burned off. They made a new one out of silicon gel and skin from his hip. Three pages of artificial body parts: eyeballs, fingernails, testicles even. A teenage girl who lost her face inside a power mower.

At the toilet, Billybones was already peeing. He looked funny, in his spider stance. Aaron began peeing right beside him. It was a game they had—sword fighting with their streams. Sometimes splashing off the side of the bowl.

"On guard," Aaron said. "Touché."

"Leave me alone," Billybones said.

Whoever lasted longest won.

"I said go away," Billybones said.

Aaron made clashing sounds, imagining blades.

"You think you're so great," Billybones said, suddenly turning on Aaron, sending a line of piss onto his knee and shin.

"Hey! Aaron said, but Billybones was already racing out the door.

A few moments later he returned, using both hands to hold a Colt .45. It had a long barrel.

"Shh!" Aaron decided to play it off. "You're not supposed to know about that." The gun was from the same maple chest that used to hold the birth disk.

"What are you gonna do?" Billybones asked. "Tell?"

The game was different. Overnight, it seemed, the rules had radically changed.

"You're not so great now," Billybones said.

Aaron buttoned up, dribbling. "Let's talk about this."

Billybones cocked the gun. "Say you'll be my slave."

Aaron swallowed.

"Say it."

"Eat shit."

Billybones pulled the trigger.

Aaron shut his eyes.

The gun clicked.

"Ha!" Billybones said. "It's not loaded, sucker!"

A single turkey vulture, wingtips spread like ten fingers, rode an air current. Franklin Wells looked at it and thought, Loss. There used to be so many. It was a phenomenon, yet never mentioned in print, on cable, or documented anywhere. The lack of coverage sometimes made him suspect this and other of his memories.

In another way, a very selfish way, the lack of coverage comforted him. In this day and age, anything private— anything at all—was sacred.

Whole flocks used to come when the sky was dirty and the tip of your tongue dried out if you spoke more than a few sentences. The birds, hardly ever flapping their wings, had black feathers and wrinkly, pink-skinned heads. They floated and swooped in graceful columns, hundreds of them, as if a single organism, looking for dead animals.

It wasn't the birds he missed.

It was Mavy, his one and only wife. Mavy Tibbets Wells.

The first day they set foot in the orange grove, a week after the reading of Mavy's grandmother Franny's will, the sky darkened above.

"Like something out of Shakespeare," Mavy had said. "Only more so."

Where did they go, Franklin wondered, blinking rapidly, looking at the single buzzard. All of a sudden, he had an overwhelming desire to go to the beach. He felt like looking in tidepools. He felt like having a moment of not having to explain himself to himself.

The buzzard swooped, attacking a smaller bird, a dove or pigeon, in midair.

Franklin almost never missed living near the beach. But when he did, he missed it fiercely.

A steak caught fire on the grill.

Franklin sprayed it with Freehealth, extinguishing the flare-up. When he looked back at the sky, the buzzard was flying away, holding in its beak the dove or pigeon, which appeared dead, by the neck.

Since when had vultures become birds of prey?

Mavy's body was never found, so there was always hope the truth would come out. Which scared the hell out of him.

Aaron ripped the gun from Billybones's hand. "Stay out of Mom's chest."

"I wish there would've been bullets." Billybones staggered away.

In the privacy of his bedroom, Aaron examined the Colt .45. It was heavy, with mother of pearl inlaid on the handle. It reminded him of something. Not Mom exactly. But Momness. He broke open the gun, looked into the chamber. There was a single bullet.

Fucking Billy.

He reinserted the bullet, snapped shut the gun, and hid the six-shooter in a slit he had cut into his mattress.

"Dad, you're not really going to rip out the trees to build condos, are you?"

"Oh Airy, this again?" Franklin asked, squirting lighter

fluid (a minor but thrilling illegal act) onto another load of briquettes—couldn't let a permit go to waste—watching the flame run in place along the trickle. The kid needed two things: a mother and a girlfriend.

In life, it seemed, most people got more than enough of one, but never enough of another. Franklin himself had to take a certain amount of blame. He'd be the first to admit—

"I'm sure your father will think it over very carefully," said Mr. Delgado. His eyes were also on the flame.

"Ahh, Manny," Franklin Wells said, giving the can a final squeeze, then capping it. "I got solar panels." He pointed them out on his roof, and nodded at the volleyball net made of interwoven six-pack webbing. "I've got good, wholesome business projects." His most recent included a company that recycled plastic soda bottles into fiberfill for ski parkas.

"Ski areas aren't exactly Earth friendly," Aaron had said.

"I'm doing it for *you*," Franklin had said. "You and Bill."

"*Superdad*," Aaron had said. It was happening all over the Inland Empire. Groves dying of thirst, trees drying up, turning dark and crispy—only after they were dead could the land be rezoned—then replaced in a year by bannered subdivisions, Orangewood Estates.

"I'm not going to *murder* it," Franklin Wells said.

For a long moment, everybody stared at him.

Finally, Manny Delgado cleared his throat.

"For chrissakes!" Franklin said, bristling. He took a good hard look at Delgado. How'd it happen that the man had no wrinkles? Franklin's own face was a map of them; a place with borders, a political history. The skin under his eyes was going fast, the veins there changed colors, and his eyebrows spindled and shot sideways. With his shaved head, classic chin, and beefy cheeks, he was more formidable than good-looking. But he was nowhere near young. The old George Orwell saying that a man had the face he deserved at forty horrified him, because now, in the wrong light, his own was proof.

"Come on now, let's have a good time."

He scraped his finger against the grill, burning it. Goddamn it, that was another thing: As you aged, pain began to feel different. Everything hurt worse, but paradoxically was easier to ignore.

He squeezed his blistered fingertip. There just isn't time. You find out.

Since fireworks were illegal, Franklin Wells celebrated by throwing plastic explosives into the gully next to the orange grove. He took one out of a brushed aluminum briefcase, pulled the pin, and flung it straight-armed— without bending his elbow. It hit the ground with a blue and yellow flash. *PBLAM!*

Aaron liked how the blast echoed in his bones.

The adults watched and seemed impressed, except for Linda's dad, Mr. Delgado, who, buckling his sandals, prepared to leave.

Aaron's father was wearing Tuscaro trunks and eye-drop sunglasses, which made him wide-eyed in the bright sunlight. Tan and handsome, by far the fittest of the adults, Dad made Aaron feel both proud and embarrassed. On this cul-de-sac, designer names bought distrust, and vanity in a middle-aged man brought suspicion.

"Want to toss one, Sweetheart?" he asked.

"No thanks," Aaron said. He wanted to confess about

the shattered disk, to be assured of—of what? Of an identity, he supposed. He felt a little confused. My mom is a laser disk, my little brother is a wolfspider, my first love is a swimming pool, my dog is addicted to the air conditioner, and my father calls me Sweetheart.

Franklin Wells reached into the aluminum briefcase and took out another grenade. Right after Mavy was gone, he had an interest in a manufacturing firm that supplied training grenades to the army bases in Twenty-Nine Palms and Camp Pendleton. He had given the military a good deal, and as a result he received a signed eight-by-ten of General Colin Powell that he was saving in the basement. He said it could be worth a lot of money.

"Here." He offered a training grenade to Aaron. "You've got seven seconds after you pull the pin."

Billybones made a grab.

Dad boxed him out by turning toward Aaron. "Let's see what you can do."

"Let Bones," Aaron said. Even though Mom was gone ten years, they were still competitive with each other over her. Aaron realized his little brother didn't understand this concept yet, and forgave him. "He wants to more than me."

Billybones wiggled his fingers, clutching for the grenade. "Lemme, lemme."

"Be careful," said Mrs. Brainard. She had tense dark eyes, black hair, and pouchy cheeks that felt like velvet when she presented one or the other for Aaron to kiss. As a kid she had spent an entire year in bed with the Rubicon virus. She said the experience made her interior life very rich.

"The kid'll do okay," said Uncle Brainy. He was tall and hunched, like a skinny giant with a long neck. "Let

Aaron throw the grenade." Uncle Brainy was eager for Aaron's father's approval, and would side with him even against his own wife. When you talked to him he continually nodded, and his own opinions were usually in agreement with yours. His voice seemed not his own, but one he wished was his. "Let her rip, big guy." But for Aaron, Uncle Brainy's need to be liked made him likable.

Aaron took the grenade. It was white, plastic, shaped like a pump-top toothpaste container.

"Me!" Billybones shrieked. "Me!"

"That's enough, Bill." Dad frowned. "Behave yourself."

"Go ahead," Uncle Brainy nodded, sticking fingers in his ears.

"Throw it, son," Dad said.

I'm your son," Billybones sobbed. "I am."

"Wait! I'm having a déjà vu," Mrs. Brainard said, rubbing her temples. "Wait. Wait. It's over."

"Heave-ho for chrissakes!" Dad bellowed.

"NO!" Billybones screamed.

"Yes!" shouted all the adults at once.

Aaron pulled the pin to make everybody shut up. Seconds ticked away. Uncle Brainy removed his fingers from his ears. The pool sweep hose squirted the BBQ making it hiss.

"Sweetheart," Dad said.

"I said don't call me that." Aaron drew back his arm as if to throw the pump-top toothpaste at his father. But it wasn't pump-top toothpaste. It was a training grenade. All the adults ducked or ran, except Dad, who stood there, beaming, proud, fierce. It was like he was happy that for once Aaron wasn't ignoring him.

Now would be a good time to teach him a lesson. Aaron

turned his back on his father, and gently tossed the grenade to Billybones, and in Aaron's mind, Billybones knew it was coming, simply because they were brothers. In Aaron's mind, Billybones caught the pump-top toothpaste grenade, spun gracefully, and flung it slo-mo into the gully where it went *flashblam* like the perfectest symbol of Independence Day.

But Billybones wasn't expecting the grenade, and he fumbled it, slapping, grabbing, and the strange thing was that he was laughing, for the first time all day Billybones was laughing, laughing hard as he tipped the grenade up with his fingers, into the air where it arced slowly, flipping over the concrete lip of the patio and into the pool. It barely made a splash.

They waited for the explosion. With it came a cloud of water. It rose up and hung there, sparkling.

"I'll be damned," Dad said, and everybody stared at him as if they knew he already was.

The first sizable orange grove in California was planted at San Gabriel Mission about 1804. By 1867 there were approximately 17,000 orange trees in the state. All Valencias, or *juice* oranges. Navel oranges didn't arrive until a housewife, Eliza Tibbets, planted the first one in 1885.

Franklin was going into marketing because he had an aptitude. But in order to graduate from college it was necessary to take classes in subjects that didn't matter. So here he was, enrolled in, of all things, Intertidal Bio, a.k.a. Beachology, no tests, fourteen scheduled field trips, write your own final marks.

Other students filed in and sat at long black lab tables. Franklin opened his textbook and tried to catch up on last week's reading assignment.

It was bullshit, complete and total, this class. But he needed the degree. His salary, if he got the Solvtex job, would be 47.5 to start. But it was the eighties, everything was booming, everywhere, especially Pacific Rim intelligence. He could be making thrice that in five years. By twenty-seven, he'd be pulling down six figures.

All week, Franklin had been interviewing with companies recruiting through the Packard Career Center. He still had three more interviews lined up, including one today after class, in—he looked at the clock—forty-five minutes. But he was pretty sure Solvtex wanted him. They could see he had an aptitude.

He ran his fingers over the knot in his tie. The creases in his slacks were holding up, and he had just polished his shoes this morning. Interviewers put a premium on detail. As soon as he could afford it, he'd wear only shirts that required cuff links. Onyx, not plastic, gold maybe. No turquoise, ever. Diamonds were a possibility, but as a rule of thumb you had to be in your early fifties to pull off wearing rocks. Or a Republican. But it was dangerous to be a Republican for the same reason that it was dangerous to be anything, on record.

"Is this seat taken?" a woman asked him. She had crazy yellow hair, and though tall, at least six feet, she had a teenager's face. In place of experience, it displayed an eagerness that was borderline goofy. It might turn pretty depending on how her life turned out. After a moment she said, "It is."

"No," Franklin said, and tried to smile. He saw she was barefoot. Her eyes were blue, uncomfortably bright, as if she were making them that way on purpose. "Not that I know of."

"Yes it is." She hugged her textbook.

"No, it isn't." He looked at the empty seat, then at her. "Really." Here he was arguing for what he didn't want. "Sit."

"It's just that you're frowning," she said. He realized she *was* a teenager, one of the AP high school kids. Six or seven of them were here. Most sat in the front row, diligent and conscientious, eager to please their parents, whom you could sense in the room (though of course they weren't), there in the back, not understanding the exploded views and Latinates on the board, but watching the backs of their children's necks, making sure *they* did. But this girl was different, wearing blue gym shorts and a T-shirt, and *barefoot.*

Though she wasn't fat, the chair creaked under her.

The teacher explained the sex lives of chitons. Sex, he said, was the crux of biology. If it doesn't reproduce, it's not alive. Chitons were hermaphrodites, male and fe-

male, depending on, the teacher speculated, mood, because, he said, if a creature could be both, well, then, that
changed the concept of *need.* "Doesn't it?"

The girl giggled. Franklin watched her out of the
corner of his eye.

Grow up, he thought. Get an aptitude.

The girl was not made for the lab, squirming in her
chair, eyes all over the room, big-knuckled hands clumsy
on the microscope but nimble on the chiton shell itself,
which she held to her nose and sniffed.

The teacher, a gracious man with a thick auburn
beard, crow's feet, and knee-high rubber boots, smiled,
and looked at her, unsure.

That started the girl off. She laughed uncontrollably
among the test tubes, bunsen burners, and buckets of
Monterey Bay water containing live plankton for microscope examination.

Because Franklin had the misfortune to be sitting next
to her, many people, including the teacher, stared at him
as well. He turned his eyes on the girl, making a face that
he hoped was nonjudgmental without being condescend-
ing.

"I'm sorry," she managed to say to the teacher. "It's not
you, it's me."

She was really immature.

The next week the class took a bus to Moss Landing to
study a rocky lagoon at low tide. Franklin went off on his
own so he wouldn't have to bother with conversation. He
preferred to be left alone with his happiness. He had just
got word Solvtex wanted him! What's more, they were
offering 49.5 to start, if he agreed to travel. Real money.
And so soon!

He told them he'd have to think about it.

If you didn't establish bluff credibility at first, you had to earn it at triple the cost later. He'd read that in a manual at PackCen. Playing Hardball, as a job strategy, was worth an average of 6.7 percent of the first offer. It was documented in a University of Illinois study.

Now, counting his uncollected sick pay from his part-time job washing lab equipment at Sparta, he already had scraped together about six thousand dollars in savings. Then there was the five thousand and change in the IRA he had established when he turned eighteen. It was good to start early on an IRA, because of the combination tax shelter and write-off, and because when it matured, if you had been contributing every year, it would net you a sum in the neighborhood of $300,000. This was tax free, by the way. No capital gains. Money saved in the early years of adulthood grows three times faster than money saved in later years. Anybody who grasped the concept of compound interest understood that.

Furthermore, if somewhere down the line you found yourself cash-strapped, you could always roll over your IRA and have access to your balance for six months or so without paying a penalty. Any fool could get one, an IRA, just like any fool could go to PackCen and get leads on a career. But people his age didn't. People his age perversely cheered the end of the middle class, the end of history, the end of nature, the end of the American dream. People of his generation sulked about downward mobility and griped about having to pay for the excesses of their parents. But not Franklin; he knew better.

In addition to a good salary, he would also have health and dental, and an expense account. Bonuses for sure. Other contacts, some free-lance ops. In two or three years there would be enough for a down payment on a nice house—modest, but nice. He'd be a homeowner at twenty-five or twenty-six!

Franklin waded into a tidepool the size of a small pond, feeling the water press against his rubber knee boots. The sun was shining, the air smelled like kelp, and the breakers crashed against the rocks, sending up little tornadoes of foam.

It felt good to get what you dreamed for.

Something bright moved through the tidepool. Hands on his knees, bending down to peer closely, Franklin had to admit that this class wasn't so bad. Oh, he had his criticisms, but what was this sleek, red, flying-carpet-like thing?

He cupped his hands in the water, which was cold— turning his palms immediately white—and lifted out the creature. Bright red with purple dots, a single undulation ran the course of its half-inch body, then another, and another, propelling it. Two feathery antennae waved calmly back and forth, tickling Franklin's palm.

"I hope you don't mind"—

Franklin turned to see the barefoot girl. She stood there, wild-eyed, teeming-haired, forsaking the boots everybody wore, sand sticking in patches to her kneecaps. She was wearing the same blue gym shorts.

—"if I share your, oh, I'm sorry. I'll leave." She lingered, probably wanting him to invite her to stay. Instead, he turned and dipped his hands into the water, refilling them. Whatever it was, the creature didn't seem afraid.

He wondered if it understood that it was in human hands. And what about Franklin himself, if he was living a life in the metaphysical equivalent of cupped hands.

Not having any, the creature probably didn't even have the faintest concept of a hand at all, much less two of them cupped. Franklin tried to imagine for himself what he couldn't picture, then gave up.

"Can I have a look?" the girl asked.

Patiently, Franklin offered his find. The girl was so tall, and her thick, yellow curls were unruly and full of knots. No way you could get a comb through them, though she didn't look unkempt or dirty or homeless or anything. She had a pleasant enough face, kind of smiley. Really in need of experience, though. You could tell looking at her that she wasn't yet capable of recognizing her own aptitudes.

Franklin wondered what his own wife would be like, what kind of car she would drive. Of course, that would be a while from now; he had years of unencumbered weekends to look forward to. But eventually he wanted a wife, and kids. Two or three. Cute ones, lots of snapshots. And toys. The house would be full of toys. They'd redo the entire basement and call it the rec room, or the playroom. Or just the kids' room. It would be so full of toys that you'd have to clear a path for yourself every time you walked through. Toys were important. No kid could ever have too many toys. Toys were a good thing.

Franklin's own first and for a long time only toy was an ice cube tray.

"Hmmm," she said, impressed. "Nudibranch."

"Huh?" he asked, unsure what she was getting at.

"Nudibranch." She put one of her hands on his, stopping water from leaking between his fingers. Very like out-of-a-movie of her. "I've never seen this one before."

After a moment, he poured the contents into her hands, and went to the far corner of the tidepool.

If Franklin stayed very still, the surface got perfectly

clear. Tiny hermit crabs lugged their shells across the pebble bottom. A fish shot out of a shadow, followed by several more. Under a ledge, Franklin could see a large anemone. Green, with pink-jellied arms that pulsed, seeming to grasp.

"Put your finger in it," she said. This girl wasn't going to leave him alone. She waded deeper, water climbing up her thighs, making goosebumps. Tiny blond leg hairs stood up and turned white in the sunlight. She took another step, and the water darkened the hem of her shorts. "Go ahead, it won't hurt."

He looked up at her and noticed that she was doing that thing with her eyes, making them bright, not caring how obvious. "Are you following me around?"

"Yeah," she said, matter-of-fact. She had a voice like that girl's in the *Wizard of Oz,* speech with an actual melody, immune to cynicism. More than enough might make you sick with sweetness. "You find things."

On field trips Franklin had been the one to spot several unusual specimens. A carnivorous worm with a red segmented body, whipping its eyeless head back and forth, needle-sharp mouthparts menacing. Sea stars. An octopus changing colors in flashes he was sure had to be emotional, camouflaging itself to look like sand, seaweed, round black stones. Once he waded into a lagoon where black seagrass grew, slimy and clutching. In it he discovered a giant sea cucumber, huge and purple, so soft his hands disappeared inside when he picked it up.

The teacher had singled him out, and one day after class asked questions about himself, stroking his scrawny red beard while listening to Franklin answer. Even his marketing professors—and he was one of the *top* students—didn't get so . . . personal.

He was doing outstanding work in the one course that didn't apply to his life.

"Aren't you going to stick your finger in it?" she asked. Now her shorts were almost completely soaked.

"No-I'm-not-going-to-stick-my-finger-in-it," he said, all at once, as if it were one long word. Then he sighed. "Look, I'm sorry, but I'm really trying to . . . to *look* here."

Admonished, she peered down at the nudibranch in her hands.

Franklin turned his eyes to the pool. He knew from the textbook (which managed to have a few interesting facts, after you waded through a lot of boring concepts) that sea anemones were harmless to humans.

Franklin wondered if the money was good in textbooks. A data base supplying company he had interviewed with, MassData, had a division that published textbooks, everything from math to multiculturalism. They offered him shit—25K—but that was for an entry level spot in their publishing department. Their marketing unit might very well be more lucrative. Anyway, he already had a great job lined up, at Solvtex. A fantastic job. 49.5K.

The way the light shone made it hard to see past his own reflection. But, underwater, one anemone stood out from the rest. Translucent green, salmon pink, rippling. Such voluptuous patience, such faith that food will come.

When Franklin touched a fingertip to a single leg, a half-dozen others closed in. They felt tacky, like liquid sandpaper, superfine. His finger slid easily into the anemone's single orifice, and the creature folded on it. At the first hint of pain, he was ready to pull out, but there was none. Inside was soft.

Franklin noticed the girl was watching him. He raised his eyebrows, waiting for her to say, I told you so. But she just raised her eyebrows, too.

"Happy birthday, hon," Eliza Tibbets imagined her husband, Luther, telling her. Instead, he said, "You can . . . achieve release now."

Eliza moved faster, and, since she was on her stomach, and the angle wasn't quite right, she began using her fingers, a pleasure that used to be unthinkable. But now things were different. Today, June 21, 1885, she turned thirty, and was beginning to panic. According to Luther's Harvard doctor, "achieving release" made the inside of a woman friendlier to conception. That was how he put it, "friendlier."

While behind her Luther pumped, suppressing himself, allowing "the saps to build," Eliza shut her eyes and tried to picture a baby in her mind's eye, but came up with her garden instead. She could hardly wait to get her hands in the soil. But it was Luther's lunch hour, and during this time of the month, they had to stick to the schedule.

Besides, she wanted this baby. As much, no, *more* than he. But what they were doing now could wait till tonight. It seemed a shame to waste an hour of such fine noonday sunlight. Her ocotillos and aloes and rock poppies. Her purple garlic and white onion and thin-stemmed celery. Her thyme, lamb's ear, and mountain sage. Each idiosyncratic and needy. Raising plants was its own kind of parenting.

Eliza doted on the plumless tree that exploded in plum-scented blossoms but never once bore fruit. She was patient with the fickle and dangerous roses; this part of southern California could produce vigorous thorns. And when she thought of birthday presents, she thought not of a baby, but of the "curious fruit" she'd read about in the Department of Agriculture catalog. Sweet-tasting seedless oranges with navels.

Of all things.

There was an illustration that showed whitecoats propagating these trees, discovered, according to the catalog, some fifteen years ago by a missionary in Bahia, Brazil. He sent a dozen saplings to Washington, D.C., where the USDA named them Washington navels. They were offering free seedlings to American growers. Free curious fruit.

"I'm sorry, Eliza hon." Luther stopped. Was this it? Had he remembered her birthday after all? She wanted him to treat her special, but not remind him time was running out. "I'm sorry, hon," Luther repeated, "but I must get back to work. Please."

He was telling her to achieve release already.

Eliza hid her disappointment in great bucking movements, pretending. She couldn't very well expect him to remember, what with his busy job at the Civil Engineer Corps. They were constructing that railroad line that would join Los Angeles to the East. It was going to slice right through Redlands, right through the backyard, practically. The train was going to change things, people said. The Chamber of Commerce had already put out new maps that called San Bernardino and Riverside counties "the Inland Empire."

Eliza gave a slight groan and relaxed. "Ready, hon."

Luther grunted, then cleared his throat. The place he had been was suddenly cool and wet as he withdrew. From her. From the room.

To help "friendliness" occur, Eliza was supposed to lie in bed with her legs raised for another full hour. She browsed the dozens of catalogs piled in the oak crib Luther had built. That was four years ago. Now it was filled with seed packets, egg cartons, and other gardening paraphernalia. Better this than empty, mocking them.

Orange trees are symbols of weddings and fertility in every culture, the catalog said, as if it were speaking to Eliza directly, because of their ability to simultaneously bear fruit, foliage, and blossoms. Turning the pages with soil-stained fingers, she stared at the fuzzy illustrations, willing them into better focus.

After Luther washed his hands and genitals, after he finished his chicken and mustard, his bread, his pickle sliver, after he shook the crumbs from his great auburn beard and blinked several times at his handsome reflection in the dressing room mirror, after he kissed her on the mouth, nicely it seemed, with feeling, after he left for the Civil Engineers Corps, Eliza leapt out of bed and put on her sundress.

Standing up made an enemy of gravity. But it was her birthday! Thirty! And she couldn't sit still. Besides, the sooner she filled out those forms, the sooner she'd get her trees. On the dotted line, she scratched out Eliza, and wrote Mrs. Luther Tibbets. It was necessary if she wanted to be treated seriously.

Also, she liked being Mrs. Luther Tibbets. She had

married because she was eighteen and it was time. Luther was twenty and no boy. He had a man's smile, a man's dark green eyes, and a man's hair. A full thick head of it, dark black, and deep red whiskers an hour after shaving. Even on his back, whole black locks she used to like to grab hold of. And there was a single muscle that rippled the center of his forehead when he laughed, which used to be often. The rippled forehead was ugly—she knew that's how most people saw it—but to her, it was his best feature. So unconcealed.

During the first years of their marriage, they took precautions. Luther wanted to establish a career, which seemed sensible. In those years, every sideways glance seemed fertile, the most innocent kiss, a simple stroke of his hand through her hair. Back then, every single day she felt female.

It wasn't entirely gone. Some aspects, like Luther's gentle shyness, would never go away. It was *Eliza* herself who initiated the new sex position. Learn from nature, suggested an issue of *Ladies Home Journal.* It's not necessary to visit a barnyard or to go on a safari, simply watch your neighborhood cats and dogs.

"Is this medically proven?" Luther had asked, a bit shocked, a bit nervous, averting his eyes when Eliza presented her backside to him.

"Absolutely," she lied.

For a while, love was fresh again. For a while, quite thrilling.

Until Luther's romance with the railroad hit. It was in his eyes, full with the weight of this iron mistress. It was in his skin, always wet and a little frothy, as if the man sweated soap.

Now their babymaking attempts were mechanical.

They had goal-oriented intercourse, by appointment. The baby had taken them from themselves.

As a result, there were no longer many bashful surprises. They didn't wait on formalities. In the stark midday sun she could look at his nakedness and feel nothing compelling, except for a mild amusement at just how purple his erection was, and feel disappointment that his rather small testicles weren't doing the job. And he, she was certain, was long past approaching her as a romantic partner, and now looked upon her not as a lover, but as a problem of civil engineering.

During her period, he never touched her. "Point is," he'd lie, "let the potencies build."

But late at night, beside her in bed, while another lost chance flowed out of her, messily, crampingly, Luther would lie beside her until he thought she was asleep. Then he would touch himself in slow measured strokes, holding his breath, squeaking. Her fluids and his, leaking out under the same bedspread, but never mixing. This was the worst kind of loneliness.

It was the policy of Luther's Engineering Department to buy a block of tickets to the annual firemen's pancake breakfast. "In the brotherhood of civil service," said Bob Gosse, the district manager.

And Luther liked going. He liked pancakes. He liked the firemen. He liked showing off his wife's fine figure. Most of all he liked the good name he'd earned with his record of perfect attendance. Gosse took notice who was present and who was not. And Luther was due for a promotion.

"Don't get up," said Gosse, approaching the Tibbetses' picnic table. He pumped Luther's hand, but eyed his plate. Then, tipping his hat to Eliza, said, "A stack like that will surely turn your husband into a lumberjack." His gaze flickered for the barest second on her tight-bodiced dress. "Ma'am. You look positively radiant."

"Why thank you, Mr. Gosse," Eliza said, flushing, though not at the compliment.

"Eat hearty, Tibbets," Gosse winked. "If you know what I mean."

"Cripes, Luther!" Eliza said, after the hunch-necked man waddled away. "What have you told him?"

Rather than explain, Luther forked up another bite of syrup-drenched pancake, and another.

On his second trip to the buffet line, he overheard plump firemen's wives' conspiring whispers.

"Who does she think she is?"

"Wearing such a thing."

They were frowning at *Eliza*.

"Practically spilling out the top."

"Vulgar as a—"

"As a—"

"A daughter of joy—"

"An *engineer*'s wife."

"They don't believe in God."

"Engineers."

"I should say not."

"Childless too, on account of the husband."

"District Manager Gosse said as much."

"The man can't *provide*."

"Oh my."

Back at the table, Luther cleared his throat, as if to say something to Eliza, but then decided against it.

He wanted what he didn't have—what came so easily to others. He wanted to impress most those he most despised.

Jimbo stood next to the pool on a tin-bright, hundred-and-thirteen-degree afternoon, and grabbed his crotch. "Prudey," he sighed, and his eyes filled with impossible tenderness.

Brainy rubbed himself with coconut oil. His parents were in Paris, so he was using their absence as a chance to forgo the SPF 124, and get a tan. Already his skin was turning pink. "I'm hungry." He stood up and left the pool area.

Aaron sat on the diving board, dangling his toes in the water, watching the glare ripples expand, reflect as sine waves on the plaster bottom, and collide with each other. No matter how chaotic seeming, there was always a pattern.

Brainy returned carrying a bottle of ketchup, a six-pack of orange soda, and a dozen eggs. He squirted coconut oil on the patio, smeared it around with his fingers, applying the extra to his shoulders and nose.

"She's so . . . *innocent,*" Jimbo said, as if innocence was the highest law. Aaron knew otherwise; in Prudey's case it was an act, a survival skill. Jimbo cupped his hand and held his fingers together. "Her sex," he said without a trace of irony, "is so . . ." The poetry didn't come, so he made a kissing sound.

Aaron sat extremely still, conscious of his breathing, of the smell of the ripe loquats, of the heat waves rising off the patio, of himself being a virgin. The hot brown sky sucked the sweat right out of his pores, keeping him weirdly dry.

Brainy cracked open an egg, carefully let it slip from the shell to the cement. It didn't spatter, but immediately turned white around the edges. "Want one?" he asked Aaron.

Aaron nodded, held up an index finger.

"Yeah, I'll take a couple," said Jimbo, displaying a middle finger from each hand.

Brainy started several more.

"She's so lovable," Jimbo said. "But I think I'm too big for her."

Brainy looked up from the eggs.

"It didn't fit," Jimbo said, clutching his genitals. When he got talking, the talking took over. "I mean, it did, but just barely."

Aaron watched as Brainy pulled a blade from a squat yucca plant. The blade was green with hard yellow edges. Brainy used it as a spatula, turning the eggs without breaking a single yoke.

"I guess I have a bigger than normal dick," Jimbo said.

Brainy served the eggs on baby palm fronds, green, accordion-like. The three of them ate with their fingers, Brainy using lots of ketchup.

The sun-fried egg was good, Aaron decided, tasting of coconut. He drank the orange soda in a single gulp.

It hadn't even started out as a date.

Franklin's car needed a new clutch so he had dropped it off at the mechanic, then, since he was downtown, he took care of some other errands. By Playing Hardball, Franklin had got Solvtex to up their offer by 18 percent, almost three times the percentage claimed in the University of Illinois study—58.9K. Just like that, 58.9K.

He stepped out of Gairs with two brand-new suits—off the rack but tailor-fitted—and onto the sidewalk, where Mavy practically crashed into him. Her rollerblades had lime-green wheels. They made her thighs stay flexed.

She invited him for lemonade. "I live right around the corner."

"How old are you?" he asked. When she didn't answer, he added, "I didn't mean it that way."

"Sixteen," she said.

"I'm twenty-two," he said, hoping to sound conciliatory, but it came off like bragging.

Maybe it was the hot sun mixed with a Pacific breeze, or her thighs, or the car repair bills, or 58.9K, whatever the reason, he was thirsty. "I haven't had lemonade," he told her, "in a long, long time."

Her apartment was a cheap stucco box in a multi-unit complex landscaped with gravel and potted hibiscus with black spot disease. Indoors smelled like roses and mildew. The rooms were square, the fixtures plastic, and the windows small with fat-pleated curtains. The walls were so thin you could hear sinks running, toilets flushing, Bob Dylan.

"How many sixteen-year-olds have their own place?" Franklin asked. He laid his garment bags on the couch, plaid, institutional, battered. Dried flowers were everywhere: bowls of them on windowsills, lavender and baby's breath and wild roses, marigold wreaths, a garlic braid hanging under a kitchen cabinet. Mobiles made from rosebuds and seashells hung from ceiling hooks. Each object spun in its own slow orbit.

Mavy sat on a crate to unlace her skates, and took a long time doing it. "I wanted my own place, and my parents said good idea." She explained how she had entered a special program in high school, SWAS, "school within a school," from which she would graduate a half year early, next December. "I have a problem with authority." Skates finally off, she jumped up and disappeared.

Left alone, Franklin eyed the thumbtacked antique magazine posters. Ladies in furs, evening gowns, formal dresses. Ladies with cigarette holders, high heels, parasols. Ladies with tiny coiffed dogs on rhinestone leashes.

"They're by my grandmother," she said, coming back into the room with a pitcher of lemonade and two glasses. "She's from New York."

"Grandmother?" Franklin asked, not so interested in the pictures themselves, but that they were commissioned by *Vogue*. Examples of commercial success held him spellbound.

58.9K, he thought.

"Sex," Mavy said, pointing out how a pair of dogs on a leash could be seen as testicles, the tall thin woman herself a phallus.

She poured the lemonade. The crack and split of the ice cubes made Franklin realize how thirsty he was.

58.9K.

For dinner they ate raw spinach and tomatoes with smelly cheese on whole-wheat sesame crackers, and drank more lemonade. She told him about growing up in Big Sur. Her father used to be a blacksmith, but in his spare time he wrote a book. *"Ripcord."*

"Ripcord? Your father wrote *Ripcord?"*

"Mmmm," she said.

Ripcord was huge in the seventies. The movie had quickly turned into sort of a cultural artifact, and now the local independent cinema played an occasional run of midnight showings.

"I never met anybody," Franklin said. Bernal Tibbets must have made a fortune off *Ripcord.* That this girl came from a family of *Ripcord* and *Vogue* people deeply, deeply impressed him.

"He's blocked now," she said. "He's been blocked for ten years." Her mother was a software theorist. "Before computers she was serious into TV." Their house was on some really beautiful coastline, in Garapata Canyon, made of redwood, glass, and, of course, since Bernal used to be a blacksmith, lots of cast iron.

The more lemonade Franklin drank, the thirstier he became.

Bob Dylan still came through the walls, and, as the hours passed, his tone grew more plaintive, more urgent. *Knocking on Heaven's Door.* There were other sounds, electronic beeping, somebody sneezing.

"How about your parents?" Mavy asked. "What do they do?"

Franklin slurped at his melted ice cubes. "My mom was a dancer and my dad I never knew him."

She didn't say anything.

He stood up. It was late, almost midnight, and he was exhausted. The last bus would pass shortly. "Well, I guess—"

"Stay," she said. Then, noticing his surprise, added, "You can sleep on the couch."

He stared at it, battered, institutional, plaid. Bob Dylan sang on and on. A dog barked once. "No thanks, really." They shook hands goodnight.

"Like a modern dancer?" Mavy asked, suddenly, as he stood in the doorway. "Your mother? I saw some Martha Graham in New York once." For a moment they both looked at the *Vogue* posters on the wall.

"Las Vegas," Franklin said, blushing.

They shook hands again.

Outside was cold. The bus was late. Maybe it had already come and left. No, it couldn't have. Franklin unzipped his garment bag and put on an extra suit jacket. Still chilled, he pulled the pair of baggy suit trousers over the ones he was already wearing. So what if he never knew his father? He had aptitude. So what if his mother was an ex-can can girl? She didn't regret it. So what if his first and for a long time only toy had been an ice cube tray. Hadn't he turned it into a dinosaur, a train, a traffic jam, the Panama Canal, 58.9K?

Still the bus didn't come. He found himself looking for signs in every pair of headlights. If it's the bus, I'm lucky; just a car will build character.

He was ashamed of himself for being ashamed of his mother. He was ashamed of his mother for not being ashamed of herself. Of course, she didn't recognize his self-pride either. In fact, she disapproved of him. "Material comfort and social standing," she had said, barely a pinprick of irony. "Damn fine things."

A group of teenagers riding by in a Camaro threw half-full beer cans at him, several finding their mark, hitting his chest and back.

"Power breakfast!" they shouted. "Junk bonds!"

"Losers!" he screamed, his jacket soaked, his shoulder blade, where an especially heavy can had hit him, aching. "Fucking Camaro assholes." The Camaro was rated very low by *Consumer Reports,* its handling and reliability chart cursed with black dots. When he saw the car's brake lights go on, he buttoned his jacket and tugged on the cuffs to get a better fit. 58.9K.

A patrol car, its engine low and throbbing, cruised up. A spotlight shone, blinding him. The policemen got out and approached him.

"There's a car full of kids causing trouble." Franklin pointed. "In that Camaro."

Squinting as it disappeared around a bend, one of the police officers turned to Franklin, sniffed, and asked him for ID. He was strange-looking for a cop, large pink cheeks, big pink earlobes, and lank yellow hair that curled at his fat pink neck. "You had a few, pardner?"

"Those kids threw beer cans at me," Franklin said. "Open container. Underage."

The other cop, a woman, approached him. She was heavyset, her shape muted by panels of bulletproof Kevlar and elastic knit heavy-gauge polyester. She wore mascara and eyeshadow underneath bulletproof glasses. Her black hair was chopped flat. Automatically, Franklin sized her up, and decided if he really was a criminal, he could get the best of her physically.

She looked him up and down, at his layered suits. "Sir, your ID please."

"You want *my* ID?" Then, knowing it was a mistake,

but not being able to stop himself, he snapped, *"They're the DUIs."*

When he stuck a hand in his pocket, the woman cop shoved Franklin against the hood, kicked his legs apart, ripping the neatly stitched seam of his trousers. He could feel her breath on the back of his neck; it was cold, and smelled like dishwashing liquid. The pink-cheeked man frisked him gently. Leaving him cuffed at the side of the car, they went back to the car to use the radio. The last bus of the night came and went.

Fifteen minutes later the woman released him, giving him a final push. "Sorry, sir," she said, "for any inconvenience."

He repeated their badge numbers aloud, trying to memorize them. Cops had an extraordinarily high rate of divorce and substance abuse. The nature of their jobs made them see the worst sides of people. That's where they looked first. But, "Goddamn it," Franklin muttered, they brought the worst out. "I'm a taxpayer."

This wasn't entirely true, but it would be in a few weeks. At 58.9K, he'd be handing over practically nine thousand dollars a year to California and to the county for the privilege of being shaken down by these thicknecks. And the shittiest thing of it was, he never had a problem with paying taxes. In fact, he'd always *wanted* to be a taxpayer, as if society, as if America itself would take him more seriously. Franklin was ready to assume the role of good citizen. More than ready.

He buttoned his reeking jacket against the cold. Shit shit shit, he grumbled, then began to walk. Camaro assholes. It hurt his shoulder blade to laugh. Cursing and such. Well, it was understandable. He was an adult. An adult, goddammit, 58.9K, and he had a right to be treated like one.

The Downtowner Motel stood at an intersection where the traffic lights, hanging on cables, swung back and forth in the wind, whistling. Franklin pulled his suit jacket tight around his neck and headed for it. The neon sign wasn't working properly, so it read "Down   er," with the "town" part flickering. The rooms faced a parking lot that was empty, except for a panel van with chrome mags and two Japanese motorcycles chopped to look American. The front door squeaked painfully on its hinges, opening to a lobby that smelled like bleach and cigarettes. Nobody was at the counter, so he rang the bell.

A woman with dyed orange hair finally showed up. She wore a pink housedress and held a corn muffin in one hand, in the other a stack of coupons. "How may I help you?"

"A room, please."

Her eyes traveled him up and down, stopping for the briefest second on the split crotch seam. By the way her nostrils flattened, he could tell she smelled the beer. "What major credit card will you be using?"

Any day now, he'd start receiving credit cards in the mail. He had filled out applications for American Express, Visa, and Mastercard, still a little amazed at how well qualified he'd become. All three companies had deals where you got the first year free of charge. "Cash."

"Sorry, sir, we only take credit cards," she said, tearing the perforated lines of a coupon. Carnegie Sunpuffs, 75 cents off, with the purchase of a first bag at the regular price.

"What? This says 'legal tender' on it, doesn't it?" He pointed to the words on a fifty-dollar bill. A marketing teacher had told him once, if people don't accept cash, show them the words. If they still don't, sue.

She regarded the bill suspiciously. Maybe she was

afraid it was drug money. That must be it. Franklin suddenly smiled. Body language, diction. He straightened, smoothed the hair at his temples. "Look, beg pardon, I mean, I beg your pardon. I've just had a hard night. Some . . . *kids* threw beer at me."

She made no show of having heard him. "Thirty-seven seventy-five plus a fifty-dollar deposit, to be returned on checkout, providing no damage has occurred." She took a bite of her corn muffin. "Eighty-seven seventy-five, please."

The way she said *please*, the way the yellow crumbs clung to the corners of her lips, the careful way she tore the Sunpuffs coupon's dotted lines; it really got to him. How like life to be refused something you don't want but really need, have enough money for but can't afford.

"Here's a fifty," he said. "The room's thirty-seven seventy-five. Keep the change. Please."

With a ring finger—gold band and solitaire diamond, perhaps a quarter of a carat, certainly no more—she pushed a single corn muffin crumb into her mouth. "I'm sorry, sir."

Franklin shouted, "Lady, I'm tired, I'm drenched in beer, my fucking suit's ripped, and I just want a bed!"

The lady glanced worriedly into the fisheye of a video camera mounted in the corner. Franklin noticed himself in the small black-and-white screen behind the desk, his two suits were bunched up and rumpled, his hair was sticking up, and both his hands were in fists. "I'm sorry, Miss, Mrs., Ms.," he said, turning to leave. "Sorry, please."

She locked the door after him, and when she came out from behind the counter to do it, he saw that she was wearing Cookie Monster slippers. Above, the neon sign shut off.

Garbage blew along the streets. A lid tumbled off a
trashcan. It clanged, rolling along. He was freezing, his
shoulder blade felt chipped, and there was nowhere to go.
He saw himself reflected in a store window, and he was
actually muttering to himself, "Camaro assholes," like
some kind of homeless. 58.9K, health and dental, a goddamn bum.

"Damn fine things," his mother had said. "Material
comfort and social standing." Then, winking, as if it was
just a stage he was going through, "Get all you can."

Maybe one day he'd get over his shame about his
mother. After all, it was sort of vain to worry about what
others might think. About what Mavy thought. But that
was only part of it.

Without planning to, he had come full circle back to
Mavy's apartment. For a long time he stood looking at
her front door. It made him think of the nudibranch
cupped in his hands, of destiny. Usually other people had
it. For him it seemed an affliction, which he himself only
got occasionally, like the common cold, no cure or vac-
cine. He seemed to be having a touch of it now.

He tried the knob; Mavy opened the door as if she had
been standing there waiting for him. Sleepy-eyed and
crazy-haired, she took his hand in her bony fingers and
brought him inside where the warmth made him shiver.

"I was dreaming Bob Dylan was my dad," she said.
"He was wearing boxing gloves." From a drawer in the
hallway, she got out a pair of sweats for Franklin. They
were folded and smelled laundry clean. "What happened?"

He told her the story, and in the telling it got funny.
But with every laugh his shoulder blade throbbed; it felt
serious.

They sat cross-legged on her futon and sipped chamo-
mile tea, surrounded by a dozen beeswax candles, some of
their flames still, some jumping. Mobiles cast a changing
web of shadows on the walls and ceiling. The scent of rose
petals was sweet and deep, where the nose meets the
throat.

She didn't seem to think any less of him for the fact of
his mother.

On the other side of the wall, a man burped and farted,
no mistaking it, then got into the shower. Franklin and
Mavy had another laugh, and when they stopped laughing, he was exhausted, and let his eyes close. Bob Dylan
was still knocking on heaven's door.

When Franklin awoke, he was shivering, outside the
covers. Mavy was under them, curled fetal, facing away.
All the candles had been blown out. He pulled the blankets over himself, took one deep, very satisfying breath,
and fell back asleep.

Only for a moment, though. Or an hour, it was hard to
be sure. Sounds next door woke him up. A woman's voice,
"You said you'd fix it, liar," followed by shrill laughter.
The man grunted. "Baby baby," he said. "I promise."
More sputtering, then some slapping. "You better," the
woman teased. "Baby baby," moaned the man. Then
mutual groaning, rhythmic squeaking . . .

Franklin reached over, let a hand rest on Mavy's arm.
That was all he wanted, just to touch her, to rest his hand
on her arm, then go back to sleep. But when he did, she
turned to him. And when she turned to him, they kissed
sloppily. And because it was the middle of the night, it
had been such a weird night, and just because, they were
kissing, kissing.

And then they were pulling off each other's sweats. But
her drawstring was tied in an actual knot, which Franklin

was incapable of untying. She undid it herself, in the fumbling, endless, panting silence.

In his arms she felt large and strong. It was hard to remember ever being cold.

Franklin put a knee between her legs, spreading them. He shouldn't have, but he did. Not using birth control like a couple of junior high kids. Not using a condom, stupid, stupid, Russian roulette.

Franklin would just get inside her, that was all, he wouldn't come there, he just needed to know how it would feel, just for a second.

She whined, groaned something, maybe "oh," and either pushed him away or clutched him, he couldn't tell which. Right then he pulled out, coming. He ejaculated in hot streaks on the sheets, on her stomach, in his own eye.

"Sorry," he whispered.

Beside him, Mavy, taking quick shallow breaths, turned neither toward him nor away.

His eye was on fire. His shoulder burned.

Early the next morning, before sunrise, Franklin woke upon hearing the next-door twosome going at it again. He had never had a one-night stand before. It left him feeling both older and younger, as if more experience could make you less mature.

Silently, he creeped into Mavy's bathroom and washed his face, soaking the eyelid open. It had crusted shut. He brushed his teeth, using her toothbrush, drying it off with a towel. Last night seemed so far away, his feelings grown cold to the point of being no longer recognizable. He gathered his things, including his beer-soaked, ripped-crotch suit, and let himself out. 58.9K, he thought, and felt a little better.

Two days later Mavy left a message inviting him to go

to Big Sur for a weekend. "There are tidepools there." On the machine her voice sounded happy and clear, and because she wasn't heartbroken or depressed, it was easy for him to ignore her.

After a week, she phoned again. He made the mistake of not screening this time. "I can't. I was going to call you," he said. "About the tidepools. It's graduation that weekend. I can't."

"You're doing the ceremony?"

Lots of students didn't *do* the ceremony, or they did do it but wore blue jeans or casual dresses, because this college was founded in the sixties, when tradition was something to be skeptical of. But now it was the eighties, and Franklin, like the rest of the prosperous world, believed in the value of tradition. It put you irrevocably in touch with where you came from, and therefore where you were going. "I sure am."

"Family and everybody?" she asked, crunching something.

"What are you eating?"

"An apple. Granny Smith. It's *so* juicy."

The call went on like this, zigzagging, pointless. He had planned to be distant to her. Cold and offputting without getting rude. "So can I meet them?"

He hesitated. "Who?"

"Your family."

"It's just my mom." He mentioned again that he never knew his father.

"I forgot. I'm sorry."

"I have no memory of him anyway, so don't worry about it." He told her he was really busy, but he'd call her soon, and they'd go check out the tidepools, even though he had no intention of doing either.

Mr. Rogers, the postman, knew intimate things about Eliza Tibbets. To her, he had delivered many oddities: fertility vitamins, black bear pancreas, an accredited mail-order law degree course for housewives. But it wasn't till the government orange trees that he saw any tangible results.

Not two years after the tree plantings, Eliza saw her first fruit.

"Heck of a thing," said Mr. Rogers, wiping sweat from his temples, even though it was December. The coming of winter had failed to relieve southern California's drought. The sun blasted down shards of heat. Mr. Rogers bit into the hard small orange Eliza ceremoniously presented to him.

"You've got to peel it first!" she said. Several neighbors' kids snickered. So far, they had spent every day of their Christmas break hanging around the strange Tibbets tree. Lacking space in the back, Eliza had planted them right out in her front yard.

"Here," she said, taking back Mr. Rogers's orange and slicing it for him with a penknife he had also delivered. "See?"

"Versatile," he said. Still embarrassed and unsure whether or not she was teasing him, he hesitated before accepting the fruit again. Eliza offered the remaining wedges to the kids, who also seemed uncertain. They squirmed and giggled. Some ran away and hid.

Because she had no children of her own, because she wore gauzy sleeves and a hat to keep her skin white, because she managed to keep these queer trees alive through the summer (while the rest of the county's plants and trees, aside from anything cactus, withered under the long dry spell), and because she wore pants and used a penknife like a man, word got around the neighborhood that Eliza was a witch. When the kids weren't standing around waiting for some further evidence, they were galloping past in packs screaming, "Ring a bell, duck the spell, the wicked witch comes straight from hell!" Once, after hearing a sharp rap, Eliza opened her front door to find a big load of excrement dumped on her porch. Not real feces, though; the youngsters had fashioned it out of mud. Such calculating humor and the effort behind it, to craft a lifelike, odorless turd, seemed to her especially nasty.

"Yummy!" they shouted now, those brave enough to risk being poisoned by "witch fruit." "Yum yum yum!"

The oranges were unimaginable, Eliza knew. And yet, here they were. The children's eyes widened and brightened as the juice hit their tongues. Sweet, tangy, volatile.

"If you're very good," she told them, "I'll let you have more," bribing their respect, their allegiance.

She'd do the same for Mr. Rogers, whom she suspected of spreading bizarre rumors concerning her and Luther. Store clerks eyed Eliza curiously, young women tittered, men offered her cigarettes. At Civil Engineers, Luther got passed over for every job advancement. Their only real friends, the Burtons, a couple they had played cards with every week for five years, had abruptly canceled the Saturday-night ritual. Mr. Rogers brought no invitations to parties, not even to the firemen's pancake breakfast. The Tibbetses were plain and simply shunned. And, Eliza sometimes thought, for good reason.

One evening Luther brought home a book written by the "modern" Harvard doctor. After a decade spent researching a certain African tribe known for their extraordinarily high birth rate, "the fertility authority" concluded the same thing as *Ladies Home Journal,* only less clearly, and in a great many more words. He also suggested other "conception enhancers." Drinking cold Silvertuft Weed tea. Taking egg-white baths. Standing on your head. Luther, purpose having given way to desperation, was all for trying every one of them.

"For the baby," he said, holding up a bulb of garlic. The doctor had prescribed inserting a clove before and after relations.

"Sure," Eliza said, aware of Luther's teeth, stained red from the Chianti he now sloppily poured (a little splashing her elbow) from a big, straw-bottomed bottle. She had never seen a bottle like that, or Luther like this, with his purple mouth, with breadcrumbs clinging to his beard. When he started to lick the wine off her arm, she knew he was drunk. "Sure. Then I'll follow it with onions and carrots."

"Eliza!" Luther laughed, feigning shock. The bone-white garlic had purple streaks. Eliza had grown it herself in the poorest of soils, coaxing it out of sunlight and dust. A single clove was strong enough to stink up the entire kitchen.

"No, *really,*" she teased, gulping. Everybody knew garlic had medicinal properties. It purified the blood, strengthened the internal organs. But the other business was mumbo-jumbo, Harvard or no. "If your modern doctor can get it in print, the least we can do——"

"Oh, Eliza." Luther stroked his great auburn beard. "Sometimes I wonder if you really want this child."

"What an unfair thing to say, Luther Tibbets!" Just when they were playing around for a change. Having a silly time.

Luther picked at the straw on the Chianti bottle. "I think we should try it."

"*We?*" Her gulp of wine shot up inside her nose. "Why don't *you try* it."

He rose, knocking over his chair. She had never seen any violence in him, though at times she almost wished she had. Violence had a persuasiveness about it that no amount of manners could make up for, especially in a man.

Was he a real man? She often wondered. It was what drove her to ordering the lawyer correspondence course. Among the contracts and sample suits was the one she was most interested in: divorce. Obviously, she had never used the kit, could not even make sense of its legalese. It was written in a style that put no pictures in her head. And yet, it made her feel better to know the documents were there. It gave her life a back door.

She was, well, disappointed in Luther. Stuck in a mid-level job for years now, kowtowing to that snide hunchnecked Gosse, doing what he was told. Why couldn't he ask for more? Why must he always wear cheap jackets? A temper was a sign of ambition, and her husband had neither.

Of course the violence Eliza wished he'd exhibit was of this abstract, metaphorical nature. She never imagined it could be used against her.

They faced each other, not moving.

His eyes were green, gorgeous, mean. He was mad at her for everything. For the dirt under her fingernails. For her knees, bruised and misshapen from so much kneeling and digging. For the beautiful plum tree in spring, for the aromatic basil at dinner, for garlic and seedless oranges. He was mad at all the parts of herself that she devoted to things other than him. And mad at the things themselves.

He clenched his big hairy fists.

But suddenly he smiled.

Eliza realized they *were* playing after all. "Well! Did you ever give me a fright," she half-lied. It was exciting. "I thought you were serious, Luther."

"I am," he said, holding the bottle to his mouth, emptying its dregs. "In the name of science." He picked up both the garlic and his wife, and carried them into the bedroom. She smiled uncontrollably, at first.

It was scary what the baby made them do. After the garlic event, whole evenings passed where the Tibbets did not speak a word to each other. Without child, without friends, Eliza began talking to her plants, while Luther purchased a Great Dane he named Bub. Even as a puppy Bub was huge. His gangly legs splaying about, never all four in concert, each holding stubbornly to its own tempo, curled toenails skittering across the tile floor. His jowls, like his eyelids, were black as tire rubber, kept moist by a ten-inch tongue and a constant slap of drool. Eliza would have hated the creature were it not for his eyes, a deep brown, trusting and infinitely sorrowful.

The pup whined and cried the minute Luther left for work. He batted his tail about and licked everything the minute he returned. His inexhaustible howls of grief kept up all night. Eliza could tell he missed his mother. Only Luther within eyesight soothed him.

And so the dog adopted the crib. To make room, Luther discarded Eliza's seed packets and catalogs.

She seethed.

She refused to have relations while the dog watched. She made Luther beg. While down there on his hands and knees, he did peculiar things to her, things with his mouth and tongue, things she was sure were illegal, immoral, irresistible.

Then the manhood enlarger arrived. On its box an endorsement by Dr. Harvard, "triumph of Western medicine" written in industrial revolution typeface. Inside was a hand pump made of blown glass, lined with rubber. When Luther came out of the bathroom, he was larger all right, but red and misshapen, puffed out in places like a blown-up balloon half deflated.

Eliza could tell the sex was painful. At the crucial moment, he screamed and Bub leapt from the crib onto him. She did not laugh. She gave him two aspirins, a raw steak for the swelling.

Of course people in town thought them weird; and they didn't know the half of it.

"Go ahead," Eliza said, and smiled at Mr. Rogers. She was long past hoping to pass herself off as average. But at least she'd show him she wasn't all bad.

Tentatively, Mr. Rogers put the orange wedge to his lips, as if it had come from a hot oven. The tip of his tongue appeared, quivering. He nibbled softly with his front teeth. At last the wedge exploded in a tremble of juice.

"Heck of a thing," he said, licking his knuckles. "Heck of a thing."

The neighbors' kids jammed the peels into their mouths, between their front teeth and lips. They grunted, jumping up and down with savage orange grins.

"Do you have a match?" Eliza asked Mr. Rogers, who brought out a box from London called Lucifers. He lit one, importantly. Being a postman gave him access to exciting products from all over the world.

The kids huddled close as Eliza held a peel a half inch from the match, and squeezed. *Whoosh!* The fine spray of citrus oils ignited and spattered flame.

Mr. Rogers ducked; the kids squealed. "Do it again!"

"That reminds me," Mr. Rogers said, after the shock had passed. "Mail." From his leather bag he pulled yet another plain brown envelope from the Harvard Fertility Institute.

"Can't imagine what that is," Mr. Rogers said, but curled his mouth in a way that suggested he was having a fine time trying.

"Do it again!" pleaded the neighbor kids. "Mrs. Tibbets, do that thing again!"

Mrs. Jaycock's eyes fluttered like beetles stuck on their backs. "Left then right, one-two-three." She clapped her finger cymbals three times, then grimaced. "Young man. You there."

"Yes, ma'am?" Aaron was dancing with Prudence, who kept spike-pumping his toes.

"Chin up, arm out," Mrs. Jaycock modeled, dancing with air for a partner. "One-two-three, with dig-ni-ty." She pulled her arm gloves up to her elbows where they bunched.

"Yes, ma'am," Aaron nodded, and Mrs. Jaycock flexed her neck, rouged cheeks pouching up. "Watch your posture."

Cotillion was group insanity.

First you had to get invited, which basically meant being born well off. Then you had to put on formal wear and go downtown to the Clock Auditorium to learn manners and protocol, how to dance, how to sit, how to bow.

Which Aaron did now, one hand on the stomach, the other behind the back, to Prudence as the song ended.

Everybody took seats on folding metal chairs, boys on one side, girls facing them on the other. It was a long and narrow room, with cherubs painted on the ceiling, chandeliers filled with flame-simulation bulbs, a marble floor fractured from various earthquakes, and windows draped in crumbling chintz. The opulence was anachronistic, suggesting a refusal to recognize the truth.

Jimbo and Brainy sat on either side of Aaron. Their suits were tailor-made. Aaron's too, but, on Dad's insistence, the material was red velvet. Or maybe it was velour. Or suede. Aaron wasn't really sure. And, with his mousse-spiked hair, he felt like a road hazard.

"Poise is as poise does," Mrs. Jaycock said into a microphone, which picked up the noise she made fumbling through a stack of albums.

"All that antique vinyl," Brainy said, shaking his head sadly. He had a very subdued camouflage shirt and tie,

Cattail, under a khaki sport jacket. Brainy could pull it off, could make it somehow hypersuburban, somehow desirable.

Jimbo said, "People pay for that shit."

Brainy said, "Analog is, like, unrivaled."

Aaron: "Anything *intuition* always gets . . ."

Jimbo: ". . . gets it up the ass."

Aaron: "Gets no legit . . ."

Brainy: "You can codify intuition."

Jimbo: "Yeah? Codify this."

Aaron: "Let's get outta here."

Brainy: "Remember 'Amazonas Sings for Grain'?"

There was a long silence.

Brainy: "Totally digital. Paint-by-numbers. No such thing as 'live' after her."

Jimbo: "Here's live."

There was another silence.

"I'm grounded." Jimbo suddenly laughed sarcastically.

Earlier, when Aaron swung by to pick up Jimbo, Mrs. Talkington was screaming at him. "Don't you *dare* call me a lizard, Jimbo!" She had a nervous tic of picking at her eyebrows; they no longer existed. Where they used to be, she stuck Band-Aids. When you looked at her you knew right off she was a victim. "That's it! You're grounded for a week!"

"Let's go to the grove," Aaron said.

Jimbo looked across the room at Prudence, who sat whispering to Linda Delgado. Prudence had on a lace blouse, and leather miniskirt. Since Jimbo and she had been fucking, Jimbo wouldn't ask her to dance.

Mrs. Jaycock picked up the microphone to publicly frown at Prudence. "A lady doesn't sit with her legs spread."

Everybody looked.

"Legs cross at the ankle. That's right. Hands fold in your lap. Fine. The key to being ladylike——" The words soared into feedback.

Brainy: "Analog's Achilles' heel."

Mrs. Jaycock dropped the mike. High-pitched whistling and sonic booms.

Meanwhile, Prudence slouched, leered, and opened her legs wide.

"Is *honor,*" Mrs. Jaycock said, finished her thought, and started it all over again. "The key to being ladylike——"

A petal fell from Linda's crown. A waltz began. Aaron took her hand—warm, dry, buzzing. Her hair smelled of pine trees and chlorine. They danced like robots.

"Aaron," she said, eyes downcast, smiling. "This sucks."

"Obey the beat, anticipate the melody," Mrs. Jaycock said, eyes closed, fingers spread as if to sense vibrations. It was strange, music with such a self-insistent melody. "Hold her, young man. She won't bite."

What Aaron liked about Linda Delgado was this:

She was nice.

She was ordinary.

She had breasts.

She put flowers in her hair, but not to make fun of the past.

She had athlete's foot.

Aaron pulled her closer. Suddenly, with one hand on the small of her back, the other holding hers aloft, Aaron's eyes watered. He wondered whether his erection was his gift to her, or hers to him.

When Franklin, in cap and gown, walked across the stage to receive a scrolled diploma and a firm handshake from the dean, and when, squinting under the white sun, he heard his name announced over the loudspeaker "with high honors," a chill ran through him and it was all he could do to keep from letting a single hot tear spill from each eye.

And when the chancellor, charismatic in a flowing black robe and crimson sash, hereby declared them graduates, a great roar went up and Franklin, along with hundreds of others, flung his mortarboard high. The sky was full of spinning black squares that seemed to hang aloft before floating slowly, slowly down. No telling which was his. If he lost it, well, so be it, the cap deposit was one he could afford to forfeit.

58.9K.

After, there was champagne and picture taking, roving videocams and Chablis in plastic cups. Cheese cubes on toothpicks. Strawberries. Cookies and carrot sticks and fruit punch. One of Franklin's marketing professors, Ms. Kersh, who single-handedly developed the Coalescent Market Theory, or the Rope Scope as it was more commonly known, with which one could gauge in surprising precision the variable strengths and weaknesses of commercial-system interdependence, was the first to congratulate him.

"My, my," she said. A silver-eyed woman with a silver
pompadour and purple Birkenstocks, she used a pressed
red bandanna to pat her forehead and nose, then forehead
again. Her portfolio was supposedly worth thirteen million. Something like that. Not a lot of liquidity, however.
When Franklin told her his plans with Solvtex, what his
duties would be, the 58.9K, she said, "I think that's just
fantastic. Just fantastic. Now, if you'll excuse me."

In its jubilance, the crowd pushed him forward, pulled
him back, sweeping him along. A champagne bottle was
thrust in his direction. He put his lips to it. The alcoholic
tang filled his nose, icy wetness spilled down his chin.

Underneath his gown he wore a suit and tie, and, even
though the material was relatively lightweight (tropical
wool), having on so many layers under black was making
him sticky. The sky was like plastic wrap, breezeless, and
the amphitheater parabolic, a giant bowl that sunshine
could not easily find its way out of. Many of the spectators
sat under umbrellas, others wore hats folded from programs, paper triangles. Franklin raised the bottle for another swallow, but this time gagged.

"Are you okay?" It was Mavy. She had applied mascara, lipstick, and wore a dress. A comb kept the front of
her hair in control, but behind, the big loopy curls broke
free. The attempt to look *put together*, in its earnestness,
had the opposite effect: Whole clumps of eyelashes were
black-flecked while others, missed, remained fine and
white, and the maroon gloss was smeared, in places over-
running the borders of her lips. She looked barely con-
tainable.

He wiped his mouth with the back of his sleeve. "What
are you doing here?" Then he heard how it must have
sounded. Words kind of got away from you sometimes.
Now that he was, well, a professional, he'd have to prac-

tice his diction. Systematically. He'd get a workbook from PackCen and practice fifteen minutes a day. "I mean, do you know someone graduating?"

She frowned.

The heat was stifling. Rolling up his sleeves and unzipping the gown didn't help much, the cloth didn't breathe. He stopped just short of loosening his tie. Anyone could read that tipoff. Another thing he'd have to work on, body language. Even the tiniest gesture could be made to speak, or to lie. As it was now, he was sloshing with communication, most of it uncontrolled. "Want some champagne?"

"Mmmhmmm," she said, still a little stung.

The way her large fingers grasped the neck as she drank made him smile; for half a second, it was almost like she was family.

"Where's your mom?" she asked.

"My mom?"

"Yeah, you said she was coming," she said, looking at her feet. "Remember?"

"Oh, um, yeah," he said. It was against the law to have sex with a sixteen-year-old. Statutory rape. A charge that could ruin his career. "I mean, *yes.*"

"So, where is she?"

Franklin scanned the crowd. So many faces. A woman who looked like his mother was dabbing her eyes with tissue. "I don't see her."

Mavy drew something in the dust with her toe.

Franklin wondered how he was going to get away from her without being *too* cruel, because no matter what, it would be obvious.

"Look, I'll go find her," he said. "Then I'll bring her over."

"You find things," she said, very softly. In the dust

Mavy had drawn something with her toe. A heart! She had drawn a heart! She was sixteen years old and had drawn a heart in the dust.

"Hey," Franklin said. He didn't want this. He never asked for this. "Hey," he said, lightly. "We'll meet right here in twenty minutes." But it was lies. It was all bull-shit and lies, and his voice wasn't worth the air it was carried on.

When she looked up, he touched her chin. There was something new showing in her face. Trust betrayed, tena-cious innocence.

He turned and left, merging into the swirl of the crowd. Letting himself be carried along, he thought about going back to her, he really did. When he turned around, she was exactly where he had left her, watching.

But just then Ms. Kersh bumped into him. She flashed her hands in recognition, "You again," and offered him a toothpick that held a chunk of Swiss. He nodded and grinned and made expansive gestures.

An outsider might have mistaken them for mother and son.

It bothered Franklin that his mom answered the phone "Yeah?" on the first ring.

"Hi," he said. "It's me."

"Well, Frankly," she said. He heard the TV going in the background, exhortations, gunfire, squealing tires. And the low whine of the air conditioner, which she ran twenty-four hours a day all year long, sometimes along with the heater. "I miss you. How are you?"

"I graduated today."

"I've got it right here on my calendar," she said, paus-ing. "And the newspaper says your weather's fine. Eighty-one." He pictured her in her high-rise staring out at the Strip ablaze in neon, sitting in her favorite spot on the white leather sofa, so favorite that it was worn, carefully extracting a Dunhill Blue from its box, breaking off the filter, and lighting it with a three-thousand-dollar lighter from Tiffany's—a gift from a big spender, one of many, it was surprising how many—in the shape of a borzoi. She exhaled and said, "I *am* proud."

"I think it was closer to ninety." He told her about the speech, about the food, the weather again, about Ms. Kersh. "She said my job was 'fantastic.' 'Just fantastic,' she said."

"Well, I should say so," Mom said, pausing to take a drag. "My, my, I'm *so* proud of you, Frankly."

"I wish you could have been here, Ma."

"Now don't start with that," she said. The TV was still going, screaming, blond, cleavage, heels, hostage. It bothered Franklin that cliché hacks had more audience with his mother than he had. "You know I love you, and I'd do anything for you except be a burden on you. I don't drive, I don't get on so well with."

"I know, Ma." He wondered if she was on a prescription, then felt guilty. She'd stopped with that years ago.

Then, surprising himself, he said, "I have a girlfriend, Ma. You'd like her." Girlfriend? You say these things sometimes, and you don't mean them. Or you try them aloud, just to hear how they sound. A girlfriend, for godssakes.

The psychologist had the same name as Aaron. He appeared wise, like a medicine man. Aaron suddenly felt like confessing to Mom's murder on Dad's behalf. Admission of guilt seemed just now terribly liberating, even if the guilt wasn't technically his own. Aaron would gladly take his father's punishment.

The psychologist glanced at the mirror—one way, Aaron realized—and asked a test question. "An Indian chief says, 'White Man lazy. He runs while sitting down.' What is the white man doing?"

Depending on how he answered, Aaron could qualify to be a "Mentally Gifted Minor."

"Is this being videoed?" Aaron asked, deciding that the psychologist was not so wise as suspicious. He felt he had to be secretive.

"No." Aaron the psychologist scratched his thick black beard. "Some of my college students are observing."

Aaron the kid waved at them, at his reflection. "Invite 'em in."

"Wouldn't you prefer privacy?"

"White Man's riding a bike," Aaron said. "But why'd you make the Indian a moron?"

"He's not a moron, he's literal minded."

Aaron considered deliberately failing the test, but he wasn't sure he was capable. If he tried to say wrong answers, they might actually be right ones, or the ones the shrink wanted, and he'd get accepted by accident. Or worse, Aaron would reveal his secret—these psychologists were trained to spot body language, verbal slip-ups, and knew what they meant. If he wasn't careful, Aaron could wind up enrolled in "At Risk."

"You lose a wallet in a square field," the psychologist told him. Aaron wondered how earlier he could have seen this man as some sort of shaman. The psychologist had a black toupee—Aaron was pretty sure it was a rug—a black beard, black eyebrows, long black nose hairs, black-rimmed glasses, black jeans, black socks, black sandals soled with almost-bald tire treads. Aaron wondered whether this man's father chose the name Aaron, or his mother. "How do you go about looking for it, in the most efficient way?"

"What's in the wallet?"

"Money."

"How much?"

"A million dollars."

"I'd never carry that much cash around."

The psychologist tapped an index finger against a front tooth. "Just suppose you had."

"I'd probably buy the orange—" Aaron stared at the mirror, wondering at the college students beyond it. A million dollars would solve almost everything. "The Orange Julius chain of restaurants."

"No, you *lost* the wallet," the psychologist Aaron said. "In a square field."

"I'd look for it the way our gardener mows the lawn," Aaron said. "In rows, back and forth."

The psychologist scratched his beard again, wrote something in his notebook. "What's your favorite TV show?"

Aaron could only think of his birth video. It made him tear up, a surprise.

"Is something wrong?"

Aaron held on tight to the armrests. His eyes felt very salty. "Nature shows."

The psychologist studied him. Then, glancing at the mirror, said, "You must really like them."

Franklin had been working at Solvtex nine months when Gas & Electric exploded. For a moment, several high-rises throbbed brilliantly. Inside, computers flickered and smoked, their protectors mysteriously disabled. Then came the blackout.

There would be no service for two weeks, possibly three in the business district. Solvtex, along with hundreds of other corporations, was paralyzed. Projects were put on hold, others vanished in scrambled programs.

Employees were at a loss, rubbing their heads, hugging each other, commiserating about their ruined enterprises, grumbling about delayed paychecks. It was almost joyful, this loss of responsibility, this involvement in a bloodless disaster of historic proportions. Office workers sat in the glow of fluorescent torches telling stories and drinking thin coffee in foam cups delivered from a crosstown deli.

"This is not a holiday," said Victoria Welch, the assistant vice-president. "This is an *opportunity.*" She arranged for eighteen-wheeler semis to park on the street. The trucks carried diesel generators the size of boxcars. Cables ran up stairwells, humming with current produced by the burning of fuel oil. The air crackled with ozone and hydrocarbons.

Employees returned to the worse aspects of their former personalities, going back to their jobs, retracing, retrenching, rebuilding. They got headaches from the fumes, achy joints, eyestrain. One of the sidewalk boxcars had been converted into a mobile therapy center, which earned a reputation for serving strong French roast in the dinky waiting room, and for the receptionist who ran a popular sports betting pool.

Boldly, Franklin beeped Victoria's office. "I've got an idea."

"Wells," she said, exasperated, but scheduled him an appointment for the following day.

Victoria often wore black, never any makeup. Mid-length dresses. Stirrup pants. Turtlenecks. Heeled boots. Anything simple and expensive. Never skirt suits, though occasionally Franklin saw her in a man's suit, with a narrow silk tie, diagonally striped. She had a closet in her office suite, and a shower, and a kitchenette.

Today, she wore black, of course, a silk blouse and wool pants, leather mules. A large pearl hung from a gold chain at her neck. She had long black hair too thin to braid, huge brown eyes, and equally huge lips, red going purple. She was never without her liter of Trinity Pure water in a plastic bottle.

"Talented, however, semi-unfocused," she had written on his last performance review. She wanted focus? He'd show her focus. But at the bottom of the document she had initialed a pay raise.

Less than a year on the job and already he was making

65K, with probably another 5K in bonuses and profit points. But these were old math numbers.

Money, now, was sequences of light pulsing through underground cables. Money was radiowaves bouncing off low-orbit satellites. Money was bit sequences transmitted from one computer to another, endlessly recorded, endlessly erased, processed and reprocessed. Money was no longer something you saved; it was something you *accessed.* How wealthy you were depended on whose magnetic identi-strip you were using, what touchtone code, which computer handshake. For a better reach, Franklin could use the company's.

His early successes earned him a reputation for casual brilliance, and for getting the job done. Noisily, he *got the job done.* Always, though, by a stroke of luck, with a scare or two along the way.

There was one other new guy who, because he was also in his early twenties, became Franklin's rival. Stoddard Manville was actually a year younger than Franklin, which was mildly irritating. A Stanford fratboy with a New York lawyer dad, Manville was getting the same bonuses and profit points, and, the fucker, he had a slightly better office. He had a thick head of hair, also; Franklin's was thinning rapidly. In fact, Manville was quite handsome, a composite of flawless features, with impossible-to-read Teutonic eyes, and his work was always dependable and executed to perfection. He grew up in a co-op on Park Avenue where apparently there were tulips and often said living in a co-op had taught him to cooperate. He wore Armani and had a tie pin for each day of the week. His solid good looks—blunt-chopped blond—and good taste and good work and complete lack of excitability made you think of him as the one who would take command in a lifeboat, getting you rescued. One thing Manville never took was risks.

"The energy surge caught everybody by surprise," Franklin began. He, on the other hand, thrived on risk, and wore clothes that gave the impression of being both absentminded and fearless. Nameless suits and nameless shirts, moderately priced. Never stripes, never plaids, never tweeds. Never geometry. Only solids, or colorful patterns, batik-like cityscapes, schools of fish, subtle paisleys, all sort of right-brain, but comfortably within the left-brain parameters of *suit and tie*. His ties were unusual enough to be noticed, but not remembered.

Today, however, he put on his most expensive suit. He got it at a warehouse sale, then had it tailored by a man with green eyeglasses named "Mr. Bill" who had a little shop under a freeway overpass. Even so, with a white cotton 220-stitch shirt, sterling cuff links, and a red tie, the package cost close to a thousand dollars. Though it fit beautifully, and accentuated his good posture, Franklin only wore the suit on ceremonial occasions, so, wearing it, he never looked entirely comfortable. Until today. "Whole businesses have gone down."

"Wells," Victoria said, her eyes traveling over the narrow lapels, the slightly iridescent red-and-green tie. "Tell me something new."

Franklin let her finish looking, then booted up his laptop and displayed his visuals. "Disaster proofing." A company could insure their nervous systems against natural disasters, acts of God, war. "Outtages, fires, floods, crumbling infrastructures, unforeseeables," he explained. Whole data bases, operational programs, communications systems could be secured at a secondary location. When catastrophe struck, the information would simply be looped back, or rerouted through previously constructed redundant networks, or reprotocolled to bounce off network satellites. All a company would need was a code and a swipe stripe, ATM banking style gone cellular. "We'll sell the complete package. And bill monthly."

"What are you telling me?" Victoria sipped from her water bottle.

"Say an electrical surge burns out a hospital's files. The hospital calls us, and we restore them. We're the second-location backup disk. And the best part is, it's all done automatically. Every keystroke there shows up here.

"We provide something like safe deposit boxes. Except they don't put *things* in it, they put their information systems in it—and it's updated and revised here *simultaneously*. We don't peek, but whenever the need arises, they pay us a visit and use their key."

After a pause, Victoria said, "How's the Phase Sizer project working out?"

Franklin frowned, taken aback. Phase Sizer was bread and butter, a bore, traffic-copping a team of numberheads and commission quacks who were cranking out a marketing strategy for remote-control garage door openers. "Okay, I guess, but. Fine. Great. It's going great." Phase Sizer fell into Franklin's lap after Manville took a grab at the Bitsumi NeuroLaser account, a fast track to bigger money, a grander title. "Sutter's keeping me busy."

"Why didn't you take your idea to him?" Victoria asked.

Sutter was the man Franklin reported to, a middle-aged, mid-level executive with purple bags under his eyes and a clipped ponytail, a cowboy boot and bolo tie guy, a lifer with a medium-sized office. On his desk there were framed snapshots of his daughters in their Little League uniforms, and one taken years—decades—ago of him and his wife standing long-haired and stoned at a Dead show. It was unspeakably depressing having this washed-up, broken-principled man for a boss.

ArManiville, on the other hand, got to report to Victoria, who was considered hotshit.

Victoria had in fact been written up in trade magazines, in the pop press, too. The *Wall Street Journal, Ms., Money, California,* the *Sunday Chronicle* business section. According to these articles she was a corporate icon smasher, a woman who favored silk, a dangerous competitor, a single woman, workaholic, child of television. No, she was not planning to have kids in the immediate future, but yes, someday. Of course.

She took another sip of water. Even though she had a desk, it was common knowledge she didn't work at it. She worked standing up, at a podium, talking into a telephone headset. She never sat. Not even for Japanese clients. CNN was always going, volume turned low, on a 27-inch TV in the corner. Just now there was stop-action video of a skydiver whose chute had failed to open.

Everything about Victoria was extreme. Rumors further built up the mystique. In her, politeness became magnanimity, bad habits addictions. Cocaine. A broken marriage to a Boston financier. Nympho, lesbo, no sex at all. Leftist politics. Real estate speculator. Silicone.

Franklin both admired and feared her. She was driven, ambitious, an East Coaster who didn't seem to have many West Coast friends. Always the last to leave, the first to arrive, she worked *more* than anyone he had ever encountered. Franklin watched her turn her back toward him with lanky grace, the tailored silk clinging behind like a whisper.

"I brought it to you instead of Sutter because," Franklin paused, *"you* know it's a surefire hit." Sometimes you had to play a role. But if you *felt* the part, was it acting?

"Surefire?" she said, wheeling to face him, smiling. When she smiled he wanted to please her. "Surefire?" When she frowned he wanted something else. "Now get out of here."

For weeks afterward he worked independently on DisasterProof. He came to know the addiction—late nights, early mornings, coffee, unwrapping waxpaper from turkey sandwiches—of work. After a string of twenty-hour days, he reached something of an altered state. He craved work, it was a physical desire, the need to feel whatever it was that information conferred upon him as it flowed into his eyes and through his fingertips.

Even when he wasn't working, he was too wired to sleep. He went to the movies. Screwball comedies, black-and-white classics, horror flicks, one-note dramas, weepy love tragedies, art films, student shorts, big-screen epics; he was indiscriminate. They replaced his dream life, and for that he was grateful.

"Surefire," he reminded Victoria when he passed her in the hallway.

"Wells," she said. "Phase Sizer is suffering."

"Put Manville on it," he said.

He worked up graphics to make the concept clear. He worked out a plan of execution. He worked on flowcharts mapping responsibilities. He worked with accounting tables to devise a feasibility study showing a formidable profit curve. He worked towards something even more valuable: a *Rolodex.* Contacts, contractors, and experts; names, numbers, and titles.

A phone message from Mom went unanswered and

suddenly two weeks had passed. His right eye started seeing blurry.

Finally, at home one Saturday evening, he sat down, untied his shoelaces, and closed his eyes for a second. Hours passed. Shoes still on, laces untied, he sat open-eyed and breathing, no images, no fantasies, no desires, just an almost orgasmically satisfying inhale and exhale.

Sunday noon he got up. There was literally nothing to do at the office, and it was too early for the movies, so he burned the time separating him from Monday 7 A.M. by flipping through channels, settling on "News Forum Quorum," a show featuring reporters and politicians and academics (names and positions and cities subtitled) insulting each other while arguing over whether good fences made good neighbors. It was fascinating, full of poetry and bluff. Franklin ate half the yogurt in a container before discovering the expiration date was sixteen days ago.

The phone rang. He grabbed it. "Wells, Solvtex." The line went dead. He should call his mom. He didn't want to talk to her, but he wouldn't want to even more tomorrow, once the workweek started. Thirty seconds later the phone rang again.

"Mom?" Franklin said. Over and done with.

"I thought I got a robot," said a high, childlike voice.

It took him a moment to place it. "Mavy," he said. He hadn't talked to her in over a year.

"Get down from there!" she yelled, not into the phone. "Mikey!"

Franklin heard the clatter of hooves. "How did you get my number?"

A door shut. Mavy was out of breath. "It's listed."

"I didn't mean it like that."

"Don't worry, I wouldn't have called except that I thought you wouldn't be home."

For a moment neither of them said anything.

"I mean," she continued, "I thought I could leave this message on your machine so you wouldn't feel pressured."

"I don't feel——"

"There's a really low tide today. Six point four or something. Full moon, you know. Plus Neptune is as close as it's ever been, not that that has anything to do with anything. But we should, just, I don't know, go."

Franklin thought, I could use that voice. Persuasive, but innocent. Like Dorothy: There's no place like home. How could he use it for DisasterProof? To accompany slides?

"Yeah," he said. "Yes." Yes, yes; get in the habit. This was the first lesson from his year of corporate employment: Say yes. You can always sidestep later. The second lesson was that you laughed at your opponent's jokes. The third: Everybody is your opponent.

"It's one of the things I'm working on, not being late, and here I am," Mavy sighed, looking at Franklin's watch. "Chronic." She had therapy in five minutes.

"Want to pull over and call?" Franklin asked. After looking at the tidepools, they got stuck in beach traffic. He shifted uncomfortably in his seat, wishing there had been time to change earlier into the clean shirt and shorts packed in his knapsack. His trunks were salty, nylon rubbing and pinching.

"No, let's just go," she said. Mavy herself had changed right here in the car, putting on light cotton trousers and a white button shirt, clean and wrinkled. Even though he hadn't seen her in a year, being with her was like being with an old friend.

There was lots of news: Mavy had graduated from high school, and was taking classes at Monterey Peninsula College. She had a boyfriend, which got Franklin off the hook.

She ran a hand gently through her big yellow tangles. "Annie's going to tell me it spills over."

Annie was Mavy's therapist. In Franklin's mind, Annie the therapist was CIA, with a little ASPCA thrown in. Annie the therapist was covertly (lovingly, he imagined) involved with Mavy's wars, whatever they were. Annie probably knew some of Franklin's own intimate details, the botched sex, the career drive, while he knew none of hers. Annie the therapist cost $50 an hour, the price of solving problems an obverse reflection of their worth. "What spills over?"

"One part of your life into another."

Traffic seemed an organism. Oozing, shimmering, plasmatic. Bare-chested teenage boys munching Tasty Kakes stood in a Jeep with a roll bar. Ignoring them, oiled girls in bikini tops sat in a convertible Cadillac and sipped Juicy Juice from straws. An extended family was crammed into the dining room of an RV, watching TV, grandma rubbing lotion on an infant, father with head in hands, elbows on the wheel. A charcoal BMW with smoked glass windows flashed its brights on and off, doors thudding with funk bass. Each vehicle jerking forward a few feet at a time, possessive in its grab for progress.

"Uh-oh," Mavy said, peering down the front of her trousers.

Franklin felt slow in the head, car-drugged. "What?"

"Me," she said, reaching down. She smelled her fin-

gertips. From her daybag, she got out a mini-pack of
tissues. "My period." She cleaned herself up and sat looking at him.

Franklin looked at his watch. Being late was a form of
aggression. He learned that in Psychology. His mother
always made him wait. Made everybody wait. Mavy must
have known that there would be traffic, a beach-weather
afternoon. She also must have known that Annie would
get paid regardless.

"Franklin, can I borrow your underwear?"

And now this.

He didn't know whether to be disgusted or embarrassed. She seemed neither.

Don't they know? Franklin himself, if he were a girl,
he would know. *He* would be prepared days in advance.
"Yeah. In my pack."

Mavy climbed out of her seat belt and into the back
seat, unzipping.

Outside, the sun glared, aluminum cans glinted among
the iceplant, bits of backlit pampas grass floated on the
heat waves.

He couldn't imagine sharing underwear with a man,
no matter how friendly. Franklin looked in the rearview.
"Did you and Annie ever discuss me?"

"I told her you find things."

Aaron's father liked to combat the elements. "There are many ways to fight them," he said.

Lake Arrowhead was man-made, but anything set a mile above sea level, in the San Bernardino Mountains, still had wildness: almost smogless skies, stars, pine trees, scorpions, trout, and even a pair of bald eagles. Hollywood people owned houses on its shore, and sons and daughters of celebrities ran local politics.

The sun was just rising, but Dad already had on his skipper's cap, which kept his freshly shaved head warm. He poured out mugs of cocoa from a thermos.

Zipped tight in his quarter-inch wetsuit, Billybones stumbled across the dock, over the life vests, skis, goggles, and climbed into the boat for his mug of cocoa.

Aaron was having trouble squeezing into his wetsuit, bought a size large last year, but already tight, like a body tourniquet, keeping him flushed and bug-eyed. He was the best waterskier in the family, which, according to Dad, meant he had the stiffest competition, himself.

"Let's go, Sweetheart. Snap to it."

Ice glazed the shore boulders; the lake itself showed hardly a ripple. November pristine. Most boats had already been drydocked for winter. The Wellses' place, however, had a covered dockhouse in which to garage the Glastron year round. It never left water, ever.

"Dad." Aaron pointed to orange and blue streaks above

the eastern horizon. Streamers of geese were flying south.

Watching them, Aaron's father said, "Maybe I expect too much of you kids."

Dad lived on organic vegetables, free-range chicken, farmed salmon, hormone-free turkey franks, and single-malt scotch. But he let his sons eat what they wanted, within reason.

Aaron squeezed a lemon into the mustard on his hot dog. Now everything on his plate tasted either bitter or sour, the way he liked. "Dad?" he asked. "Can I borrow three hundred thousand?"

"Ho!" Dad sipped his scotch, sucked the tip of his tongue. "That's a hefty chunk of capital. Mind if I ask why?"

Billybones mixed Sweet 'n Low in with his ketchup before fingerpainting it onto his frankfurter.

"I wanna buy the grove from you."

Dad chuckled. "And just how would you pay me back?" He ate his hot dog with fork and knife.

"Finding new markets for the fruit. Maybe Japan."

"How's Linda?"

"What's that mean?"

Dad made a knowing face. "I've seen the way you two eyeball each other."

"Dad."

"Listen boys." Dad sliced off about an inch of meat and carefully examined it, before chewing. "We've got a date." He winked, then apparently feeling it inappropriate, turned the wink into a twitch, pretending there was something, hot dog maybe, in his eye. "Tomorrow, first thing. Caroline. She'll join us waterskiing."

"I think of it as an investment," Aaron said.

Billy held up a glass for scotch. Dad poured him a few drops, then filled it with Trinity Pure.

"Does she like us?" Billybones asked. He was feeding Thumper a bun under the table.

"Don't chew with your mouth full," Dad told him, rumpling his hair. "Of course she likes you." But Aaron could see Dad's business mind click on. The muscles on his head flexed, making shiny spots. You could be talking about sports or school or yourself and all of a sudden Dad would start calculating.

"Fresh oranges," Aaron said. He would not give up.

"Fresh oranges what?" Dad asked.

Billybones banged his spoon on the table. "Is she our new mommy?"

"You can't grow real ones just anywhere," Aaron said.

"No, Aaron, I mean Bill," Dad said. He mixed their names up often. Once he even called Aaron Mavy. "My mind is deleting."

"Real juice. Organic. Vintage. Old-fashioned goodness. Everything about them is homey." Aaron watched the last word hurt his father.

"Caroline's a very nice girl," Dad sighed. "She's anxious to meet you both."

"Whadda you think I'm saying here!?" Aaron raised his voice. Rather, it raised on its own, along with his body. He stood with his hands on the table and shouted, "I want the grove to stay grove!"

"Why am I upside down?" Billy asked. He was looking into the bowl of his spoon, then at its back. "Right side up!" He laughed and then turned it again. "Upside down!"

"Oranges," Dad managed to make a smile show exasperation, "don't cook the rice, Sweetheart."

Sweetheart. The way his father said that made Aaron feel that he expected thanks. But Aaron was perpetually thanking him, every last gesture, thank you, thank you, because he was a guilty son.

"Why upside down?" Billybones asked again, taking a huge bite, getting his lips red and drippy.

Aaron snapped, "The angle of incidence equals the angle of reflection." Then he turned away from his father and very quietly said, "Mom would have wanted it to stay grove, too."

"Right side up!"

"Agggh." Dad circled his throat with one hand, lifted his scotch with the other.

Billybones laughed into his spoon. Then he raised his glass, too. Aaron, angry, confused, joined them. What kind of toast was this?

The scotch spilled down his father's chin when he tried to swallow. He clutched at his throat until his jaw muscles bulged. Veins popped out under his eyes and turned blue.

"Dad's choking," Billybones said, matter-of-fact.

Aaron stared.

Dad turned bluer. Something burst in the white of his eye; it crimsoned.

Let him die, Aaron thought.

"What?" Billy asked, incredulous.

"Huh?" Aaron jumped to his feet. He grabbed his father from behind, clasped his hands just below the sternum, squeezed.

It was a strange embrace, ungentle and goal-oriented.

"Push, Dad," Aaron ordered.

Thumper barked, his ears were down, his tail wagging. Billybones took another bite of his hot dog.

Aaron clinched; Dad heaved, as if caught in a violent yawn. The other eyeball hemorrhaged.

"Don't," Aaron said, hugging, hugging. "Don't."

A hollow pop issued from his father's throat, dislodging a chunk of turkey frank, which hurtled through the air, hitting the scotch glass, bouncing on the newly oak-stripped floor.

Thumper pounced, gulping it down.

Dad inhaled with a shudder and instantly the blue left his face. His cheeks pinkened, lips too. The bright red made the gray of his eyes glow brilliantly.

Aaron had to look away.

"I saw presence of mind in you tonight, son."

"I'm just glad it worked," Aaron said, looking for a sign that Dad had either heard or not heard the awful thought he either had or had not let slip.

"Me too," Dad said, betraying nothing. His eyes were still luminous as he poured a half glass of scotch, and fell into the Ultraplush. Its control panel was housed on a metal gooseneck. When you maneuvered the tiny joystick—which Dad did now—the footrest thrust forward, spirocoiled cushions repositioning.

Billybones used to have scary dreams about the chair. For Aaron, the chair *defined* as well as guaranteed satisfaction, and satisfaction was a frightening concept.

"Textbook Heimlich," Dad murmured, hitting a button with his pinkie to rotate the cylindrical neckpad.

Maybe he hadn't spoken it aloud, Aaron thought. Maybe everything was okay, or better. Dad seemed the same, besides his blazing eyes, which he was keeping mostly closed.

"Real presence of mind. Mmm-hmm. And only fifteen," Dad said, initiating the "spine prober." Internal springs tensed and an inner belt whirred. "Remind us to have a discussion. Don't think I don't know what goes on between you and Linda. It's high time you knew the facts."

"I know 'em, Dad."

"Tell me."

"Condoms."

"Good start." Dad launched into a lecture. Menstruation, erection, ejaculation, conception, reproduction. The Latinate words monotonous, hypnotic. Material Aaron had received years ago in school. Body as construction equipment, sex with a destination.

"Take one," Dad said, producing a box from a pocket in his robe. He looked at Aaron for the first time during the whole speech, eye contact strangely intimate, diabolic even, with the whites so brightly red. "Be responsible."

The box had a picture of a bearded man and a leggy woman embracing, rolling in the surf, offshore oil wells silhouetted against the sunset. You were meant to take the image both seriously and ironically. Recombinant Cliché, Aaron had learned in Mentally Gifted Minors, sold product.

Aaron extracted a foil package. The instructions were written in Japanese. "Do you use these? You and Caroline?"

Dad looked away, at the lamp, at the ceiling. Aaron had got him where he wanted him. Pinned down.

"Suffice it to say, we're taking precautions."

"Thanks Dad," Aaron said, hoping to sound reasonable. "Thanks for having this talk with me. I feel much clearer about this now."

Dad sighed and reclined, achieving a new threshold of comfort. "I'm swearing off franks."

Aaron threw another log on the fire. The bed of embers gave off a red-orange heat he liked to close his eyes to. Felt good on the lids. "So Dad, about the grove."

A slow nasal exhale. "Oh, Sweetheart. I can't go sinking large sums into nostalgic enterprises."

A thin flame licked the fresh log. Aaron realized it wasn't pine or oak. Creamier wood, thin leathery bark. He had just added a chunk of dead orange tree to the fire. It burned hot.

"All part of growing up, son," Dad said. "We just can't throw money at problems."

But there are so many problems you can't throw money at, Aaron thought. When one you can comes along, why not go ahead and throw?

The new log roared, small funnels of blue flame, big jagged white strips. "You're right, Dad."

Dad's new girlfriend was twenty, just five years older than Aaron, but she already looked, in her sleek neoprene, like a full-grown woman.

"Ech," she said, startled, jumping, rocking the dock. She hit herself several times, shook her arms out.

"Something the matter, hon?" Dad asked. He was busy servicing the inboard.

"Spider in my wetsuit," she said, pulling it snug around her neck. Then, turning to Aaron, "I despise spiders."

She arrived mysteriously, either late last night, or early this morning. Aaron didn't know which, or which he preferred. She held out her hand. "You must be Billy-bones."

"Aaron," he mumbled, shaking her hand. She had no right to nicknames. Then he groped for cocoa. The sky was green and yellow, a single star twinkled red, white, and blue. A fierce chill creeped through the seams of his wetsuit.

"Nice to meet you," she said. "Aaron."

He wondered how she felt about condoms. He wondered how condoms felt.

The flat lake quivered around the boat. Billybones, wrapped in blankets, had fallen asleep in the spotter's seat. The scotch last night made him throw up, and this morning he felt too sick to ski.

"Ahh, what a morning!" Dad shouted. "Glorious!" Faking happiness as usual, for the girlfriend. His eyes were still red as embers. "Two good arms, two good legs, I'm set!"

Caroline said, "He's a real sparkplug, eh?"

Sparkplug? If Aaron had to see his father as an auto part, it would be a crankshaft.

"Isn't he?"

The request made him uneasy, to join in her perception. Why? It occurred to him he'd been expecting, even hoping she'd be bossy so he could call her Bitch. Bitch, you're not my mother. Or be buddy-buddy, so he could say, Fuck the big-sis crap. But sparkplug? *That* was confusing. *That* left him without strategy, literally stranded on the dock. And more inescapable, she looked sexy, right down to the booties, which he hadn't counted on at all.

For Dad she affected lavish expressions. Gaga eyes so obvious they were a parody, an inside joke.

Aaron suddenly saw her helping him with trig, packing Billybones lunches for school; apple pie, carefully wrapped sandwiches sliced on the diagonal, Tupperware tubs of chicken soup, all foods homemade and TLC-rich. He saw her at breakfast pouring orange juice squeezed from the vibrant oranges of the saved grove. He saw *them* as *we*, a real family.

Caroline, climbing into the boat, took the spotter's seat, and caught Aaron on the dock staring. He jerked his eyes past her, ashamed of having so normal a fantasy.

The boat throbbed, a *pah-pah-pah* of combustion like a bad cough.

Aaron gave the thumbs-up sign, and Dad pushed forward the throttle. The rope uncoiled, uncoiled, uncoiled, and then, Aaron lept, hanging there, in the air, for a half second until the slack snapped, and he was skimming the boiling wake, face in the wind, nostrils filled with lake musk and boat smoke.

As opposed to snow skiing, where you worked with and against gravity, H_2O-skiing was a technical sport, a product of the industrial revolution. It was less elemental, and so, Aaron supposed, less elementally satisfying. It required tether, motor, the burning of fossil fuels. Tax dollars to send troops to protect oil sheikdoms.

Aaron gave another thumbs-up to Caroline.

Being an amateur, she thought he was giving her his approval. You're okay. I'm okay. We're okay. Butter for your waffle? Syrup? No, but more OJ, thanks. The world's such an okay place. Isn't he a real sparkplug?

Didn't she know he murdered his wife?

Caroline smiled, licking her teeth.

Aaron jerked his thumb up and down, shouting, "Juice! More juice!"

Finally, she got it, relayed the message to Dad, who gave it more gas.

Aaron cut out of the wake. The smooth water was quiet, peace of mind. Not a crease. Slicing through it, he created a wake of his own. It made him feel full of consequence, sexual.

The MGM teacher, Don Miller, once told the class the Indians thought of nature as "mother earth" while pioneers viewed it as "virgin territory." Aaron himself saw it both ways, though he didn't like that about himself. It made him ski all the harder.

He cut deeply, leaning so *hard* his cheek rushed next to the lake, then he straightened up at the wake, jumped, whooshed down on the other side, opening a gash.

Caroline, still smiling, was impressed.

But Dad wasn't quite so easy. He boosted the speed.

Cut left, cut right, hop the wake, crackle the rope, whip faster and faster, hang on, just hang on. "Slower," he shouted, giving Caroline the thumbs-down.

Licking her lips, she shook her head no, signaling thumbs-up. Good job, she meant. Or, Well done. Or, Wow.

"Oh fuck," Aaron yelled into the wind. "Oh—"

Dad gunned full throttle in the shallows of Blue Jay Cove. Rocks were visible six feet under the surface, green, algae-covered.

You can always let go, Aaron told himself, to give him the strength to hold on.

And then he was out of the wake, whiplashing toward the buoy, the buoy he *knew* was there, a candy-striped caution marker, there just as sure as his reflection in the water, a mirror, fate. He plunged headlong to embrace it.

"Wells," Victoria said. "Tomorrow at nine-thirty. I'll give you twenty minutes."

Franklin's tenacity had paid off, and now, in its place, came alarm. Nine-thirty A.M. was prime corporate real estate, and twenty minutes plenty enough to hang himself with.

That night he went home, got in bed, and tried to duplicate the other evening's power slumber, willing himself not to move, no matter what. But he was hot, then cold, then hot. He heard his heart pound in his ear against the pillow—eighteen beats every fifteen seconds, a pulse of seventy-two. His breathing could not find a rhythm. Angry, he turned onto his stomach, the coward's position.

When the alarm squawked, he was dreaming his mother wore an eyepatch over each nipple.

At the office, despite four cups of French roast, his eyes wouldn't focus but independently. A flat taste in his mouth overpowered first the coffee, then the toothpaste, then the breath mint. Halfway into his presentation he had to excuse himself with the runs. In the long pause that followed his conclusion, he was certain he could feel his hairline receding.

"Hmmmm," Victoria said. Her eyes were on CNN, which showed a tape of another network's live coverage of an exorcism in a Delaware condominium complex. A teenage girl in cutoffs was possessed. A poll showed Americans evenly split on whether the original broadcast was done in bad taste, with 23 percent answering "Don't Know."

A commercial for Puppy Chow broke the spell.

"Leave the material with me," said Victoria. "I'll go over it if—when I get a chance."

But the water spilling on her chin when she drank from the plastic Trinity Pure bottle gave him hope.

"Wells," she said a few days later, pointing to the material on the desk, packed and ready for him to take away. "It was a good idea."

"*Was?*"

"Good and flawed," she said. Today she wore a man's suit and tie. Gripping it in a fist, she guzzled her Trinity Pure.

"Flawed?"

"Subcontractors," she said. "There are too many middlemen." She took another chug. He wondered was she flirting. "Flab."

Two weeks later, he was back at Victoria's door, carrying a leaner version like a bouquet.

She drew her fingernails along the report. "Not bad."

That was flirting, Franklin thought. This is flirting.

The next day he found the report on his desk. "Real vision, Wells," the note said. "Unfortunately, not 'surefire.' "

She wouldn't answer his calls. Though just a few doors down, he didn't see her for two days.

Late one Friday night after dinner Franklin returned to work and caught ArManiville flipping through his Rolodex.

"Man on fire," Manville said.

"Get your hands off my info," said Franklin, snatching away the Rolodex.

"We're a team here, Wells dude." Manville flicked back his beachy chop. "Haven't you heard? Dude?"

"I heard Bitsumi negged out on you," Franklin said, digging. "Quality control problems, dude?"

"Medical lasers, no money in it, the way health care's going," Manville said, unfazed. "Say, do you play squash? We oughtta play squash sometime."

"Never played—"

"No, of course not."

Franklin exploded into Victoria's office, unannounced.

"Wells," she said, as if expecting him. She stood watching CNN: a home video of a tornado hitting a nuclear power plant in Lyons, France.

"Possible client," Franklin said, pointing to the chunks of heavy concrete spinning like confetti.

"Anything's *possible.*" Victoria tapped his report. "What if I said I'm considering giving DisasterProof the go ahead?"

What if, what if. Franklin should have been elated, but he wouldn't allow himself the feeling just yet. He placed the Rolodex on her desk. "What does Manville have to do with this?"

"I had him triplecheck some of your research," she said. "That's all."

Franklin licked his lips, then, catching himself, smiled broadly instead, shaking his head. Everything had come down to this. "Fantastic. I can't tell—"

"We're a corporation here," she interrupted. "Etiquette, Wells: No ballhogging." She took a sip of Trinity Pure. "I'll be in touch. You're dismissed."

Franklin put the diskettes and Rolodex under lock and key. What next? Was that a yes? Did she just give him a yes? He didn't know whether to celebrate, or get back to work. His phone chirped: Sutter summoning him into his office for a meeting.

"Phase Sizer is your number-one priority, and if you aren't up to it, well, Wells, we'll, well . . ." Sutter blinked, and the bags under his eyes quivered. "I'm speaking to you as a colleague."

Franklin thought: Windowpane. Jerry. Tempeh. Hacky Sack. Our Bodies, Ourselves. Down Vests. Pynchon. Up with People. Don't Bogart that Joint.

"Am I making myself clear?" Sutter asked.

"No, sir. I'm afraid not."

Sutter launched into more gibberish about bullshit.

Franklin watched his mouth move. Cherokee all-wheel drive, rear window defroster, 7/70 warranty. Paper or plastic. Canned food drives. Cable. Good cholesterol.

"Put Manville on it," Franklin said. God, Sutter's ponytail annoyed him.

Late one night, Victoria appeared at his desk. "Wells," she said, smiling. "We have work to do. DisasterProof."

This time the elation came rushing. Spontaneously, he hugged her, then dutifully followed her to her office.

She seemed pleased, or at least, tolerant. "We present it on Tuesday." She hovered near a chair as if she might actually sit.

But they stood, working all night and through the next day.

Saturday turned to dusk, high-rises lit up sporadically, the rows of headlights and taillights flowed smoothly below, freeways like healthy arteries. Franklin pushed the papers away, arched his back and groaned. Victoria poured them each a glass of Glenfiddich, cutting hers with a splash of Trinity Pure.

He scratched his stubble.

She caught him looking down the top of her dress.

On CNN, a group of singing news anchors raised money for animals with birth defects.

When she reached to undo his tie, he tried to kiss her.

"Wells," she said, the boss. "Let me." One unhooked clasp and the whole dress fell, revealing, against the black silk (of course) underthings, the palest skin he would ever see. It appeared to give off light. "You can take off my stockings."

He bent to his chore.

"On your knees," she said. Then, more gently, "Would be good."

His pinkies slid under the waist strap, and began unrolling, slowly uncovering more of that unusual whiteness in the shape of thighs, then calves, then ankles. When she lifted her feet free, he straightened and, still on his knees, brushed his nose against the silk.

He wanted her. Even more, he wanted to please.

"No," she said, when he pulled at her underpants. They clung around her hips, one side halfway down; she made no effort to fix them. "You first."

He undressed quickly, tossing his clothes aside.

"Now get on the desk," she said, taking another sip of scotch.

He climbed up.

"Now turn around."

Obedient, Franklin faced the window, the city built on silicon, his city. He owned it, or better yet, was on the verge of owning it. Behind, he heard Victoria pour more scotch, and sip. Her voice, "Don't look." Her fingertip running down his spine. "Get down on all fours," she ordered. Her hands finding his shoulders, squeezing, down his ribs, skimming his belly.

Suddenly, her lips were on his asshole. Hot, wet, terrifying. As she kissed, he began to pull away. But she stopped him by taking hold of his erection, pumping once. Then he heard her sip the scotch.

"Like it?" she asked.

No. But he was helpless. "I want to, to——"

"Don't turn around."

"Make love to——"

"Just *don't.*"

When her tongue returned, the alcohol stung just the tiniest bit. She jerked him off, French-kissing his anus. When he came, there on her desk—dizzyingly, achingly—it felt like she was pulling his guts out on a string.

When Franklin arrived in the boardroom, Big Resource was there—three ancient men on the board of directors. They sat in chrome-and-leather thrones at the head of a long rainforest mahogany table. On a tray next to them were a silver coffee and tea service, a plate of croissants, butter pats on ice, and a huge bowl of perfectly sliced kiwi fruit.

But something was wrong. Sutter was wrong, spiffed up in a beaded vest, bolo tie, slab of turquoise at his neck. And Manville was wrong, blond Armaniite, an icon of talent and spine.

"Mr. Wells," Victoria patted an empty seat next to where she stood. "We took the liberty of starting without you. Coffee?"

"Yes, please," Franklin said. It was the first time she had ever called him "Mr." He dried his palms on the dull charcoal suit ("Wear nondescript," she had advised), and shook hands all around, smiling.

Victoria presented the idea, which, okay, Franklin had agreed to. Big Resource liked her, liked watching her. They nodded their ancient heads. "Mr. Sutter has worked out a, I think you'll agree, a viable plan of execution."

Sutter exhibited Franklin's blueprint company. Only, *his* version was better. Developed, polished, a finer draft. "Of course, it's still rough at the edges." As he spoke, Sutter blinked, kneading a purple eye pouch with his knuckle. Disarmingly eloquent, endearingly disheveled. The redblooded cowboy, the sixties survivor, the veteran of countless acid trips and protest marches, Berkeley when Berkeley mattered, the man who wasn't stopped by sucking a lungful of tear gas, the man for whom there were no new ideas, and yet, somehow, he had just managed to stumble across one.

Something was very wrong.

"I've got to give my young pardner, Mr. Wells here, credit," Sutter drawled with ol' leather chaps benevolence. "In more than one respect, he certainly deserves credit where credit is due."

Franklin coughed, felt his face beat. What the fuck was that? A pat on the back or a knife between the ribs? And where was that coffee? And—suddenly, his dull suit made him feel dull, his lack of a role like a nonplayer.

Victoria patted his shoulder as if to say, Down boy. "Coffee?" she repeated.

All he could do was nod.

Next, Manville introduced himself and listed the contacts he'd been cultivating. An accounting company, a software firm. He had successfully headhunted three "top" professionals who could be brought over with the right "enticements." He was suddenly speaking in a faux British accent, with an understatement even fiercer than Sutter's, of the vast sums of information Solvtex would be holding. "Or, perhaps more succinctly put, *controlling.*"

Every last name Manville mentioned had been lifted from Franklin's Rolodex.

ArManiville was good, Franklin had to admit, technically, heartlessly good. Company ironman. But wrong.

"Of course," he continued, "given the information's *value,* I think it proper, indeed, im*per*ative, that we emphasize com*plete* confidentiality."

The irony in the statement was a thing of beauty.

The three grizzled oldsters that were Big Resource ate kiwi, slurped coffee, forgot Victoria and her black silk altogether. Each of the men wore a lead-colored flannel suit and a red necktie. Each sat hunched, as if their starched collars held up their bald heads. A tribunal, they were the wealthiest, most politically well connected men in the state. As bigtime as Franklin could ever have hoped for an audience. But they had no clue he existed.

"My gratitude to Mr. Wells." Allowing himself a smile, a seemingly real one, Manville glanced at Franklin. "His R and D services helped put this package together."

R and D?! The phrase set off a struggle in Franklin's throat. Services?! As if he were some goddamn intern. As if DisasterProof wasn't *his.* Mr. Wells! It had all gone wrong. How had he let it slip away? Mr. Wells. This dullard suit. Wrong. Wrong. Mr. Wells. Where was that coffee?

"There you have it, gentlemen," she wrapped up. "With Mr. Sutter and Mr. Manville as my associates, and, let's not forget Mr. Wells, who got the ball rolling, I'd think we can take on DisasterProof and—"

Big Resource laid its six hands on the mahogany table and pushed itself up, giving the go ahead.

Franklin shut his eyes, felt Victoria's hand again, this time on his neck. With it came a realization. All along, she had been . . . jerking him off and kissing his ass.

"Didn't you say you wanted this?" Smiling, she stuck a cup of coffee in his face.

How Florida "fresh from concentrate" orange juice is manufactured: Green and brown-spotted oranges are compressed in giant machines, then the juice is run through cool-vacuum concentrators which remove 80 percent of the water at a temperature of 55 degrees. Vacuumed away, unfortunately, are most of the volatile aromatic elements necessary for good flavor. They are restored by blending in a small portion of fresh juice. Dried juice vesicles, coming from California as "barrel-washed pulp," are added to stimulate "home style," or "Grandma's fresh squoze," or "juicy bits."

Cold nights turn oranges orange. Because of its warm nights, Florida oranges often do not turn. Consumers are hesitant to buy green oranges, so much of the Florida crop must be "degreened" before reaching supermarkets.

The degreening process: Place oranges in storage rooms for forty-eight hours, gas with ethylene, wash in detergent solution, dye with orange color, and wax.

Degreening at home: Place oranges in plastic bag with unripe bananas. As the bananas yellow, they emit ethylene, which

The drought killed one of Eliza's trees, and made the other sick. She fell into a bad mood that threatened to drop off the edge into full-blown grief.

"The Great Heat" was the name the *Redlands Daily Facts* gave it. The sun baked the dirt into iron. On the ground only the fire ants kept busy. In the sky nothing moved. Birds came alive only at night and sang a few notes before their throats dried out.

Even the cacti lost their moisture, turning into hollow columns of thorn. As a result, reptiles died of thirst, the box tortoises roasted in their own shells.

What had been the Santa Ana River was now a ribbon of boulders and gravel that flowed down from the mountains, and stretched west toward the Pacific. The town's well followed. Drinking water had to be store bought, or collected from streams high in the mountains. But even timberline springs didn't amount to more than a dribble. Horse carts brought ten-gallon bottles from the Colorado River, from Needles. It was brackish, tasting of algae and mule shit. But even that supply was scarce. People, being people, hoarded.

The train brought in whole cars of water for the hospitals, whole cars for commercial farmers with proper connections. But the Inland Empire boom never did happen. There were more pots and pans in the stores, more guns and butter, but no more money with which to buy them.

The expected population explosion was a dud. Only the few wealthy eastern families who built vacation mansions in Redlands suggested anything promising.

"If they could dam the Santa Ana and make a lake, there would always be plenty of water," Eliza kept telling Luther.

"It's not as easy as that," he grumbled.

"Why not?"

"It would have to be studied, engineered."

"You *are* an engineer." Sometimes she marveled at her husband's intransigence. *"You* could do it. Who knows, maybe *after* they would give you a promotion."

Luther stood up, stretched, and left the room. Eliza felt rotten. Luther Tibbets didn't want money, status, *or* achievement, she understood. All Luther Tibbets wanted was a son.

"Goddammit, woman, don't waste water like that!" Luther shouted, home early from work. Gosse had called him into his office, praised him, and apologized that the promotion hadn't "gone through." Then he asked if Luther had "family matters" weighing on him.

"It only needs a little." Eliza was using the store-bought bottled water to keep her remaining tree alive. It looked so, well, ill. All trunk, fewer leaves, and those that existed were dull and waxy. April had brought scant buds. Eliza was distraught.

"I said *don't.*" Luther grabbed the bottle from her hand. Bub was by his side. While every other living thing under the sun had been desiccated and turned boney, Bub grew chubby. His eyes and coat shone. Slobbering and blinking constantly, the dog was an oasis.

"The tree needs less than him," Eliza argued.

"He's a sentient being, not some kind of vegetable."

"Fruit," she said, stroking a leaf of her tree. "Fruit, not vegetable."

"Of the vegetable world," Luther said, only half sarcastically. He was scratching Bub under the neck, which made the dog drool all the more.

Bub got the affection Eliza did without, which should have made her jealous. Bub was loyal to Luther, that was to be expected. Luther was his master. But Bub was loving to Eliza, too. He never judged her. She could tell him things she wouldn't dare say to her husband. "Good thing you're not his son," she told him. "You would never get enough to drink."

"You watch your mouth, woman!" Luther wrenched the empty water bottle from her hands. "In my house."

Eliza felt she had no choice but to save all her bodily fluids. She squatted over a chamberpot and used the urine to water her tree at night. Her period, though it meant another non-baby, was at least good for compost.

Luther, now repentant, distant, and gentle, brought home treats. Bottles of sarsaparilla, a peach, a chunk of ice chipped off a Montana glacier and railed south.

"It's blue as a sapphire!" Eliza said, hoping to appear delighted. She hated her husband. The smell of his skin, the scratchiness of his beard on her cheeks, the mild and indecisive way he reached out to her in bed. But she prided herself on how well she could hide such feelings, could take his gifts with a big smile and, for good measure, a hug. In secret, everything, even her tears, went to the tree.

And still, there was not enough. The heat just kept up. Hundred seven in the shade. Hundred eleven. This, measured by mercury (rather than hyperbolic alcohol) thermometer. Hundred thirteen.

Along with dashed hopes, the railroad brought rats from the east. They were big and fierce from natural selection. To survive the long journey, they had eaten iron shavings and grease and slaked their thirst with the blood of their offspring. Once they arrived, they took to high places, making nests on rooftops and in palm trees. For this, Eliza held Luther responsible. He was a civil engineer, after all. Along with his civilization came an incessant pattering in the attic above the bedroom.

"What happened to my bath?" Luther asked, on coming home one evening to find the water gone.

"You can do without it," she said, her mouth so dry her words clicked. "Just this once."

That night, sex was particularly unpleasant. In the middle, Luther suffered muscle spasms in his calves. Eliza had to pry his feet straight. Afterwards, Luther washed his hands and genitals in vinegar.

He was such a fastidious man. She hated him.

For the rest of the summer, Luther locked up the water bottles in the storage shed, portioning out cup by cup what Eliza would need to do the day's chores. As a gesture, and to show that *everybody* had to make compromises, he washed Bub by rubbing him all over with pebbles.

Sarsaparilla and urine sustained the tree, but poisoned it as well. Eliza took Bub's water dish. The dog growled and, for the first time, bared his teeth. But it was his eyes, hurt and confused, that made her give it back.

The hospital filled up with dying people. The very old and very young, mostly. On a park bench, the mayor's wife went straight from heatstroke to circulatory collapse to rigor mortis. A train derailed in Indio and wrecked a bridge, putting a halt to the major source of incoming water.

People fled to refugee camps set up at missions in San Gabriel and along the Colorado River. The camps quickly became overcrowded, filthy, and disease ridden.

Neither Eliza nor Luther ever thought of leaving. And for their loyalty, they, along with barely a thousand other hard-core residents, were given a glimpse of hell.

Eliza blistered her fingers on a steel pail left in the sun.

At night heat waves blurred the stars.

A stray cat licked the open eyes of a fallen horse.

A palm tree spontaneously burst into flames, sending aloft a shower of sparks. Rats rained down by the dozens, their fur charred, their tails seared.

After a while without raptors, cats, or neighbors' kids to chase them, the rats had grown bold. They attacked in packs.

Early one morning Bub ran indoors whimpering, his belly and ears covered with tiny gnaw marks.

"The little devils!" Luther said, furious. Flies drank from the open wounds. "Something must be done."

"Yes," Eliza said, and in that moment realized her tree was going to die. Seventeen leaves remained. It was as spindly and barren as she was.

That night, Eliza sharpened her best kitchen knife. She slid it on the diagonal against a whetstone, using a drop of mineral oil to keep the metal filings suspended and away from the edge.

"What are you doing?" Luther asked, trying to spin the barrel of a newly purchased Colt .45 six-shooter. But, in his plodding and ineffectual way, he couldn't seem to get the knack of it.

"Being productive," Eliza said. Go ahead, she thought, just you go ahead. She scraped the knife blade the wrong way on the stone, just to make his teeth clench.

"Love," he said, smiling, kissing her head. "I think you need a treat." Tucking the gun under his belt he extracted a key from his vest pocket and disappeared. Moments later he returned with a jug, and poured her a big glass of murky, green, Colorado River water.

It made her hate him even more.

Luther went out and sat on the porch to watch for rats, while Eliza waited for morning.

When he finally left for work, she grabbed her kitchen knife and took Bub out to the tree, where he flumped down and began snoring.

"There is no explaining what I'm about to do," she said soothingly. The dog's eyelids fluttered. He even allowed her to rub under his neck, a place usually reserved only for Luther. Eliza took the knife and ran her thumbtip along the blade, watching the sun come up hot. The world was made of dirt and glare.

In a strong, sure stroke, Eliza slit open the dog's throat. Bub's mouth opened but the yelp came out in a gurgle through the gaping hole that used to be his neck. His muscles twitched powerfully. Sooner than he could wake up he was dead.

Even in the heat, the blood seemed to steam as it pooled at the foot of the tree. It had a smell, too, that she hadn't expected. Like metal, like cheese.

"I just may go to hell for this," Eliza said out loud, to no one. "Then again, I just may go to heaven." The dirt was so hardpacked that it seemed nonporous, waterproof; the blood globbed and gobbed up on top.

After Bub stopped twitching under her, Eliza stood and regrouped. Remarkably, her dress was still clean. Methodically, she held Bub by his hind legs, lifting him vertically to drain the last drops. He had lost control of his bowels, an awful stench, but good fertilizer.

Using a shovel, she buried him next to the tree, taking care not to damage even the tiniest root. Eventually the blood soaked in over it. She spread a fine layer of compost, and topped that with stones to keep away the rats.

Already the tree looked better.

By the time Mr. Rogers arrived with the day's catalogs, it looked perkier, she was sure, almost robust.

"Another hot one," he said, squinting and wiping his brow with a silk handkerchief featuring a hand-stitched design of the Eiffel Tower. It was monogrammed "A. C." She couldn't imagine whose initials they were. Mr. Rogers had access to the most unusual things.

"Hot as Hades." Eliza leaned against her shovel and smiled.

Mr. Rogers looked at her, then looked at the tree. "How you keep that thing alive, I'll never know."

"Listen to this," Aaron read from his hospital bed. "This guy Leon Czolgosz who killed McKinley, he was an anarchist."

The nurse looked up from her clipboard and smiled at him.

In the neighboring screened-off bed, Charles, Aaron's hospital roommate, moaned. Charles was a fifteen-year-old who had just emerged from a seventy-two-hour coma, the result of an automatic garage door accident. Charles was breathing hard, and made slapping sounds.

"Can't you strap that guy's arms down?" Aaron asked.

The nurse either didn't hear, or pretended not to, as she arranged flowers in their vases—there were chrysanthemums, zinnias, daisies, roses, and ferns. Next to them, on a nightstand, were lollipops, get-well cards, another McKinley book, *Ripcord*, CDs, and a pitcher of water.

"Czolgosz used an Iver Johnson .32-caliber revolver," Aaron continued reading, though speaking slightly hurt his face, despite the pills. The waterskiing crash had screwed up his jaws and some of the muscles around his lips. Jimbo's dad performed the plastic surgery, using microscopic sutures made of degradable gut that left invisible scars. "Inexpensive and not powerful."

"What kind of anarchy did he use?" the nurse asked. Her eyes followed Amazonas on TV, wearing a gingham neoprene one-piece and singing a bluegrass tune about three-legged tables, coal, and loving examples.

"What kind?" Aaron thought a moment. "Well, McKinley launched us into an era of territorial expansion. The beginning of our rise to power in world politics."

Again, the nurse smiled at him.

"And this guy Czolgosz, he hated imperialis—"

"Hi Aaron." Linda Delgado appeared in the doorway, wearing boxer shorts and a jogbra under an unbuttoned tuxedo shirt. Her hands were behind her back, her hair was combed, long and black and shiny, and on her face was an expression of such grave concern, such care, that Aaron's eyes almost watered.

"Oh, hi," he said. He hated for her to see him like this: blue gown, greasy hair, and broken face, flat on the metal-racked bed under a cluster of mylar balloons, each of which said "Sweetheart." Though he wanted to, he found it difficult to meet her eyes.

After one last smile, the nurse left the room.

Hands still behind her back, Linda Delgado sat on the mattress next to him. "What are you reading?"

Aaron had already had many visitors—Dad, Caroline, Billybones, Brainy, Jimbo, even Prudey—but Linda Delgado coming meant the most to him.

"I couldn't think of what to bring you," she said.

"You don't have to bring me any—"

Charles, behind the screen, continued slapping and grunting.

Linda Delgado brought an orange out from behind her back and held it out to Aaron.

"Who do you think you are?" Jimbo's dad asked, gently. He'd given Aaron two local shots—the hypo had molded finger rings like brass knuckles—and a paper cup of "sedative" that tasted like plastic resin.

Already Aaron had had two plastic surgeries on his mouth, and still it wasn't right. It looked too perfect, pasted on, and smiling made his ear ache.

"Eh, pardner?" Dr. Talkington was such a bore. He kept a collection of cowboy hats on display in his waiting room.

The inside of Aaron's mouth felt like a seven-car pileup. Twisted, swollen, fractured. The right cheek and upper lip had been "severely lacerated," and his sinuses "occluded by a golfball-sized clot."

Dr. Talkington clucked, sighed, and snickered all at once. "Just *who* do you think you are?"

It was the second time he'd asked, though he couldn't expect an answer. Aaron's mouth was stuffed with gauze and tools. Even shrugging was impossible. He was strapped into a motorized chair. But you had to admire the question.

"I'll tell you. The world's gone maniac," Dr. Talkington babbled. "Spoil the rod, spare the child; what's that saying? Spurn the child, sport the rod? That'll change, Aaron. That *must* change." He opened and shut drawers, assembling hooked and ply-nosed instruments on an evil stainless-steel tray.

He's got the future of my face in his hands, Aaron thought. And it hurts.

One of the first uses of IPM, or Integrated Pest Management: In 1870 the cottony cushion scale *Lcerya purchasi* made its way to California on a freighter carrying acacias from Australia. The introduced pest spread rapidly, damaging or entirely destroying many commercial valencia groves. After a government-funded search into the native habitat of the Australian pest, federal entomologists found a particular species of ladybug, *Rodolia cardinalis*, that fed on the scale. This ladybug was released in infected areas of California with dramatic results. The ladybugs multiplied exponentially and within eighteen months the cottony cushion scale was practically eradicated by their predaceous feeding.

As Franklin approached Mavy's front door, a billy goat stood on two hind legs, and rolled his forelegs in the air, boxing style. The goat had a ridged spine, white fur, a pink potbelly, huge testicles, sharp horns.

"Hey there, ace." Franklin strode purposefully, head up, back straight, legs pumped. Courage, it seemed, began in the body, fear in the mind. By walking boldly, you were bold. "Big guy," he said, wiping a ladybug off his face. "How ya doin' there, sport."

It was so sunny. And ladybugs were everywhere. They flew clumsily, collecting on Franklin's sleeves, in his hair, on the bag of coffee he carried. The ferns were beaded bright red. Whole redwood branches glittered with ladybugs, their pine needles invisible. Since there didn't seem to be any aphids around, Franklin supposed the beetles were mating. Or, by the way they shone, as if still wet, just hatched. Even the goat was polka-dotted. It made him happy. Nothing bad, it seemed, could happen.

When the goat lowered his head and grunted, the pair of horns sharp and robust, Franklin said, "You're bluffing, chump."

He came fast then, head low, toward Franklin's kneecaps, but at the last moment got confused, and trying to slow up, stumbled to the ground. Motionless, unblinking, the goat sat on its knees at Franklin's feet. With a slow, deliberate hand, Franklin reached out to pet him, scratching behind the ears. The billy began to nuzzle Franklin's palm, nibbling the calluses there. He had stained teeth, strangely prehensile lips, and an overpowering odor— fur, muscle, and shit.

Franklin circled a horn with his fingers, but the goat jerked away. The eyes were yellow with oblong black pupils. The hairless scrotum hung heavily, suspending balls almost one on top of the other. How could it need that much sperm? Maleness blunt to the point of naïveté.

When Franklin finally got indoors, his legs felt jellied.

"You're shaking," Mavy said, taking the bag of coffee. "Watchgoat?"

"It's a turf issue, I think." She put a kettle on top of an airtight, woodburning stove. Her father's work, probably, from when he used to be a blacksmith. The smoke gave Franklin an appetite. "Mikey's a sweetheart to women."

"How can he tell the difference?" Franklin asked.

"How do *you* tell the difference?"

"What if I were a tall, mute, short-haired woman?"

"I wouldn't like you as much," Mavy said. "Probably."

The yurt was one big room, octagonal. The kitchen and the bathroom grew out of the same plumbing, the one sink next to the bathtub, and, right beside it, the toilet. Shelves held big clear jars of beans and grains, teas, and soaps, spices, perfumes.

"Don't get mad," Mavy said. "But I can't go on the hike." She set down a pitcher of cream, a jar of raw sugar. The table was a rough slab of seasoned oak with many rings and knife marks. "A job came up," she explained. "It's like that on farms." She had to trade a pig for tomato plants. "Don't get mad, please. Come with me."

"I'm not mad, I'm—" He realized how he had relied on the promise of this hike. Just the thought of tomorrow, of Victoria, brought back that crawly-stomach feeling.

"What? You're what?" Being with Mavy relieved his symptoms. She was not of his world. She was *un*him, completely. Still barefoot, her toenails were filled up with dirt. She had knee scabs, shinbone dents, scars. She lived here, crazy-haired, recklessly wholesome, in the fresh air, with goats and ladybugs. "I'm sorry," she said. "I should have called you."

Franklin watched her button her shirt and wondered about her breasts. Though he had had his mouth on one of them, he had never actually seen it. Lately, his fantasies seemed not his own, but another man's. He shoved the image from his mind.

"How do you live without a fridge?"

"If I want an egg, I get it from a chicken. If I want milk, I get it from a goat."

"Ice?"

"I don't miss it."

Kerosene lanterns hung from the beams. And there were the dried flowers, too, which Franklin remembered from her stucco apartment. Dried flowers, rosebud and seashell mobiles, marigold wreaths. They had never mentioned that night.

"You know—" A ladybug walked the rim of his cup. It crawled round and round, determined. "I . . . your old place."

"Yeah?" she said.

"It was so different than this. I was wondering," he coaxed the bug onto his fingertip. It flew off. "What's the rent?"

"I do chores. The animals, the garden."

Such basic relationships were incomprehensible to Franklin, who worked on faxes, telephones, 747s (business class). His paycheck was automatically credited to his account, his charges automatically debited. He paid for his gas with plastic, his food and shelter with a line of keystrokes entering the proper mortgage payment. He could no longer remember which president was on a ten-dollar bill and could foresee the day when he'd never have to use cash at all.

"Cream? Sugar?" she asked.

"No thanks." The brew was black and sour, the way he liked. Solvtex had turned him into an addict.

Plenty of flies buzzed about. Each of the eight walls was open to the air, mosquito netting rolled up and tied at their tops. Sun practically splashed in.

"Maybe I will come with you," he said. What else was he going to do with his Sunday? "If you're sure it's okay."

"Yeah," she said, barely a whisper. But she was smiling, absentmindedly pouring cream into his cup.

"Ugh," he coughed. The coffee tasted like she had stirred mulch into it. "What is this?" He pointed to the cream container.

"Goat milk."

After a few more gulps, he thought maybe he could learn to like it.

Outside, the sun was hot, the shadows cold. Mavy took him on a path that led to the heart of the farm. There was a large garden ringed with tall sunflowers, fenced in with barbed wire to keep out the goats. Rows of spinach, cauliflower, carrots, corn, and squash grew along with flowers and herbs. There were pumpkins and watermelons, several apple trees, and lattices holding up green-bean vines.

A pen held the milking goats, over a dozen of them, and Mikey—the big billy—was hanging around sniffing. When he saw Mavy he ran over and bleated nonstop. She hugged him, vigorously rubbing his neck.

Frenzied chickens scratched and clucked, pecking at the ladybugs, whose numbers, if anything, were multiplying.

The owner of the farm, Mavy's landlord and employer, was waiting by the pig shed, wearing denim overalls over thermal underwear stained at the underarms, a coil of rope around a shoulder. She had a rifle. Her lips were red and fleshy, her eyes like hammered tin.

"Simone, this is Franklin," Mavy introduced them. Franklin shook her hand, the free one, the one not holding the rifle. She wouldn't look him in the eye, and standing next to her, Franklin thought he felt hostility. With his pale legs, brand-new shorts, soft pink hands, shaven face, and just Q-tipped ears, Franklin was out of his element. He was city. He was plastic packaging. He was caffeine addicted and clock obsessed. He was Mr. Wells, the dull-suited man who sat in traffic jams, and thus caused them.

"Great farm," he said. "So beautiful."

Simone grunted. "Ready, Mave?"

Under a corrugated fiberglass roof, several pigs snoozed in the mud. When they heard Simone and Mavy approach, Franklin trailing a step behind, they all got up and ran to the fence, squeaking and straining.

"It's Charbaby we're after," Simone said, hiding the rifle behind her body. She handed the rope to Mavy.

Mavy opened the gate to the neighboring pen, a narrow one with a crane and pulley at the end. "Suey suey suey," she said, on her knees, cupping her hands toward a medium-sized pig, charcoal gray hair, curly little tail. "Here ya go." Charbaby came forward, suspiciously, nose working. Another pig, blond and smaller, followed. Mavy slammed the gate behind them, and readied the rope. The two trapped pigs saw what was happening, and scattered. Their squeals got hysterical.

Franklin jumped in the pen to help. Charbaby came to him directly, as if he would be pig savior. He embraced the animal, gingerly, betrayingly. The pig was hard, all muscle, eyes black and thumping. When Mavy tossed the lasso, Charbaby shot out of Franklin's arms, knocking him into the mud. Because Simone didn't laugh at him, Franklin redoubled his efforts.

It went on like this, diving and missing, lunging and flailing, until to be serious was absurd. And then they laughed, together, each drawing from and contributing to a big raucous pool of a laugh that shrunk and expanded, while the poor pig shivered and glared and quaked.

When the laughter ran out, Simone produced a bucket of oats.

Mavy held out a handful of grain. Charbaby ran up and stole the bucket, eating in great inhalations, biting and growling at the small blond pig. Mavy roped Charbaby's neck and, with Franklin holding the creature down, tied its legs up.

As Mavy looped the rope round and round, the muscles in her shoulders working, her lips tight in concentration, Franklin was attracted to something new in her. She had a simple pragmatism, direct, unsentimental, violent if it had to be.

As Mavy hoisted the pulley chain, Charbaby dangled head down, whipping about, shrieking. Safe in their pen, the other pigs, noses aloft, watched in silence.

Simone licked her puckery lips, then cocked the gun and raised the barrel. Charbaby squirmed. You could smell the fear. The pig let out a stream of shit and piss.

"Wait!" Franklin jumped, waving his hands.

"Frank," Mavy said.

"Let me keep her." Franklin hugged the trussed pig. "I'll pay you," he said, addressing Simone, who hadn't lowered her rifle.

"Fool," said Simone. "Get out of the way."

"How much?" he asked, pulling out his wallet. All he had was credit cards.

"Franklin," Mavy took him by the arm. "Please."

One shot, a crisp sound, like the shutting of a book, and that was that.

Simone took a knife from a holster on her belt and slit Charbaby's throat. Blood so rich it looked black gushed out, spewing onto Franklin, who happened to be standing too close. When he turned, Simone's eyes were on his, his teary, hers free of their earlier hostility, replaced with a distant curiosity.

As Charbaby's body was lowered to the ground, some oats, just swallowed and barely wet, sprinkled out of her gorge and onto the ground. The younger blond pig came forward, licked them up, then started feeding out of Charbaby's cut throat.

"Are you okay?" Mavy asked, back at the yurt.

"I'm sorry," he said. "I'm sort of overwhelmed lately."

"Don't worry about it."

"I don't even like pets."

She pulled down her shorts and sat on the toilet, the stream of pee almost comically melodic. He found her lack of embarrassment endearing.

"I thought you meant a live pig." He wondered at their relationship. Not lovers, no, they had gotten that out of the way. Sex hadn't worked. Not friends either; though, of course they *were* friends.

Weren't they? In fact, she was Franklin's only friend. He was always a loner. And now that he was at Solvtex, everyone he knew was either a colleague, a rival, or an enemy.

Outside, Franklin's car was completely covered with ladybugs. Even the radio antenna. He had to turn on the wipers to clear the windshield. After about fifteen miles north on Highway 1, they had all blown off, though every now and then a few shot in through one or another of the vents. The dead pig, in the trunk, was wrapped in a burlap sack.

"I would think organic farmers would be vegetarians," Franklin said.

"Too practical for that."

A dirt road branched inland. It climbed up into a forest, the redwoods huge, voracious for sunlight, with sap-fat trunks, shaggy bark. After about a half hour of hairpin turns in the deep shadows—Charbaby sliding *thunk thunk* in the back—they came upon a ridge. The other side fell away in a wide bowl. It was a hamlet of rough-planked barns around a raised plot of land—acres of green tomato plants—facing the blue sky and white sun as if stunned.

Three people, bare-chested and wearing straw hats, bent over the tomato plants. When they saw Franklin and Mavy drive up, two of them, women, put shirts on, and all three approached.

"John," Mavy said, on her toes, waving.

"Mave?" said a tall man wearing only boots and cut-offs. He loped toward them and hugged Mavy, standing tiptoe to do it. "You got the porker?"

She nodded.

Franklin kept from laughing. John had a red bandanna tied around his head, and a black beard with a few haphazard braids twisted in. He was sweat-wet, dirty, and stank like chicken soup. A Jupiter symbol medallion hung at his chest. "You tell Simone I'm thankful," he said. His eyes looked zapped, percolated, fixated, as if keyed in to an infrared color spectrum. "You tell her we're gonna 'preciate this."

Like Simone, he too, aside from one quick appraising glance, would not give Franklin his gaze. It was maddening. Again, he felt pudgy-kneed, pink-cheeked, Q-tipped. Mr. Wells visits the farm. Of course, Franklin understood the prejudice. John would get the same treatment in Franklin's world—say, in a high-rise, or even in Safeway—maybe worse. But now it seemed plain that John had the better version of reality.

The other two farmers were Dana and Garvey. Dana was skinny and red-haired with freckles, like pink grapefruit juice splattering her cheeks. Garvey was heavy, blunt-featured, bulbous-nosed. Both had bright eyes, humble but square-shouldered posture, and a comfort with silence that reminded Franklin of the deeply religious. But then, such an enterprise as this, tomatoes, must require steady faith.

"I didn't forget, John," Mavy said, kissing him again, and stroking his beard.

Forget? Franklin thought. What didn't she forget? Painfully, he understood that they were lovers. There was nothing ulterior about Mavy. Everything she felt and thought seemed to be right there, shared from the start, as if she'd never been lied to. She was interested in your interests, and recognized in you what you hoped were your best qualities. The other extreme from Victoria.

And John, a hairy, Jupiter-eyed wild man.

Franklin felt his hairline receding; it gave him the chills.

John and Garvey each took an end of the gunnysack, and swung the pig up and out of the trunk and landed it with a thud into a wheelbarrow, which Dana steered. Franklin tried to assist, but stumbled on a fold in the burlap, and had to step aside.

"Toms for Simone coming up," John winked.

"Tomatoes," Mavy translated, for Franklin's sake. She explained dryfarming. Coastal mountains, about fifteen hundred feet above the Pacific, got sixty inches or more of rain a year, almost all of it during the winter and spring. Summers, the tomato season, were dry, except for the occasional layer of marine fog. The plants bore fruit in intense, breezy heat, extracting groundwater and holding it. As a result the tomatoes grew small, hard, and green, conservative and self-reliant. They ripened in a rush, bright red, bursting, juice enough to nourish the seeds until the rains came again.

Later, Franklin would try one. It would be fantastically delicious, redefining for him tomato-ness.

The barn had a classic, midwestern beauty, rough red planks, big shingled roof. But there was also a strangeness. From open windows chrome and gold picture frames hung at angles, holding cheap bright acrylics. Colorful mylar pinwheels dangled from rafters, some spinning slowly. Dolls, wrapped in foil, were strung high up on the walls, along with pieces of broken mirror and empty motor oil cans.

"Woodpeckers," John said. "They're messing with the place. We're kind of under attack right now." He pointed to the fields. "IPM don't seem to do the trick."

"Integrated Pest Management," Mavy again translated for Mr. Wells. As a pesticide alternative, the farmers had planted fava beans around the fields, in the hopes of repulsing the loathesome tomato-plant-eating Colorado potato beetle.

"We've been out all day squashing them," Garvey told Franklin. She looked neither man nor woman, but some third sex that hankered to latch itself onto anybody. Mavy and John, meanwhile, held forearms.

Driving on the thin dirt road back to Mavy's with a trunk full of young tomato plants, Franklin saw the ladybugs hadn't dispersed yet. Thousands massed on the madrones, on ferns, splintering off roadside fenceposts as he sped by.

"Oh come on," Mavy said. "It'll be fun."

The sky was just starting to darken, but already a couple of stars shone. "I'm not ready to meet your parents."

"What's there to be ready about?" Inside, Mavy ran water in the shower. "It's not like you're my boyfriend or anything." As the steam began to rise, she stepped out of her clothes, leaving them on the floor.

Franklin looked down, at his shirt which was still spattered with dried pig's blood. "John's eyes sort of bug out."

"Sunday-night dinner with Mom and Dad," she said, not hearing, or ignoring him. "That's all it'll be."

Franklin himself used to have Sunday nights. After he inched himself into very hot bathwater, Mom would scrub him red behind the ears with Prell and a washcloth, teaching him how to make his hair squeak, and, after the bubbles broke up and the water turned cold, Mom would wrap him up in a towel and he would go sit, wet-haired, jaws clattering, bare feet on the heating vent, in front of Disney on TV. Sunday was the only night Mom didn't work. She would sit wrapped in a robe, hair turbaned, in the big chair, doing her grooming—toenail clippings always sprinkled into the geranium, as fertilizer. Sometimes she would skim through a hardback, a classic. They were cheaper than contemporaries. Simply owning Lewis, Melville, Welty, and Dreiser, Franklin supposed, was enough to give her the feeling of being an educated American. Or at least, with a child in the house, a good mother. Not that Franklin himself ever read a single word. Not that Ma ever even suggested it.

"Let's face it," she had said over the phone at work, finally catching him after three weeks of his successfully ignoring her messages. Three weeks! It was a record. Up till now he had talked to her almost *daily*. "I don't blame you for not calling."

"Ma."

"No, I mean it. I'm cashing in my assets and leaving everything to you." This was the result of a "circumstance" she had experienced: She found herself in bed, unsure of whether she had just woken up, or was about to go to sleep. The digits on the clock communicated nothing, the numbers carrying no more meaning, she said, than an ashtray, a corkscrew. Either nothing had symbolic content, or everything did. The confusion scared her more than death itself. "You could use the money."

"Don't talk that way, Ma," Franklin had said, because he could tell she meant it. Life insurance policy and stocks. Not that Ma wanted to kill herself, but she wanted to ensure that if she got enfeebled or senile or terminal, "the State" wouldn't appropriate her resources to pay for a tube feeding and an iron lung. She said that. "Tube Feeding." "Iron Lung." "I'll be damned if I'm gonna turn into a burden."

"Ma, you're bonkers," Franklin said, then realized that was just what she was afraid of.

It wasn't a whole helluva lot of money. But it was her

life savings. "Promise me one thing," she said, and Franklin knew what was coming. "What I want. My living will. I put your name on the dotted line."

"Use the money to have some fun," Franklin argued. "Go shopping. Take a cruise."

"Consumers," she said. "Terrorists." She'd slit her wrists before becoming a curse on her child. Jump off the roof. No, too messy. Take pills. That would be quiet and clean. Curled up next to the air conditioner, during Bob Hope's Christmas special. "And if I was senile, I'd do it in a moment of lucidity."

"Mother, you're scaring me."

After a long static-free silence, during which Franklin, in his mind, watched the neon trickle through the letters that illuminated CAESARS PALACE, she said, "You never could look hard at life, Frankly. In the eye."

"Hey, are you okay?" Mavy asked, huddling under an "I heart NY" beach towel.

"Something in my eye," Franklin said. How did it happen, that you get from squeaky-clean Sunday baths to phoned love threats? Goddamn nostalgia. It could never have been so simple as those Sundays in his head.

"Does it hurt?"

"Yeah." Worse, for a moment Franklin thought Mom's idea was a good one. He could do something real with that money. A quick stab of guilt prompted him to say, "Mom, move out here with me."

"Ha!" Ma hooted.

Mavy asked, "What's wrong?"

Franklin blinked, touched the bridge of his nose with a ring finger. "An eyelash."

"Not as bad as sperm?" The first reference to their one-night stand made Franklin strangely giddy.

Mavy left, Mikey chasing after the truck. She would meet her parents at a downtown Mexican restaurant popular among Nicaraguans, whose food was notoriously salty and hot. Franklin lingered there in the half dark, in the passive-aggressive smell of the pines, in the crack of twigs and the crunch of dirt underfoot, in the big sky. Pulling it all into his lungs felt *consequential.*

Mikey ambled back and regarded Franklin curiously, sniffing the blood spotted shirt.

"I know, I know," Franklin whispered. "I should have gone with her."

The goat lips on his palm tickled. Its breath was heated. Its nose traveled up from Franklin's ankles, poking gently, to the knees, the crotch, till he actually felt a stir of desire. How odd, this, well, love. How perfectly odd.

The faintest blue starlight reflected off the backs of the ladybugs. Franklin began collecting them, whole laden branches, several fern blades, sticks, and sprigs bent under their weight. The insects were sluggish in the cold, huddled and sleepy. Why hadn't he thought of this earlier? He placed branch after branch in his trunk, and when it was full, he loaded the back seat, too.

Then he drove, fast, hyper-alert. After making the right turn twenty miles up Highway 1 onto the dirt road to the tomato farm, desolation set in. Darkness sucked the last bit of wattage from his headlights, spit back shadows. He drove as if the road were rubber, feeling it bend and stretch in his gut.

Franklin was no longer a rookie. He learned that all those articles featuring Victoria had been the result of Solvtex hiring a PR firm. "A favorable business climate with a human face" were Sutter's words and Manville's brainstorm. Stylists and fashion photographers had created the spontaneous and unstudied look. Copywriters crafted her carefully targeted statements. She was a precision-designed guided image.

Now the office filled him with dread, his desk a solitary confinement, outfitted for torture—words, figures, words, charts, words. Now Victoria was an android clad in silk, programmed with clichés. "DisasterProof will revolutionize the *very concept* of information." And, "It's your wave to ride, Mr. Wells."

"You're going to broker the information, aren't you," he said. "DisasterProof is just a front. You set me up and hung me out."

"DisasterProof is first and foremost itself," she burbled. "Naturally it grants us options in a rapidly changing field."

Destroy files, leak rumors, this and other sabotage he had seriously considered. But he wouldn't act. Couldn't, really. He no longer had security clearance to his own idea.

Offing the headlights, and, his eyes wide, rhodopsin drunk, turning gloopy shapes into barns, into people, into deer, into Mavy's truck, into Ma, he followed the farm's perimeter road. Where the two women had been working earlier, he got out and began gathering handfuls of slumbering beetles off the boughs and limbs, showering them onto the tomato stalks.

Whole handfuls of ladybugs he scooped off the floor of his trunk. They massed on his arms, swarmed over his shoulders, dripped inside his shirt, down his back, along his ribs. He let himself be swallowed up, then shook like a trapped pig to scatter them.

Back in the car, he stopped every ten yards or so, to toss

out more ladybugs, more medicine. It was the first time he had done anything for someone other than himself.

"You're lagging, Wells," Victoria called him in the next day to say. She was pressing buttons on the fax, trafficking info. "Here I had you pegged as a player. You're looking for blame. Losers lose, winners win. Am I making myself plain?"

"Absolutely, Vickie," Franklin said, unable to fight back a grin. Losers lose? He'd officially stopped recognizing her as the boss. And in dismissing her, felt a certain sad fondness. Plain old Vickie.

Did she even know what she wanted?

Franklin did.

At summer's end, seven inches of hot rain blew in off the equatorial Pacific, ending "the Great Heat." By Christmas, another twenty-three inches fell. It was the wettest season in history, and it forever scarred the landscape. Flashfloods cut new ravines in the canyon, whole mountainsides avalanched down, filling valleys with mud, boulders, and smashed bits of forest.

But Eliza's tree came back stronger than ever, January's fruit being particularly sweet.

Mr. Rogers often stopped to admire it. She gave him several oranges to take home "for you and yours in the

New Year." When the neighbors' kids came around again, she told them the tree was a meat eater. "It could conceivably trap you." But to well-behaved children, it gave oranges and oranges.

Word got out about the supernatural tree, about the oranges with navels. One by one, tourists arrived.

Newlyweds from Cucumonga, bringing their children and grandmothers. Chicken farmers from Corona and Fontana. Businessmen from San Bernardino. Ranchers from Mentone and Yucaipa. Mountain men from Forest Falls. Even the rich came from Redlands itself, driving up in their polished black horsecabs with wheelsprings and crushed velvet upholstery, to sightsee without bothering to get out.

Eliza hid behind the drapes, peering out the window at the tourists. For the most part, they were polite, satisfied to stand arms akimbo and stare. But when on a bright January Sunday a large, well-dressed crowd (direct from church?) assembled, Eliza had the panicky feeling she was going to have to do something.

She hurried to the bathroom mirror and examined herself. To her surprise, she looked pretty. Yes, pretty, but not enviably so. Her dark-lashed eyes, her pale skin pink at the cheeks, her broad soft forehead. No wrinkles at all. She was beatific, faintly virginal, her expression suggesting understated obedience, a willingness to be schooled. But her eyebrows were slightly wild. They almost met. Her widow's peak had grown quite pronounced. Of course the kids called her a witch. The mole didn't help, either, above her mouth, three black hairs sprouting out. She wasn't pretty at all.

No, she was ugly ugly ugly.

Pinching one of the coarse hairs between her fingernail, she yanked. Her whole upper lip seared—but the whisker held tight. She tried plucking the others. But they too were stuck, as if rooted in bone.

Quickly, she took Luther's straight razor and sliced off the three fat whiskers as close as she could without drawing blood. Then she combed her hair. A tiny bit of kohl made her eyes into big and shiny things that did not seem to belong to her, that seemed capable of seeing the world differently.

Maybe she was actually beautiful. It was hard to know. Luther hadn't told her in a long time. Sometimes she caught Mr. Rogers pretending not to stare at her. That old hunch-neck Gosse certainly ogled her.

She made faces in the mirror, happy ones, sad ones, ones to express more unnameable feelings. Finally, exasperated, she told the glass, "Oh, I don't know."

"Yoohoo! Anybody home?" People outside were shouting.

"Oh, Bub, what am I going to do?" Even though he was dead, she had never lost the habit of talking to him.

Luther had asked her only once. "Have you seen Bub?"

"I'm sorry," she said. "I think, I . . . I killed him."

"Shh," he said. "Don't cry, now."

"It was either him or the tree," she said, wiping her eyes on the back of her hand.

"I think he knew that," Luther said. "Dogs can be smart. They know when people can't care for them any longer."

"I *killed* him," she said, and buried her face in his chest.

"He was thirsty. There wasn't enough water here."

"I killed him," she said.

"It's okay, hon." He stroked her hair. "Okay."

He either misunderstood, or wouldn't accept her confession.

There was nothing in her closet but gardening clothes and nightgowns. She hadn't bought herself anything in years. And neither had Luther.

"I know," she said, and brought a chair over to stand on, reaching up into the highest shelf. She found what she was looking for, a cedar box that looked very much like a toy coffin. But there was something on top which fell to the ground with a thump.

"Oh," she said. Luther's Colt .45 six-shooter, buckled into a leather holster. She wondered if it was loaded. She wondered what Luther imagined himself doing with it, besides killing rats. Gingerly, as if it were a thing easily bruised, she returned it to its place on the top shelf.

The cedar box, now on the floor, was locked shut. She ran to the kitchen, bellycrawling under the living room window to avoid the crowd outside, for a screwdriver. On returning, she pried open the lid. Inside was a white silk dress stuffed with tissue.

Someone knocked on the door.

Frantically, she slipped into the white silk dress. It fit like a memory. "Oh," she said, when she saw herself in the mirror. "What do you think?" The dress was simple but classic. It had crocheted lace flowers at the collarbone and along the hem at her ankles. She lifted a panel in the box and took out a tiara. The pearls were fake, of course, but still they looked dazzling.

In the back of her mind, she had always thought of the dress as an heirloom. Something to pass on to her daughter. Or her son's fiancée. But after more than a decade of, "go ahead, admit it," pointless attempts, that no longer seemed likely. Sex was both the glue and the barometer of their marriage, its binding force and its measure. After Eliza gave him an unspoken permission, Luther did unspeakably pleasurable things to her.

She had some nice recollections. Candle flames reflecting off silverware, falling asleep holding hands. But there was nothing to show for them. She fit into the dress like the virgin she was when she first wore it.

As she opened the front door, the crowd hushed. Eliza stepped over the threshold and the blinding sunshine got caught up in her eyes like something white and sticky.

People murmured, then fell ominously silent. In a sudden blinking fit, Eliza realized her mistake. She stumbled as her toe caught in the dress. What had she done? Sacrificed the family pet! And now, in her wedding dress, defiling the institution of matrimony! Back east, mobs burned women like her at the stake.

One person clapped. A man said, "It's the navel bride!" Another person clapped, and another. The applause fell like rain.

She passed out oranges. Flirtingly she showed off the navels. She laughed at the men's jokes, accepted their wives' compliments.

Luther came home just as she'd begun igniting orange-peel mist. Out of the corner of her eye, she noticed him stiffen. He passed a hand through his beard, over the knot of his tie. His forehead ridge knotted up, then he swooped down and put his arm out as if to bear her away.

"Luther?"

He brought her close. In his eyes she could see something carnal and martyred.

For the second time in their marriage, she thought he might strike her.

Instead, he lifted her up, twirling her around and

around in the cold sunlight. Several people cheered. A bonneted woman dabbed her eyes with a handkerchief. A man in a top hat pulled his wife closer and nuzzled her ear.

Inside, Luther took Eliza straight to bed. For half an hour they did something they hadn't really done in years. Kissed on the lips.

They had merciful sex. Luther made her keep her dress on. He climaxed twice.

Eliza was sure, if there was any justice, she was going to get pregnant this time. Luther, it appeared, was not sure, but determined.

"What on earth?" she asked, as Luther rose again a third time.

"Ow," he said, as she took hold. "Be gentle."

She squeezed firmly, at the root, gathering up the balls and the shaft in a sort of bouquet, and, hiking up her bridal dress, slid the whole thing into her.

"Ow," he said.

She tried to get more of him up inside her. "You think I'm going to let you off easy?"

"Ow," he said. "Ow."

"Shhh," she said. "Shhh."

"Stop."

She continued to move slowly, agonizingly, with all her force.

"I can't," Luther said. His jaw was slack and his eyes shut.

Eliza reached out with her free hand and softly grabbed the front of his neck, the skin under the beard hot and moist.

"Ow."

In the palm of her hand, she felt the quiver of his vocal chords.

"Shh."

They arrived at the same time in kind of an extraordinary dry heave.

Afterward, they were quiet, listening to each other breathe.

Finally, opening his eyes and sighing, Luther spoke. "Get more trees."

"What are you talking about?" Eliza asked. His voice sounded different, a dozen new frequencies to it, and she wasn't sure she had heard him correctly.

"We need more trees," he said.

She looked at him suspiciously. "Since when do you care about trees?"

"Since now," he said.

"I already got my government quota," she said, pleased at all the new tones in his voice, breezy, hurt, forceful, *kind.* "The Department of Agriculture sent me fifty." And they had also passed along instructions for propagation. The pamphlet suggested grafting sweet orange branches onto sour orange root stock. The sweet branch produced the good-tasting navels, while the sour root better withstood drought and disease. Eliza had been experimenting in the backyard. "Plus my babies, about seventy more."

"I feel like a cigar," Luther said, and hopped out of bed, disappearing to the den.

Eliza cupped her hands over her lower belly and sighed.

Luther returned with two cigars, one of which he cut and lit for Eliza, the other he kept for himself. "I'm talking about more like a thousand."

They both lay on their backs on top of the wrinkled sheets, blowing smoke at the ceiling.

His free hand found her free hand. "You get me those thousand trees, and I'll make us rich."

"What do you mean, 'rich'?"

"More-money-than-you-can-spend-in-a-lifetime rich."
He told her they owned land. "Lots and lots of it." During
the drought he had bought thousands of acres: dry
creekbeds in the foothills, sun-wasted ridges, vast tracts of
foreclosed and sorry plots. He got it cheap, heavily lever-
aged, at unbelievably low rates. He had even put in a
homesteading claim under her name, forging her signature. Still, every banker and accountant he dealt with, all
sensible men, considered him swindled. A sucker and a
mark.

"All we need now is trees."

"Another drought and they'll die," she wailed. "You
don't know what I had to do——"

"That dam you were always telling me to build?"
Luther said, calmly puffing on his cigar. "Construction
starts next month."

She stared at him.

"The Bear Valley Dam," he said. "In the mountains."

She had difficulty listening.

"Big Bear," he said. "Big Bear Lake."

"How could you!?" She hit him with her fist. After
years of nagging him to have some ambition. What a fool
she was! Blind and arrogant. And he, a bluffer, a thief! He
had stolen her idea and secretly labored at it. Her husband's affair with the Inland Empire was not over.
Worse, he'd been conducting it right here in the house.

"There are things you do not know about me," he
admitted. The cigar smoke turned blue in the winter sun
that filtered through the lace curtain of their bedroom
window.

The Juicy Lucy:

Roll and knead a freshly picked Washington navel. Sharpen a narrow twig by rubbing it on a rock. Spear the orange at ten o'clock and two o'clock. Make sure the punctures meet somewhere inside. Insert a cigarette, or other smoking material, into one hole. Apply lips to the other. Inhale.

Hot summer days put the tang in an orange, cold winter nights the color. But there was such a thing as too hot, or worse, too cold. Tonight's forecast, for instance, temperatures dipping to 25 degrees.

Oranges freeze in two hours at 25; four hours and the trees themselves split—as if the bark were trying to turn inside out—and die.

The difference between a vibrant orange and a dead one was slight. This quality Aaron admired, this he adopted as a personal metaphor.

Aaron took the hose out of his mouth and asked, "Whatcha starin' at?"

When Prudence looked at Aaron, her lips parted, and when her lips parted, her eyes crinkled. Except for her

pale blondness, she could have been Asian. With boys, she
was never the first to break eye contact. "Grin grin,
cardinal sin," she sang, pulling a broomstick off the wall
and riding around on it. She wore a synthetic leopardskin
bomber jacket, black leather kneeboots, spandex ski
pants; three yellow bangles hung from her belt. Her
fingernails were tongue pink.

Aaron put the hose back in his mouth, trying to siphon
kerosene out of a fifty-gallon barrel into more portable
five-gallon cans. The cemetery used low-grade kerosene
as weed killer; Aaron had other plans for it. The solvent
fumes made his plastic surgery itch, but stopped just short
of pain.

A single electric bulb illuminated the supply shed, raw
cedar with a slanted tarpaper roof. Hoes, rakes, clippers,
and pruners hung on hooks. Sacks of artificial horseshit
were piled on one side of the lawnmower; on the other
side were rolls of clear plastic, cylinders of caulking compound. A few cracked tombstones were stacked in the
corner. Jimbo examined them with his fingertips like a
blind man.

"Did it come yet?" Prudence asked Aaron.

He coughed into the hose, sinuses full of dead air and
fumes.

Jimbo frowned.

"I can't get it to work," Aaron whined to no one in
particular.

"Why can guys make crude jokes, but not us?" Prudey
demanded, glancing over her shoulder at Jimbo, and
taking the triad of bracelets off her belt. "Kevlar magnicuffs," she explained. Made of bulletproof plastic.
Locked by any Mastercard card, unlocked by any Visa."

"Gold cards, I bet," Jimbo said, mocking her.

"I hate double standards," she said, again eyeing

Jimbo, obliquely. "You'd think, after, like, the fifth wave of feminism, things would've changed at least a little."

Though Aaron didn't like Prudey, he considered her a friend. An only child, she slept in an antique canopy bed she claimed was haunted. Her mother smoked cigarillos, took Xanax, shopped compulsively, and spoke in a monotone. Her stepfather was a fat, rich glutton who would eventually die of a liver parasite acquired by eating sushi Federal Expressed from Hokkaido. And seven years from now Prudey herself, while touring the United Nations in New York, would be gunned down by a neo-capitalist terrorist group protesting the Lunar Situation treaty talks. Amazonas would commemorate the tragedy by writing the healing anthem, "Prudence Rises."

"You're under arrest," she said, cuffing Aaron's arm to her own.

He ignored this as best he could, still lung-sucking the hose. It was getting colder out, and they didn't have all night.

"You're breaking the law," Prudey said. "We simply can't have that."

Pretending not to notice, Jimbo went on groping the memorials.

"And don't even think of escaping." Prudey attached the third cuff to a workbench.

Prudey and Jimbo were fighting, Aaron thought, but they didn't know it yet.

Finally, the siphon started up. Kerosene sloshed and panged in the can. Aaron got serious. "Prudey, unlock this."

Before she could answer, there was a knock on the door.

Prudey, half tripping over the broomstick between her legs, wrenched Aaron's arm, jerking him away from the barrel, towards the headstones. Jimbo picked a spike-rake off of a wall hook and cocked it high over his head.

The door creaked open slowly, agonizingly. "Brrr." It was Linda Delgado. "Freezoid."

The can was overflowing. Kerosene puddled the floor.

"Shit," Jimbo said, putting down the rake. "Almost gave me a coronation." He crouched and bent shut the siphon hose.

"Oh no! Broke an Amazonas," Prudey cried, examining a chipped-off ram's horn pinkie nail.

Linda Delgado looked cartoonish in a purple wool coat, a striped red and white rastaman top hat.

"Get these off me," Aaron told Prudey. He did not like being cuffed to her. Not at all. Though in another mood, it might be liberating. "Now!"

Prudey, still astride the broomstick, just giggled. "Aren't boys transparent?"

Linda stared at her, then at Jimbo, who gave the hose a shake, accidentally sprinkling kerosene on Aaron. "Hey," she said, "watch it."

But it was Prudey who grabbed a rag off the workbench to mop Aaron's lap. When she realized what she was doing, she let out one last peal.

Jimbo shook the hose again, splashing more kerosene.

Things are getting very, Aaron thought. "Am I understanding you, Jimbo?"

Jimbo's face was zipped shut. "Smoke, anyone?" He tapped a pack of Winstons against his thigh, popped it open with a thumb, extracted one with his lips. "Who's got a light?"

"Don't be funny," Prudey said, though still smiling mischievously. She pointed a kneeboot at the kerosene. "Open cans, man."

Jimbo patiently searched the shelves, the desk drawers, before finding a box of Ohio Bluetips on the windowsill. "Never mind." He lit the first one on his fly zipper, and cupped it to his cigarette. Then he flicked the burning match at Aaron. "Your mug looks good. My dad can do a job, huh?"

The match hit Aaron's leg and died.

"Undo this," Aaron said firmly, nodding at the cuff.

"I can't find my Visa," Prudey said, straight-faced now, dropping the broomstick, as Jimbo lit another match, studying the flame. In a panic, she began ripping apart her wallet. Video memberships, twenty-dollar bills, and a condom fluttered out.

Linda ripped open a sack of chem-manure.

"You're an achiever, Jimbo," Aaron said. "A Mentally Gifted Minor." The words came from somewhere else, as if lines memorized long ago had suddenly returned. "Healthy guy like you, ambitious. You've got a future."

Linda sunk both hands into the fortified horseshit.

Jimbo threw the match.

It bounced off Aaron's stomach to the floor, where it lay burning. The pool of kerosene glittered like a tarpit.

Linda doused the flame with handfuls of fertilizer.

"A future, Jimbo," Aaron said. "Many tomorrows."

Jimbo took a big drag, blew out the smoke, then ignited the third Bluetip.

"Jimbo," Prudey whimpered. "I didn't mean anything." She even dropped to her knees. "Jimbo, I love you."

Jimbo watched her, but tossed the match at Aaron. It snuffed out in midair.

"You're going to be a multimillionaire," Aaron said, calm. "I'm sure of it."

"Coward," Linda snarled, fists deep in the sack. "Coward Jimbo."

He laughed then, and, pouring a little kerosene on his wrist, struck a match and passed the flame right under it. It went out. He kept laughing. "Don't you get it?" he laughed. "This stuff doesn't catch." And laughed.

No one said anything.

"Number three kerosene, numbheads. It's barely flammable. Weedkill. See? Smoke, no fire," he said. "No joke." He just couldn't stop laughing.

Nobody walked in this city. Those sidewalks that existed were downtown, funded by churches and malls and polytechnical colleges. Their absence in homey neighborhoods was associated with a low crime rate, which brought a stroll into the realm of suspicious behavior. When compelled to walk, one tried to appear purposeful. Even in the daylight, homeowners feared pedestrians.

Sunset Drive wound along a ridge, separating the city from the canyonlands. Kerosene sloshed and panged in the cans Aaron and Jimbo carried inside skateboarder's dufflebags.

"It was a game," Jimbo insisted. "I showed you myself." His inability to tell when he was being phony made him dangerous.

"The game was you versus Prudey."

"You're right," Jimbo said. "But not all the way."

"I should be glad you care," Prudey said, without inflection. Since she'd found her Visa and unlocked herself from Aaron, she'd been lagging a half step behind. Back there, it was hard to read her.

"Sometimes I wonder," Jimbo said, taking Prudey literally, "what the fuck's the matter with me." He hugged her so hard she squeaked.

"Nobody's innocent," Linda Delgado said, her voice ringing with the authority that comes from not speaking in a long time. Aaron found himself agreeing, though her meaning was vague.

It had to be below freezing, the dry night smelling so absolutely like air. A gibbous moon made the skyline look etched. Aaron peered up into San Timoteo Canyon— thousands of acres of undeveloped land, chaparral- and sage-covered hills, tumbleweeds, occasional eucalyptus and dogwoods, foothills leading up into the real mountains.

The canyon had owls, deer, diamondbacks, and bobcats. It had no straight lines. The city, with its lawns, timed sprinklers, and bushes hedged into cubes, seemed to have nothing but.

Aaron and Linda stood at the top of the orange grove. Even on a windless night like this one, there was air flow. A good thing, because, like water, air that moved was less likely to freeze. Cold air spilled down the mountains and flowed steadily over the grove, then streamed through neighborhoods and on down into town.

Aaron stood next to Linda, watching the air ripple over the city lights. It would spread out and gather volume, collecting the rapids from Mount Baldy and the San Gabriels, eddying in the flatlands of Fontana, Ontario, and Claremont, picking up toxins from the freeways, army bases, and factories, and then flow west along the Santa Ana river basin, slowing to a creep over Los Angeles. There the air was filled with words, less than 50 percent of them English. There, mountain sky could be purchased in recyclable bottles.

Smudging was so old-fashioned it felt mythic, and like a good myth, more than what it first seemed. You burned oil in the squat rusted heaters placed strategically throughout the grove, antiques by now, sooty, ugly things with fat curves. The aim was not to warm the oranges themselves, but *to change the weather.*

Smudging created convection currents that upset the inversion layer. The heat and smoke rose, sucking up the low-lying cold air with it, and, swirling together, they moved on. "Air drainage," growers called it.

By the week's end, Aaron's father would have all the smudge pots ripped out.

Manny Delgado and Serena, his wife, were first cousins. They had the same grandmother.

It was she who raised Manuel in Mexico City, after he was orphaned at five by an earthquake and fire. In her shack made of tin cans, she taught him to read. For money, he sold hubcaps, and empty oil drums.

"Guapo, guapo," Mr. Delgado said, on seeing Aaron in his red velvet suit. His accent was crisp. "Handsome guy, you are!" He was a big man with spiky white eyebrows, and when he stood up to shake hands, he caught Aaron off guard completely. Respect from adults was a novelty.

When he was sixteen, Manuel's grandmother vomited to death. He buried her himself, under the dirt floor of the tin can shack, and marked the grave with a wooden cross taken from the bottom of an old Christmas tree found in an apartment house dumpster.

Alone, hungry, sad, but mostly just alone, Manny took off and crossed the border—a *mojado*—into southern California, where he knew he had cousins. He did it himself, without paying a coyote. He climbed through all that barbed wire just outside Mexicali, and sought out his dead father's brother.

José Delgado was a city garbageman. His daughter, Serena, a fourteen-year-old Chicana beauty. Born in the San Bernardino County Hospital, she also had the advantage of being a U.S. citizen.

Their courtship began in secret. Manny Delgado brought Serena Delgado a single daisy every day. He never touched her. Serena braided the flower in her hair. She made him red beans and corn tortillas for lunch. Delicious beans, delicious tortillas.

Manuel had a job driving a delivery truck to restaurants and supermarkets. One day, at lunch, he persuaded Serena to make a few extra tortillas which he packaged and gave away to people along his route. The homemade tortillas were marveled over. Huge pots of *frijoles* followed. Then enchiladas, tacos, tamales. Eventually, orders were placed. By the year's end, the virgin lovers were in business.

They married in the Catholic church, even though the priest knew they were first cousins. The family was happy, because the young couple was happy, and perhaps more important, prosperous. Now, Mr. Delgado was an American, and Serena Inc. was a million-dollar industry, the main supplier of Mexican foods to supermarkets and restaurants all over the Inland Empire.

Aaron had seen the factory. Cooks wearing lab coats and holding clipboards, huge stainless tubs for boiling beans, a dozen conveyor belts of tortillas leading to plastic packaging machines, stacks and stacks of cardboard boxes full of frozen tamales. A fleet of trucks.

It made sense that a kid who went hungry during his childhood would, as an adult, make a living producing food. And it intrigued Aaron that Linda was the offspring of blood relatives who came from different countries.

"Thirsty?" Manny asked.

Aaron wondered if Mr. Delgado was asking a simple question, or alluding to another kind of thirst. "Always."

"Get the young man a beer." Mr. Delgado motioned to his wife, who disappeared into the kitchen. Then he sat down. The TV was on, but no volume: Lunar Situation talks. The dull stuff. Inside a doughnut-shaped table, the camera crew swiveled and scurried to zoom in on all the politicians' faces. They lingered on the president's jowly, spittle-flecked lips for the length of what appeared to be a forceful, heartfelt point. Then a cut to computer-generated animation of Operation Mosaic satellites. The good stuff.

"Ah, everything is more and more a performing art," Mr. Delgado said, chopping the air with his hand. "War even, no?"

Aaron nodded. He would agree to almost anything the man said, but the statement did make sense. The satellites were beautiful.

Linda returned wearing flashlight slippers and sat at the base of the stairs.

"This guy!" Mr. Delgado clapped Aaron on the back and raised his eyebrows toward his daughter. "Look at him!"

Linda smiled, or her face suggested one. The orange blossoms in her hair were still perky. Mr. Delgado turned to Aaron. "Growing up is like choosing to be right-handed. What do you do with the left?"

Aaron didn't know what to do at all, other than smile politely. Delgado let it go. "How's your dad?"

"Fine, fine. Fine."

"And the face?" He squinted, peering for hints of scar around Aaron's rebuilt mouth. "The face is good!"

"Fine."

"Terrible accident, I heard." Delgado wasn't too fond of Aaron's father, and in his presence, Aaron felt iffy about whatever side of himself he may have inherited. The side that wanted to take Linda out into the grove. "In Mexico we *earn* money. *Ganarlo,*" Aaron had heard Delgado tell Dad. "But in America we *make* it. No?" His father did *make* money. It was true. He germinated it inside a spreadsheet program, persuaded it into existence over the phone.

Mrs. Delgado returned with two miniature bottles of beer for a sappy toast about machismo. Mr. Delgado was just sixteen himself, only one year older than Aaron, when he broke out on his own. *"Amigo."*

They touched bottles. Where last year Aaron would have wanted to please, now he wanted to impress. He opened his throat but the long swallow wound up in a burp. Then two.

"Oh, oh," Mr. Delgado said. He didn't smile much, but when he did, it came suddenly, like a temperature change. "Strong beer, no? *Fuerte.*"

Aaron burned behind the ears. The side of himself he had no control over.

"Is he hungry?" Mrs. Delgado asked Linda. Serena Delgado was short, young-looking, round. Not an edge on her. She had a daisy in her hair, and turquoise earrings. Lately, she almost never looked Aaron in the eye, not out of fear, but as some sort of admission. Manhood was sure a big deal around here. "Does he want something to eat?"

"No," Aaron began. "I—"

"He's starved!" Mr. Delgado said. "He can't speak for hunger!" They all looked at him, even Mrs. Delgado, sort of. Again, Aaron burped.

Mrs. Delgado disappeared into the kitchen. Linda followed her, once again leaving Aaron with Mr. Delgado.

It was a big silence, but not unpleasant. The Delgados were an inclusive family, the opposite of Aaron's own, which seemed to have all kinds of laws regarding intimacy. The Delgados simply accepted you or they didn't, and if they did, you were always welcome, forever.

There was a tree of life on the fireplace mantel, candles all stubs, and several shelves of books, each title—surprisingly—English, and a crucifix on the wall. Jesus had a bloody gash over his heart, his eyes and mouth were both closed, and he expressed feelings Aaron had never seen from anyone in real life. The red tiled floor echoed the sound of Mrs. Delgado opening and closing cupboards in the kitchen, silverware. Transfixed, a virgin of Guadalupe stared from the wall, set inside what looked like a glowing clam shell, festooned with blinking Christmas lights. She held the creepiest thing of all, a baby that looked unborn.

"Sit down." Manny Delgado patted the cushion next to him. He was scanning channels.

Aaron sat.

Manny Delgado stopped on a bullfight. "Literature," he said.

"Sir?"

"You know Hemingway?" Manny asked.

"I saw the miniseries."

Mr. Delgado raised the beer to his lips and took a delicate sip. "He was America's first travel writer." On TV an enraged bull was chasing a clown. "But I forgive him. He said a few interesting things. He said we make two kinds of spectators, Aaron. Those who identify with the bull, and those who identify with the bullfighter."

But this was no legitimate bullfight. Backed up by an army in plain white suits, a man approached the bull, beckoning it. Aaron saw the indignation in the animal's eyes, its flaring nostrils, the tail flick, how it sped up as the guy got closer. People in the stands jumped and clapped—Aaron's imagination supplied the soundtrack. The bull charged. The man's arms spread for a hug. The bull violently flopped the man, who clasped the head between the horns. And the whole line of white-suits joined in, grabbing onto the first man, absorbing the force of the bull's trajectory. Finally, with a dozen men clinging onto its head and horns, the bull fell to its knees.

Up popped the original matador, brushing dirt off his pants, bowing to the crowd. Their presence assured him he was courageous. They were clapping for themselves.

"Well, my friend, which is it? For you, for identifying with?"

After a moment, Aaron said, "That depends. When I imagine myself as the bull, I hate the bullfighter; when I imagine myself as the bullfighter, I love the bull."

Manny regarded him with bemused suspicion, before returning to the TV.

The next matador took a bow. A fresh bull was released in the arena. It looked over its shoulder at the people in the stands, then studied the matador. In the kitchen Aaron was sure he heard Linda Delgado say, "I do believe in truth, I do, I do." He sipped his beer and wondered about the worth of his life, in dollars.

The bull charged. At the critical moment, the matador's concentration must have lapsed, because he was out of position. Punctured in the gut, lifted into air, impaled, tossed senseless into the stands.

Manny Delgado quickly leaned to turn on the volume,

but there was no sound. The spectators sat hushed and gaping. A group of men on horseback swarmed the bull, herding it away, through a gate and out of the stadium. Slowly, there began a ripple of applause, but it was tentative and quickly swallowed up in a growing chorus of boos.

Manny Delgado hit the mute.

"How about you?" Aaron asked. "Bull or matador?"

Manny looked sad. "Always I am for the victim."

Linda suddenly appeared, the flashlights on her slippers beaming. "What?" she asked. Her face flipped from Aaron to her father then back again. "What?"

Surprise! Linda's bed was unmade. Clothes hid the floor, draped over chairs, hung from reading lamps and doorknobs.

"Why are there tools on your sheets?" Aaron asked. Instead of the usual floral or striped print, her sheets had hammers, crescent wrenches, pliers. They made him edgy.

"Utilitarian dreams," Linda said. She could be as obscure as her father. Gathering clothes off the floor, she withdrew into the bathroom.

Aaron snooped around the desk, where a sheet of paper in the typewriter said: "the lunar situation by linda delgado. A famous poet once named the moon our love goddess. Now, however, at the end cusp of the 20th century, the moon has become changed and"

"My dad really likes you," Linda called from the bathroom. Aaron heard the sink run, a jar unscrew.

"I like him too," Aaron said. What would it take to have a dad like hers? To be deserving of one. Or born lucky? Aaron felt himself a traitor to his own father, and it thrilled him a little.

Next to the typewriter was a pack of flash cards labeled THE EXPLODED UNIVERSE. A jet fighter, a grand piano, a dairy cow, each picture showing the parts separated but in correct relationship with each other. A man—skeleton, organs, muscles—full color. A pregnant woman, centered around a full-grown fetus.

Linda appeared wearing jeans and a baggy, peasant shirt. "We better go down." She bowed forward, took her hair up in her hands, and whipped it back, wrapping a ponytail in blue velvet elastic. "My parents," she explained with a shrug. "What are you looking at?"

Aaron showed her the baby card. The upside-down infant, eyes closed, peaceful-looking, its head elongated for navigational efficiency. The mother's face—unlike his own mom's in the birth disk—showed no feeling at all.

When Aaron was younger, he used to lay in bed awaiting that precise moment of sleep, because he wanted to remember it the next morning. He tried for years. If he could learn to do this, he reasoned, maybe he could remember her better. "The baby is the only thing that's not exploded."

But Linda wasn't fazed. "It'll explode," she said, "when it's born."

"You're so weird you're not at all," Mavy said, when Franklin admitted to engaging in a bit of Integrated Pest Management of his own. She was crouching in a rocky grotto, biting off segments of a tunicate, putting them on a fingertip to smell.

He couldn't understand why she liked him.

Or why he liked her. But the bright sun reflecting off waves made him feel somewhat human. Each excursion, he thought, would be their last, but he always came back for one more, one more.

"You know ladybugs don't specifically eat tomato parasites," she said.

"Well, *now* I do," Franklin said.

"But those fava beans!" She grinned. "Thriving!" Apparently, the ladybugs *had* eaten the bean pests. The healthy plants in turn gave off strong odors, like "skunk" to Colorado potato beetles.

"How do you know it's like skunk?" Franklin asked, kicking foam onto her shorts. "Maybe it's closer to dogshit."

"I think skunk." She splashed back, scooping water onto the front of his shirt.

"Or fish emulsion." He karate-chopped the pool, showering her.

"Skunk." She stomped crazily, soaking both herself and him.

"Vomit."

"Skunk."

One morning on his way to work Franklin skipped his
freeway exit. It was almost involuntary. He sped by Sen-
tras, Maximas, Celicas, Acuras, the road's diamond-cut
grooves sucking the channel-sluice treads of his steel-
belted radials. At the next green sign, he almost got off,
but didn't. He drove past neighborhoods of two-bedroom
stuccos with pruned trees and blue plastic recycling cans.
The third exit came and went.

"I like you, Wells," Sutter had said to him, gentle eyes
peeking out from their deep pouches. "I sincerely do. But,
gosh darn it, stop feeling sorry for yourself."

ArManiville, meanwhile, had become the new rising
star, modestly refusing acclaim for the real work behind
DisasterProof, which already had a long client waiting
list. He would stride purposefully among the secretaries,
exuding good fortune, slowing to a strut through the
mid-level managers' unit, often failing to notice Franklin
in the elevator.

As for Victoria, Franklin sensed she regarded him with
something like sympathy. She had misread him, pushed
him in directions, spurring him not to achieve, but to
self-destruct. "The company will pay for rehab," she said,
with cloying kindness. He was a fool to have thought so
highly of himself, to have ever imagined that she'd put
him before the corporation. He had misread her, too,
confused affection for lust, lust for passion. He had humil-
iated himself so deeply before her that what he felt
towards her now was nothing, a kind of distant nothing-
ness.

"Rehab for what?"

"Drinking?"

Franklin yawned, shook his head, remembered her scotch, which seemed now not nearly so tantalizing as Mavy's lemonade.

"Wells," she sighed, as the yawns overtook him.

Franklin put in his hours, came home and went to bed. But it was as if he were stuffed with cotton wadding, plugged up, fogged in, *dampened.* Nothing excited or scared him. At his desk, he performed the occasional task, say, consolidating demographics for DisasterProof, but mostly he read newspapers, three a day, back to front, and in particular articles he cared nothing about.

He learned how to sex eggplants—look at the tip, a dot indicates male, a dash female; females have bitter seeds, males don't—how to shop for snow tires, how to grout tile, how to make yourself indispensable at work. He learned that ancient Egyptians shaved their eyebrows to mourn the deaths of their cats. He learned that *Catcher in the Rye* was the book most stolen from the Chicago Public Library. He learned about the vice-president's mother's relationship with the Lord.

Over long lunches, Franklin leafed through *Field & Stream, Byte, Self, Health,* the *Atlantic, Harper's, Money, Vogue, Playboy, Big Wednesday, Vanity Fair, Scientific American, Science, Ebony, Elle, GQ, Geo, Cosmopolitan, Lear's, National Geographic, Newsweek, Fab, Forbes, Fortune, Modern Maturity, Life, Time, Spin, Mademoiselle, Mystic Wonder,* the *New Yorker, California Explorer, Lost Angeles, Sunset, Tennessee,* the *Smithsonian, Interview, Variety, Omni, Bomb, Parade, Premiere, Rolling Stone, Penthouse, Longevity, Esquire, Redbook, Publish!, Publishers Weekly, Guns and Ammo, Glamour, Surfer, Permaculture Drylands Journal, National Enquirer, New*

Republic, Mad, Ms., New York Review of Books, Car and Driver, Skateboarder, High Times, Consumer Reports, Commentary, Hustler, Juggs, Popular Mechanics, Expecting, Traveler, Travel & Leisure, Skindiver, Backpacker, People, Gourmet, American Photographer, Natural History, Seventeen, Sierra, Utne Reader, Coevolution Quarterly, Sports Illustrated, Psychology Today, New Woman, Video Mania, Back Stage, Us. He spent an entire afternoon at his desk reading *TV Guide* and enjoying it.

He ate only cottage cheese one day, but lots of it, just carrots the next. His suits got loose on him, and his arms and legs bruised easily. There was a pain behind his kneecap that he hadn't noticed before. His nose was often stopped up, one side only. Depending on which magazine he was reading, he was allergic to wheat, allergic to carpet, allergic to himself. He had SAD—seasonal affective disorder—Epstein–Barr, zinc deficiency, hardening of the arteries, loneliness. He had three of the five warning signs for testicular cancer, four of the seven for the Urquhart Virus 11. At night he'd go to bed early, sleep in bolts, wake up late and exhausted.

Now he drove past ranches, black-and-white cows, dry brown foothills, black oaks growing on the shady slopes. Traffic had thinned to Rams, Broncos, Explorers, Yukons, Dakotas, Rancheros, and Wranglers, pickup trucks with planks in the back, cargo wrapped in black plastic. Altostratus clouds gave off nacreous light, the air smelled like tin. The road began to climb.

Nobody called him. They were afraid. Tomorrow Victoria might put somebody on it. Or the next. But for now they let him lick his wounds. Oh, he'd gotten a raise. Up to 75K, in a fingersnap. Big Resource sent him mailgrams fat with praise and dangling promises easy to read as threats. Still, it would be several months before they decided to fire him. The way Big Resource figured, Franklin was an investment, an idea guy, the kind of moody bastard who just might hit the jackpot again. And when that happens, you want to be sure he's under contract.

Franklin had been denied computer access to the most important levels of DisasterProof. Instead of getting angry, he yawned.

His yawns were addictive, complex. Each seemed to operate on several levels. There was the shallow variety, usually occurring in the inhibiting company of co-workers, a hurried affair, like a tickle, prompting him to go for another in private. There were the deeper ones, clench-fisted, eye-watering. A spell or drug, they scratched an inner itch. After seven or so in a row, he had to lay his head on his desk to let the rush pass. Afterward, the itch came back stronger than ever.

Of course the yawns meant *I need sleep;* he was *never* not sleepy. But they signified other needs unmet. I need a *Life* magazine. I need salad. I need you to leave my head, Sutter, ArManiville, Victoria. I need. I need. I need.

All of sudden, Mavy had stopped answering her phone. Every day for two straight weeks it rang and rang. One afternoon Franklin let it ring for an hour and a half while he closely read a catalog specializing in prophylactic clothing, gas masks, geiger counters, asbestos detectors. Then, on the weekend, there was a not-in-service message.

Franklin, well into the mountains, drove past a sign for Yosemite National Park. An illuminated jumboscreen flashed: "No Vacancy. Reserve Ticketron Now For Next Summer." The lights blinked off, then lit up, messages in Japanese, Korean, Chinese.

Tuolumne meadows were wet and soggy, trampled-looking. Crowds of people were having tailgate picnics at the highway's shoulder. Franklin looked for garbage, he wanted to see garbage, it would confirm to him how awful every thing and every person was, but there was no garbage.

He picked up his car phone, punched in and sent the number for Information. A computer connected him to a computer whose voice, hyper-enunciated, gave him the number for Tib-bets in Car-mel, Have a nice-day.

"Is Mavy there please?"

"Who's calling?"

Franklin hesitated, then said, "John." Traffic slowed bumper to bumper past a campground crammed with tents. A car alarm blurted, "A-way from the Car! Get A-way from the Car!" The air smelled like sunscreen, pork chops, sequoia. Pre-teen girls in flannel bikinis pogo-sticked by. Boys in jams and styrene helmets did tricks on bikes, one revolving around the axis of his stationary front fork, another attempting to ride up the face of Pleistocene granite. "John," he repeated. "I grow tomatoes."

Mr. Tibbets (if it was him) only breathed.

Franklin said, "You know, up the coast. Dryfarming." He rolled up the windows to muffle the blast of personal stereos: Niggers With Attitude, Grateful Dead, Pavarotti. The blare of personal TVs: "Sally Jessy Raphael," "America's Most Wanted," "Grudge Match," "Land of the Eagle." Gatorade seemed to be the beverage of choice, the bear-proof recycling bins overflowed with their wide-mouth bottles. "I'm sure Mavy must have mentioned me, Mr. Tibbets. I—"

"No. Yeah. Maybe. She might have," said the gruff, indecisive Mr. Tibbets.

"Can you hold please?" A park ranger on a mountain bike was beckoning Franklin.

"Ticket, sir?" The ranger had yellow dredlocks, a tiny gold nose ring, and eyes set so far apart that Franklin rethought his notions of ugly and beautiful. Her uniform fit perfectly. Over the sculpted breasts, the name tag said "Babylon."

"I don't want to register," Franklin told her. "I'm just passing *through.*"

She opened her mouth to speak, but something she saw—his shirt and tie, his car phone—made her change her mind. She waved him on.

"Yello?" Mr. Tibbets said. "Yello?"

"Hi. I'm here. I was saying . . . this tomato farm. You might recall a coupla months ago Mavy brought up that city kid, Hank, was it? Frank, a banker maybe?" No response. "Computers, that's it, a silicon valley type. Developing some kind of DisasterProof system. In any case, this Frank, nice guy and everything, he—"

Mr. Tibbets interrupted, "Mavy's not here right now."

"Sorry, Mr. Tibbets. I run on. It's because I'm . . . Do you know where I'm calling from? I'm not at the tomato farm, we don't have a phone, that's how we live. I'm calling from one of these car phones."

"Hmmm," Mr. Tibbets said. A hairline fracture in the ice.

"Amazing, isn't it?"

"Usually it goes in and out," Mr. Tibbets said. "With static."

"Like next door," Franklin said. Now that he had passed the campground, traffic began to flow. A valley opened up, forests and granite cliffs. "Huh?"

"How 'bout that."

"We live simply on the farm, but I'm calling on the car

phone to thank Mavy. But I'm not in a car, I'm at the seashore." He held the phone out the window to catch the sound of air. A view of Half Dome opened up on his right, the vista iconographed by Ansel Adams. Buses and campers were parked in a rest area, aluminum forever. Hundreds of people stood on tiptoe, taking turns videotaping. "Can you hear the waves?"

After a moment, Mr. Tibbets said, "Yeah, how 'bout that."

A biplane flew past drawing behind a banner that said something in Japanese.

"It's really something, isn't it?" Franklin asked.

"When I was young we had to fucking *dial,*" Mr. Tibbets said. "You had to get the operator to connect you. Kathleen Ryan was the gal's name. She knew all the secrets in town. I almost married her for that."

"What town? Where was that, Mr. Tibbets?"

"You never heard of it."

"Try me."

"Coronado.

"Sure I have. Sure. An island off San Diego. Am I right? Did you grow up there?"

"No, no, no. New York City. This was after."

"Why, if you don't mind me asking."

"Navy—"

"Mavy?"

"N, navy, n!"

"N! I got ya. N!"

"I was seventeen. They were drafting." In the silence, Franklin thought he could hear the man shrug. "You wanted to leave a message for Mavy?"

"This guy, my friend, he's got a solar panel for charging the phone battery."

"It's a new world," Mr. Tibbets said.

"Even in *my* lifetime," Franklin said, reaching the crest of Tioga Pass. Far below was Mono Lake, and several volcanic craters. Beyond them, Nevada. "VCRs."

"Car alarms."

"Cash machines."

"Laser disks."

"Bar codes."

"Smart bombs."

"Sun Protection Factors."

"Nonfat fat."

They both laughed, not from funniness, Franklin felt, but because it was a shareable language. After a moment, Mr. Tibbets said, "My wife bounces computer signals off shooting stars."

"No kidding."

"Well, she may be exaggerating. I don't know her, her real thing. I—"

The connection hummed, voice converted into radio waves then into electricity and back into voice. A live entity, waiting.

"Material wealth, social standing, I've learned these things don't matter. As for technology, well, anything to add to the toolbox, I guess.

"I remember the first Mr. Coffee," Mr. Tibbets said wistfully.

"As long as it doesn't possess you."

"Joe DiMaggio—he was selling the damn thing on TV—looked confused by it."

"Kind of makes a person, I don't know," Franklin said, now thoroughly John. He liked being John. As John, he had gone ten minutes at least without yawning. "Doesn't it."

"When things were knowable," Mr. Tibbets chuckled.

"When things were themselves."

"When things were things."

Franklin's ears popped as he descended. Air thickening, heat building.

"Mr. Tibbets, sir, I don't preach or try to push my way of life on people, but I gotta ask you one thing."

"Bernie. Name's Bernie, John."

Again, the connection hummed. At work, Franklin's fax would be pouring out documents, his secretary stressing over so much paper, wiping her thermographic-ink-stained fingers on tissues. Franklin's knee resumed hurting. Tiny stabs that made him want to yawn. "Which war was it? The one you were drafted for?"

"No war. Korea."

"Of course. I know that. Your book, of course. Assigned reading in college."

"Well, thanks, John. Thanks a lot."

"Core course, humanities breadth requirement. *Ripcord*'s up there with Homer and Shakespeare and Maxine Hong Kingston. Damn good movie, too."

"John," Mr. Tibbets said, voice hardening again. "Mavy has moved. Up to the highlands. No phone. My daughter's living in an airstream."

Franklin hadn't heard that expression before. Airstream, shooting stars, a writer's family. "Will you tell her I called. Tell her thanks for the ladybugs. Practically saved my farm, her and that Frank guy. She'll know what I mean. Mavy, she's very intuitive. She—"

"Sure thing, John. Will do."

"Oh, and tell her that, that Frank guy is okay, even if he seems sort of clueless."

Franklin reached Las Vegas at sundown. Even the gaping sunset could not compete with the neon. Light sprang and swelled and spun fantastically, splashing reds and flowing blues and yellow fountains and geysers of white, so luxurious, so wasteful, so unredemptive, so so utterly fuck-you.

It felt good to be home.

He left his car with a valet he didn't recognize and stood outside the hotel lobby, enjoying the forgotten smell. Cactus, blacktop, money. You go places and you go places and you go places, Franklin thought, then you come back.

"It's Frankly!" said Horatio Myers, the elevator man, saluting. He wore a toga and crown of silk laurels, in keeping with the hotel theme.

"It's Hornblower!" Franklin smiled wide and threw a few fake punches. "Lookin' fine, Cap," he lied. What a stoop—the guy must have lost three inches. His eyelashes had gone gray. His complexion resembled a plate of cheese and crackers. No mistaking, Horatio had gotten old.

A tourist couple, each holding a disposable camera, boarded the elevator. Behind them, a gambler in a suit and tie, fingertapping "shave and a haircut, two bits," on his briefcase. The door closed with a beep and they rose.

"Long time," said Horatio sheepishly. Eons by the looks of it. "Some big exec, now, eh? Your ma tells me. Pullin' down the real dough, the beaucoup bucks, the big S on a pole. Protectin' the world from acts a God, eh?"

At six the tourist couple got out. Six was for people on bus packages from the San Fernando Valley. Six was small, boxy rooms, drippy air conditioners, canary acrylic bedspreads and curtains.

"How *is* Ma?" Franklin asked.

"Glamorous as they get."

At fourteen the gambler got out. Fourteen was really

thirteen, bad luck—proofed. Reserved for comps, fourteen was suites with bathroom spas, amply stocked minibars, complimentary robe and fruit basket.

Horatio suddenly faced Franklin and said, "She forgets. I seen it happen in my aunt." His breath smelled like vitamins. "Tuesday Mrs. Wells's in the elevator? I think she knows up from down. 'Horatio?' she's sayin' to me. 'Horatio, I got groceries here. I got minestrone.' I think she's seein' the sack in her arms for the first time. 'Horatio?' she's sayin'. 'But I don't like minestrone.' " Blinking rapidly, his eyes stuck closed. He had to wrestle them open. "I seen it happen in my aunt. I did."

The elevator stopped at the top, twenty-seven, and the door whooshed open.

"You remind her you can order room service," Horatio said. "A nice bowl of chicken soup, eh?"

"Okay," Franklin said. After Mom got too old for stage work (thirty-nine), she became head secretary to Van Galona (born Ivan Ogalonaski), the hotel and casino owner. After she got too old for desk work (sixty-three), Galona set her up here on twenty-seven. A duplex suite with a sunken whirlpool overlooking the Strip. Why this free room and board for the rest of her life? Loyalty? A tax write-off? Simple kindness? Ma never gave him a straight answer. And Galona, a big man who wore wing-lapel suits and had a hair weave prone to scalp infections (once he was hospitalized for two weeks), was never around long enough for Franklin to ask. There were moments when he wondered if Galona might be his father. After all, Franklin was going bald, too. He had Galona's thick beard, Galona's hairy arms, Galona's weakness for money.

Horatio was still sputtering, "You remind her, she

don't need to go breakin' a hip in any darn Safeway."

"She doesn't take advantage," Franklin said.

Horatio nodded by shaking his head from side to side. " 'Horatio,' she says to me, 'minegoddamnstrone!' The next day she's back to normal, full a vinegar, tellin' me to get a haircut, the usual."

"Thanks, pal," Franklin said, offering open palms for their usual high-ten. Horatio obliged, but held on, squeezing Franklin's hands with just a touch of desperation.

"Frankly!" Ma yanked him into the foyer and hugged him roughly. Then she leaned back to examine him with a horrified grimace. "Oh, Frankly!" She finally smiled as the doorbell played out the last few bars of "My Way." "Let me, let me, my, get a look at ya."

Ma herself was, as Horatio said, as glamorous as they get. Her hair, just dyed, hung in damp charcoal squiggles over the collar of the hotel's plush robe. She blinked, startled, a tear brightening her good eye. Over the other, she wore the familiar gold lamé patch. At seventy, she was finally cashing in on a lifetime of narcissism. With her smooth, nut-brown skin and big white teeth, she could easily pass for fifty.

"You look like a bag of shit. A fuckin' corpse," she said, pulling Franklin in by the ears, kissing his lips.

"I like your perfume, Ma. What is it?"

"Perfume? I don't know what the hell you're talking, perfume." She released his ears and looked behind, around him. "Where's Maybe?"

"Mavy, Ma, v, as in vvv, Mavy."

"Her, too? She can have your old room. You get the couch."

"But Ma, she——"

"What? You think 'cause I bared my tits to give you an upbringing I've got no morals?"

"No, Ma, no." He sighed, felt a click in his throat. It still bothered Franklin that she did not breastfeed him for fear of ruining her figure. For money, audiences always got what they wanted. For love, he never got even what he needed.

"When you're married and not a day before."

Plush gray carpet, white leather living room set, the sofa with its worn spot, chrome-and-glass tables. The suite was neater than he remembered, and more overrun with knickknacks, like candlesticks made of pennies and crystal pets. On the huge TV, soldiers in snow white uniforms were shooting surface-to-air missiles.

"Got a root beer or something? Ginger ale?"

Ma regarded him for a moment with her one good eye. Then she disappeared into the kitchen, where Franklin heard something drop. "She dumped ya, didn't she!"

He stood up, rolled out his neck, sat back down, stood back up, sat.

Ma returned, set the fizzing glass on an eight of hearts coaster, and toweled her hair delicately. "For a second, I thought I'd forgotten you were coming."

"No, Ma. You couldn't have. I didn't know myself. It was a surprise."

"But I was convinced I'd been expecting you." She put down the towel and picked up a pack of Dunhills.

"No, Ma."

"Sure. You and Maybe, v, May-vee, over there with your valises"—she carefully broke the filter off the cigarette before lighting it—"and then of course it's just a. Like a memory that hasn't happened yet. But that I want. Next it's. Well. They're starting to blur, those two. Right, I'm back to my senses now."

"Oh, Ma."

"Did Horatio tell you about the minestrone?"

"He said it was no big deal."

"If it was no big deal he wouldn't have said it." She used a pinkie nail to scratch just inside a nostril. "I may be living in a déjà vu, Frankly, but I'm not crazy."

"No, Ma. You're just—"

"Don't 'No Ma' me!" Twin streams of smoke ribboned out her nose then rose in loops and mixed together. "I've got a regular self and an irregular self, and the irregular one's gettin' more regular. This is fact." She scratched her nose again. "This does not go away." Kept scratching though her nose was red, kept smoking though the cigarette had already burned down to her knuckles. She delicately poked it out in a roulette wheel–shaped ashtray. Kindly, admonishingly, she added, "You always were such a fraidy cat."

"I quit my job, Ma," Franklin both said and realized at the same time.

"Always airbrushing over that scary stuff." She patted his hand. "I understand. The girl dumps ya, job fires ya, a mean week."

"She didn't!" Franklin snapped. "Dump me."

Ma raised an eyebrow, looking impressed. *"You* dumped *her?"*

"We're closer than ever." Franklin amazed himself. But then, depending on how you looked at it, he and Mavy *were* closer than ever. Hadn't he (well, as John) just bonded with Mr. Tibbets?

Ma appeared thoughtful. She pulled a nail file out of the air, and asked, "How's the sex life?"

Franklin sipped his root beer down to the ice cubes. "I'm not going to discuss sex with my mother."

"Prig!"

"You're the one that wouldn't let us sleep in the same room!"

Ma laughed, but Franklin wouldn't allow himself to.

"Doesn't go wild enough, hmm?" She swiped the file too violently across a thumbnail, breaking it. "Or you don't. Otherwise you wouldn't—"

"What?!"

"Be so—"

"What, Ma?"

"Wan."

Franklin folded his arms over his chest. She had that permanent Las Vegas suntan, that Wild West stubbornness, that completely irrational way of looking at the world that comes with living among a surplus of neon and unreported income.

"I suppose we mustn't underestimate companionship," she said, adding the broken nail to her potted geranium. For a moment they both stared off out the window, where luminous bulbs and tubes pulsed, spastic and shadowless. Then Ma wrinkled her nose again in what Franklin thought must be a new twitch. "And a course, I want grandkids before I get tube-fed and brain dead and all shrunken like Horatio."

"Ma!" Franklin said, angry. "Will you stop with that, please? You keep telling me you're this, you're that, irregular, regular, about living wills and dotted lines, about me being chicken. You think I'm not looking at things, and here I am looking and all I see is just you, Ma." Out of breath, he picked up the glass and accidentally swallowed an ice cube.

"My nostrils itch," Ma said, twitching again. *Inside.* That's a sign of a brain tumor."

Franklin sighed. He'd actually read that in *Prevention.*

"I'm sorry, Frankly," Ma said. "Here we were discussin' your job."

"My sex life."

"That's right, your sex life." Forcing back a smile, dimples nevertheless appeared in her cheeks. She tapped another cigarette out of the pack and sliced off the filter with her remaining thumbnail. "Don't get worked up, I'm just having some fun." Cigarette clamped in her lips, she spoke out of the side of her mouth. "So what happened that you got quit. Let's hear."

When Franklin was a teenager, he had broken in half every single Dunhill in the house. Another time he had patted out the tobacco, and refilled the paper with oregano, parsley, thyme. On a third occasion he drew lines with a red felt tip around the middle of each cigarette, because smoking only halfway, the TV actor famous for portraying doctors said, lessened tar and nicotine. "I want the tar! I want the nicotine!" she had raged. "Tar and nicotine are the goddamn point!"

"If you're so worried about your health, quit smoking."

He was still jealous of her addiction. He was still bitter about the ice cube tray. He was still envious of the paying audience.

"I'll stop," she said. "I'll stop when you have a grandkid. Deal?"

"What kind of deal is that?"

"A fair one."

"I gotta have a kid first?"

On TV, the snow guerrilla show had given way to a program about wildebeest migration in Africa. The endless herd stampeded across the savannah; some of them had ear tags and personalities.

Franklin waved off a patch of smoke. Around Ma, he

always felt prim, meticulous. He was the rulemaker, she the rulebreaker. With her ailing health, neurotic fidgeting, and impending death, there was no weight to his aching knee, his yawning spells, his bruises. He wanted to impress his symptoms upon her. He wanted her to take care of him. "I was driving to work this morning and I just kept going," he confessed. "That's what happened. I was driving and I drove."

She nodded, eyes on the TV. "Good thinkin'."

"I exhausted my opportunities there."

"What in hell does that mean, 'exhausted my opportunities'?"

He explained DisasterProof, how it was his, how they took it from him, Sutter, ArManiville, Victoria. Solvtex was turning his humane idea into a weapon. Solvtex planned to sell confidential data—whole nervous systems of Forbes 500 companies, the credit histories of telephone customers, the personal preferences of video renters, the health records of children raised by single mothers, you name it—to demographers, R&D firms, the government, whoever bid highest. It was more valuable than all the oil in Louisiana. "And probably Texas, too."

"You lost me," Ma said. "I'm lost."

The electronic transfer of personal information was not protected by the Constitution. Privacy would be compromised. People hurt, manipulated, bribed.

It was all Victoria's fault. She had betrayed him. She was without integrity.

"Did you sleep with her?" Ma asked. This she understood.

Franklin lifted his glass, cracked an ice cube on a molar filling. "Everything doesn't have to boil down to sex, Ma."

"Since when?"

He thought of himself on all fours atop Victoria's desk, her crooked underpants, her raspy, icy tongue— If Ma only knew. But of course she did. "This is a *job* I'm talking about. Work."

"Oh, baby," she said. "Job's not the sum total of who you are." She stroked his hair, and out of nowhere he nearly cried. "You're heartbroken, aren't ya?" She ran her nails over the back of his neck. "Frankly."

Franklin gave in, to crying, to yawning up that itch, on and on, in mucous-gooey sobs. It was like coming. Like sneezing. Like sweating. Like breathing.

After what felt like a long time, Ma said, "How do ya like my new eyepatch?"

The gold material was the same as always. "I really like it."

"Courtesy of Mr. Van Galona."

On TV, wildebeests swam across the rapids. Many drowned. Ma turned up the volume. With the hotel's rooftop megadish, you could access hundreds of channels. You could get Kabul. King Mustafa, or his younger brother Ahmed. "Car 54" dubbed in Italian, clog dancing, penetration, Holocaust. You could get plane crashes from every corner of the globe. Occasionally you'd get the tape of a man filming his own death, by gunshot, hurricane, car wreck, self-immolation. But Ma seemed to prefer narrative.

After the wildebeests cross the Kalahari, encountering lion, tiger, cheetah, hyena, vulture (beak tangled in eyeball strings), after a substantial percentage of the wildebeests ("herd animals," the mellifluous narrator reminded, "think of them as *a plasma*") actually reach their destination, a beautiful wildflowered valley, "shoots and sprouts!", with "babbling creeks!", and "nary a spit-at-the-mouth carnivore to peel an eye for!", after all this, the credits began floating upscreen over a pair of wildebeests (plasma!) nuzzling, and Franklin recognized the name of a girl with whom he had gone to school, a girl who'd worn red Converse high-tops and stuck her tongue out at him often and for no apparent reason at all.

"Hungry?" Ma asked softly.

"Yeah." How about that? It was an alien feeling, tiny and sharp and so easy to deal with. He wondered if she still had that can of minestrone. He liked minestrone. But for Horatio's sake, he said, "Let's order in."

"A celebration!"

A celebration it was. Escargot, wood-fired pizza with anchovies, spinach salad, chocolate mousse, a bottle of sparkling cider in a hammered silver bucket.

"I hate happy endings," Ma said, chewing. "Goddamn wildebeest heaven." As she aged, Franklin observed, her personality seemed to have condensed to a concentrate: love, smoke, spite. "I never knew they were *plasma*. Did you know that?"

"They're not *plasma*!" Franklin snapped. "That was just a concept."

"Concept?! Concept?! You want concept?" she said. Then, matter-of-factly licking garlic butter off her wrist, "The doctor says I need a peacemaker."

Franklin stopped chewing.

"It's my fibrillating heart."

Franklin swallowed.

"I already got a fake eye for my birthday. From Mr. Galona. From Venice. Actually, an island off Venice. Murano, Burano, Verano, the famous one. But a goddamn chunk of Nagasaki in my chest I don't need."

"Mother." He held the napkin to his lips, it was hard with starch. "A pacemaker's not so bad, really." But how to sound convincing when his own mother may, in fact, be starting to die? "Don't worry——"

"I'm not worried." With her pinkie, she scratched inside her nostril. "Frankly, I'm pissed."

Nurse Twyla had her name badge pinned to the breast of her white smock, and a dye job that made her bouffant an iridescent polyhedron. Aaron had never seen her out of uniform, or without her name badge. Even when she grocery-shopped, or drove downtown, or picked Jimbo up from school or cotillion. Aaron imagined she cleaned and watched TV and dreamed in uniform.

"Morning, handsome," she said, pressing the foot pedal that reclined Aaron's chair. She aimed a parabolic mirror into his face, and began asking what she supposed were harmless questions. "How's your father?" Her geometrical red hair did not match her black and wooly eyebrows, which were the opposite of Mrs. Talkington's pluck spots. It was common knowledge that Nurse Twyla was, as Jimbo put it, Dr. Talkington's "side dish."

"Fie," Aaron said, his mouth jammed with mirrors, picks, and a greasy medicine swab. "N yours?"

"Ah, the young," Nurse Twyla said, coffee and toothpaste breath, pores on her nose plugged with blush. "You heal so nicely."

"Amazonas Sings for Grain," the Muzak version, trebled through perforated metal circles in the ceiling. A rheostat controlled the volume, which Nurse Twyla boosted for a sing-along. "Even Amazonas admits to having had a little plastic done. She's not above it."

"Well, well, well." Dr. Talkington entered, snapping on rubber gloves. "If it isn't Aaron, the carin', rarin', Baron." His voice boomed, making something crawl in Aaron's insides. "Tearin', scarin', waterskiin' American!" Dr. Talkington admired his work, pulling back Aaron's lips with cold fingers. "Hmmmm." Then he ran a fingertip along the upper gums, let Aaron's mouth flap shut. "Fabulous."

He fumbled with some instruments on a tray. "How's your father?"

"Fine," Aaron said. "Yours?"

Dr. Talkington probed at the jaw hinge with a blunt pulsator. "Hurt?"

It felt like metal on metal, an electrical smear of pain. "Hurt?"

For a second Aaron was convinced Talkington was torturing him on purpose. And strangely, he respected him for it.

"How's Jimbo?" Dr. Talkington asked.

Aaron preferred this question to "How's your father?" It was weird having to tell a man how his own son was, but not that weird.

"I worry," Dr. Talkington said, and put a small clamp on Aaron's earlobe. It made the side of his skull buzz. "Bite. He seems, well, tormented."

Triangular head. A mom with no eyebrows. An adulterous father. A girlfriend who'd fuck anyone that told her "you're skinny." No wonder.

"Open." He removed the clamp, the buzzing stopped.

"Our generation," Aaron said. "We're not going to do as well as our parents."

"Bonds, pardner. Zero load coupons. Strips, Twyla!"

Aaron heard her scamper in, turn on the faucet, and stir a bowl of something. Meanwhile Dr. Talkington produced a syringe. The needle slid painfully into the neck muscle behind his ear, and the back of his nose filled with medicine vapors. "That oughtta get numb in about a minute and a half."

It was a feeling Aaron felt familiar with, this initial warmth, the tingling, the promise of one thing, but the delivery of quite another.

"Open," Dr. Talkington said. Twyla stuck a tube into his ear, and with a slim nozzle, sprayed something inside. The problem with having an artificial face, Aaron suddenly realized, was that it would need constant maintenance.

Luther thrust a hand into the dirt, made rich, made dark red, by gallon after gallon of Big Bear Lake mountainwater. Crews had just grafted thousands of Washington navel sapling trunks onto the root stock of sour orange trees. Seven thousand to be exact.

"Strangest damn color," said Gosse. He wore a white shirt, narrow black bow tie, and white cowboy hat with crisply rolled side brims. It was the uniform Luther insisted upon for all his field managers. "So *red,*" Gosse said, as he jabbed the blade of shovel, meanly it seemed, into the ground. "Like blood——"

Luther stood, hand still clenched around a fistful of mud. He narrowed his eyes, checked Gosse's for hidden meaning. Of course, Gosse had a poker face. You could learn from Gosse's poker face, if you knew what to look for, and looked instead for something different.

Gosse snickered. "But that's, I guess, why they call it *Red*lands."

"Iron," Luther said. He let his eyes fix on Gosse's rolled-up sleeves. That was all it took.

"Yes sir, chief, I think you're right." Gosse extended his neck, gooselike, and flapped his arms, getting the sleeves to unravel simultaneously. "Yes sirree." He retrieved cuff links from his pants pocket, and inserted them. "Iron, and lots of it."

Being Gosse's boss had not provided Luther with the satisfaction he had hoped for. Rather, it made him feel that, though their social positions were finally correct, their relationship was essentially unchanged. Here Luther was—owner and overseer of thousands of acres of freshly planted groves, with thousands more a decade old now and producing as beautiful oranges as you could ever want to see—and yet here Luther was, once again dependent on the hunch-necked, snide Gosse for managing day-to-day operations, for giving orders, though now in the form of dispensing advice. "Iron and, oh, I don't know what else."

"The saplings are taking," Gosse said, again snickering. Luther had to give him credit. Eliza took the idea from government botanists but Gosse executed it: Sour-root stock was disease resistant, drought resistant, fungus resistant—it was essentially a weed. Not only did it stand up to abuse, it thrived on abuse. While up top, sweet sapling produced the whitest, finest, full-blown blossoms, amazing, but in themselves inadequate precursors of the glorious fruit to come. "Sour-root's going to make you . . . *father* of the Inland Empire."

Luther let the comment pass unacknowledged. He dropped the handful of mud at Gosse's shoes, polished nicely black. "What are you making now, Bob?"

Gosse frowned. "I'm not asking—"

Luther held his hand up, palm stained earth-red. "Humor me."

Gosse, eyes stuttering closed, told him.

Good, Luther thought, taking pleasure in Gosse's small humiliation. "I'm giving you a fifteen percent raise, starting last month."

"Thank you, chief," Gosse said, eyes going one direction, lower jaw the opposite.

At home, Luther tethered his horse, told the workmen to take the rest of the day off, and went inside. His house was unfinished, but it was going to be grand. It was going to be the finest in the land. He had made sure of that. "Eliza!" he shouted. "Eliza, honey!"

He walked through the hallway. Chunks of Vermont marble were piled up, awaiting installation.

"Eliza!" his voice echoed in the unfinished dining room. Mahogany from Brazil had just been fitted to the walls. The wood had a deep shine and a fine grain, but it smelled thin, like a solvent. A chandelier outfitted with electric wire—for light bulbs—hung suspended from the ceiling. It was a new invention, and came from Italy via inventors in New York. There were no chairs or table yet, and no china or silverware to speak of. "Eliza, where are you?"

The living room was completely finished. Silk wallpaper from Japan had the sheen you see in butterfly wings. The Chippendale secretary looked rather pedestrian next to the Italian sofas and Belgian tables. The Scandinavian chairs had chilling, though classic, wooden structures, like bones holding black leather pads. "Eliza!"

He climbed the sweeping staircase, carpeted in a custom Persian with brass rollers keeping it flush, up to the master bedroom. The bed was unmade—a bad sign, Eliza slept when she was angry or depressed—and there were dirty dishes on the Russian nightstands. "Eliza?"

He noticed the balcony French doors were open. Corsican lace blew slowly, like whispering made visible. Outside, the sky was so blue it was almost green. Acres and acres of orange grove, in varying stages of maturity, unfolded below. Beyond them, palm trees swayed in the most gentle way against a backdrop of blue mountains convoluted by shadowed arroyos and barrancos.

Eliza had her eyes far away, focused on nothing, or on something imagined.

"Eliza? What are you doing out here?"

"Luther, my sweet," she said, turning toward him suddenly and with great force. She embraced him, and kept hugging until the hug turned into something more, a clutch perhaps, or a promise.

Luther understood. Despite himself, he wiped his eyes with the back of his hand. "The curse again."

Ground beef crackled on the stove with onions. It smelled appalling, but started Aaron's mouth watering. Each girlfriend brought new foods, and new food attitudes, which revealed something about her appetites, while making him feel vaguely unsettled about his own.

Caroline was a pretty standard carnivore, though she had a habit of sneaking frozen pastries, which she ate out of the box standing at the freezer. Aaron caught her more than once slamming shut the door and swallowing fast.

Not the most attentive cook; while her meat simmered she was downstairs exercising on the virtual bikepath. Dad was still in Houston, till tomorrow.

Aaron opened the fridge. The door's squeak and whoosh attracted Thumper, who ambled over for a sniff. He knew he'd be fed slices of double-processed American cheese and praised.

"You're such a *good* dog."

But his ears curled down at the groggy, sticky sound of Aaron's voice, post-antibiotics, post-nap.

"Say cheese, Thump."

American cheese was topical. The president, encountering congressional opposition in his push for the Operation Mosaic satellite-based missile system, accused the House majority leader of being unpatriotic because, among other things, he preferred goat cheese to plain old American. The dairy lobby used the situation for a major

PR push—TV spots where slices of cheese jumped up and turned into waving flags—and started letter and phone campaigns. The majority leader's popularity quotient had plunged, and the weapons go-ahead now seemed assured. Meanwhile, American cheese was enjoying something of a renaissance, featured in sitcoms and comics, with irony of course, but affectionate irony. The hot new retro thing. Artists were melting it and molding it and cutting it into the shapes of all fifty-one states. At school, kids sewed square orange patches over the ripped-out knees in their jeans. "Cheesehead" had become something of an endearment.

Thumper got a hard-on, wagging his tail.

Aaron reached for the last orange, but Billybones ducked under his arm and swiped it. He was back to being Wolfspider after a brief stage during which he was, in turn, a computer virus, a speech flake, a theory.

"That's my orange," Aaron wailed, and his mouth clicked. The medicine had dried him out. His tongue felt bent.

Billybones held the orange low, out of reach. "Don't resist what you most desire," he said, employing one of Wolfspeak's high-voltage Zen platitudes. Wolfspider merchandise—toy action figures, candy, cereal—was lately endorsed by poets and historical figures like William Burroughs, Chief Joseph, and ex-president Jimmy Carter. The cereal boxes themselves featured aphorisms, chants, and truncated sonnets. As a result, legions of five-year-olds spoke thus: "You are merely battling yourself."

"Look, you've already had about a million." Aaron pointed to the dozen oranges sucked dry on the counter. Billybones's method: Knead them, roll them around, palpate, loosening and juicing their insides. Then insert the mail-order pincer straws and suck out the liquified guts.

"Be a pal, give it here," Aaron said. He wouldn't care so much if it wasn't the last one. He was already nostalgic for it. Plus he could use the C. His orbiculariplasty was killing him. His perfect smile.

"Negative."

"Give it up, Birth Defect."

"Uglyface," Bones dropped the orange. It rolled along the Mexican tiles.

It was scary how fast they could hate each other.

Aaron picked up the orange and put it to his nose. "Sorry, Billy."

"Billy? Who is Billy?" Bones asked.

"It's just I need the vitamins." Aaron rubbed the orange over his little brother's many-eyeballed head. Being bigger made you addicted to power and corrupt. "For my uglyface."

"Fear nothing so much as thyself," Bones said.

"I hear you, pal."

Of the several ways to peel oranges, Aaron found the thumb method was best. Cupping the fruit in your fingers, you plunged a thumb under the navel, removing the embryo at the blossom end. (It was usually granular, asymmetrical, and sour, bad for eating.) Then, with a minimum of wasted motion, you spiraled off the rind, running the single thumb under the skin. This particular peel was thin and resilient, small pores, a rich flat color, the sign of a fine weather season.

"What's for dinner?" Aaron asked. They both stared at the simmering ground beef.

"Olfactory distress," Billybones said. He was careful never to say anything bad, or anything at all, about the girlfriends themselves.

"Caroline tries," Aaron told him. He split the peeled orange in two, cleanly between sections, handing Bones half.

Billybones regarded the offering suspiciously.

"Nutrify." Aaron squeezed his Wolfspider head again, friendly this time, and forced a wedge into the mouth between the pincers of his mask. Billybones crammed an orange section into Aaron's ear.

"No roughhousing!" Caroline shouted, still a little out of breath and freshly sweaty from the virtual bikepath. Her workout-proof makeup, eyeliner and lipstick, brought out her features too vividly, like a lingering afterimage.

Billybones stared at her.

To break the weirdness, Aaron stuffed another section of orange into Billy's mouth. He squealed with delight and collapsed in giggles.

"Enough!" Caroline banged a wooden spoon on a copper pan hanging from a hook. "Someone could get hurt!"

Aaron saw her confusion, her fear of spiders, her contact lenses afloat on the slightest of tears. She didn't ask to be a mother of kids not all that much younger than herself. After pedalling a simulated bike through the San Juan Islands or Prague or the Dordogne Valley countryside, she didn't want to referee and serve up unappreciated meat. She was lonely. Dad was still in Houston.

Stirring with one hand, she ripped open a flavor packet in her teeth and frowned at all the sucked-out oranges on the counter. "Billy?" she said.

"Who is Billy?"

The living room was entangled in a giant web. String connected the Christmas tree to the card-table leg, to the fireplace mantel, to the HDTV, to the ironing board, to a plant hook in the ceiling, to another lamp, ending with Billybones, who was holding the roll of monofilament.

Caroline ate her sloppy joe at the ironing board, in the midst of the web. She drank jug wine out of a jelly jar, dabbing the corners of her mouth with a paper towel after every single sip. The Amazonas Christmas special was on TV. Like Prudey, Caroline seemed enchanted with Amazonas.

Ignoring his food, Billybones began stringing her legs together.

"Cut it out, Bones," Aaron said, balancing his paper plate of joe and spinach–tomato salad, careful not to trip or get tangled.

Billybones kept spinning the web. "We are every one of us everything that is, everything that ever was, everything that ever will be."

Caroline looked like she was making an effort to be a good sport, as if that would bring Billybones's respect. But, Aaron knew, its effect was just the opposite.

"Let her go, Bones."

"I don't mind." Caroline sipped, dabbed, sipped.

It was then Aaron noticed the pickle jar on the coffee table. It was full of spiders. Brown, hairy, fairly large, each the size of a newborn baby's hand.

"Don't shake it," Billybones warned Aaron. He tied Caroline's arms to the chair.

Frightened, she peered over her shoulder. "That's not—are those spiders?"

"They are within," Billybones said.

On the news it was reported that the Alabama state legislature was boycotting companies which advertised during broadcasts of the Wolfspider Saturday-morning series. They cited Wolfspider's celebration of the dark force, which they said was Satan-like, and his "pernicious language abuse."

The front door blew open.

"Bonester!" Jimbo said, grinning at the threshold. "Nice web, dude. Very nice."

"Come on in," Caroline said. "Warm up by the fire."

"No, don't make him run the obstacle course." Aaron tried to stand, but when he did, he tripped over the string, and fell, causing the lamp to fall, causing the coffee table to jerk, causing Billy's sloppy joe and jar of spiders to fall onto the carpet where the joe purled and the jar smashed, and spiders began crawling everywhere.

"Uh-oh." Caroline jumped, but the slack tightened and pulled her down, strapping her in as her chair toppled over. The ironing board flipped onto Caroline's dinner. Billy and Aaron were tangled up, too. The harder they struggled the worse it got.

"Goddamn you, Bones," Aaron said, watching a spider advance. It held up its legs, using them as antennae, sensing the layout of the shag carpet.

Jimbo laughed.

Caroline whimpered. Several spiders, seemingly attracted by her panic, moved toward her, in staccato starts and stops.

"Jimbo," Aaron said, trying to bite through the nylon, "get a knife."

"What the fuck," he said, and was gone.

On TV, the president was a guest of Amazonas, along with the first lady. They had joined the show live, via satellite from the White House.

"Many of us love the moon," Amazonas said.

The president nodded. "Oh, I can sympathize." Behind

him, a Christmas tree twinkled. An electric menorah, all eight days full, blazed. A fire crackled in the executive mansion's hearth. The first lady prodded Suzi, the first cat, embarrassed that it was licking its genitals before hundreds of millions. "I think we *all* can."

Caroline began to scream as a spider crept onto her shoulder. Another circled her foot. Another navigated the blond strands of her hair.

A Pentagon file tape showed a smart missile seeking and destroying a less smart missile. The moon in the background had picturesque craters. Next, a teenage girl in a leotard slid down a banister, poured blue fluid into a biodegradable sanitary napkin, and kissed a uniformed man who opened the door for her, allowing indoors the sound of children playing.

At last, Jimbo appeared with a steak knife. After cutting the lines, he plucked up spider after spider, tossing each into the fire where it popped and sizzled.

"Don't!" Billybones protested.

"Will you define that for us, 'friendly aggression'?" Amazonas asked the president.

Caroline flailed on the carpet like the epileptic Aaron had once seen at an American Youth Soccer Organization bake sale.

"You little impostor," Jimbo said, grinning and tossing spiders into the fire. "Wolfspiders don't even use webs."

The president said, "Things being what they are, yes. That's not to say no."

"Oh my God!" Caroline screamed, chest heaving. After she got the last spider off her, she wiped away her tears with the napkin, and faced Billybones. "Is it true? They don't even use webs?"

Without looking at her, Billybones said, "They hunt by pouncing."

For the first time Franklin could not see into his future. This was like being rich only different.

He bought a Deko Max board and a 5-mil wetsuit and surfed, everyday, especially the stormy ones. Explosive swells rolled in from the south as high as you could want.

But he kept at it tenaciously, braving faceplants, instant deaths, wall breaks. It was like learning how to walk, and for now seemed just as practical.

Until now, Franklin had prized a structured life. He had mistaken ambition for desire. The pursuit of money and power eventually supplanted the goal. Mom was right all along. The fraidy cat had been airbrushing out the scary shit.

Now he craved what he used to fear most: free time.

The other surfers called him Jones, Homes, Wadface, tried to thrash him with their boards, crowd him out. But when Franklin staked out his own patch of ocean and stuck to it, when the other surfers saw him paddling furiously to greet even the ragest breaks, they understood he was a regular, and cheered on one insane wipeout after another.

Two months passed. His bank statement continued to show paychecks being deposited into his account. Still, no one from the office ever phoned him. I'm a homeowner, he thought, and employed. A professional with real consumer muscle. Underneath, the blue sea rolled.

Every now and then—once buckling his seat belt,

another time licking a stamp—he'd feel a quick but fierce rush of panic. He didn't know its source, or how to begin to listen for its message.

One morning, while straddling his Deko Max, a sea lion bit Franklin's leg, ripping a gash in the wetsuit, puncturing flesh. It sent him to the clinic for a tetanus shot, then to Mavy's for sympathy.

"Ow," she said, blinking rapidly, looking at the wounds on his calf, where he had peeled back the bandage. One puncture was particularly deep, puckered at the edges, still bleeding. She had a plaster-and-gauze cast over her face, hair wrapped in a towel-turban. Her eyes, gazing out of the white mask, were glacier blue. Somehow it seemed that she, the person, disappeared with each blink. "I never heard of a sea lion biting a person."

"Canines," Franklin said.

She popped off the mask. White flecks clung to her eyelashes, and her cheeks and chin were glossy from nonpetroleum jelly. "Excuse me a sec." She returned with her diaphragm and from it began fingerpainting menstrual blood onto the still-moist plaster.

Franklin no longer knew what was weird, what was disgusting, what was what.

"Um," Mavy gestured toward the blood on his calf. "Mind if I use some of that?"

"I'm not sure," Franklin said. Her mask, a reddish fresco, smelled like raw chicken. Without eyes or lips or any play of features, the face in her hands was, if not offensive, certainly severe, faintly religious. "What for?"

"It's not like voodoo," she said.

"Aren't you worried it's poisonous?" There were so many viruses now. Other things too. Polymers.

"What's it gonna hurt? The mask?"

"Is this a group project?" He knew. She had joined a *coven*, what they called themselves anyhow, a *coven* of women who met weekly after self-defense class. "What do you all do there anyway?"

"Talk," she said.

"What about spells and chanting?" He had met only one of the women, a sexy health food clerk who scowled at him for using up his pennies, twenty-seven or so, on a purchase of blue corn chips. Franklin didn't really know any of Mavy's friends. She and he were like emissaries from different countries, bringing cultural exchange, but always on the brink of giving offense. "Witchcraft?"

"Noooo," she said. "Not like you're thinking." She reached over and touched his wound, then hesitated before applying the blood to a spot on the mask forehead. "I broke up with John, you know."

"Sorry to hear that." The health food store sold his tomatoes.

"He found your underwear in my bedroom."

"Sorry to hear that," Franklin repeated, in exactly the same tone and speed. "Didn't you tell him we were just friends?"

"He doesn't believe *just friends* exists, between man and woman." She held up the mask in the dying sunlight. It was brown, crusty, like a scab.

"That underwear was in your bedroom a long time."

In the years he'd known her she'd changed in this way most: opened up. In her expression, Franklin now recognized what he was incapable of seeing earlier: trust. Her one great aptitude.

"Do you?" Mavy asked.

"Do I what?"

"Believe."

Franklin peeked at his wound again. He wanted to say that it really didn't matter. What he believed was irrelevant. But it was easier to answer, "Yes and no."

All machinery seemed too small for her. Seat back, head jammed against the roof, she leaned into curves and hummed; Franklin could easily see the child, Mavy. Gangly, oversized, huge with needs. It confused him, convinced him she must be taught to protect herself. People would try to take this from her. He would try.

"My dad thinks you're stealing from me," she said, as they drove through Carmel highlands. Her parents' house was just up in the woods to the left. After he'd grudgingly accepted the invitation to dinner, they'd canceled, feigning other plans. "Not my money or anything."

"Your what then?"

"I don't know. My something."

South of Big Sur there were no more cars on the road. Pairs of eyes got caught in the headlights. Primary colors frozen open. In them, Franklin saw terror—quick, impersonal stabs—like his old panic had been refined and upgraded. He needed another job, but didn't want one. His mother was getting worse. The violent beauty of this coast. The Perseid meteors.

Mavy's humming wasn't musical, just one continuous sound. She pulled off the highway and wrestled the steering wheel a few hundred yards down a dirt road, parking in the dark under a splay-rooted oak, where cows slept.

They stood outside the still-ticking white Toyota pickup—a surprise gift from her New York grandmother whose *Vogue* magazine covers had so impressed Franklin. Granny Franny had not spoken to Mavy in over a decade, and the truck arrived without a card. Just above the delivery sticker's bar code was the following message spit out in ink-jetted letters: "ALL MY LOVE GRANNY FRANNY."

Cows groaned and shifted, sinking back into their night selves. Franklin smelled the ocean air, the straw, shit, the poppies, oak leaves, the dirt clods, brake linings, lichens, the granite. Out of the city even rocks have a scent.

No moon, the Milky Way plenty visible. "There's one," Franklin said, but it may have just been a glare in his eyelash. His eyelashes frequently shed.

"Hurry up and wish," Mavy said, and, crouching under a line of barbed wire, followed a thin trail back to the highway. It was a flat blue strip of asphalt built long ago by prisoners and just now empty of cars.

Franklin's mother had become a prisoner of sorts. A prisoner of her body parts. She was losing things, befriending strangers, sometimes inviting them over. She'd call and beg him to explain about the wildebeests to Joe or Etta or Mr. What's-his-name. Meanwhile Solvtex was Fed-Exing letters. Come back, they said, or you'll hear from our lawyers.

"Did you?" asked Mavy. "Wish?"

"Yeah."

"What for?"

"Won't come true if I tell you."

"Lots of shooting stars are space garbage," Mavy said. "Excrement, disposable razor blades, powdered drink wrappers."

At a stone-and-mortar wall, just past the Esalen sign, they snuck in to avoid paying the five dollars for the hot springs. It wasn't serious money, of course. It was the principle. Mavy thought you shouldn't have to pay for nature.

Once inside, the wildness gave way to flower beds,

stone gardens, cottages; inside them support groups laughed and wept.

"My dad used to give a workshop here," she said as if just remembering. "See Yourself, Live, he called it." She was barefoot, her hands were free, no purse or pockets even, her license and wad of dollar bills were stashed back in the glove box. But it was her sheer largeness that most surprised him, that kept surprising him. An athleticism so raw you could hear it in her voice. "Auto-video was the idea. Set up the tripod and tape yourself. Eating, sleeping, having sex, reclining in front of the ballgame. At first, the camera becomes your conscience. You're on your best behavior. You smile, you recycle, you do not slouch. Then, typically, you rebel. Show the camera it cannot control you. Flash it, moon it, curse it. Next, you realize this all-seeing eye has tremendous power over you and your behavior. You dress up and deliver tender, forceful speeches, presenting the self you want others to see. Finally, you understand the camera is like God; it forgives by the simple fact of recording."

"Then what?" Franklin asked, fascinated.

"You stop acting."

"Doesn't sound too practical."

"Try it," she said. "See yourself, live."

She went on to the tubs, while Franklin entered the locker room. Cement benches ran under bare light bulbs, but an eclectic crowd gathered for the cosmic fireworks gave the room personality.

A long-haired woman in lacy lingerie and red plastic-rimmed glasses struggled to pull a notebook computer out of a shoulder bag.

Someone popped the cork from a bottle of champagne and screamed, "Let's get fucked up!" He had an evangelist's pompadour.

"Naahhh," shrugged still another man. This one covered with tattoos. Umbrellas over his nipples, an aircraft carrier on the belly. A suspension bridge connected his shoulder blades. An evil-looking Eden scene in which Eve bulged with scar tissue. He held up a thermos. "Iced coffee."

"Twelve-step program?" asked a hairless man.

Tattoo Man nodded once, then sat next to Lingerie Lady, who was booting up the laptop. Franklin wondered at the almost cartoonish aim of her sex appeal. You didn't see too much of that anymore.

"Me, too." She looked perpetually on the verge of a wink. The computer beeped twice. "Not booze, though."

"I hear you," said Hairless One, peering over a fat sheaf of papers. "I admit I'm powerless over certain behaviors."

"TV," said Lingerie Lady. "Anything hard and rapidly unfolding. When I got my hands on that clicker, oh, I lost myself. Staring at experts discussing oil painting, one pan cooking, Brownian movement, architecture of the Bauhaus, nonracist joke-telling techniques. I learned South American weather patterns, Croatian folk songs, chaos theory as it applied to the gold standard. I entered the head of a Van Nuys teen who raped and dismembered his stepsister, then cooked her cheek muscle in a microwave and ate it on rye bread with mayo. I remember the soundtrack, a bar chord and glockenspiel arrangement of 'Bridge Over Troubled Water.' I could witness the boy's execution by injection. Through coloscopy I could see, and did see, the dysplasia on the first lady's cervix. Her parents, corn farmers shifting from petrofertilizers to organic methods, gave commentary from a hookup in their living room in Oshkosh, Nebraska; you could tell the mother had her hair dyed fresh, red from a box. I believe

Clairol was one of the show's sponsors. Oh, I learned how to install storm windows, to play 'Oh Susanna' by popping my lips, to drill and fill cavities, to perform arthroscopic knee surgery, to pilot a Stealth bomber, to make several hundred thousand in Florida real estate, and somehow, just *watching how* relieved me of *my desire* to actually do any of them."

"I hear you." Hairless One rubbed moisturizer into his elbows. "A fearless moral inventory."

"I developed personal and gratifying relationships with TV anchorpersons, especially women who had to overcome some form of victimization—divorce, middle age, infertility, physical disability, speech impediment, motherhood, over-the-counter drug addiction, go ahead, name it—in order to achieve a continuing presence on the airwaves. Jane Pauley, Linda Ellerbee, Bree Walker, Bobbie Battista, Connie Chung, Barbara Walters, and, oh, especially, totally, Oprah."

Tattoo Man shook his head, eyes downcast, grinning. "So now it's computers?"

"Remember that Michael Landon period, near his death, when he was on every single channel? In all his incarnations? His life flashing before our eyes. Well, what I experienced was so . . . it matches how I feel toward my own daughter."

"Ah, Babs, it wasn't that bad," said Tattoo Man. He sandwiched her hand, fresh and pink skin between his own, blue and green with roses and thorns.

"*Now* you say that." Then, soberly, she added, "With that thing in my hand, I was, oh, I don't know. A nonrippled pond."

"Comfort food," said Hairless One, rubbing both elbows at once. "I eat to self-medicate."

"Anything can be a drug," the woman said.

"Mashed potatoes, ice cream. That creamy-mouth feel. Once I start, that's it," Hairless One continued. "Potato chips, pretzel rods. Anything crunchy with salt."

"I can't own a TV. If I watch even for a minute, I slip."

"The middle of the night, it hits me. The peanut butter calls out. 'Get out of bed,' it says, 'Come.' "

"Banks of TVs in department stores, all on the same channel."

Hairless One: "Only to hate myself in the morning."

Lingerie Lady: "There should be government warnings."

"One day at a time."

"One day at a time."

"Well ain't we a boatload of victims," said Pompadour Man, gesturing with the champagne bottle.

There was a lengthy silence which seemed to call out for more confessions.

Pompadour Man suddenly thrust the champagne bottle toward Franklin and asked, "Okay, what's *your* problem, Mister?"

I'm young, Franklin thought. He'd just stepped out of his clothes, and now all eyes were upon him. Young and without secrets. Young and innocent even to himself. The future was fraught with missteps, addictions, multi-tiered redemptions. The most innocuous-seeming thing—a talk show, a can of minestrone, a sip of bubbly—posed a spiritual hazard. The terror came back to him, that pure edge.

"Huh? You gonna tell us or what?" Pompadour Man asked, between guzzles.

"Leave him alone," said Tattoo Man, then to Franklin, "Something wrong, son?"

Franklin had been staring. "Nothing, no. Sorry."

"Bernie," the man said, offering Franklin a handshake. His palm bore an eighth-note tattoo. "Go ahead, take a good long look."

A girl on a swing. The Mad Hatter. The Garden of Eden, the snake and Adam, and Eve, who was ripped in half by an appendectomy scar, her face purple and abulge. A Mack truck bulldog, a bald eagle, a bicycle on fire. Franklin wondered if the images served a larger narrative. There were even tattoos on Bernie's buttocks and genitals, which Franklin wouldn't allow himself to look at.

"You get used to 'em," said the woman, who appeared to be putting a waterproof housing around the computer. "When you love a person."

Outside, under the moon, the tubs steamed. A series of four of them were cut into the hillside, rectangles of cheaply poured concrete. They overflowed with spring water that stank of sulfur.

One contained several teenagers smoking, drinking, chewing gum, and listening to a rap sermon turned low on a boombox, "No work, no work, d-d-demolition of the ethic." The boys were naked, most of the girls wore bathing suits, though a few were topless. In the neighboring pool was a woman teaching three plump toddlers to swim, an Oriental man assuming a trance position, and two young Fort Ord buzzcuts, beer cans in fists, eyes straight up. A meteor streaked overhead, blue tail lingering for a whisper of a second, and the whole group went, "Ooooooh."

Even if the shooting star was a disposable razor, even if the crowd was uncollective, you could feel healing taking place. Something alive in the air, something open-hearted. Maybe it was religion. Nothing could stop the beauty of the place, and Franklin felt sure that the more beauty you soaked up, the more you'd shine back, a thought which seemed, at the moment, social and important.

"What took you so long?" Mavy asked. "This one is the hottest." She was already up to her neck in the least crowded pool, the first to catch the curative waters as they bubbled out of the mountain, directly above the rift where two continental plates were colliding at phenomenal speeds, geologically speaking.

Franklin hesitated, then dropped his towel. He felt not shy, but naked, which, he realized with a certain satisfaction, was exactly what he was. He put his toe in, then yanked it back out. "Scalding."

There were two other people in the tub, silently bobbing heads. Franklin jumped in splashing to get rid of them; no room in paradise. It worked, they climbed out and left.

It was the first hint of a problem that would stay with him forever, not wanting to share her. Later, Franklin would look back and realize that it was then he wanted Mavy totally and completely—her ears and eyes and, oh yes, even, especially, what he hadn't been allowing himself to imagine. Without being conscious of it, he began devoting levels of himself to her.

The water was so hot it felt like being cooked. Stew me, boil me, make me broth. Mineral deposits slicked on his bare feet, briny salts stung his scrotum, anus, armpits. It felt unpleasant but good for you.

"You should let it out by screaming," Mavy said, in her breathy voice. "That's what I do."

"Show me," he said.

"Mmmmm. I have to feel it first." She cupped some water over her shoulders. Big shoulders from wrenching mussels loose, catching pigs, driving the truck, but there were no bulging veins in them, not one.

She plunged underwater, and came up screaming. Loud and craziful, happy.

People from the other tubs looked over, puzzled.

Franklin didn't know any better than they did what to make of her. But here she was, and here he was, here *we* are, in this almost-twenty-first-century cathedral of naked strangers at 3 A.M. on the ferocious coast where shooting stars made of space garbage shine on waves breaking against the cliff a hundred yards below.

Franklin climbed up on the concrete massage table. Though it was breezy, neither he nor Mavy had bothered to put their clothes back on.

She stood below him in the dark, large as ever. She put her hands on his feet, rubbed up. Maybe he *wouldn't* steal from her.

He reached down and took her head with both hands. "I can't let you touch me that way," he said softly.

Mavy clasped his legs and began kissing his knees, one then the other.

"Hey," he said, stumbling off balance.

She squeezed harder, steadying him, and nosed up his thigh.

"Mavy," he said, trying to pull away, thinking, yes. "Don't."

She squeezed tighter and closed her eyes, chin aloft.

"Mavy!" It felt wonderful. But shouldn't they at least be kissing, hugging, something soft-core? He tried to move away. But she bit slightly, holding him still with her teeth.

Well, okay, he thought. She took his balls in one hand and squeezed gently, while with the other she pumped slowly.

"Mavy, don't," he said.

Accidentally, his knee jabbed her neck. She fell back, gripping her throat, choking.

"Listen to me," Franklin said, suddenly angry.

She got to her feet, hugging his legs again, kissing his shin. He tried to push her head away, but she was strong, and bulled forward, tackling him. His head smacked concrete and bounced.

"Why'd you let me, then?" Mavy asked, on top of him. "Jerk!"

Franklin shivered. The stars, all of them, were runny smears. Some were growing, others dying. All of them were moving at unimaginable velocities, in different directions. The light hitting his eyes was seven years old here, seven centuries old there. Staring at a past that no longer existed, a present that was somewhere else's future. Nothing was fixed. Nothing was anything it seemed. Some of it was garbage.

"Pulling that shit," she ranted. "Letting me, then pushing me away. You think you can have both at once? You can't."

He struggled to his feet, gulping, snotnosed.

She made as if to spit, then swallowed. "Oh my God."

Franklin looked at her, and made a decision.

"Act normal," she said, shaking out her hair, then patting it down, then examining her split ends. "Franklin, my parents are here."

It was the man with the tattoos. It was Lingerie Lady, the one with the laptop who used to be addicted to TV.

Franklin looked at them, and made a decision.

Luther shaved his beard and took to wearing a handlebar mustache. He twirled and waxed it every morning, then examined his work in the mirror from several angles. It became his signature look. On a lesser man it would appear like wishful thinking.

President McKinley's mustache was bigger, but shapeless and bushy. The whiskers were long enough that they ruffled in the light wind.

"A fine place," McKinley said. "I see the God drama of it all, southern California, yes sir." The tip of his tongue flicked along the bottom of his mustache. "Why, there's nowhere prettier."

"West of paradise, Mr. President," Luther said. The two stood in a gazebo, surveying the Tibbets domain. Thousands of acres of grove rolled in terraces below, in full blossom.

"Their fragrance could knock a man down," said McKinley, briefly glancing at Luther's before tasting his own mustache. "Yes sir, sure is pretty."

The mountains were purple, starkly convoluted, the palm trees swayed in the crisp desert breeze. Red, white, and blue festoons graced the house, and a rippling banner proclaimed "McKinley 1901."

"Awful gracious of you to host this campaign festival," McKinley added.

People had begun collecting in the open yard below.

The mayor was here, the owners of businesses. Councilmen, politicians from neighboring counties. Chamber of commerce, the Kiwanis, the CEO of Southern Pacific. Gosse, Luther's right-hand man, saw to it that each got their individual requests into the hands of the candidate.

The Inland Empire had finally boomed, and Luther, at its center, was its most prominent citizen. He had engineered the railway line opening commercial trade. He had engineered the dam that quenched the thirsty valley with fresh cold mountain water. He had engineered the planting of hundreds of thousands of orange trees.

There was money in everything:

Blossoms went to France, where they were crushed, their essences extracted for the manufacture of perfume.

The oil in the peel, what Eliza ignited to impress the tourists, turned into turpentine when exposed to light and air.

From the albedo—the white underside of the peel— came pectin, a necessary ingredient for the manufacture of custard, candy, and jelly. Even the "worthless" by-product of the process could be sold to pig farmers as a feed supplement.

Luther was a powerful man. He had powerful friends.

"So this is the lovely lady who planted the first Washington navel." McKinley kissed the top of Eliza's gloved hand.

"An honor to meet you, Mr. President." Ever since the afternoon of the wedding dress, Eliza wore only shades of white. Ivory, shell, milk, snow, moonlight, bone. Silk and linen, decorated with lace. She still had the tight hips of a woman who has never given birth, flawless skin, and that virtuous, slightly reserved expression.

McKinley licked his mustache and grinned at Luther.

"Don't tell me you got a corner on the fountain of youth."

By now, Eliza was used to men and their flirting. But the president?

"Perhaps you'll grant me a garden tour after the speech," McKinley said. "I'd like a peek at the original tree."

"Pleasure," Eliza touched his arm lightly, "would be mine." It surprised her that he was flesh and bone.

"Department of Agriculture likes to take credit for that tree. But I say credit belongs right here," Eliza said, feeling bold, feeling Bub. "The Tibbets navel." The original tree was going strong. Eliza had propagated over a hundred others using its sweet branchings. It still produced the best oranges, only ones she'd eat, the ones bringing prizes and reputation, the ones bringing presidents. "What do you say, Mr. President?"

"I'd say you're a lucky man," McKinley told Luther.

Luther was now an influential man. He had influential friends. But he was not a lucky man.

As everyone knew, he had railed west Dr. Harvard, who concluded his wife had "a hostile cervical environment."

After the speech, the crowd dispersed. Vice-President Hobart and Luther answered questions from reporters.

McKinley turned to Eliza and asked her into his carriage.

Grandma Goretex was grinding the coffee beans again. No matter how many times you told her, Grandma Goretex insisted on killing herself. Aaron pulled the pillow over his head to shut out the noise. Dad should be the one keeping an ear out for her. She was *his* mother.

Something glass smashed.

Aaron sat up, straining to hear. What was her cardiac care emergency number? Just as he put a foot on the floor came the sound of more beans grinding.

No matter how many times you told her.

"Imagine a ball of writhing worms in your chest," she'd told Aaron. "That's fibrillation."

The tea kettle whistled.

Aaron hated this room, the ex-den, small and half underground. Kitchen noises amplified in the wall. Shag carpeting and cork paneling harbored the smell of every animal, mineral, and vegetable that had ever passed through. A single transom window opened to a view of the iceplant, spikes in the dark.

Aaron had volunteered his bedroom six months ago, after Grandma Goretex had her last surgery. But now he regretted it. Like Dad, she never said thank you, or sorry.

She never even got his name right.

She never stopped drinking coffee.

"You'll fibrillate," Aaron warned her, uselessly.

"Good morning, you." She sat in a cone of light at the

brushed aluminum table, both hands around an Amazonas coffee mug, a nicorette—a cigarette-shaped nicotine delivery system—between her teeth.

"You know you're not supposed to drink coffee."

"I'm only smelling it, see?" She inhaled deeply. "I never wanted to live in a major population center." Pointing with her nicorette, she added, "And look me in the *good* eye!"

It was dull blue, and the white of it appeared calloused. Her bad eye was so much prettier.

Aaron stepped over shards of a porcelain cup and saucer she'd dropped on the kitchen tiles, then checked the burner to make sure it was off. Another job that Dad should take charge of—safety.

"You still haven't cashed my rent check, I noticed." Grandma blinked several times. Her voice was tough and stringy. "I'm no freeloader, Frankly. I pay my way."

"It's me, Grandma. Me, Aaron."

She studied him with her good eye. Then she sighed. "I know. I'm just rehearsing."

Aaron assembled his breakfast: Quinoa Crisp, Rice Dream, banana. A line of ants was traveling very slowly inside the fridge, along the egg rack to a sticky maraschino cherry jar. The maraschino cherries another habit of Grandma's.

She had made herself up this morning. How you appear reflects how you see yourself, she liked to say. Which meant, Aaron decided, she didn't see herself too clearly. In addition to her special blue eye—the one from Venice or Soprano—she wore psychotic pink lipstick and her hair was teased up, sprayed, and stiffened into a puffy russet shell. Aaron found her vain and needy and slightly repellent. He asked, "Did you have any dreams?"

"Like I tell you and tell you," she said. "I don't dream."

"Everybody dreams."

"Who says?"

"Scientists."

"Scientists." She sucked her nicorette. "Scientists don't know *me.*"

Aaron tried not to laugh. He ate his cereal.

"Your mom used to drink that stuff," Grandma said, jabbing the nicorette at the carton of Rice Dream.

She had already told him this many times. But she was stingy with other memories.

Aaron lapped up a spoonful, imagining how it must have tasted on his mother's tongue. But it was an old game, and didn't work anymore. "What else did she like?"

Drawing a deep breath through her nose, Grandma absorbed the coffee steam, and said, good-naturedly, "God gave us this coffee."

"But——," Aaron said. "What else——"

Thumper appeared, ears down, tail wagging, the *L.A. Times* clamped in his mouth. When he saw Grandma, he bowed his head and stiffened his tail.

"Good boy, Thump," Aaron cooed, scratching the dog's head, taking the paper. A front-page headline: *Boredom with TV Stirs Discontent in China.* Who cares? What he turned to first were the Air Quality Charts. Ozone (O_3) would be over 200 parts per million today on the pollution standard index. A first-stage episode, unhealthful. Ozone was invisible, but it hurt your airpipe. Nitrogen dioxide (NO_2) would reach 150, only moderate, thanks to the haze, which cut the sunlight necessary for NO_2's creation. Nitrogen dioxide, the brown stuff L.A. was famous for, made the edges of your lungs itch. Carbon monoxide

(CO) would hit about 30. Invisible, odorless, painless, monoxide reduced the blood's oxygen. "Lots of ten-micron particulates today," Aaron said. "Over a hundred." Particulates—dust, metals, polymers—embedded themselves in alveoli. Once there, they took root. "Do you remember how to use your bottled oxygen, Grandma?"

"Scientists! Oxygen!" she snorted. "What about you, Mr. Rice Dreamer. What did you dream?"

"Mom," Aaron said, suddenly remembering. Mom was beating up a grocery clerk. "Grandma, tell me what else she was like?"

Grandma Goretex slapped her calves. "Damn ants. It's that bedroom of yours. Ants, and biting spiders, too. They live in the drains. Look between my toes, you'll see."

Look between her toes? Never. If *his* bedroom was so infested, why didn't she give it back?

When she first moved into his room, she demanded a bird feeder. Dad made Aaron hang it for her, right outside the window, and Grandma instructed him to fill it with real maple syrup and red food coloring. The maple syrup *had* to be from Vermont. At night, rats came down from the palm trees and sucked the tube.

Still, Grandma refused to believe they were rats, instead calling them shy birds. And after she learned oleander blossoms were poisonous, she cut them to stick in vases on her nightstand.

"Scary?" she asked.

"Huh?"

"Your dream?"

"No."

"Not scary is good." Grandma held the nicorette between two fingers. Sometimes she smelled like cigarettes, though she denied she'd been smoking.

Another headline said, *Muscle Is Turned into Bone by Researchers in St. Louis.* Aaron suddenly remembered Grandma's cardiac care number. It made him feel powerful, in control.

"I want to know about my mom," he said. "Now."

"Will you look at that!" she said, nodding toward the pink and yolky sun out the window. "God gave us sunrises!"

Maybe it was wrong to expect anything heart-to-heart from her. Maybe it was impossible not to.

Aaron resumed studying the pollution forecast. Redlands always had the highest numbers; today was no exception. One surprise—the Mojave had tons of ten-micron particulates. Sandstorm, probably, and jet propulsion experiments.

Grandma slapped at her calves, exaggerating to get his attention. "Damn ants," she said. "And pill bugs, too." She kicked Thumper, who was eating one under the table. "Vermin all over the place."

"Here, Thump," Aaron said. But Thumper ambled over to the cabinet and began licking up ants.

"The roaches of the West Coast."

"They're not roaches."

"Just like 'em. Wiggling. Eating crumbs."

"Pill bugs don't eat crumbs."

"I've seen them eating crumbs. And getting into my fancy soaps." She'd changed his bedroom all around. Now it was full of smelly gels and creams and perfumes, prescription bottles, casino chips, bags of Mint Milanos, which she hoarded. It was frustrating sharing with a person who didn't share back. Especially your grandmother.

"They're sort of cool." Aaron had seen pill bugs walking on the pool bottom, waving their antennae underwater.

"You used to play doctor and make your little brother eat 'em," Grandma said. "He'd swallow two or three pill bugs with a glass of water, rub his face, and say, 'All better.'"

Aaron didn't remember. He wondered whether she was making it up.

"You were always the doctor, Bill always the patient. Your mother found this hilarious."

Aaron was jealous that she knew his mother. And suspicious of any memory that wasn't joyful or tender.

"God gave us pill bugs," he said, and nearly choked on Quinoa Crisp when Grandma smiled for the first time in weeks. "And God gave us rats," he said. "And smog."

"Yes She did, didn't She, yes."

Thumper went to the air conditioner and lay down. That was *his* place of worship. Aaron got up to rinse his cereal bowl.

"And God gave us Goretex and Teflon and plastic cigarettes." Not smiling any longer, she actually sipped her coffee.

And God took Mom from me, Aaron thought, and left you.

"Your father loved her, I'll tell ya that."

"The last time you saw her."

"He hasn't recovered."

"Did she seem depressed?"

"It eats him alive."

"Grandma!" Aaron slammed down his spoon. She looked up at him, startled. The good eye was blinking, the glass eye open and drooling. "Please stop drinking that coffee."

"I bet I know what you'd like." Standing slowly, stiff in the knees and back, she shuffled in her thin foam American Airlines slippers to the cupboard. With both hands, chin high, she reached up to pull down flour, brown sugar, baking powder, chocolate chips, walnuts, vanilla extract, and, spinning around, set each neatly on the counter. From the fridge she got Butter Buds Spread and eggs.

"What are you doing, Grandma?"

"Sit down." After creaming the Butter Buds and sugar in a large white bowl, she cracked an egg in each hand, expertly letting the gooey insides dribble into the bowl. She flung the shells into the In-sink-erator.

"I have to go to school."

"Nonsense." Moving faster now, she shook the bag of flour, launching a white cloud. As if casting a spell, she tossed in a five-finger pinch of baking powder. Next, she opened drawers and slammed them shut, one after the other, like rifle shots. "Bosh!" she said, holding up a BBQ fork. She used it to stir.

"Your fibrillation!" said Aaron, gaping at the way she whipped herself around the room.

"Toll House, your favorite," she said, clawing out tiny gobs of dough and plopping them down in rows on a baking sheet. "I don't forget."

"Grandma, it's *me*, Aaron."

Jamming the tray into the oven, she swung around, one slippered foot crunching a porcelain shard.

"I," she said, and froze.

"Grandma." It surprised Aaron that her blood, leaking onto the tile floor, could be so bright and healthy-looking.

"I." She convulsed, once, bringing her fists to her chest. The BBQ fork was sticking into her neck, drawing two pinpricks of blood like a vampire bite. Aaron pried it from her fingers.

"Nonrehabilitatable," she said, or something that sounded like it. She had disturbed the line of ants, and now they swarmed mercilessly over her ankles. Grandma heaved again, once, and folded in upon herself, tiny.

It was Aaron's worst fear.

The defibrillator kicked, making her lash back and gasp. But it must have failed. She crumpled again, this time into a fetal position. The puddle under her bleeding foot grew quickly to drown hundreds of ants.

Aaron ran for the phone, punched in the hospital number, and waited. Grandma's eyelids were blue. She was panting.

A female computer's voice said, "Enter your transtelephonic defibrillator code now for reprogramming, now."

Aaron punched the buttons. His hands did not shake.

"Now place the speaker to the pacemaker, now."

Now.

Now.

Aaron thrust the Sony cordless against his grandmother's heart. Her good eye was shut, but her hand-blown glass eye sparkled like a marble.

Tones came from the phone. The pacemaker answered in tones of its own. A language of real authority, non-rhetorical, emotion-free, digitized.

Purple cracks showed through her psychotic pink lipstick. Sweat turned the rouge on her cheeks filmy.

"Did Dad kill her, Grandma?"

"I'm a body mover," she said.

"Dad killed Mom," said Aaron.

On cue, Franklin walked in—head stubble, pillow creases lining his eyelids. He saw the blood on the Mexican tiles, he saw ants paddling in the blood, he saw the neck punctures, and Aaron, Aaron still somehow holding the BBQ fork, the Sony cordless, and Grandma in a head-lock.

"What did you do to my mother?" Franklin asked.

The smell of chocolate chip cookies was almost dainty.

Grandma Goretex recovered, but lost all her remaining mental faculties. She could no longer think rationally, was confused about the passage of time, and her speech rarely made sense. Sometimes Aaron would catch her holding the Sony cordless to her chest, punching buttons and smiling. She seemed to particularly like 1-8-3, 1-8-3, 1-8-3.

Daddy did not like Franklin. "He's so much older."

Mavy knew that what he meant was, he's sucking your youth, and when he's through, he'll spit you out older, sadder, burnt at the edges.

Plus there was the slut factor. Having premarital sex was all you had to do to qualify. As if Mavy had only so much sexual mileage before being *used.* Franklin, on the other hand, accrued virility with each fuck, a kind of macho equity. This was what Mavy's father thought, she knew. She saw through him where others did not.

But *he* could not spout at the mouth. *He* was Bernal Tibbets, author of *Ripcord*—the blunt seventies classic ruled obscene in Dade County. It was still taught in expensive liberal arts colleges, part hard-core lit, part novel, essay, rant, and one thousand percent graphic. It was the only book in history that the *New York Times* urged its readers not to buy because *To do so*, they warned, *is to pay homage to the death of literature.*

Mavy herself loved *Ripcord*, and loved her father for writing it. But he couldn't spout at the mouth.

Bernal Tibbets the author was an American icon ("to smash," he told graduate writing students who brown-nosed him at Berkeley, Stanford, and U.C. Irvine).

Bernal Tibbets the man was plainspoken—"an ordinary joe, a baseball fan."

But Bernal Tibbets the father was a hypocrite.

"What do you see in that yuppie?" he asked.

"Shhh," Mommy said. She was working with a jeweler's screwdriver and pliers at the back of her laptop. Her recent project involved sending radio signals into space using a computer and a communications dish, directing them at shooting star trails, which had just enough density to reflect radio waves. You could only get about 750 bytes per star, but it was cheaper than launching communications satellites. "Be nice."

Franklin was just now in Mavy's room, under the covers, trying to keep his hands off his hard-on.

"To you everyone in their twenties is a yuppie," Mavy said.

"Is that supposed to be an answer?" Daddy asked. He was tipping back in his chair and drinking black coffee out of a thick, home-thrown mug. "That kid tossed his juice bottle in the trash."

Mavy took a breath. "You have to educate people."

"Not recycling is worse than yuppie," Bernal grumbled. "What about that tomato grower, Farmer John? There's a nice guy. I spoke with him on the phone. A real find. What's wrong with John?"

"Do we have any aloe vera, Mom?"

"Burn yourself?"

"My hands are chapped," Mavy said. "In your bathroom?"

"I'll get it," Mom said, putting down her tools. She returned with a mason jar filled with the clear, deceptively viscous aloe vera. "I wish you'd learn to put the toilet seat up, sweetie pie."

"If I put it up, you get mad when I forget to put it down," Bernal said.

"It's the man's job."

"The woman's."

"Thanks, Mom." While her parents bickered, Mavy took two plastic sandwich bags off the drying rack—Dad insisted the family rinse out and reuse even these—and hid them down her shorts.

"Your aim's not so good," Mom teased. After all these years, Mavy could see that her parents were still in love. Not romantically, perhaps, in the way of flowers and chocolate, or fire and ripped underwear, but in another way, one always about to happen.

"Happens," Bernal said. He used to pee a straight full stream, a thick head of foam in the bowl, and get the chills at the end. Now he sprayed a low-pressure spatter, finishing with a dribble. And there wasn't a goddamn thing he could do, neither wish, exercise, nor pay to get it back. A small thing, until you thought about it. A half hour after sex, the stream came out forked, one going into the toilet bowl, the other splashing onto the floor. His prostate hurt, too, like heartburn, only at the core of his hips. "I hate being old."

And now there was a young man in the house, in his daughter's bed. Looking at Mavy, he asked, "Is this, serious?"

Mavy shrugged. Partially to antagonize him, and partially not to jinx it.

"That's what I thought," he said, wincing and rubbing his appendectomy scar.

Daddy had almost died in Mexico of a burst appendix, and even to this day, it pained him whenever he had big emotions.

"Give me your hands, hon." Mom began rubbing the aloe into Mavy's chapped hands. It had a mild cucumber smell.

"Gimme some of that," Daddy said, dipping his thumb into the jar and patting it onto his scar.

Of course, the scar had a place in American letters. Most English majors knew the story:

Sucking Cuervo from the bottle, Bernal had been trying to forget his thirtieth birthday when the cramp struck.

A bad taco, he thought. Spit-fired pork, corn tortilla, gamey beans, jalapeños. It tasted damn fine, but he barely got out the back door before it came back up. Every last chile seed.

The pain doubled him over and told him he was just another fuck-up about to die. Until now, he had been forging metal and bending iron—a trade he had learned in the navy. He hated the work, but the smelting and hammering did satisfy a part of him, the part that was angry at his privileged New York boyhood, at his distant mother, at the fraudulent tycoon who posed as his grandfather.

A pair of Federales wearing khaki suits and shiny badges seized Bernal by the shoulders. He was happy to give them all the dollars in his wallet. Between barking heaves, he offered to trade them his American Express card for their badges.

The Federales dragged him to a building made of cinderblocks and corrugated tin. In the front door, a goat and dog fought viciously. The Federales shot the dog.

Inside the *clinica* pregnant women sat on pallets of Coca-Cola empties, some cradling babies too sick to cry.

The very young *medica*, a skinny teenager by the look of her in the baggy white lab coat, pretty, ordered the Federales to bed Bernal down in the delivery room. The gurney had a sheet of protective butcher paper, stirrups, and faced a wall with an anatomical poster of a giant vagina.

"I'm going to cut you open and take it out," she said, looking so touchable that Bernal tried to kiss her.

The Federales hooted. They puckered up their lips, strapping his ankles into the stirrups.

"What a lot of tattoos," she said, swabbing an oil derrick on his arm with alcohol.

"Just one kiss," he roared, grabbing the tail of her lab coat.

"Be a gentleman," she said, and stabbed the oil derrick with the syringe needle.

Bernal's hangover was like getting religion. The slightest movement of his head sent quiet howls echoing into the up above. His veins itched. On his back, legs stirruped, he opened his eyes to the giant vagina.

When he scratched his belly, his fingernails caught the sutures. "Bitch!"

That teenybopper doctor had sliced Eve in two!

Now, twenty years later, Eve's top half was slightly displaced, and her midsection was a ropey, keratosis-thickened blue. Adam and the tree and the snake remained intact, but the way the scar pulled at the skin altered their expressions. Now Adam had the sunken eyes of Boris Karloff and the snake resembled Bryant Gumbel.

"Buenos días." The *medica* handed him a jar. Inside was his appendix, pink, slimey, and bursting.

"Any normal person would have cut the snake," Daddy said, for the zillionth time. The *medica* would turn out to be Mavy's mom. She and Bernal got married only a few months later, after a bullfight in Tijuana. On their honeymoon in Mexico City, they were coming out of an ice cream parlor when a terrorist group with no clear cause blew the place to bits. Bernal dropped his cone and plunged into the flames, skipping over an injured nun and priest to save a toddler. *"Por favor,"* the nun said, her bloody arm outstretched, her habit ripped and torn, *"ayuda el Padre."* She pointed to the unblinking Father, his legs bent terribly. Clutched in his hands was *Alive*, the paperback. Only after bringing the kid out onto the *zocalo* did Bernal realize that he was already dead.

The building collapsed, killing everybody else, including the nun and the Padre. The experience made Bernal hate God, which meant he at least believed. The experience made his new wife suddenly want a child.

"I would never have cut the snake," Mom said, as always. Who knew what would happen if she strayed from her lines.

"Thanks, Mom," Mavy said, stroking her newly soft palms and fingers.

Bernal liked the story, because it kept people preoc-
cupied, preventing them from looking for others. The
story turned him into a hero, when really he was an
emotionally dishonest teacher (See Yourself, Live! He'd
rather die), a secretive husband, a bullying, hypocritical
father. He held up his empty mug. "You don't need a new
tea bag every time, Mavy."

"Da-ad," she said, two syllables. The peppermint tea
steamed.

"It's wasteful."

"I like it strong."

"Then let it steep a little longer. What's your hurry?"
He saw his wife and daughter exchange grins, and felt
unwitty and patronized. "Everyone's in such a hurry."

"It's just a tea bag, Dad," Mavy said. "Not—"

"You don't need it."

"Want, Dad. I *want."*

"In *your* house, you can use all the tea bags in China."

Mom kissed him on the top of the head, but winked at
Mavy, too.

"It's just a tea bag," she repeated, but obeyed. She had
more important battles coming up.

Mom did not approve of Franklin either, Mavy knew
that. But Mom understood Mavy was in love, and something about it pleased her. Maybe she was hoping the
change would rub off on her and Daddy.

"And I don't think everybody in their twenties is a
yuppie," Bernal said. "I think anybody who thinks glass
is trash, anybody who works with computers to invade
people's private lives, to sell them, and makes sh—truck-
loads of money doing it, and has no weight on his soul,
and thinks he can control—"

"Shhhh," Mom said. "You're shouting."

"He doesn't think he can control," said Mavy.

"I was the same way," Bernal said. This kid Franklin had a mug, an expression full of chin. There was something too gung-ho about him, a disobedient bigness. You could see the youngster was some kind of spiritual mercenary. The look of a boy who'd turn man too fast and die violently. "What do you need those Baggies for, Mavy?"

The plastic bags had slipped. They were hanging out of her shorts. "Nuts. I'm gonna put nuts in them." She was usually honest with her parents; it saved time. One on one, she could say anything to them, but together they were somehow different, somehow no longer *us*.

"Nuts?"

"Yeah, almonds." Before having to explain further, Mavy took the aloe vera and the Baggies into her bedroom.

Bernal farted.

"Bern."

"It's the bean. I should get off the java," Bernal said, farting again, then grimacing after the last bitter swallow of coffee. "It makes me grumpy and it makes me fart. I love it."

First drug he had to give up was aspirin. After the appendicitis, even the baby variety gave him stomach pains, made him fall down. Next it was grass and hallucinogens. Pot turned him stupid for whole afternoons, and psychedelics incapacitated him with mathematical, thumb-twiddling reveries. Then came a chemical-free spell of almost manic clarity during which he wrote *Ripcord.* Success followed, and with it money, and a whole lot of booze. The alcohol he had recovered from, though he hadn't touched it in thirteen years. An ice-cold beer on a hot day scared him more than the face of death.

Now, bowels misfiring, back full of knots, it was about time to cut out the joe. It seemed like his life was a progression of beating one addiction after the next in a struggle to find in himself another book, another point of view.

He had just two rules for writing: 1. Tell the truth. 2. Use only words he'd heard spoken. That was all. That was *Ripcord.* A cinch. But lately, he could not write three sentences before a lie appeared. Or, worse, something that might be a lie or not; he wasn't sure.

The novel inside him was like another poison he'd eventually have to give up. But to yield it would hurt both him and his family. There was something he'd never told his wife, his daughter. Something important.

He lifted one buttock off the chair to coax out another fart. Hadn't he once appeared in *Rolling Stone* in full and glorious tattoodom? Hadn't he been a guest on "Johnny Carson"? Hadn't he been a sex symbol to a whole generation of "coeds"? It was worse than bad, being old.

People were surprised when they found out Bernal Tibbets was still alive. The board game Trivial Pursuit put him in their Baby Boomer edition as Bern*ard* Tibbets.

He stood up, put his arms around his wife's waist, his hands into her pockets, smelling her hair. All he had to do was tell the truth. And now that his daughter was getting to be a serious person, he might well have no choice but.

"What took you so long?" Franklin asked as Mavy dove under the covers, beside him.

"Mmmmm," she said, licking his ear, hugging him. His body was hard, and all hers, and right here.

They had already done everything but. But Mavy wanted more now. She slathered aloe vera on his erection. "Marry me."

"No," Franklin said. He had already come three times.

Mavy put the two plastic sandwich bags over his dick. He couldn't possibly have much left, but all it took was one. And there was safety to think about, common sense. It was either this, or a trip to the drugstore; finding a parking place would break the spell for sure. She lubricated the bags with more aloe vera, wondering if she appeared business-like. "Why not?"

"Why not not." Franklin bent down. He put his tongue up into her as far as it would go.

"Here," she whispered, tugging him back up by the scalp.

He entered her in slow, slow increments. For a moment they lay joined but for the few millimeters of plastic. Quietly, calmly, Franklin said, *"You* marry me."

"No," she said, beginning to move underneath him. *"I'm* the one asking."

"You're only sixteen."

"Seventeen."

"You're only seventeen!"

She came, but he couldn't.

"Okay," Franklin said, flopping back. "I do."

"Oh." She kissed his nose, eye, his chin, the corners of his lips.

"Oh?" he said.

Then "Oh," again, because in the Baggies was a tiny blinking split. He figured it didn't really matter, since he hadn't been able to ejaculate anyhow.

But, though they wouldn't know it for months, Bernal and Barbara Tibbets, while making slow, expert love in

another part of the house, became the grandparents of a
Mentally Gifted Minor.

April brought warm nights and a sun-fed haze. May
started hotter, drier, days of white skies, a government-
classified drought. The Army Corp of Engineers had covered the California aqueduct with mylar to prevent
evaporation. Quotas were imposed. In one case, a seventy-
seven-year-old man who repeatedly broke the injudi-
cious-use law for washing his Pontiac received a
six-month jail sentence.

All over town, homeowners sprayed their lawns with
Revironment, a dye that stained gutters green when rain
finally came. Landscapers advised planting blossoming
ocotillo, flowering yucca, red bloom aloe, poppies and
other desert flora.

Surviving orange groves looked lean and sinuous.
Dying ones looked dead. Mom's, though, was thriving.
Each tree was almost completely white, blossom-flocked,
the creamy flowers' undersides just turning hard and
green.

It was strange to see them, buzzing with millions of
honeybees, their population having exploded as a result
of the weather.

Across the room, Linda Delgado wore a crown of orange blossoms. In the grove, they'd be buzzing with millions of honeybees. But on Linda's hair they held a different sort of attraction.

Aaron wondered why romance got like this—the more he began liking her, the shyer he became. They looked away and at each other, at and away.

"Ladies and gentlepersons," Mrs. Jaycock said, clanging her finger cymbals. "Refreshments are served."

The bright red fluid in the simulated crystal punch bowl did not look at all refreshing, but Aaron ladled some into a Dixie cup anyhow.

Jimbo approached, wearing a blue pinstriped suit that did justice to his triangular head. "Fuel." Jimbo drew a half-pint bottle of bourbon from a jacket pocket. He unscrewed the lid, topped off his own cup, then poured a splash for Aaron. The liquor turned the punch fiery.

"You're fucking her, aren't you?" Jimbo said. He meant Prudence, who'd just winked at them. She slouched in a shoulderless, sleeveless, backless dress. For jewelry she wore her magnicuffs, of course, the triad on the same wrist. All evening she'd been harassing Aaron, pinching his ass, whispering lewdities; he could not help associating the cuffs with the way a leash will give a certain kind of dog permission to be ferocious.

Jimbo's eyes were bloodshot and his breath stank, but still the suit suggested an illusion of credibility and manners. For a long time the two of them just stood there. Then Jimbo smacked his lips and stroked Aaron's red velvet lapel. "Well, Wells?"

"Young man!" Mrs. Jaycock fluttered her eyelids, coral-shadowed to match her dress. The skin on her neck hung in folds. "You there, Mr. Wells."

Aaron curled his fist tight around the wadded cup. Jimbo slid the bottle back into his pocket. A record was going *ktch-ktch-ktch.*

Mrs. Jaycock curtsied and bared her dental implants. "Honor us."

Jimbo jabbed a thumb into his ribs. "Dudesterism."

"My pleasure, ma'am." Aaron bowed, offering Mrs. Jaycock his arm.

Mrs. Jaycock giggled like a woodpecker. "Oh, heavens no. Not me. Ask one of these comely young ladies here."

Prudey licked her lips; Linda looked at the floor.

"Well? Go on," Mrs. Jaycock said. "She can't read your mind."

Despite Jimbo's eyes reaming into Aaron's back, or because of them, he asked Prudey.

Arroyo Grande Cemetery was never particularly creepy. Plentiful eucalyptus, palm, and cypress trees that grew in spires. The lawn was immaculate, the roads curving and sloped, no telephone poles, gutters made of carved rock and mortar. It felt storybook; its ghosts—if they existed—were familiar, wholesome, without complicated psychologies.

Aaron took off his red velvet suit and laid it down on the grass, cut low and plush like a golf green. Revironment at work. You'd never know the lawn hadn't been watered for months.

His mother's tombstone was deluxe, with a guitar-strumming cherub and orange blossoms cut into marble. But the fact that she herself wasn't buried here made the thing seem shoddy. It was a monument to Dad's guilt. To relieve it? Or memorialize it?

No, no, no. There was no way on earth Dad killed

Mom, and Aaron was a horrible son to even think such a thing.

Prudey kept her tight mini on while they had sex.

Aaron didn't mind. He was never not horny, addicted to orgasm, perpetually scheming how and where to get the next. He beat off first thing in the morning, last thing before sleep. Right hand, left hand. He beat off to centerfolds, music videos, mirrors, in the orange grove, on Dad's bed, in front of Thumper. He beat off into Kleenex and tube socks and Caroline's underwear, imagining girls at school. Only Linda Delgado did he save for special occasions.

"Hey," Prudey said, after Aaron pulled away. "I'm not done yet."

He lay on his back, breathing wildly. The moon was yellow and bloated. Aaron studied it for signs of disease. He didn't know what he expected to see, exactly. Twinkling lights, smog, firestacks. There was nowhere you could look, now, on land or in space, that wasn't already sampled, bagged, tagged, and—

"I said I'm not done yet," Prudey said. She plucked off the rubber and tossed it aside. Then she started in again, stroking him with her mouth.

It was a horrible thing, losing your virginity to a girl you faked liking on your mother's fake grave. That's why it turned him on. That's why now it was getting boring. "Jimbo knows," Aaron said.

"There ya go," Prudey sang. She rubbered him up with another of those Japanese condoms from the Price Club. Like tourniquets, 49-millimeter diameter compared to the American 52.

Aaron pushed all the way in; Prudey shivered.

"Say I'm skinny," she said.

Aaron stopped.

" 'You're skinny,' " Prudey said. She frowned fiercely. "Tell me!"

Aaron started again. He watched her satellite dish earrings swing. "You're skinny."

"Say I'm gorgeous," she whispered. "Say it!!"

"You're a total babe. You're exquisite."

"Tell me you lust me." She smelled spicy, and looked him in the eye as if she were helping herself by the handful to something personal. "More than *any* girl. Say it!"

Aaron's excitement scared him until he stopped resisting it. "You're everything to me," he lied, but it sounded like the truth.

Minutes later she came. So did he, at the same time, but silently, trying to keep it private.

"I told her," Prudey rasped. "Linda knows."

On the walk home, there was a freshly dug grave, prepared for the coffin, no marker yet. The dirt was red and clumpy. Aaron jumped down into it.

"Come out of there!" Prudey's voice had that same hysteria as the night he was here, cuffed and doused with kerosene.

"Why'd you tell her?" he asked, picturing that Bluetip, lit against Jimbo's fly, burning.

"I just wanted to see what it felt like," she said.

Somewhere in the dark, a bird hit the same high note again and again.

Frances Tibbets, five years old tomorrow, was already one of the richest citizens in the Inland Empire. For Eliza, having had a child was a simple miracle. Eliza sat in a fat chair before the fireplace, feeling thanks.

Theirs was a happy family. She and Luther had only hurt each other deeply twice. Maybe three times. But those were bygones.

On this cold December evening Frances slept cozily under a gigantically poofy eiderdown comforter. Outside the trees were heavy with the orange crop. There was money in the bank. Money enough to stand several banks.

A few months after Franny was born, Luther had begun selling off parcels of the grove, diversifying, ensuring a good future. A very good future.

Since Franny, Eliza had lost interest in gardening. But every now and then, it came back, in pangs. A catalog picture of crimson tulips would set her off. The smell of wet newsprint. She hadn't gotten her hands dirty in a long time.

"Franny in bed?" Luther asked, sneaking up behind her with a bottle of orange liqueur, one of several new products in development.

"Get away from me, you animal!" she said, with exaggerated virtue. "She wants a birthday kiss and for you to sing the 'Goodnight Already Song.' "

He growled mischievously, pecking her gently on the cheek. She put down her catalog, and, hugging him around the neck, kissed his newly regrown beard in four places.

The fire popped and sparkled as if on cue, and they both laughed. Luther rose and poured out two snifters, singing in a surprisingly melodic baritone, "Goodnight already, you little maniac, goodnight already, you bird of paradise on stilts, goodnight already, you longstem rose eating gorilla." Then he waltzed out of the room to go kiss their daughter goodnight.

Eliza sipped her orange liqueur—not bad—and felt unimaginably peaceful. It didn't even bother her that Franny seemed to like her father more. He was better with her, knew when to be firm, when silly. No, it didn't bother her. Luther was such a deserving man.

Once or twice she imagined she saw something other than fatherly love in his gaze. Not anything evil or, God forbid, *psychological,* but something critical. Perhaps that was too strong a word. *Appraising* was closer. And *wondering.*

"She's so perfect," he said now, returning. "Remember when . . ."—and Eliza could swear she saw his eyes tear. It was Bub.

Luther added a Y-shaped log to the fire. Then he sat on the ledge at Eliza's feet and took a sip of his liqueur. "Mmmmm, I like it," he said. "I like it."

She'd confessed several times about her crime, but Luther refused to take her at her word, insisting her meaning was metaphorical. "Do you ever think about that party?"

"What party?" He frowned and poked the fire. "You mean for McKinley?" The flames kicked up, but he kept on poking. "What about it? That was years ago. Why? What about it?"

She started to speak, but didn't know what to say, or what she meant by asking.

"He tried to kiss you," Luther said at last. "Right? The president tried to kiss my wife."

"It was us I was thinking of," she said. It was hard to believe she'd ever hated him.

"If you add water it changes colors." Luther showed her. "See?" The liquid was a pale, creamy yellow. They sipped and watched the snifters, the fire, the floor, everything but each other. "Did he kiss you? You never actually told me. But of course he did. Did he?"

"I just don't want anything to happen to us," she said.

"Impossible. He's already . . . we're still here, aren't we? Together?" He hugged her, poker still clenched in his fist. "We had our times," he went on. "I'm embarrassed, oh, I'll admit. That damn manhood enlarger!"

"The dog!" Until he believed her, she could not be redeemed.

"Oh, don't say anymore," he said, laughing abruptly, laughing! He took a sip and looked at her. "God, what kids we were. What utter imbeciles. Me, anyway."

"Oh no, no, no! Me!" she argued, pulling away to lift the glass to her lips.

"Both of us," Luther compromised. Then after a few moments, added, "Then again, for all we know they worked. I mean the garlic."

For a long time they were silent, sipping their liqueurs. The fire burned steadily.

"How you kept that tree going—"

"Yes," Eliza interrupted. "He did."

"Did what? Who did?"

"McKinley. He kissed me."

Luther poured them each another glass. "I thought he only *tried.*"

Eliza knew she should stop. Stop drinking, stop talking. Her nose was filled with nectary fumes.

"That's what you told me before."

"I have always told you the truth, and now I'm telling you he *kissed* me."

The air had a piney snap. The corners of the room glowed. The flame, blue in spurts from knots in the log, hid the ridge in Luther's forehead, but Eliza knew it was there.

"A curious fruit, you are," Luther said, rubbing her silk robe, a *kimono* Mr. Rogers the postman called it. A gift on the birth of Franny.

"Franny's birthday, can you believe it?" Eliza said. "Already five."

"Mmm-hmm," he said. "What else happened, Eliza? With you and McKinley."

"She's so smart," Eliza continued. "Today she waited out front for an hour for you to come home from work because it would be the last time she was waiting for you to come home from work as a four-year-old. Now isn't that smart?"

"It's smart all right," Luther repeated, holding his glass up to the light. "Do you think this is too sweet? I think it's a little too sweet."

"Oranges *are* sweet," she said. "That's what they are."

"I don't know. I think it may be a little too sweet." He set down his drink on the bricks and held both hands up to the fire. "Come on, Eliza, tell me. You can't let my imagination—"

"Okay," she said. "To shut you up." But a chill ran

through her, the Japanese silk on her nipples. "He was
big and fat, you know. He drank a lot . . ."

"And?"

"Well, he got kind of . . ."

"Any man would. That's the truth."

"I suppose I was tipsy, too. All the festivities. You were
off entertaining that Hobart person—"

"The vice-president," Luther reminded her.

"—and McKinley, well, he was just this big and
fat—"

"You said that already."

"—with a great big fat mustache—not like yours, of
course, yours is nice—and I remember thinking, *this* is
the president of the United States? This big, fat, drunk
man?"

"Why do you have to keep saying that?"

Eliza shook out her hair and allowed herself a small
smile. "Well, it was on the tour of the orange grove that
he kissed me."

"That's all?" Luther asked. "That's the story?"

"Pretty much."

"No one could find you two for quite some time. Hobart was *insinuating*. It's no wonder he disappeared from
politics, fast."

"Well," Eliza said, dismissively.

"Oh come on, hon. It's the past. What can hurt us?"

Eliza imagined the orange liqueur swirling through
her head. Outside, the cold night was ripening her
oranges, bright and juicy. Inside, their daughter was
asleep, and turning five. The chair she was sitting in was
made by hand in Italy. The snifter lead crystal from
Finland. If here wasn't safe, nowhere was.

"He'd have been crazy not to try anything," Luther

said, as if talking to himself. "A woman like yourself."

The fountain of youth. That's what McKinley called her.

"Well," she repeated; this time the word had possibilities. "He had brought out this bottle of I don't know what, from New York and very strong."

"You had some?"

"To be polite." She held her glass out to Luther. He filled it dutifully, then his own, and they toasted, smiling weakly at each other.

"Oh forget it," Luther said. "What's the difference? I'm sorry I ever brought it up in the first place."

"*I* brought it up," Eliza said.

"We love each other." It was unclear whether this was a statement or a question.

"Yes," she answered, just in case. "Yes." For a while they were quiet, watching the fire. "He had the funniest way of talking, I mean, I couldn't get it out of my head that this person was the president. He kept asking me my secret. Of youth." The fire crackled, then died down a bit. The allure of darkness kept her talking. "What was I going to tell him? Wear a hat in the sun? Eat fruit? He was so big and fat. It was stupid, Luther! You know I wouldn't hurt you."

He gulped his drink, but Eliza could see the swallow didn't go down. He coughed into the fire; the spray of liqueur sizzled and sent up remarkably well-formed smoke rings. "I see," he said. "Okay, I see."

"I'm sorry," Eliza said, suddenly panicked. What had she done? "Oh Luther I'm so sorry."

He squinted into his liqueur. "I'm not sure I even like this stuff."

"It'll never happen again, I promise you that. Ever."

She rubbed his shoulder, waiting to feel relieved. "I *love* you, Luther Tibbets." She vowed to prove it, too. "Look at me."

Luther's eyes stayed on the fire, vacant, but his fingers absently twirled in her hair. "And I actually gave money to that guy." He laughed sarcastically. "I hate this stuff!" he blurted, flinging his glass into the fire where it shattered beautifully. "It's too damn sweet!"

For some reason, this made Eliza angry. "For heaven's sake, Luther!"

He looked like a man choking on his own lungs. "Eliza, I want the truth. *The truth,* do you hear?"

He threw himself down on her in the privacy of the grove, the rows and rows of Washington navels. Just as quickly he rolled away. "I'm leaving it up to you," he said. "I'm the president of the United States of America, and I'm leaving this decision up to you."

"I wanted to say no," she said. "I really wanted to."

"Never," she said. Or maybe it was "You're drunk." Or "Wait till my husband hears." There were a million things she could have said, only one she should have said. But her hands, disobeying her, unfastened his belt buckle. Something in her had to see how far she could take this.

"They said I couldn't have a baby," she said. "All the doctors said."

"Thatta girl," McKinley said. It was so large. So much larger than Luther's. And it was so ugly, horrifying, big and fat, thicker than her wrist, with ropey blue veins and a tiny blind head. His balls were enormous and lopsided, practically hairless, and they had a sweet rank smell. It appalled her that she liked it.

"Never seen anything like it, huh?" he asked.

She squeezed as hard as she could to show him she was

no easy conquest, but he only groaned with pleasure.

The rest was awful. It was so awful she thought she would be sick. Instead she climaxed. McKinley laughing all the way through it. His belly was blubbery, jiggling, his mustache squirming like an animal on his face. The skin on his cheeks was thick with big pores—orange peel texture.

"Oh my God," Luther said. "You let him!"

"Luther, don't!"

He chortled as orgasm possessed him. Afterwards, he patted dry his forehead with a handkerchief and politely straightened the collar on her dress for her. "Thanks, Mrs. Tibbets. I've had a refreshing dip in the fountain of youth. And you, my dear, have a story for your grandkids."

"Oh my God." Luther pounded his temples with open hands.

Three months later an assassin shot him in the head.

"Don't think that!" she said. Franny was born eight months after the party. Eliza had done the math in her head a thousand times, she was almost positive it was probably only eight. Since the doctors told her it couldn't possibly matter she never bothered to keep track. "I was *al*ready pregnant," she said, sounding hopeful rather than definite. Then there was the fact that Franny was nearly *seven* pounds at birth—well, one ounce shy (six pounds fifteen ounces). And perfectly healthy, other than that little cough (accompanied, as you would expect, by a fever) which cleared up after a month. And with Luther's gorgeous green eyes, his resolute disposition. "She loves you—"

"No!" He turned his back to her. Broad and strong, twitching with sobs. "I can't believe this is happening."

"—more than me!" Eliza said, out of breath. "She loves *you* . . . more."

The fire died, reappeared as a single flame curling slowly, tentatively—tenderly, it seemed—along the crux of the log.

"It's me. *I'm* the one who can't . . . who should have." His voice trailed off. His face was like a wave-battered rock. "First thing tomorrow, I'm to the doctor, have myself checked."

"Shut up, Luther," Eliza said. "Just. Shut. Up."

But he was already out of the room.

Luther unlocked his desk and took out the Colt .45. He broke the gun open and spun the chamber. Six bullets. It was his habit to always keep the pistol fully loaded. For rats, at first. Later, after he became rich, for dangers yet to reveal themselves.

Luther quietly entered the bedroom. McKinley's daughter lay curled under the lofty eiderdown. Light streaming through the doorway fell gently on her cheeks.

Luther pointed the barrel. Her eyelids quivered. McKinley's daughter. Dreaming.

She was so beautiful. Luther kissed her forehead and, without opening her eyes, she murmured, "Daddy."

Luther stuck the muzzle against his temple. He could not help himself.

Eliza was not surprised when she saw Luther storm into the living room clutching a cocked pistol. What surprised her was that in his other hand was a box of bullets.

"You shut up," he growled, aiming at her. "You just shut up." He put on a heavy coat, biting the box and shifting hands to keep the gun on her. "You just keep your goddamn lying mouth *shut.*"

Outside, Luther stomped up the terraces until he got to the largest tree, one of Eliza's original government-sent.

Thick-branched, rich with foliage, laden with fruit. Luther aimed and fired.

It took him over an hour to kill all her oranges.

When Don Miller, the MGM teacher, interrupted his talk about flags of South America to tell him he looked "peaked," Aaron said nothing. He turned and peered out the window at the orange grove across the street, ringed with palm trees.

"Are you with us?" Don Miller asked.

It was sad because now you had to look at every grove as if it was the last time you'd be seeing it. Everything was like that.

"What's on your mind? Come on, tell us." Don Miller was a big man with bulging cheekbones and chin, as if the skin was stretched over three cue balls. Black curls fell over his ears, and wire-rims magnified brown eyes that pointed in slightly different directions. This morning he wore a fat striped tie with a plaid shirt, and a fringed suede jacket that made him look like a futon salesman.

"Fun," Aaron said.

"Fun," Don Miller repeated kindly, and wrote it on the chalkboard. "Fun, the noun?"

Aaron nodded.

"What about fun the noun?"

Aaron shrugged.

Other kids shifted in their chairs. Linda Delgado gazed at him, her hand resting on her chin, delicate. After Prudey in the graveyard, he didn't deserve to be in the same room as Linda Delgado. He was not worthy of meeting her eyes. What am I doing? Aaron suddenly wondered. What am I saying? "I can't explain it."

Don Miller came over and knelt next to Aaron's desk. He had an extremely large head. The rest of him was sprawling too. Over six feet tall, two hundred twenty pounds. He seemed too physical to be a teacher, too big for a classroom.

"Pull your desks into a circle," he said. Behind him, a poster vibrated—orange and yellow and black. You looked and your eyes teared, unable to hold the three colors at once.

With the desks rearranged, everyone saw everybody else to some degree in profile; nobody was just the back of a head anymore.

"Let's scrutinize the word itself," Don Miller said. *"Fun."* His huge dark eyes groping. "We'll go round the room and each say it twice. Fun, fun. Aaron?"

"Fun fun," Aaron said. Pretense, pain.

"Fun fun," said Jimmy Zydecky. Squeaky clean.

"Fun fun." Tammy Sandersson. Serious damage.

"Fun fun." Bernard Yalkovich. Unkind.

"Fun fun." Lupe Manzano. Delicious food.

"Fun fun." Cicero Jones. Exercise.

"Fun fun." Brainard. Swimming pool.

It was like a striptease, the word revolving, shedding layers as people cheered it on.

"Fun fun." Linda Delgado. Sacred, foreign.

Don Miller rubbed his stubble. The whiskers gave

the impression of sprouting. "All together now. Fun. Fun . . ."

"Fun, fun, fun . . ." They chanted in unison. Soft at first. Shy, tentative, faltering. "Fun, fun, fun." Building momentum. "Unf unf unf." Various movements. Resonance. Girls' voices harmonized with boys', tempos changed, syncopations developed. "Nfuh nfuh nfuh."

Afterward, Aaron felt warmth, togetherness, as if as a group they had survived a crisis.

Fun things you can do with oranges:

Bake with maple syrup.

Spike with cloves and dangle from string for a sinfully delightful-smelling boudoir ornament.

Cut into wedges (lengthwise, navel-to-stem, for better appearance and chewability) and lightly glaze with olive oil.

Grate orange peel into bran muffin batter for extra moisture, texture, and tang.

Mix orange juice with distilled spirits. Float thin slices in glass pitchers of spiced red wine.

Roll cool orange across forehead and neck.

There was a time in college when Franklin used to watch a doctor show. It was about a kind, fatherly doctor, white at the temples, plainspoken, without an ounce of irony.

Franklin used to sit up late at night and watch the syndicated episodes. They were from two decades ago, so the color was slightly off, the surgeon's scrubs a washed pastel blue, the big-fendered cars unfamiliar shades of red and yellow, highly enameled.

The shows he liked best were when young people came in with secret afflictions. Sometimes they also had potentially fatal diseases. The doctor never lied, but if there was even the slightest (and there always was) hope, he encouraged the patient to focus on it. Inevitably, a cure would follow, and along with it a magical clearheadedness that allowed the patient to confront and exorcise all personal idiosyncrasies. They were invariably the demons, the idiosyncrasies.

It was such a reassuring show.

The doctor's first name was from classic Latin and bespoke authority and learning; his good, solid, Protestant surname suggested well-being. He had a secretary who went by her first name, an easy-to-pronounce, mellifluous one that, loosely translated from the Mexican, meant "with dreams." She had red hair, extravagantly coiffed. Often she failed to pass on pieces of crucial information, through no fault of her own (flat tire, busy signals, e.g.).

But in the final moments she was always there to hold the patient's hand, or to offer a box of (the advertiser's) tissues.

Franklin knew every episode by heart.

Every episode gave him a perfectly satisfying dose of fatherhood.

The problem with having lots of money, Luther realized, was that people were afraid to tell you no. Everybody became a yes-man. Spineless, despicable, shoe-lickers.

He had to go all the way to Los Angeles to find himself a doctor unfamiliar with the Tibbets name.

The doctor confirmed Luther's worst fear. "Normally, sixty percent of spermatozoa are motile and demonstrate purposeful forward movement," the doctor said. "A normal ejaculate is one to five millimeters, a density of twenty million sperm per milliliter. You've got fewer than fifteen million, and fifty percent of the spermatozoa are amorphous, double-headed, or immature."

"Can I father a baby?"

"Miracles are possible."

Bernal Tibbets was unhappy. Why?

Sometimes he said:

"In fiction, everything that searchers for the important tend to leave out is left in, and what they would have in is left out. Thomas served devotedly under Grant and was one of the most lucid thinkers in the New World, but what Smith, in *Education of a Young American*, makes of the battle of Bull Run is sheer confusion, highlighted by a running conversation with a widow steering a horsecart of her dead husband's moonshine through the thick of musket fire."

Sometimes he said:

"Plot is where you put the finish line. A marathon has a plot. Life doesn't. Fiction in its truest sense mimicks both the plotlessness of life and the drama of the marathon. Its shortcoming is that, though the best can leave you breathless, it can never leave you dead."

Sometimes he said:

"I'm competing with the VCR, and, goddamn it, it's kicking my ass."

Sometimes he said:

"I hadn't heard she won it. How much money does that carry nowadays, anyway?"

Sometimes what he said was:

"Show me a critic who understands me and I'll show you me feeding my dog. Show me a bad review and I'll show you me feeding my cat. My only real reader is my mother."

To get away from the novel that wouldn't write itself, Bernal Tibbets compiled a book of victim impact statements. They were all taken from real life, mostly legal affidavits and court transcripts. The art was in recognizing how to put them into proper form, to ritualize.

First evoke pity and horror by showing the wounds. The more gruesome the better.

Next, turn the reader into a confessor figure.

The reader grants the victim absolution, which the innocent need more than the guilty.

The victim asserts she/he is a "survivor." Then he/she explains how she/he has, paradoxically, grown from the said horrifying experience, and is now reborn.

Victim Impact Statements hit the *New York Times* bestseller list on its week of publication. Though the book never climbed to number one, it lingered at spots five, six, and seven, for a total of seventeen weeks.

Bernal was invited to the White House, along with several of the victims.

The menu:

Justice Soup
Sesame Tickets

———

Roast Loin of Veal Rodriguez with Wild Mushrooms
Liberty Potatoes
Green Asparagus and Baby Carrots

———

Equality Salad
Herbed Mexican Cheese

Caramel Mousse with Roasted Dried Pears, Orange
Sauce, and Cookies

Thax Sauvignon Blanc 1980
Napa Park Pinot Noir 1984
Ramona y Alessandro Late Harvest Riesling 1982

The first artificial snowmaker was invented in the 1940s by
a man named Joseph Tropeano, an engineer employed by
Tropicana. His job was to devise a fogging machine to
protect orange crops from frost. But in freezing temperatures, the fog his gun made turned into snow. Useless for
orange groves, the snow gun has experienced great success
in numerous ski areas around the world.

When the PUPIL TRANSPORTATION UNIT carrying
the Gifted pulled into Arroyo Grande High, dozens of
students were already crumpled on the lawn. The emergency bell screamed. Girls clasped and comforted each
other. Boys held gauze to their own bloodied heads. Several kids occupied stretchers, IV tubes attached to their
arms. An EMS crew gave a cheerleader CPR.

When the bell stopped, the silence had an echo, like a

just-vacated dimension. The Gifted filed off the yellow bus, led by Aaron Wells and Richard Brainard.

"You're all victims," explained Don Miller, "of a hypothetical disaster." He passed out adhesive labels for sticking on chests and backs. "Preparation drill." Aaron got HEAD TRAUMA. Brainard got INTERNAL BLEEDING. Each preferred the other's, so they traded.

For himself, Don Miller kept ABLE-BODIED ADULT. Aaron observed that students had COMPOUND FRACTUREs and LACERATIONs and CARDIAC ARRESTs and other serious injuries, while most teachers were ABLE-BODIED ADULTs. Not at all how it would be in real life.

"I gotta get footage," Brainy said, and went to the classroom for a camcorder.

"Camping?" asked Don Miller, noticing Aaron's backpack. "Are you men in training?"

"Not exactly," Aaron said. He liked Don Miller, with his goggled eyes and black curls, his thick wrists and lime cologne, and by mistake sometimes called him Dad. "I've got a problem." He took off his pack—now loaded with thirty pounds of freshly picked Washington navels—and gestured toward the view. It was vintage Redlands: cold, still, and succinct. Not a frond shimmered on the tall palm trees lining the avenue. Beyond the grove, brightly polka-dotted with fruit, rose the San Bernardino Mountains, purple, jagged, white-spined.

"Problem?" asked Don Miller. His eyes shifted from the mountains to Aaron. In addition to the backpack, Aaron wore a down vest over a chamois shirt, blue jeans, and boots. He had let his hair grow, and now it was an awkward length, hanging over his eyes. "Shoot."

Aaron didn't answer, instead pulled a couple of oranges

out of his pack. Small-pored, fragrant, eye-watering, grown out of the same red soil used in the adobe bricks of Aaron's house's old wing. "Take a look."

Don Miller studied the orange. Possibly among the last the grove would ever produce. Dad was excited by tonight's prospect of severe frost. Dead trees were unprotected by zoning laws, and would allow him to get the necessary permits from city hall. Plow and subdivide.

"From Mom's grove," Aaron explained.

"Mom's?"

Aaron plunged his thumb into the core and pulled out the navel—actually a secondary fruit growing inside the main one. Pulpy and sour, it was edible, but you had to be desperate. Over the years Aaron had learned to match oranges with the trees they were picked from. South-facing trees produced the zingiest fruit; they got the most sun. Top branch fruit was sweetest. "Blossom ends are the best part."

Don Miller liked hearing this stuff; it was education. He removed a section and delicately nibbled. The wedge exploded in juiciness. "Wow!"

"That's a Tibbets," Aaron told him softly, seriously. From the healthiest, strongest, best tree in the grove, the one he'd named after his mother's side of the family. "Have another."

"Lemme finish." Don Miller held the dribbling orange away from his suede jacket. Over the roar of a camouflaged C-5 transport jet descending into Norton Air Force Base, he yelled, "How do you know all this?" A military presence made the disaster seem more plausible.

"Family history." Aaron knew a lot more. Once he penetrated the "Off Limits Closet," it all opened up. There were lots of pictures and clippings, there were funny clothes, a dog collar, a petrified bottle of orange liqueur, and more bullets for the Colt .45. The six-shooter was still stashed in his mattress. "There's something I have to do," Aaron told Don Miller, talking first to one eye, then to the other.

"An oral report?"

"And this thing," Aaron went on, ignoring the comment, "will get me in a lot of trouble."

"Whoa," said Don Miller, turning severe. "Ask yourself, do I need to know." He had already been the subject of letter-writing campaigns for being immoral, incompetent, and racist. Many parents didn't like the Gifted at all, and found Don Miller's unorthodox methods threatening. He distributed condoms, he made available unrated videocassettes like *I Am Curious—Blue*, and the class library included *American Psycho*. Now he was getting flak in the newspaper for bringing musicians over from Cuba. Every article mentioned that he was thirty-seven, vegetarian, unmarried. " 'Cause maybe it's better I don't."

After a moment, Aaron said, "You're right."

"Now I'm really curious."

"I *am* sorry to interrupt," said a flame-haired lady in a blue business suit. Instead of a label, she had a plastic identi-card clipped to her lapel, Ms. Terkle. "But we're running late here. Assume your injuries, please." She stepped aside as an EMS technician in a white coat leisurely wheeled by a CORPSE on a gurney. A Red Cross van occupied the school plaza next to the flag where nurses circulated with clipboards, dispensing medi-packs, issuing orders through megaphones: "Ten units Lactated Ringer's! Transport! Transport!"

"Sure thing, Ms.—," said Don Miller, offering his hand.

"Terkle," she said, and then spelled it. Then she was gone, scuttling on high heels towards the Bloodmobile.

Don Miller shrugged, and wiped juice off his chin with the sleeve of his jacket, suede fringes riffling.

"Earthquake?" Brainy asked, returning with the camera. He paused, taking his eye out from behind the viewfinder, and pasted down another chest sticker. "Flood?" Now he had LESIONS as well as head trauma. "Or industrial disaster?" He took off his pack, an old khaki external with excessive aluminum tubing. It contained only a few oranges, along with a space blanket, a topo map of Redlands, and an unauthorized bio of David Geffen. "Love Canal. Three Mile Island. Valdez." Brain was wearing waffle-stompers, his Stucco Stealth Camo fatigues, and, except for the cords in his neck, he looked Wyoming wholesome. Ten years from now he would be the cowboy on the billboards selling cigarettes which would lead to featured spots on game shows and later, an attempt on his life at a tobacco festival held in Del Mar, California. The would-be assassin, a female cancer patient breathing on half a lung, would shoot him with a 9-millimeter semiautomatic pistol. The bullet would bounce off his cranium, leaving Richard Brainard with a brief spell of amnesia, and a serious concussion. "Bhopal. Chernobyl."

Another C-5 transport rumbled overhead, its jet engines making a sucking sound that swallowed all other noise. Brainy followed it with his camera.

"Nagasaki. Beirut. Baghdad. What are we looking at here?" It was always surprising to hear Brainy speak. People expected macho, not his effeminate, almost stylized drawl—no flattened consonants, no dropped g's. "I know. Operation Mosaic." His careful enunciation, combined with the HEAD TRAUMA, made him seem prophetic, an idiot savant. "Chemicals? Biologicals?" He gestured toward a nurse who, wearing one herself, began dispensing surgeon's face-shields to a group of freshmen. "I give up. What kind of disaster am I documenting?"

"I think we can rule out natural," Don Miller said.

Early this morning Aaron and Brainard had attempted to buy a firehose at the hardware store, but the man wouldn't accept their cash. First, he said, they had to fill out forms, register intent of ownership.

"Want one?" Aaron asked, offering an orange to Brainard.

"Ugh," Brainard planted his face in the crook of his arm. "Don't you ever get sick of them?"

Aaron ignored the question. "Where are the fire trucks?"

"Bank of America, perhaps. Redlands Federal," Don Miller said. "Where the money is, is generally saved first. Besides, these buildings can't burn."

In fact, these buildings redefined state codes: cement reinforced with reebar and steel-mesh, automatic shutoff valves on gas and water mains, safety-glass windowpanes, fire-retardant carpet and curtains. Each wing had an alarm, a standpipe, and firehose. Escape plans were posted at every door, first-aid kits stocked in every room. There were even bottled oxygen and emergency water supplies in the janitor's storehouse. Arroyo Grande was a survivalist high school, and that gave the concept of security an ambiguous edge.

"Picture minor damage," Don Miller said. "A charred desk here, a smoldering book there, steaming puddles."

Ms. Terkle returned, wearing a severe expression—as if her face were accelerating at 4 Gs while the rest of her stood still. In the smile on her identi-card she was licking her teeth.

"I'd really like to help, ma'am," Aaron said.

"What do you have in mind?"

Aaron thought it strange that a Disaster Specialist would wear flammable clothing, a molded hairdo, and high heels. He gave her the orange in his hands. "I thought I'd put out that fire."

She blinked at the orange, then asked Don Miller, "What fire?"

Don Miller smiled flirtatiously. "There are two kinds of people: the rescued and the rescuers."

Aaron identified with neither, but had a queasy compassion for both. Which, he supposed, made him a third kind of person. "The hypothetical fire."

"Precocious," Nancy Terkle said, addressing Don Miller as if Aaron weren't there, her voice like fingers on a lock.

Being Gifted was like wearing one of these sticker labels. On the one hand adults credited you with more intelligence than you deserved; they wanted to follow your lead. But on the other hand they got offended when you were confused, annoyed when you were witty.

Until Don Miller, Gifted used to mean being bused to Arroyo Grande School and given harder math problems. Poor kids were almost never Gifted. Now things were different. No textbooks, no tests, no flag salute.

Don Miller built them a darkroom, acquired editing equipment, rented a shuttle van, passed out real oil paints, hung up a banner saying *Love Is Humankind's Highest Law*. He opened Gifted to any kid who had a special interest outside of regular school (Aaron's was President McKinley, Brainard's in vitro). But first you had to write a true story about yourself. Then you had to have your parents, or whomever you lived with, write true stories about you. Then you had to have one other person, a friend, a storeowner, a dentist, whoever, write

one true story about you. Not recommendations, but stories. Unflattering carried weight.

Not a lot of kids went to the trouble, and, after Don
Miller rejected the bullshitters, there was only a short
waiting list. Now there were rich, poor, black, white,
Latino, Asian, Indian, Arab, and one Inuit in the program, which was still called The Gifted. Colleges sought
them out to fill unofficial recruitment quotas.

"I'll organize a team," Aaron said, blowing the hair out
of his eyes. "We'll start——"

"*I'll* tell you what you can do, hon," Nancy Terkle said,
in the midst of another blinking fit. "What type are you?"

Type? The type that was desperately eager to please,
that had strong, inchoate convictions about right and
wrong, that saw nature as evidence of God's existence,
and that—so Aaron imagined—would either turn out a
criminal or a hero.

"A? B? O positive?" Ms. Terkle asked, her voice ex-
pressing great patience. "If your parents signed the release form, you're going to donate blood."

There was a release form, last September; Aaron remembered now. Dad had said, "Blood! That's giving of
yourself. It's not the thought that counts, not ever," and
enthusiastically checked Yes.

"A haircut and slacks and he wouldn't be half bad-
looking," Ms. Terkle observed, again as if Aaron weren't
there.

He groaned, the rebuilt smile on his face like a personality disorder. He wanted his blood. He needed it. All five
liters' worth, for tonight.

Near the Gifted classroom there was a fireplug. Directly
above it was an alarm and the cabinet containing a firehose—flat, woven canvas, folded accordion-style on a

series of pins that pulled out of a rack—capped with a foot-long nozzle. When Aaron tripped the latch, the alarm blared, and the glass door popped open. Brainard removed the hose and crammed it into his pack. Aaron shut the glass cabinet and when it clicked, the bell went off.

Checking her watch again, the CPR nurse snapped, "Your friend is dying."

Aaron hesitated.

"Clear his passage." The nurse hooked a red-nailed finger and dislodged a chunk of steak from an imaginary gullet. "Go on, clear it!"

Following the steps outlined on the chart, Aaron pinched Brainard's nose shut, clamped a hand over Brainy's mouth, and applied his own lips to the back of his own hand. It wasn't like kissing.

"One breath, five beats," the nurse said.

Aaron pressed his palm to Brain's chest, over his heart, which had supposedly stopped, but was, on the contrary, pumping fast and loud.

"Now practice for real," said the nurse. She pointed to the Annie and the Andy, both just then available.

Aaron chose Annie, who lay on her back. She wore a thick gingham dress over tights, had blond hair, missing lashes, and dazzling blue eyes. Kneeling over her, Aaron felt very tender.

Brainy got it on video.

Giving blood was easy. Aaron lay down on a starched green cot while a medic stuck a needle in his arm. The tube filled with black that trickled red into a vinyl pouch. It felt like being creative.

"What's in the backpacks, boys?" Ms. Terkle asked,

attempting a smile. She held a jelly doughnut in the very tips of her fingers. "Well?"

Aaron sat up, pulling the tube taut, causing the needle to shift painfully inside his vein. Reflex made him jump, jerking the tube from the vinyl pouch. Blood squirted, splashing Nancy Terkle's doughnut. Brainard twisted to avoid getting splattered, and broke free of his pouch. His tube began dribbling onto the pavement.

Aaron stood up in a puddle of blood, fought off a ferocious headrush, and began to sob. But it came out as a laugh. He felt as if the plug was pulled, his life was draining away. And he was going "Ha ha ha."

Brainard pulled the IV out of his own arm and calmly leaned over and bent shut Aaron's tube, stopping the flow. "Give me your arm." Brainard slipped the needle from Aaron's white—too white—skin, and pressed his mouth to the swollen puncture.

"Helicopter chum," Brainard said, referring to Aaron's large, optic yellow raincoat, which Aaron wore over a wool sweater and his down vest. Bright colors generally attracted the police chopper, which made its nightly rounds spotlighting anything—aside from cars—that moved. Brainy himself came prepared: He had camouflaged the space wrap he wore with spray paint and Magic Marker. "Tree Stand, modified."

"I can't stop shivering," Aaron said. Though he'd eaten beets, an extremely rare hamburger, and a couple of glasses of chocolate milk for dinner, he still felt a quart low. Grumpy, fatigued, unloved.

Loss of blood didn't seem to affect Brainard one way or another. He turned on his videocamera. It was wrapped in scratch resistant vinyl. A tungsten light threw a narrow beam that, even from a few feet, was hot on Aaron's cheeks.

They entered the grove. Fifty acres, each row of trees occupying a terrace, each terrace serviced by an irrigation runnel. Brainard flipped open his digital thermometer. "Twenty-nine."

Aaron looked at the Tibbets. The tree, fat with oranges, seemed to wave at him, Hello. Last year it had yielded five field boxes, fifty pounds each, more than twice the average tree. And this year, cross your fingers, would be even bigger.

Aaron pulled rubber dishwashing gloves over ragwool liners and, crouching before the cement irrigation fount, fit a plumber's coupler to attach the hose. "Crank it."

Brainy jerked the lug wrench.

The hose coughed, bucked. Chunks of ice shot out, the jet of sleet strip-mining the ground.

Brainy grabbed onto the hose behind Aaron, and they got it under control. "It's snowing!"

And for a moment the nozzle *was* spraying snow. It fell not in flakes, but in white pinpoints that hurt. Brainy's tungsten lamp hissed, his tongue jutted out from between his teeth.

They began snow-gunning the nearest tree. After a few moments, the snow turned to slush, then to water, knocking off a dozen oranges, so Aaron redirected the nozzle to a more distant tree, drenching it.

As water freezes, it gives off heat. The temperature of the oranges themselves would not drop below 32 degrees. A simple concept, but risky: Unless the air temperature rises with the morning sun, the trees, as well as the fruit, will die.

Air and Brain, moving the firehose up and down each row, coated all fifty acres.

The sun didn't rise; it slid up fast. Not one cloud. From his pocket, Brainard took a couple of Stimudents, handing one to Aaron, keeping one for himself. They both huddled against the cold, sitting on crates at the crest of the ridge.

Aaron pushed the tip between his front teeth. "How's your head trauma?"

"Getting to like it," Brainard said, sucking his Stimudent as if it were juiciful. He changed the battery in his camera, which was set on a tripod. "Now I understand what you're up against everyday."

Aaron felt his lips crack, wiped them with a knuckle that came away bloody. Now that he'd given some, he viewed the fluid differently, wondering how much of Mom was in it, compared to how much of Dad.

Dad Dad Dad would kill him. But, "Check it out!"

The grove sparkled, the green leaves glossy, light-lacquered. Ice fingers hung from branches, floes oozed between roots. Lucent blue cascades poured motionless down the terraces. Aaron picked an orange, broke off its icicle, split the enameled rind with his thumb. Juice ran.

When the detectives arrived, Aaron was dreaming each hand was stained with a bar code that would not wash clean.

"Air, these men say they want a word with you," Caroline said. She stood in the bedroom doorway, holding an Amazonas CD to her forehead. She didn't like being in control. That's what Dad saw in her, aside from that she was blond and twenty-one.

"It's okay," he said, sitting up. He checked his hands, relieved they were unmarked.

"Should I call Frank in Houston?" she asked. "I should call Frank in Houston."

"Nah." Aaron was glad Dad was gone. It wasn't anger he feared, but nonsense. If Dad were here he'd threaten the cops with lawyers, and the situation would deteriorate rapidly.

The detectives stood awkwardly in the dining room.

"Uh, Aaron Wells?" one said. His acrylic suit, sharp and tinsely, seemed a wisecrack in this neighborhood, where even coffee filters were made of natural fiber. "Detective Parks. And this is Detective Martinez."

Martinez was more casual, in a sweatshirt and zippered boots. He had ingrown whiskers on his Adam's apple, and cologne that smelled like pineapples.

"Seat, please. Have one," Caroline said. She was still clutching the CD. "I mean, can I get you gentlemen coffee?"

"Love some," said Parks. "Thank you." They waited till she was gone to continue.

"I think you know why we're here," Martinez said.

Aaron leaned back in his chair so he could see out the window. The sun shone madly, having already melted most of the ice, leaving the grove a mess of puddles and mud. But the fat, bright oranges were incriminating.

"Your classroom burnt down," Parks said.

"Yoo-hoo!" from Caroline in the kitchen. "Milk? Soy-milk? Sugar?"

Martinez sighed. "How do *you* like it, Aaron? Very hot, I gather."

"Black," Parks said.

"I'm waiting!" Caroline called. "We're waiting, sirs!"

Parks repeated, "Aaron."

"Arson," Martinez said. "Torch job."

By the time Aaron got down to Arroyo Grande High, it was deserted, except for a single security guard who sat in a parked car, motor running, probably to keep the heater on.

Aaron slipped past, easy enough, crossing the flagpole plaza where the hypothetical disaster had taken place yesterday.

What he saw made him shudder. Only the Gifted room had been affected, windows blown out, the cement surrounding them scorched black. Even in the chill, the smell was rank, overpowering, carmelized. A single yellow tape ran from sawhorse to sawhorse, marking off the premises. Aaron noticed the empty firehose cabinet.

He had told the detectives nothing. They didn't really suspect him, they were just bullies, and he was another name on their list. According to the newspaper account, which Aaron had read after they left, the fire marshal wasn't even sure the fire was deliberate. "It appears to have been an electrical fire," he was quoted as saying. "Starting in the wall." There were, however, some "articles of suspicion," which he declined to specify.

Aaron crept around to the back. An industrial dumpster was cloaked in smoke and mist. Chairs and desks and cracked blackboards were piled inside, still smoldering. Bent lamps, broken glass. An eraser. Withered plants, uprooted. Globs of molten plastic that were once stereo equipment, headphones. Diskettes, books, games, all for the most part ashes. A single Monopoly $500 bill, intact. Part of the Kwitcherbellyachin' wheel, splintered and warped, but still on its axle. The wooden pegs were warm to the touch. Aaron gave the wheel a spin. It ground to a stop immediately, on Yesterday's News, Tomorrow's Future.

It was harrowing.

Aaron stood at the doorway. Inside the air was thick with soot and smelled like soy sauce.

A noise startled him. Someone was crying in the quietest way. In what was the meditation corner.

When Aaron knelt beside Don Miller, he seemed neither surprised nor embarrassed, and made no attempt to conceal the tears, the contorted mouth, the snot.

As Aaron's eyes adjusted to the dark, the damage revealed itself. The walls, seared, latex paint blistered. The clock reduced to whitish streaks. Pink chemical retardant covered everything. One ineffective fire-sprinkler head squirted like a Water Pic.

"Love ma highest law," Don Miller read. It was all that was left of his banner.

"It'll look good again," Aaron tried. "When we clean up the mess and—you can replace most of this stuff."

"Me," Don Miller said, sweeping his hand across the ruins.

"I'm really sorry, Da—Don. I'm—"

"It's not your fault."

"Yes," Aaron said, and it all came gushing out, about the grove, about stealing the firehose, about the detectives, and Caroline, too, holding the Amazonas CD. The whole time, Don Miller sat with chin resting on folded hands, eyes straining ahead on the dumpster, which glowed every now and then, tiny flames sucking gasps out of *National Geographic*s.

"It's not your fault," Don Miller repeated, after Aaron wound down. His eyes were groping and nonaligned. "Water's not gonna stop an electrical fire."

"Electrical?" Aaron could almost believe that.

Franklin was running out of money. It had taken the bank less than two weeks to contact him about the missed mortgage payment. He paid it with a Visa check, then paid off his Visa account with the Mastercard. Deficit spending made him wonder if he actually owned anything, including his actions.

His panic attacks had resolved themselves on their own. In their place came sudden inexplicable flutters, like joy.

"Congratulations, Mavy," he said. "Eighteen today!!" In place of a gift, he videotaped her.

"You mean sex with me isn't breaking the law?" Mavy asked, as if reading the question from one of the workbooks in front of her—SAT and achievement tests. She stretched her arms out, hugging him backwards.

"No," Franklin said. "I mean happy birthday. Smile."

Mavy was in her eighth month, big and round. When she saw he had the camera, she frowned. "I hate when you point that thing at everybody."

"Tell me you love me," Franklin said, taping.

Mavy shook her eyes and clamped her jaw.

"Come on."

"Only if you turn that thing off."

It was a curiosity to Franklin that she could get pregnant when he didn't even come. Living proof of what they always warned you against. Her cheeks were big and round, too, and bright, not red, but peach-colored. In fact, everything about her was fruity. Her smell, for instance, like grape juice. Her breasts! Her belly! So big and round! When she walked she held her arms to the side and sashayed, swaybacked, rump raised. And she was so hungry! Today's lunch, still in progress: almost a pound of peanuts (in the shell), two heads of redleaf lettuce, a half gallon of goat's milk, and four oranges. Four!

After he got done panning, he put down the camera. "Okay it's off."

"I hate that thing."

"Okay, it's off. Have you decided on a name?"

" 'Aaron'?" she suggested. The sonogram had showed the baby was a boy. A black-and-white radar blip image of a baby with pointy ears, waving. "Aaron Wells."

"I don't like 'Aaron,' " Franklin said. He held up several ties, a red one, a green one, a blue one with yellow telephones. "Choose one for me." After not having worn a suit for so many months, he found them foolish and restrictive. The seams pinched if you did anything other than march. In the crotch and shoulders especially, areas in need of special discipline. "How about William? Billy Wells."

"Wear the blue," she said, nibbling the white underside of the orange peels. A new food she claimed to crave. "No, the red."

He put it on before she could change her mind again. Maybe he'd buy her an organic watermelon. You looked for wasp bumps, where wasps bit the rind, to find the sweetest ones. Her mother told him that. Or maybe he'd get her a handful of wildflowers. Or a honeycomb. She was easy to get presents for.

"I like 'Aaron' better." She stood up and kissed him full on the lips.

Franklin took a sip of her ice water, but the coldness hurt a tooth on the upper right side. Dentist, he thought, money.

"We'll have a birthday dinner tonight, right?" she asked.

He nodded.

"Good luck, baby." She had never called him *that* before.

At a Gift & Gas Plaza he bought Mavy a heart-shaped knee pillow (she had bony knees and couldn't sleep on her side without something between them), a copy of *The Joy of Sex* (because they didn't need a manual), and (in honor of the kid) a box of Godiva chocolate cigars. At the last moment, he threw in a box of Girl Scout cookies, on sale at 33 percent off. Probably stolen. Thirty-six dollars on his Mastercard. His minimum monthly was up to something like $125. Soon enough he'd be employed; one hefty paycheck would kill the outstanding balance.

There had been two bids on his house. The first one came early, but low. He would have broken exactly even. The second one was an insult. Now he wished he had taken even that.

Outside, while filling up the car with unleaded, he poked his tongue against the painful tooth. Dental benefits. A family plan. Suddenly, the nozzle coughed and gas shot back at him, soaking his hand and suit sleeve. No matter how many soap squirts he used in the men's room, the smell wouldn't go away. Twelve-sixty-five on his Mastercard.

"Ya oughtta spot your wheel wells," said the gas station attendant, a smiling young Korean woman wearing greasy overalls and a Sugar in the Raw cap. She pointed out where rust was eating through the car body.

"I only have sixty thou on this thing."
"Tell me about it." She had perfect teeth.

"Well, well, well," Victoria said. Black silk and Trinity
Pure as usual. But something was different. But Franklin
couldn't say what. "You look good, Wells."
"Yes or no, Vic, do I get my job back?" Franklin asked.
There would be no bullshit starting now. But something
was different, something he just couldn't place. Cowboys
rode horses and threw lassos up and down her stockings.
"Have a seat." She sipped the last of the water, then
said, "I need more. One sec," and left the room.
While she was gone, Franklin read the empty bottle:

pH: 5.4
Radioactivity Mache Units at 20 degrees C and 760
    mm Hg: 2.05
Conductivity at 25 degrees C: OHMS $-1 \times$ CM $^{-1}$
                    5.25×10^{-5}

Calcium Sulfate:	.0022 gram/liter
Calcium Bicarbonate:	.0105
Magnesium Chloride:	.0007
Sodium Chloride:	.0049
Sodium Nitrate:	.0099
Potassium Nitrate:	.0029
Silicon Hydrate:	.1112
Evaporate Residue:	.049 @ 180 degrees C

"Why the frown?" Victoria asked, on returning.
"This water's radioactive," Franklin said.
"Is it?" She opened the new bottle, took a sip.
"Yes."
She sat in a leather chair with brass rollers that he
recognized from the long nights of DisasterProof. Every

line on his suit was crisp, willful, for which he was
suddenly glad. But the smell of gas clung to his arm like
bad history. He had always loved the office, and, looking
around, remembered why. The thrill of contracts typeset
on 50 percent cotton bond in polished eelskin folios, each
anticipating a signature. A half-dozen Mont Blanc pens.
The click and hum of transpacific faxes. The laser printer,
the photocopier, the TV featuring interlaced scanning, a
digital process that produced highly defined images. All
invaluable, all replaceable. It was beautiful, this temple
of bluff and spectacle where to behave as if you were
risking your soul for a deal had seemed to him so shallow
less than an hour ago.

"Go ahead, touch it," Victoria said, noticing him stare
at the computer.

Franklin reached toward the tiny laptop, which was
cabled to the mainframes in the basement, which in turn
accessed seven E-Systems data storage towers, each six
feet tall, robotically managing the equivalent of 150-
mile-high stacks of typed data, which in turn amassed the
stream of satellite-guided intelligence funneling in
through the Big Swell Radio Dish, and the microwave
dish, and the Image Relay Systemics Dish, all on top of
the building. Seventy-some civilizations' worth of information waiting to be tapped, delivered in nanoseconds.

"Put your hand on it."

Franklin's fingertips itched. He punched a key. Then
another. Then a few more. It felt like breaking laws of
nature. The VGA light on his face felt better than the
sun. "My files are still here."

"Access," Victoria was stroking the polished leather of
her briefcase, "is, oh, I don't know. It's what gets me out
of bed."

Franklin looked at her over the screen. "I'm changed."

"I felt terrible for you," she said, slowly closing the briefcase. "I really did. Your episode."

The manic-depressive tag had kept him from being hired by several other companies in recent months. Franklin could imagine the delicacy with which Victoria divulged the info when department heads called to discuss his dossier. "Who said anything about an episode?"

"The company is not without compassion. But your disappearance—"

"I'm—"

"Let me finish." She stood up, smoothed out her dress.

"You're sitting!" It suddenly hit Franklin. He had never seen her sitting. "That's what's different!"

"I'm standing." She eyed him as if he were deranged.

"I mean you *were* sitting," he said. Franklin, shut up.

"This isn't just a job," she thankfully continued. "We at Solvtex are working toward a larger goal."

She paused, watching Franklin's expression.

"Put it this way." She began to pace, the Victoria he remembered, high heels clicking on the oakstrip floor. "You thought DisasterProof was yours. DisasterProof, by Franklin, whatever your middle name is, Wells. But it's not yours, any more than resident memory's the computer's."

"Who has the copyright?"

"Information as a commodity cannot be copyrighted," Victoria said, then added sarcastically, "Though it can be taxed, of course." She sipped the radioactive water. "Any teenager with an Apple can do what we do, albeit on a much smaller scale."

"Albeit?" Franklin said, immediately regretting it.

"There are no moral all-stars in this enterprise. A keystroke here and Southwestern Bell is DisasterProofed, a keystroke there and we're paid. Does a pencil manufacturer agonize that the Department of Defense uses his pencils to design atomic bombs?"

"Defense Department."

"What?"

"You said Department of Defense. The name is Defense Department."

"I see."

"Yes or no, I've got to know, Vic." Even though he had expected punishment, Franklin was hoping it would be more direct than having his nose rubbed in company doctrine. "I'm changed." He thought of Mavy at home, laboring with a Number 2 pencil over SAT questions.

"I see attitude."

Mavy, Mavy. So big and round and biologically active! And just eighteen! How much she and the baby would need. "I'm married," Franklin said, and counted her blink, one, two, three, four, in extra slow motion. Then her leg began to swing, starting up the stocking rodeo. He envied and wanted her. He'd fuck the information age, access and get revenge all at once. If he wasn't a happily married man, he'd . . . If it wasn't for Mavy, Mavy, big round Mavy! "And there's a baby on the way."

"Congratulations." Victoria held her smile a fraction too long, and it stuck.

"A son," he added, and because she looked puzzled, "Ultrasound."

"I'd want to know, too," she said. She turned toward CNN. A high-level PLO official was claiming he had unprotected sex with an Israeli air force pilot at a Peter, Paul, and Mary concert in Tel Aviv.

"Most people don't," Franklin said. "I'm the other way. If the data exist."

"Well, we have that in common," she said. Finally, the smile died, leaving behind white lines.

In the long lull that followed, Franklin watched the fax spool out thermographic paper, the computer screen's patient radiance, the phone lines blinking on and off. It was all so incredibly beautiful.

Until Victoria said, "You smell like gasoline."

Until Franklin's coffee made him wince. The tooth was heat sensitive, a danger sign he had read about. He took another sip, swishing to be sure. "Look," he said. "I need a job."

"There *is* a position," Victoria said, eyebrow raising just barely. "With Satocracy. A video party line. You beam up your home videos, you beam down other people's. It's very democratic."

"Go on."

"The position starts at forty-five."

About half his previous salary. He'd make up the difference quickly enough. "Tell me more."

"You'd have to be a team player."

Meaning they'd steal from him again. "I can live with that."

"You'd report to Manville."

ArManiville, that fashion bulldog, that ivy-and-red-brick fuckface, that upright walking handjob. "Hmmm." Maybe Franklin had made the wrong choices. Certainly all the signs indicated so. If he had strapped down his ego, he'd be a two-car man by now, owner of a house behind a coded gate, holder of several insurance policies. His rep as the original yet unsung creator of DisasterProof would have given him real status within the industry. He'd pick and choose his projects, all the while sitting on a fat piece of corporate equity. He'd take Mavy and the kid(s) whitewater rafting in Bali.

Instead, the bank was threatening to foreclose on his puny stucco bungalow, his tooth stung, his sleeve stank of unleaded. Waiting for him in the back seat of his rust-bucket import were chocolate cigars, *The Joy of Sex*, and a valentine knee pillow, all bought with money he didn't have at 19 percent interest. And unless things started looking up, his son was going to have no toys to play with except for maybe an ice cube tray.

It wasn't until this moment that Franklin felt anything other than love for the unborn child. Little Aaron, vortex of need, unborn dictator, conceived without orgasm. Franklin associated him illogically with ArManiville. "Not to save my life."

Victoria spread her hands wide, to show generosity, or to show they weren't shaking, or to show him the way out of the room.

"Goodbye," Franklin barked. "Don't bother getting up. It's been such a pleasure sitting with you."

"Please," Victoria clutched her Trinity Pure. "Please don't take it personally, Franklin."

"Of course not," he said, still disliking and admiring her. She had paid him a compliment. If not friend, then enemy; he was too good to allow to defect. "Donner."

"What?"

"My middle name," Franklin said. "DisasterProof, by Franklin Donner Wells." Then he tore the water from her fist and took a good, long swallow.

Franklin parked his car on a cliff overlooking the ocean, and rolled down the windows. The air smelled clean, salty, just in after thousands of miles off the Pacific, fresh as it gets. The waves were good. Not great. But there was a left break that had decent face.

It was uncrowded, only three surfers, all of them out

far, waiting for the next big set, their green and pink neoprenes full of unbiodegradable light.

A cormorant flew by, neck outstretched, skimming the waves.

Franklin didn't know what to do.

He wanted his Deko Max. He'd go out, feel the cold water between his toes, taste the foam dripping off his lips. He'd lay on his board while the big ocean surged under him, and that might be enough. He'd climb on top of every smooth-rumped swell and remember what hope felt like. He'd do serious tube and learn to forget.

But he didn't bring his Deko Max. So he reached for *The Joy of Sex*. He had bought the book *because* he and Mavy didn't need it. The manual was a curiosity, an ironic acknowledgment of what they already shared.

Inside were sketches. A bearded man and a short-haired woman. A drawing of an uncircumcised penis that was so uninspired it could have been anything, a sock, South America.

A pelican folded in on itself and fell like a shot in the water.

Cunnilingus, fellatio, golden showers. In some pictures the woman appeared slack-eyed, sleepy or drugged, the man as if he had his mind on something else. In others they both had a soft, stainless-edged dreaminess that suggested passion, tenderness, maybe even love.

The book was set up as a gourmet menu. Mavy would insist on trying it all: slut sex, French-maid, strangers-on-a-train, nylon-over-the-head rape fantasy. Props were emphasized: bedposts, bathtubs, feathers, cash.

Despite not being all that interested, Franklin got a hard-on.

Natural body odor is the best perfume. Dental benefits.

Maternity care bills. It was as if he had built a life out of romantic lies. He had mistaken pursuit of leisure for soulful yearning. Surfing, sex, being in nature, what did they lead to? Even spending all his time on good things—love, family ties, being emotional—had cost him. Two years ago on paper he was worth 100K. Now he didn't even have the $2,000 per month it took to keep his head above water. The baby would sink him. People don't spend enough time on kissing. He needed a job bad. Blow job, hand job, fist job. Climax should not be the goal every time out. Put the essence of your being into your lips. Smell your partner's inner elbow. Unemployed head of household. Let her in through your fingertips. Be playful. Plot, pose, pretend.

Franklin masturbated just to ejaculate, to get rid of that nagging urge. Then he ate most of the Girl Scout cookies.

After the cookies, he ate the chocolate cigars, one after another, sugar like acid on his tooth, the pain only driving him to chew quicker until just one cigar remained. This he saved for Mavy, at home, pregnant, and, no doubt, barefoot.

Mavy's face filled the viewfinder nicely, Franklin thought. "But the camera loves you, really," he said, zooming and unzooming, autofocus in a continual state of lag or overcompensate, never quite getting her eyes sharp. Now and then a tight, clear shot of her teeth clenched, or the sweat trickling from her temples.

"Ow!" Mavy said. She crouched in the corner of her bedroom, next to an illuminated plastic globe suspended between electromagnetic poles. "I." When the pain hit, it was both vague and full of edges, like a hand thrust up inside her, fingers clawing, untrimmed nails. But she bore down. She was stronger than it. Women used to give birth without resorting to drugs. Evolution was on her side. Besides, the brain produced its own endorphins. When the pain subsided, which it did—it always did— her head cleared. Everything *her* receded. Tiny things stood out: the red threads in the bedspread, the oblong bubbles in the windowpane, the perlite in the house-plant soil. Transparent hairs all over her body stood aquiver, tuning in, she felt, to the electromagnetism that kept the globe suspended. And the globe itself, too much to imagine, but nothing compared to what was inside her, and to her urge to expel it. "Don't video me."

"Breathe," Franklin said, his Cylcoptic eye whirring and clicking. "Don't forget to breathe."

"Turn that thing off, please."

"Sweetheart," he whined. "It's a once in a lifetime—"

"Turn it off—!"

"Okay—"

"Easy," said Josefina, the midwife. She was a pleasant-looking woman, beautiful brown skin, without even one wrinkle, and snow-white hair. "Your boy will be coming shortly."

Suddenly free of pain, Mavy almost giggled. But her hard, full belly turned the giggle into sort of a cough. "How do you know I'm having a boy?"

"You are having a boy?" Josefina said. "How wonderful!"

"No, I mean, yes, but—"

"Damn it!" Franklin snapped, slapping the side of the camera with an open palm. "This fucking Disc-corder wasn't even on. I really wanted that footage—"

"—how'd you know I was going to have a son—"

"Piece of junk. I should have gotten a Japanese model—"

"Eyes of woman open, she make son," Josefina said. "Eyes of woman close, she make daughter."

"—Japanese make foolproof. How do you think they became *the* world power? *User friendly,* that's how."

"Turn that fucking thing off!" Mavy practically screamed. The pain etched into her mind, giving her consciousness, it seemed, an acute and for her rare ability to recognize the obvious. She did not like her husband. Fooling with that battery-operated piece of distraction instead of seeing for himself. How could he ever understand the red bedspread, the globe, the violent fact that a human was making his way into the world? A premonition shook her, and she refused it audience.

"I'll just point it at, oh, I don't know, out the window," Franklin said. "That way, you won't be in the picture and it'll just pick up the sound—"

At the wedding, she had the first hint. He was consumed with recording the moment. As if owning it was somehow more meaningful than experiencing it. He attended to the camera with such an obedience, with a subservience even, that one would have expected the videocamera was his mother (who, by the way, couldn't make the trip, on account of a heart murmur—was that Freudian? Mavy didn't know Freud).

"You found things," she had whispered to him, as the

justice of the peace suggested that young lovers recognized in each other each other's best qualities. "Remember the nudibranch?"

Franklin had made a puzzled face, then, quickly, checked that the camera, on its tripod next to the only other guests—her father and mother, both serving as legal witnesses, Dad in a turtleneck that hid almost all his tattoos, Mom in a lacy dress and, surprise of surprises, braless—was operative. And Mavy didn't even get angry.

"I'm sorry, Sweetheart," Franklin said, ducking as he took the camera strap off his neck. "I had no idea you felt that way."

"I," she said, pain returning. Maybe her anger was out of place. She wasn't even really sure how to recognize specific emotions, or how much importance to grant them.

"You are almost," Josefina said, her voice soothing.

"Easy, there ya go, Sweetheart," Franklin said.

Something ripped. A scream tore out of her.

"You are beautiful," Josefina said, taking in her own hands Mavy's pain, delivering her. *"Hermoso."*

"Don't forget," Franklin chattered, "to breathe—"

The baby cried. Her baby. Josefina clamped the cord. Josefina put the baby into Mavy's arms.

Baby Aaron groped for a breast. Such hunger! It made Mavy attempt a giggle, but she didn't have the breath for it.

Suddenly, the what inside her had become a who.

She became aware of the whir of the camera. Franklin had been videotaping the whole time. He missed it all.

Franklin passed the camera to Josefina and had her shoot him holding the baby. When he made his son give the finger, the who of him, of Franklin, somehow became a what. At that moment, something in Mavy's heart changed quietly, irrevocably.

One day a letter arrived. It was addressed Mr. and Mrs. Mavy Wells. The postmark was from New York City, dated a week earlier. Inside was a $10,000 check. It was from Mavy's grandmother, Franny Tibbets. Her signature was a squiggly line, showing a faint tremble.

Also in the envelope were three airline tickets. First class to Kennedy.

"A car will be waiting for you on your arrival. So looking forward to seeing you. Love dearly, Granny Franny."

"Is this some sort of guilt situation?" Franklin asked, stretching and yawning.

Franklin had just finished his day shift as Data Dumper at the Del Monte canning factory in San Jose. It was his job to dispose of confidential files and electronic records. For this, they only hired temps. Regulars, after a while, knew too much. It was boring work, but money was money. First Franklin scrambled files, then he fused programs in a process called mosaicism, which fragmented them and reassembled the whole out of many. This prevented coherent trails. After that, he overwrote. He was basically a high-tech garbageman, free-lance.

"I'm not making any apologies for her," Mavy said. Besides the Toyota truck, the most Frances Tibbets had ever sent before were Hallmark cards, one to mark their wedding, another on the birth of their son, Aaron. She regretted that her osteoporosis prohibited her from making the long journey west. But she had drawn in xxxx's and oooo's and happy faces.

"Ten thousand," Franklin said, just to say something.

Mavy made him promise not to tell Bernal. "He'll insist I return it."

"Ten thousand," Franklin repeated.

"I don't know if I even want to go to New York," Mavy said.

"I know *I* don't." Franklin was on the lookout for better work, real work. He had no patience for xxxx's and oooo's and happy faces. "I gotta make money for Sweetheart." What he'd taken to calling Aaron.

"Ten thousand," Mavy said, this time. "I think I want to go."

"No you don't." He began to unbutton her shirt. In their early years of married life, they had had sex every single day. This Franklin was proud of, this not everybody had. This required effort, discipline, vigilance. This offered unexpected rewards and assorted insights. This had lately changed, though Franklin denied to what extent. "You want to stay at home and make passionate love to your husband."

"Franklin."

"I want you," he pulled her down in the living room.

Mavy said, "Don't——" She removed a plastic toy action spider from underneath her neck. "I want to go to New York."

"We haven't in so long."

"But—"

"Oh come on," he said. "Tell me something."

"Franklin—"

"Humor me."

"Okay," she finally sighed, allowing her legs to spread slightly. "Go ahead."

"Something else."

The thought of being in New York alone with Granny Franny was very inviting. "I love you."

" 'More than ever.' "

She decided to go herself and cash in his ticket. It cheered her up, gave her something to look forward to.

"Say it," he begged.

"More than ever," she said.

Though her heart wasn't in it, *because* her heart wasn't in it, Franklin experienced an odd mix of gratitude and resentment. Toward the end—the toy action spider seeming to stare at him, a scornful, mocking expression molded into its eight-eyeballed face—Franklin's passion slipped into desperation, and he felt as if he was trying to resuscitate something already dead.

Eliza died, poisoned by secretly drinking an entire pot of Silvertuft Weed root tea, a supposed fertility booster.

Luther buried her on the hill behind the house. From

the grave, only a few hundred yards from the original tree, he could see a panorama of the entire Inland Empire. Her empire, really.

"Dead?" Frances asked. Six years old now, she was a tall little girl, with bony knees, a yellow ponytail, and two missing front teeth. She stuck her right index finger into the gap, probing the gum, while with her left ring finger she made tiny circles inside her bellybutton. "But *why?*"

"It was time, I suppose," Luther said, hugging her. "Now she'll go to a place that's safe and warm."

"But it's *cold* in there," Frances said, pointing at the mound of freshly turned earth. She wiped a tear with a knuckle, then licked it.

Luther waited for his own grief, but it wouldn't come. He was still furious. Livid at Eliza's infidelity, at her dying, at his inability to shake this rage.

Two days later the mayor paid his respects. After setting a bouquet of orange blossoms on her stone, he put on his top hat and wrote Luther a summons. It was against the law to bury dead people yourself, the mayor explained. Even on your own land. "I'm real sorry about that, Mr. Tibbets. Real sorry."

"That kind of thinking will ruin this country," Luther grumbled. Rather than dig Eliza up, he donated seventy-five acres to a foundation establishing Arroyo Grande Cemetery.

Gradually Luther's anger subsided. He began finding himself a stranger to his house, his grove lands, his commercial pursuits, himself. He didn't recognize business associates. Slicing an orange, he cut his finger badly but experienced no pain. He never felt thirsty, and had to force down water.

"I'm scared of my dreams, Daddy," Franny said, late

one night. Eliza was right, McKinley's little girl had Luther's bright brooding eyes. "Can I sleep with you?"

From then on, they shared his bed.

One night Luther, aroused by a dream about Eliza, woke up to discover Frances in his arms.

Horrified, he sprang out of bed, sprinting into the grove. Wearing only pajama bottoms, he knelt at the original tree. Bub. Tourists. Railway. Bear Valley Dam. Money. McKinley. Gosse. Target practice. The tree that started it all. Eliza's tree. Eliza. Eliza.

The tears finally came.

The next day, Luther put his holdings up for sale— everything but the house and a hundred acres—and, with Frances, moved to New York City.

Luther and Frances Tibbets were married in their Park Avenue apartment by an Irish Justice Department clerk with only the clerk's wife as witness.

In New York, in the late nineteen thirties, it was not illegal to marry your adoptive father. Frances Tibbets had looked into it.

And she was already in her thirties, a graduate of New York University, a professional artist, doing covers of *Vogue*, living at home, and in love with Luther.

When they first moved to Park Avenue, Luther had explained everything. Frances understood McKinley, the twenty-fifth president of the United States, to be her real father. She didn't hate her mother. Rather, she was proud of her, in a way. And forgiving.

And this man Luther, who had doted on her since the beginning, who had loved her unconditionally, this man Luther she desired. Whether or not it was natural to have these feelings for him, she didn't know, only that it was natural to act on them.

The man holding up the "TiBBeTs" sign at Kennedy Airport wore a blue Orlon suit and a white turban. Piña colada air freshener fumes filled his car. A turban-wearing yellow Happy Face decal was stuck to the dash. "Where you are going, please?"

Mavy said, "My grandmother told me you'd know."

"City?"

"Park Avenue." Mavy fumbled for the address in her pocketbook. She was relieved and exhilarated to be rid of Franklin. Though the thought of him at home alone with Aaron worried her. Franklin had no sense. He let the child skateboard in the supermarket. He didn't know how to *watch*.

"I don't know this place," the driver said, handing her back the slip of paper. His breath smelled yeasty.

"Park Avenue," Mavy said. "Everybody knows Park Avenue."

"Yes. I remember, now." He slapped his turban, then pulled away from the curb, into traffic.

The road was crammed with sedans carrying only one or two people, dented vans tagged with spraypaint, drivers ignoring lane stripes, gunning and braking. A wrecked and stripped armored truck sat among the weeds in the median strip. Graffiti was thick and unreadable on a hundred-year-old bridge made of handcut stone.

The sky was having an identity crisis, one moment steam, the next smog, now and then a glimpse of blue. Raga music issued from the speakers at low volume. Needing air, Mavy cracked the window. She felt like throwing up. She felt like she'd forgotten something. She felt like she was pregnant again. And her period *was* late. And her sense of smell was heightened, as it had been the first time, with Aaron. Right now it was a tar-filled canal, reeking of fried eggs.

In vain, Mavy quickly scanned the back seat for something to vomit in, then very quietly used her pocketbook. When she was through, she put her face into the wind and slipped both hands up under her blouse to feel for the telltale swell.

They drove by a Jack LaLanne fitness center with multicolored plastic banners that rose out of a crumbling tenement. "White Man Is the Devil" said one wall with big paintbrushed letters. They drove by a row of magnolia trees, each shedding fat white petals. They drove by garbage and garbage—plastic bags, car batteries, tennis rackets, televisions, unspooled cassette tape—piled a foot deep against a ripped and sagging fence topped with razor wire. They drove by a parked police car just in time to witness an arm throw a single slice of bologna out the window.

"It's the Puerto Ricans, Miss, you know?" he said. Mavy saw his eyes on her in the rearview. "They make the garbage."

His turban, she thought, was a nice-looking thing. She'd like one.

"You know how I'm talking of?" he asked. "The Puerto Rican peoples?"

Mavy hadn't a clue. "Where are you from?"

"Far away," he said, honking at an imaginary obstruction.

Another wave of nausea hit. No doubt about it, she was pregnant. Her back stuck to the leather seat. The raga music had given way to Irish folk, or maybe it had been Irish folk all along, fiddles playing the same riffs over and over, like a tape loop. Since she was three thousand miles away, she allowed herself a sinister little thought: She had married too young. Daddy was right.

The car disappeared into black smoke. The driver slammed on the gas and jabbered into his car phone, not slowing down or shutting up until the air cleared. In an empty lot behind them, hundreds of tires were on fire. And nobody was doing anything to stop it, except a kid, about Aaron's age, spitting.

A terrible, terrible place, Mavy had just decided, when suddenly Manhattan sparkled into view. "Oh!" she said. "I see." An island of skyscrapers.

Mavy's first time in New York, Granny took her to the ballet at Lincoln Center. *The Nutcracker.*

"Look, Grandma, your name is in the program." Frances Tibbets, Principal Benefactor.

More enchanting than the performance to Mavy the tomboy were the other little girls in the lobby. With their hair pulled back in black ribbon, with their open-chested, splay-footed ballerina walk, they made New York seem theirs. In the city itself, every object suggested conveyance: sidewalks, taxis, elevators, trains, carriages, escalators. All illuminated. Here there was no *there*, no California, no outer space, no other universe.

Later that night, Mavy, practicing ballet steps, plied

into Franny's bedroom without knocking and saw, where her mother had breasts, her grandmother had a chest rack that held two plastic mounds, nippleless and blind.

A radical mastectomy had saved Franny from breast cancer, but left her with this apparatus, this scaffolding, this technical representation of mammalhood.

"You have seen Akbarhabad?" asked the driver.

"Yes," she said, not understanding him.

Blinking signs and orange cones chaneled traffic off the FDR at Fourteenth Street. What looked like a huge chunk of road had fallen into the river. Construction men stood about, drinking from cans wrapped in brown bags, eating sandwiches, watching a passing prison barge. Nobody seemed to be working.

It took half an hour to reach First Avenue. At the clogged intersection, a man with a squeegee started on the windshield. The cardboard sign around his neck said, "No begger. No drugs. No AIDS. Working for an honest dollar (or 2)!" A black-skinned, box-cut-wearing Happy Face button was pinned to it. The man's hair was also boxed and had zigzags shaved into each side.

The driver hit the electric lock, even though all four doors were already locked.

The squeegee man finished and came to collect. The driver scooped a handful of pennies and nickels and dimes out of the ashtray, and poured them through a few inches of open window.

"I don't want your fuckin' trash!" The man flung the coins, hard. "Take your fuckin' curry rice up the ass!"

The driver honked at the truck in front. In response, the truck blew its airhorn, and traffic ahead and behind went crazy. The vibrations set off alarms in nearby parked cars. The noise was full of textures.

The man hit the window with his squeegee, trying to

crack it. "Fuckin' cow worshipper! Fuckin' toilet paper head!"

The driver cut sharply left, up onto a sidewalk, knocking over trashcans, nearly hitting a kid whose mother had him on a retractable leash. Above, men's briefs hung from a branch of a dying elm. The Irish fiddles were going faster and faster.

They cruised past blocks of whitebrick and redbrick apartments. After turning the volume down, the driver eyed Mavy in the rearview again. "The black peoples, they have no *get ahead.*"

Mavy realized she still felt sick. She had never thought of a handful of small change as trash. At least, not literally.

"You know?"

"I don't know what you're talking about." Mavy had come from a family that wasted nothing. Not electricity, not water, not chicken bones or tea bags, not foil, charcoal, Baggies. Dad was dogmatic. He watered the plants with spaghetti water.

She wondered if he got it from Franny. There wasn't a lot she knew about her grandmother. What did people on Park Avenue eat? Did Frances Tibbets believe in God? What were her bad habits? Those, everyone had.

Franklin, for instance, was a control freak. He got his way by bullying and threats. He'd always been that way, but she'd only lately begun to recognize it. Mavy's own— well, her own biggest secret—she wasn't ready to name it.

Behind them, an ambulance whined, red lights flashing. "You are famous movie star, no?" The driver cackled, not bothering to pull over. The sound changed to something like a strobe foghorn. Still no one budged. Pedestrians crossed the street, not breaking their strides. Finally, the ambulance turned off its lights, but not its siren, and waited in gridlock like everyone else.

The smell of stale vomit rose from Mavy's pocketbook. This was not at all the glitter city she remembered.

If Aaron were here, he'd be screaming, laughing, bouncing sideways. It seemed his natural affect to be in a state of total stimulation, then to lapse into comatose exhaustion. Pure boyness. She missed him already.

She didn't miss Franklin at all. He'd be videotaping the whole time. But it wasn't the camera she hated. It was something else that had come between them, something profound that the camera only symbolized. A way of seeing things.

"In Akbarhabad, I am germ engineer." The driver pulled to the curb in front of Franny's apartment building. It was grander than Mavy remembered, constructed of chunks of marble, each one larger than the house she grew up in. Smiling griffins and snarling cherubs perched near windows high above. A group of pigeons clustered around a plastic owl.

"Be lucky," the driver said, like a warning.

A telephone company crew was ripping up the street with jackhammers. Collapsible tubes extended from a manhole. Some of the workers wore optic orange bodysuits and goggled helmets.

"Miss Mavy Tibbets!" shouted the white-haired doorman. He had a green suit with gold stitching, epaulets, and a conductor's hat. It was funny to her, and thrilling (just as it had been when she was a nine-year-old), that a grown man could wear such a uniform without irony. "Am I right?"

"Wells!" She showed him the ring on her third finger.

The gesture reassured her on some level. "Mavy *Wells* now!"

"Congratulations!" he said but winced.

The jackhammering stopped.

"I recall you as just a little ballerina." He winced again, and she realized it was a nervous tic. "What's that, about ten years gone?"

"Maybe more," she said, and all of a sudden, she couldn't wait to see Franny. Grandma. She'd call her Grandma, for the first time.

The doorman pulled out a pocket watch. "You're prompt, Mrs. Wells. I like that." Capillaries spattered his cheeks and nose as if someone had shaken a red fountain pen in his face.

"Thank you," Mavy said. She felt conspicuous in her summer drawstring pants, sunflower print blouse. Blond hair and West Coast tan seemed out of place, almost rude in a visitor. Was it obvious that she was pregnant? Did she smell like vomit?

The driver popped open the trunk from a button on the dash.

"Sir," the doorman addressed him, "may I remind you it's in our union contract that we take the bags from the car to the door, and it's in your union contract that you remove the bags from the car." He was winking now, like mad. "If you'd be so good as to——"

The driver turned up the radio. The music had changed to zydeco accordion. Or maybe it had been zydeco all this time. Then again, maybe it really was a raga. Actually, it was more than likely Irish.

The jackhammering resumed.

Brown mist rose from a manhole.

The driver examined his invoices.

"Forget it," Mavy said, grabbing the bags herself. She needed to be sick again, but all the trashcans were steel mesh.

The driver sped away, trunk door open.

"Goddamn Arab!" shouted the doorman. "Terrorist! Fanatic!"

Mavy set the bags down in the lobby, then ran back to the sidewalk, bending over the mesh trashcan. For a moment she stared into it. It was full of telephone answering machines from Radio Shack. Yellow jackets were buzzing agitatedly. After vomiting, she felt much better.

She noticed that a homeless woman on a Maytag box in the gutter was watching her. Mavy felt for some change in her pocket, then, remembering nickels and dimes and even quarters were garbage, she opened her wallet and took out a one-dollar bill.

"Here!" she yelled, offering it to the woman.

The woman looked at her cup, then wrinkled her face, fished at the coffee-soaked bill. "Sweet," she barked, eyeing Mavy up and down, taking note of the sunflower print blouse, drawstring pants. "That's real sweet."

"Oh, I'm sorry," Mavy said. She saw the woman had the beautiful face of the baby boomer mom in the Nutri-Grain ads. She wasn't homeless at all. She was famous. "But why are you, I mean, in the gutter?"

The jackhammering started up again. Across the street, the median strip was full of tulips that seemed to be illuminated red and throbbing.

"I'm waiting for my driver!"

"Driver?"

"What country are you from?"

Back inside the lobby, the doorman slammed down the intercom and frowned with exasperation. "Damn thing's on the blink. Oh well, go on up. I know she's expecting you." He escorted Mavy into the elevator, then used a key to send it to the penthouse.

"Give her a peck for me, eh?"

A man with a briefcase squeezed in just as the doors shut. He had sun-bleached, blunt-chopped hair, the most gorgeous suit Mavy had ever shared an elevator with. A United Nations name tag said Manville.

After a few moments of ascent, the elevator stopped, the lights inside dimming to black. Mavy pressed every button, even Emergency, but nothing happened. Nauseated all over again, she sat down and panted in the dark.

"Miss, are you okay?"

"Yes, just——" I don't love my husband, she thought. I love my son. She cupped her belly. Sons? But Franklin I don't love. I hate him.

The elevator lights went back on, and it began to ascend.

The United Nations man got out at eighteen, obviously relieved to be rid of this troubled girl lying on the elevator floor.

The doors opened directly into Grandmother's apartment. Mavy stepped out into the air-conditioned foyer, and stumbled, vomiting for the third time onto the marble-tiled floor.

For a moment she lay there. It was wonderful, the cool on her cheek, the quiet. She hadn't been this sick with Aaron. Had she?

"Grandma?" she called, standing. The word felt tentative in her mouth. "Grandma?" Mavy tiptoed down the hall.

At the far end Franny Tibbets lay face down, clutching

a bottle of Anacin. She wore an antique silk kimono and one high-heeled slipper; its match lay nearby among a scattering of white pills.

"Grandma?" Gently turning her over, Mavy saw those plastic, nippleless breasts. But this time they weren't frightening, only terribly sad.

Frances Tibbets was dead.

Mavy raced down the hall and picked up the phone. No dial tone. She punched 911 anyway, and got a busy signal. She tried again. Busy. Busy again and again. For five, ten, who could tell how many minutes, busy.

When finally it rang, that too was interminable. It rang and rang.

"Yes," said the woman who answered after all.

"My grandmother is dead."

"Emergency calls only."

"She just died, maybe an hour ago."

"There's no emergency, then?" the woman asked.

"Well, not exactly."

"Natural causes?"

"Yes," Mavy said. "I don't know."

"Is your mother home? An adult I could speak with?"

"I am an adult," Mavy said.

"Violent crime?"

"No. Nothing like that."

"You need the coroner, Miss."

"But—"

"Address please?"

Mavy gave it. She heard keystrokes.

"My computer shows no such listing."

Mavy had no idea how to respond to this.

"My computer shows no such listing," the woman repeated.

"It, it *is* a place," Mavy stammered. "I'm here now."

She heard more keystrokes.

"The information has been routed to the coroner," the woman said. "The coroner will contact the address you gave me within eight hours."

"Eight hours?"

"Yes, Miss."

"But what am I going to do?"

There was silence.

"I'm not *from* here. I mean—"

"I'm sorry," said the woman kindly, before adding, "but 911 is for emergency calls only."

The line went dead, without reverting to a dial tone.

Mavy punched her parents' number, and got a recorded loop: ". . . All phone systems in your service area are temporarily down while we reprogram switching circuits, meeting our commitment with the office of the mayor to make your New York a better New York. In case of emergency, use 911 . . ."

Not expecting it to work, Mavy picked up the intercom and began pressing buttons. All she could get was a Muzak version of "Those Were the Days."

Next she ran to the elevator and leaned on the button. Nothing happened. Nothing happened. She pressed Emergency. Nothing happened. The stairwell was locked.

Back down the long hallway, Mavy looked at her grandmother. "We're on our own," she said, and started laughing. But it was chilling to laugh alone.

Mavy began by kneeling down. She shut her grandmother's eyes. It was harder to do than she thought. Franny's eyeballs had sort of dried out, and the eyelids made a noise sliding over them. Mavy had to use more pressure than felt comfortable. She realized she had never seen a dead body. Ever. It seemed a peculiarly American deficiency, if you came of age in the eighties, if you grew up on the central coast of California. On TV she had seen tons. Literally, tons. Shot, stabbed, sawed into parts, hatcheted, hanged, boiled in acid, squashed under tank treads. But in real life, not one dead body. It was very very still, and not smelly like they say. Not yet.

Mavy slid her arms under Franny's shoulders, and dragged her grandmother a few yards into the bathroom. The toilet seat was up, which Mavy thought strange for a woman living alone, until noticing the bottle of Pepto Bismol on the tank. Perhaps Franny had lifted the toilet seat to vomit, and at that same time as Mavy had opened her pocketbook. That would explain the pink corners of her otherwise blue lips.

Mavy realized she was humming "Those Were the Days."

If never seeing a dead body was a typical American experience, then *this* one was particularly un-American. And one for which Mavy was suddenly thankful. It was fortunate that 911 hadn't responded, a crew of rubber gloves hadn't zipped up Frances Tibbets in plastic and wheeled her away. It was fortunate that Mavy's first sight of a dead person was *in the family*.

Franny was so small and light, the effort barely winded Mavy, who felt every inch of her own six feet, every pound of one hundred forty-five, strong. Franny, it seemed, weighed not much more than Aaron, and looked a little like him.

It still mattered what her bad habits were, her favorite colors and desserts. It mattered *even more* now that it didn't seem to. "You could have been dying," Mavy said, and the acoustics of the bathroom gave her voice a strange authenticity. "While I was wondering whether you believed in God."

She pulled off Franny's silk robe and put it on herself. It was fragile, threadbare in the armpits. It mattered that Franny had worn it specially for Mavy. That her legs were unshaven, curly white hairs thick at the ankles. That underneath the fake cleavage, her chest was flat, caved in even, scarred. It all mattered.

With hot water and a loofah, Mavy began by washing the Pepto Bismol and dried saliva off her grandmother's face. Then she washed her neck, her shoulders, her back. Delicately, she passed the warm sopping loofah over Franny's chest, over the haphazard incision scars that crisscrossed the ribcage, and down her back to wash the shriveled buttocks. Then, dipping the sponge again, she cleaned her grandmother's privates, the sight of white pubic hair somehow foreign and forlorn.

It seemed odd, this intimacy, though Mavy had done the same countless times to Aaron. A squirming son should be different than a lifeless grandmother. But not so. The wonder and trepidation she'd felt bathing an infant for the first time were the same she felt bathing an old woman for the last.

And, too, there comes a certain liberation in doing the thing that most terrifies you.

After she got Granny Franny cleaned and dressed in light cotton pajamas, and laid out on the bed, Mavy explored the apartment. The walls were covered with framed antique *Vogue* covers, like the ones she herself owned, each signed and dated by Franny. All the furniture was leather and oak. Crystal potpourri bowls sat on various tables, giving off an aroma like honey and cedar. There was no dust, but the windows had a patina of dirt that made the light gauzy.

Mavy noticed the blinking answering machine. A pack of cigarettes was set on top. Benson & Hedges. Franny's. She extracted one and lit it.

The message was from Franklin. His mother had fallen and been rushed to Las Vegas Mercy. They were giving her an artificial hip. "Teflon. Really bad."

No "I love you," no word about Aaron. Is this what family was, one crisis after the next? Death, Teflon, unwanted pregnancy?

The phone chirped, scaring her.

"Hi Mommy," breathed Aaron.

"Hi, love." She heard him grope the receiver, too large for his tiny hand, one end higher than his ear, the other lower than his mouth.

"I'm fine," he said.

She remembered she was pregnant, and, horrified, smashed out the cigarette.

"What's wrong, Mommy?"

"Nothing. I'm fine, too. It's nothing." The truth. Franny was nothing now. "Did Daddy dial for you?" she asked, carrying the cordless to the fireplace. On the mantel were daguerreotypes of Eliza and Luther Tibbets, Aaron's great-great-grandparents. They stood on the promenade of a mansion surrounded by orange groves. Eliza resplendent in white lace, Luther in top hat and tails, beard, and slightly sinister handlebar mustache.

"He put yours and Granny Franny's pitcher next to the button," Aaron was saying. "In case of 'mergency."

Speed-dialing, of course. Again, she heard him struggling to hang on to it.

"Am I in trouble?" he asked.

"Of course not, angel." Among the portraits, there was one of Franny's wedding. A joke, it must be. The man in the picture was Luther. Older, gaunter, but unmistakable. The same biblical beard.

"Does Granny Franny like me?"

"She loves you," Mavy said. Could it be? Other pictures confirmed it. Mavy's own father, Bernal, being led on a pony by Luther. Luther with his arm around Bernal holding a fat-fingered baseball mitt. "Very very much." Trembling, Mavy lay down on the cold tiles.

It all came clear: her father's tattoos and writer's block, his insistence on her sonograms and amnio. *Ripcord.* But what did that make Mavy? McKinley's granddaughter or a product of incest? What did that make Aaron? Why hadn't anyone ever told her.

"Mom? Can we get a dog?" Aaron asked. "I really want a dog."

"Ta-da!" Caroline said, and placed a steaming meatloaf in the center of the table. Tiny shimmering globules trickled down its crusted surface. Even on the trivet, it continued to sizzle, as if self-powered.

"Elbows off the table, Sweetheart," Franklin told Aaron, who grunted, but removed them. He was hunched over an Atakashita notepad, punching keys, despite the clearly established rule against using computers at the dinner table.

Slack-assed and impudent, Franklin thought. Typical teenager. Just look at yourself, Franklin wanted to say. Mopey, self-mooning, evasive bloodshot eyes. And that hair! He wasn't *against* long hair, per se. He understood the adolescent need for symbol. But Aaron's stringy yellow tangles stuck to his shiny forehead. His ears poked through. There were pimples even on them. Sure, oily skin clears in time, and even the slumped shoulders were bearable. But the hair, statement or not, was just so *sulky*. Franklin was convinced Aaron would be a happier person if he cut his hair.

"And *you*," Franklin moved on to Billybones, also playing with a palmtop. "We're having mealtime here."

"But *Dad*." Billybones glanced up for a second. "I'm in the middle of an operation." He was wearing his favorite shirt, the one bought with the birthday money from Grandma Goretex, with the stitching and the hologram buttons: Billy the Kid drawing a six-shooter. Actually, Franklin had been the one to fold cash into the card his mother made in Crafts, she being so *elsewhere*, as Aaron put it, or according to Billybones, *completely electoral college*. Franklin had even forged her signature, an act that she still had enough presence of mind to refuse to do.

The card was made of green construction paper and had a single crayon squiggle through the center. Red. Billybones really really liked it. The simple *choices* implied: red, green, squiggle. When you thought of her physical and mental constraints, and the limited materials she was working with, the picture was complete. The life she had lived; it was all there. Franklin had to agree.

"Sweetheart, would you like to cut the meatloaf?" Franklin tried.

"I hate that," Aaron mumbled. " 'Would you *like* to?' You always do that. I hate that."

"Well," Franklin said.

" 'Would you like to clean your room, would you like to wash the car, would you like to be my slave?' Why don't you just say, 'Do it'?"

"Who," Billybones peeped, eyes fastened on the screen. Aaron could see on it a depiction of an open knee, patella and tendon, veins clamped with hemostats. His brother was controlling a scalpel with a tiny joystick. "Sometimes he says 'Who.' 'Who'd like to sweep the pool?' "

"Besides," Aaron added, holding up his 686, 2X VGA, 5-meg memory. "I have homework."

"Salad," Caroline said, leaving the room.

"Cut the damn meatloaf," Franklin snapped.

Aaron sighed, saved his document, and shut off the machine. Then he picked up the knife, pinching his nose as if the pan in front of him were full of roast dogshit. It wasn't that he hated meatloaf. It smelled good actually. It was that he hated being so flipped for Linda Delgado.

"Ground control to Aaron," Franklin said, sipping his scotch. "Commence with the carving duty, *por favor.*"

Caroline returned carrying a wooden bowl filled with redleaf lettuce and carrots sticking up like spikes.

"It's treated with hormones," Aaron said. "I can smell."

"That's absurd," Franklin said. "Caroline, you got it at Perelandra, didn't you?"

"They were out," she said, shrinking. "The drought, you know. Not a lot of organic cows this year, and—"

"Bill, quit with that thing already!" Franklin shouted. Billybones's computer was beeping in the code red alert, the words "cardiac arrest" blinking at the screen's bottom.

Aaron cut extra-large slices, coaxing them gently off

the spatula onto plates. He watched Dad stare at the slab in front of him. He was a stickler for organic meat, or at least hormone-free meat.

Mainstream cows were treated with growth hormones taken from the glands of people, he said. According to Dad, there was a measure of human in this steaming meatloaf.

"I'm sorry," Caroline said. "I thought, just this once." She had purple eyeliner and curling-ironed hair that fell in coils on either side of her face. The steam rising from the meatloaf relaxed their hold. It gave her a melting appearance, as if her bone structure were turning to cartilage. "I'm sorry."

"No need," Franklin said. All this aggravation was bad for the blood pressure. "I'm sure it'll be fine. This time."

Caroline paused, fingers to lips. "I feel just awful."

"I'll be mad if you feel bad," Franklin said.

Bully, Aaron thought. Imperialist.

For a while, the family chewed in silence. The candle flames jumped nervously. Thumper the dog's jaw clicked as he yawned over and over, the way he did when he was hungry. Silverware clanked against potter's-wheel dishes. Aaron booted up the computer in his lap and went back to work, eating and keypunching. Billybones, seeing Aaron get away with it, did the same.

"I—" Caroline and Franklin both said at once.

"I'm sorry," said Franklin.

"You go."

"No, you," he said.

But neither of them said anything. Aaron was distracted by the image on Billybones's screen: female genitalia. The tool menu included picks and scoops.

Franklin slapped the table. "What is this? We're a

family here. A family having dinner. Aaron? Aaron!"

Aaron looked up, through his hair. A cluster of pimples on his forehead itched. *"What?"*

"Would you like to share your, your homework, with us?""

"He doesn't like when you say, 'Would you like to,' " Caroline said.

Aaron offered his computer. "You can have the whole thing."

"Would you please share your homework?" Franklin rephrased.

Aaron jutted out his lower lip and let out a puff of air, sending a stiff ripple through his waxy bangs. "A host, a host, my kismet for a host."

"What's that?" Franklin asked. Cut that god-ugly hair, son. "Is that homework?"

"Shakespeare." Aaron nodded.

"Not William."

"Yes," Aaron sighed. "But in Hypertext."

"Hypertext?" Franklin asked. "Hypertext? Hypertext? What on God's green earth is Hypertext?"

"God's green earth?" Aaron said. "God's green earth?"

"It's an expression," Caroline offered hopefully. "I think."

"Listen." Aaron explained how he could call up any speech from any Shakespeare play, use another window to get a schematic blocking of the play in the original Globe Theatre, use still a third to get newspaper reviews of whatever production he wanted, and use still another to get critical studies. "I can get a historical digest of the war. I can get the price of coal at the time of Edwin Booth's dying words if I want."

"What the hell does that have to do with William goddamn Shakespeare?"

"Just forget it, okay?"

"Why don't you just *read* the play?" Caroline asked sweetly.

"That's what he's doing," Billybones said. Aaron saw his little brother was using a vacuum and lots of cotton gauze to stop a small hemorrhage. Surgery was a very sophisticated program. Before being turned into a game, it was a training program for med students. *"Reading,* like, *getting* a reading."

"Could have fooled me," Franklin said.

"It's *homework.* All right?" Aaron said. "An assignment."

"No it's not *all right.* " Dad made him explain.

"I use algorithmic formulas, say noun-plus-four using the Microsoft Word version seven-point-seven dictionary, subject to maintaining the original iambic pentameter, to substitute for the original noun." The computer checked its lexicon alphabetically for the fourth noun down from the one "Shakespeare" used, continuing on if the fourth didn't fit the meter. "Kingdom to kismet, horse to host."

"Ahh, like Mad Libs," Franklin said, turning toward Caroline. "Remember Mad Libs?"

She shook her head no, and they both looked pained the way they always did when some trivial thing reminded them that no matter how much sex they had, they were still from different generations.

Caroline's curls were now completely limp, and her makeup had lost its edge. In fact, there was no longer anything sharp about her. She was blurring, as if losing possession of herself into the wallpaper. She had really aged, Aaron observed. From nineteen to early thirties, skipping her twenties altogether.

" 'To be or not to be,' " Aaron recited, reading from his tiny screen, " 'that is the quibble: Whether 'tis nobler in the mines to suffer the slips and artists of outrageous forums, or to take arts against a seal of truants, and by opposing end them?' "

"Wow," Caroline said. "That definitely *sounds* poetic."

"But it's *not* Shakespeare," Franklin said.

"Maybe it's better," Billybones said.

"Then I call up a critical reading of the new version," Aaron went on, furiously jabbing the keyboard. "There's a whole roster of names I can call up for 'in the style of': Northrop Frye, William Aldis Wright, blah blah. Or I can employ the theories of Joseph Campbell written in the style of Hunter S. Thompson. Yeah, that would be a good one." He looked up smiling for a change. "Or I can make up my own, using Urban Housing Project or Valley Speak, to get what's called an 'interp.' "

"What's the point?" Franklin asked, losing patience. Get a haircut. At least, shave. Though he could see how that must hurt passing a razor over those chin pimples for a scarce harvest of scraggly whiskers.

"I can use N-plus-five next time and get a whole new version, and a whole new set of critical readings, and they're all as profound or classic or masterful or hip or natural or professional sounding as the first." Aaron was out of breath, twitching and blinking at the hair in his eyes.

"But what's the point?" Franklin asked.

"It makes him be like in charge," Billybones said, "of lots and lots of intelligence." His computer was making code white sounds, meaning his patient was losing blood pressure rapidly.

"The point is this *is* the point." Aaron hugged the computer. He could know more about "Shakespeare" right now while they were eating meatloaf in suburbopolis than all of history combined knew last year.

"I still don't see why you just don't *read* the play," Caroline said.

"He can make up his own," Billybones said. "Him and the computer."

"And whoever else is programmed in," Aaron said. "Okay, it may not be a totally pure collaboration, you may get a few machined sentences, but it works pretty well. This gives me infinity-minus-one options."

"So does a typewriter," Franklin said.

"Yeah, but I'm using bigger building blocks than letters of the alphabet."

"Smaller actually," Billybones said. "Zero and one. The binary—"

"But what is the gosh darn point?" Franklin asked.

Aaron sucked on his hair. Gosh darn, Dad was stupid. "Want me to look it up for you?"

After dinner, Dad and Billybones went to the store for ice cream. It was Aaron's turn to help with the dishes. He loaded them into the rack while Caroline put away the leftovers.

"I liked your Hypertext thing," she said. She had the meatloaf on the cutting board. "The first time I ever cared one way or the other about Shakespeare."

"One, or the other?" Aaron grunted, jamming a handful of forks tines up into the silverware basket. "Which is it?"

"Look," she snapped. "I know you think I'm a bimbo 'cause I'm not that much older than you." She took a big big breath. The box of plastic wrap in her hands was shaking.

"Take it easy," Aaron said.

"And I'm not Mentally Gifted, I know it. And, no, we

wouldn't be friends on the outside, most likely. But I'll tell you something." With her fingernails, she pinched frantically at the edge of the plastic sheet that had merged into the roll. "I'm family now, so whatever you think of me, I'm—"

The box jumped out of her hands. "Damn it, I'm bleeding."

The serrated metal strip edge had sliced open her wrist. She held it, trying to cup the blood in her good hand, but the blood spilled over, falling in an unbroken stream to the floor.

"Ouch," she said. "Why doesn't it hurt?"

Aaron unrolled some paper towels, wadded them up, and applied them to the cut. He had to use considerable pressure to stop the bleeding. The towels had little pictures of Santa Claus, even though Christmas was months ago, or months ahead, depending. They soaked through immediately.

"Dizzy," she said. "The Glenlivet-like. Your father always makes me say that. *The* Glenlivet."

She was bleeding terribly, her face looked like it was thawing. Dad had the car, and wouldn't be back for probably a half hour. Thinking she could die, Aaron dialed 911.

"I wish you liked me," Caroline said, sitting on the floor, back against a cabinet. The blood reflected the halogen overheads in the most peculiar way.

By the time the paramedics arrived, Caroline had soaked a whole roll of paper towels, and half a bath mat.

A video crew scrambled in behind the medics, their white lights cold and unforgiving. One man held a boom mike, while another held a light meter against the blood.

"Who are *you?*" Aaron asked.

" 'Reel Life Drama,' " a man said, holding out a consent form in a manicured hand, clear nail polish. "Dad and Mom around?" His hair was gold and fine as monofilament.

The medics, wearing plastic face plates and rubber gloves, bandaged Caroline's wrist and hooked her to an IV.

Dad rushed in a few minutes later. After telling Caroline he loved her to pieces, she was going to be fine, just fine, he pushed the video guy up against the wall. "Get out!" he screamed into the guy's face. "Get out of my house *now*!"

Caroline was discharged from the hospital the next day. Her wrist had been cut to the bone. It was a scar she would have to cover for the rest of her life, because people saw what they saw, no matter how adamantly she insisted that no, she did not try to commit suicide.

"Reel Life Drama" aired the episode anyway, as journalism, which didn't require consent forms. In order to protect their privacy, the Wellses' address wasn't revealed, and nothing overtly identifying was shown. A tilting, expanding mobile black shape blocked Caroline's eyes, and Aaron's head was disguised as a fuzzy honeycomb mosaic. Voice had also been slowed and lowered, the words recognizable only if you already knew them. "I do like you, Caroline," Aaron said. "I do."

The blood, however, was in focus and very colorful. So were the paper towels, down to their tiny Santas. But Caroline's sliced wrist, lippy and garish, was the best. It dared you not to watch, like pornography.

For the first time in her life, Mavy and her father met as equals. They sat at a polished table in the office of Williams, Ernest, & Hagmeyer, for the reading of the will. Franny stipulated only Bernal and Mavy be present. The lawyer was late.

"I always thought he was *Grandpoppa,*" Bernal said. He wore a corduroy sports jacket, the same he had worn at the funeral yesterday at Arroyo Grande Cemetery in Redlands, California. His square-tailed tie seemed to be choking him. Edges of tattoos peered above his shirt collar. "I didn't know he was *Dad* till I was seventeen."

Franny's pine box had been lowered into a plot next to Luther's, opposite Eliza's. There was additional space for Bernal, and for Mavy, too. It made her feel conscripted and of small importance.

"It's not my place to forgive you," she said. Mavy, also, wore yesterday's dress. There had been so little time to pack.

"I'm not apologizing." Bernal stood up, then sat back down. Under the corporate fluorescents, he looked aged and repressed. "You'd think they'd have coffee, a place like this." The floor was red granite, the table mahogany, the chairs black leather.

Mavy tried not to be nauseated. She had already scouted the bathroom, just in case. "I'm pregnant again, you know."

Bernal closed his eyes and pinched his nose. "No, I didn't. That's great news, hon. Great."

"Don't worry, I'll definitely get tests."

"I was trying to protect you," Bernal said. "Goddamn it!" for emphasis.

That she needed protection from the truth made Mavy doubt herself, her life, as if for all these years she'd been some kind of impersonator. At last, she saw her father as he really was. A weakling with long scraggly hair in a shell of tattoos. A spiritually enfeebled, middle-aged man. Instead of pity, she felt rage. He was to blame for his child's history, and for her children's futures. "You were trying to protect yourself."

"Every fucking day," he muttered. "Every fucking minute."

When the lawyer finally arrived, he offered a box of tissues, assuming the tears had sprung from a more orthodox grief.

Frances Tibbets left Mavy a large trust fund, a house surrounded by fifty acres of the few remaining orange groves in southern California, and a chest containing ancestral documents, photographs, a wedding dress, and a mint-condition Colt .45 six-shooter.

She left Bernal the Park Avenue apartment.

Both inherited burial plots and season tickets to the ballet.

Mavy was six months pregnant when she next visited the lawyer.

"Don't," she said as Franklin tried to reach inside her shirt. She would let him put his arm around her, or hold hands, as long as they were in public. But at home, in their room, when he tried to stroke her hair, or rub her back, she'd laugh and pull away as if they were playing a tickling game.

"What is going on with you?" He couldn't understand it. For the first time, they were okay. They had their health. They had each other. They had, thanks to Granny Franny, no more money worries and plenty of space.

The new home was made of mud and straw, with a Spanish tile roof set on round log beams. Sticks of hay showed in the cracks of the red adobe. The house was small, but each room seemed larger than the next, each seemed to occupy a slightly different level. This gave better access to the range of one's own moods.

The orange grove was similar. Franklin didn't like the fruit especially—oranges hurt his sensitive teeth—but the trees sure were pretty.

Except for the hot, smoggy summer months, the lack of a nearby ocean and surfing, and the crowded freeways, the conditions could not be more ideal.

"I don't use the videocamera anymore," he said, feeling almost timid. She was so beautiful pregnant. Her cheeks got pink, her movements stately, assured. "So why won't you tell me what's eating you?"

"Me?" Mavy asked. "You're the one who's in a tizzy."

"Is it this place?" Franklin could see she was somewhere in between giving Redlands a try and giving up on it.

"No, no, no," she said. "No."

He kissed her, partially to get away from the imprecision of words.

She kissed back, which surprised him.

"Is it me, then?" he asked.

"No, no, no," she said, a little too insistently. The

lawyer said the divorce papers would take a couple of months. "I'm just going through something here."

Franklin paid the money for a private hospital room, even if Mom didn't want it.

"Doctor said I could get out of this fucking death pit tomorrow," she said, arranging her hair in a hand mirror.

"She said, 'We'll see, tomorrow,'" Franklin said, holding a videocassette. "How's the hip?"

"Better than the old one." Surgeons had replaced the joint with a Teflon-coated hard plastic ball and socket, grafted onto bone transplanted from the cadaver of a nineteen-year-old Korean girl raped and killed at her job as an attendant at a Gift & Gas Plaza. "What's that?"

Franklin inserted the videocassette. Onscreen, the tape showed a thousand shades of silver, liquid and contracting. A shape suggested itself.

"Your grandson," Franklin said. "What does it look like?"

Aaron was convinced Mavy was carrying a big puppy in her round belly, and no amount of patient explanation could convince him otherwise.

When instead out came a baby brother, he was devastated. He refused to crap. The only power he had, it was quite compelling. He got gassy, smelly, cranky, and mean. Days went by without a smile from him, without a sound.

In the end, Mavy broke down and took him to the animal shelter, where he picked out a six-week-old Samoyed that licked him until its tongue bled.

Later that day, Aaron took such a happy dump that it plugged up the toilet.

Billybones was a fat baby. He fed so much, so vigorously, that scabs formed on Mavy's nipples. And her breasts ached all the time. She couldn't remember them ever being like this before. Full of pebbles, they felt, and not round ones. Billy couldn't get enough of them.

It was really time to wean him, but she didn't have the heart. And continuing to breastfeed gave her an excuse to keep Franklin away.

"Uh-uh-uh," the baby said. He was flat on his back on the kitchen table.

Ever since New York, or maybe since the birth of her first son, she saw her husband in a new light, or more like, didn't see him. Her fantasies revolved around him being gone . . .

Anything needy in Franklin filled her with disgust. His lust, especially. It wasn't as if she *wanted* to find him repulsive. She just did.

Aaron shot into the kitchen, skidded to a stop, and, holding a toy spider and an orange, rubbed his face into the baby's. "Billybones!"

The puppy, Thumper, ran in a few seconds behind and right away crashed headfirst into a table leg. Franklin had discovered the pup seemed to have three testicles, an attribute Mavy found mildly amusing, mildly disturbing.

Now Aaron was stroking the baby's bent collarbone, a curve that seemed about to pop through the skin. The doctor had told them the clavicle would return to normal, but it hadn't, and wouldn't.

Mavy took it to be a message. A message she was sent but not meant to understand. "Be gentle," she said.

The baby coughed whenever his defect was touched. Aaron tried to jam the toy spider into Billy's tiny fist. "He's trying to eat it!"

Mavy took the spider, and gave it back to Aaron. It was probably unfair that the seat, and with it most of Billy's belongings, would be the very ones Aaron outgrew. There would be very little original territory for the second born.

"Doesn't he know anything?" Aaron was still angry at the baby for not being a dog.

"He's only three months old," said Mavy.

"Ah-ga ah-ga." Billybones waved his arms in the air, then stopped, distracted by his hands.

"How come there are no freckles there?" Aaron asked, eyes on his mother's breasts.

"I've kept them out of the sun," Mavy said. Though she didn't like breastfeeding in front of her husband, she had long stopped worrying about whether it was right to perform the task in front of her son.

"I'm hungry, too," Aaron said, watching. He was sun-tanned, huge blue eyes, with her crazy-out-of-control hair. Her oldest boy didn't walk but ran, didn't sleep but fell unconscious, didn't eat but gorged. He was fiercely physical, super-oxygenated, terrific.

"Eat your orange." The grove was the one thing she loved about living here. Everything else about southern California scared her.

The desert light was freakish and addictive. The trees were all from somewhere else: cypress, palm, orange, eucalyptus. The places far apart and alien. To the east: Yucaipa, Banning, Cabazon, Needles. To the north: Mojave, Tehachapi, Gorman, Garlock. To the south: Perris, Temecula, La Jolla. To the west: Rialto, Fontana, Van Nuys. What kinds of names were these? What did the words mean?

In fact, she had to learn a whole new vocabulary: ten-micron particulates, Pool Sweep, Santana winds, cloverleaf, sonic boom—proof glass, cul-de-sac, Washington navels.

Sometimes the sky got crowded with buzzards. They flew in a giant cloud, rarely flapping their wings, just circling and circling, their shadows scraping along the ground. It was one of the only things Aaron feared.

Cars another. An endless glistening beast, threading past stucco churches, warehouse shopping clubs, parking lot horizons, mall petting zoos, fifty-pump gas stations, blue-mirrored insurance buildings.

Mavy had no friends, besides Aaron. "Peel," he said, trying to give her the orange.

"You can do it yourself." She knew it would take him about ten minutes. He loved the grove as much as she. They slept out there sometimes, set up camp with a mattress and a board. It had never rained on them. Not once.

"This not food," Aaron said. He ate so many oranges that he had vitamin C for blood, and the citric acid had eaten away most of the enamel on his baby teeth. She was convinced it was what turned his hair so ungoverned, his eyes so audaciously blue. Franklin suggested putting him in commercials. When she realized he wasn't kidding, Mavy had become appalled. "It's for thirsty."

Mavy took the orange and started it for him, breaking the skin with her thumbnail. He watched so intently, as if etching the gesture into his memory.

"Eeeee!" Aaron said, maybe meaning Thumper the dog now inside the diaper bin, chewing a soiled one. Maybe meaning Billy suckling, still gumming and grasping and slurping.

Where Aaron used to linger, nuzzling, tasting, Billy clutched, seizing, gnawing. But she didn't love him any less for it. Born in a swirl of static and radiomagnetism, Billy was a stay-inside boy, allergic, it seemed, to anything bright. He was mucousy, an insomniac, sharp-fisted, upset.

"What is it, Billy? Show me what's wrong." She never spoke babytalk to either son.

"I wish he was a dog," Aaron said, Frisbeeing orange peels at his brother.

"Stop!" Mavy said, and Billy coughed, spitting up. It was nothing unusual. The baby had a delicate stomach, and was always spitting up. But Mavy was alarmed to see blood on the nursing blanket. Billy spit up again, more blood. Billy's color was fine, but— He seemed to have no fever, but— He spit up a third time, less blood, but—

"Is he gonna be dead?" Aaron asked, mouth full of orange.

"Course not," Mavy said. Internal bleeding, she panicked. Ambulance. Poison. Decoagulant.

"Aaron," she said. It wouldn't be the first time he tried to kill his little brother. "Did you see him eat anything funny? Something under the sink. Your toy spider?"

Aaron continued chewing, eyes wide on hers. Then he swallowed and, mouth open, approached her left nipple to taste the milky blood.

Common enemies of the orange tree: mites, aphids, thrips, scale insects, grasshoppers, whitefly, Mexican fruit fly, and, most notably, the Mediterranean fruit fly, better known as the Medfly.

Aaron bounced excitedly on the bed. "Mom, Mom, candy, candy!"

Mavy opened her eyes, clasping the pillow above her head. "Aaron, Aaron, slow down."

"Come see the candy!" He took her hand and pulled her out from under the sheet.

"Okay, okay!" She put on Franny's silk kimono, and followed her son outside.

The sky had pink in it, and brown. The mountains looked like uncrumpled aluminum foil. Light clung like a glaze of honey to the leaves of the orange trees. Her hand stuck slightly to the handrail on the stairs leading down from the balcony, her bare feet left prints.

"See?" Aaron said. He offered her an orange tree leaf. "Candy!"

She smelled it. "It *is* honey."

"What?" Aaron said, jumping up and down, rolling around on the ground.

"No," she said, tasting again. "It's honey."

Later she learned helicopters had come in the night and dropped malathion-laced honey over the Inland Empire in order to kill the Medfly. There had been announcements; she had just missed them.

Puppy Thumper, licking the fender, wagged his tail fiercely.

The days of tomatoes, Integrated Pest Management, and sweet naive Franklin seemed long gone.

Mavy's mother-in-law weighed eighty pounds. She had been in bed for a month. Nurses turned her body every four hours to prevent bedsores. She didn't have enough strength to cough.

She lay in bed, every sheet and blanket stenciled "Redlands Community Hospital," lest she try to forget. The linoleum shone and the venetian blinds smelled like ammonia. Oprah was going on a TV mounted to the wall. Her guests were people who had no identifiable feelings.

Mrs. Wells coughed and tried to say something. Her eyepatch had come off, revealing a wrinkly, sunken socket. Nobody ever bothered with the glass eye anymore.

Mavy replaced the patch, and put an ear to her mother-in-law's lips.

"Make them stop," Mrs. Wells said, cringing. A wave of pain turned her white. When it passed, her cheeks reddened.

"You're going to get better, Mrs. Wells," Mavy said, stroking her hand. Doctors didn't know what was wrong, aside from a lung infection. They suspected it was caused by microbial fungus living in the central air conditioner at her Las Vegas hotel, because dozens of others had also fallen sick. The strange thing was, no one shared common symptoms.

"Aaron, you're a good boy," Mrs. Wells said, accepting a kiss on the cheek from a hallucination. Lately she had been going in and out, sometimes coherent, sometimes not. "Don't let your father climb ahead of you."

"Mrs. Wells," Mavy said, "Aaron's not here." She believed it was important to tell it like it was, right to the end if necessary.

Mrs. Wells looked confused, blinking her one eye. "Where is he?"

"At his swimming lesson."

Onscreen, a guest panelist said, "*I'm* not saying I don't have feelings. I just can't *differentiate* between them."

Mrs. Wells closed her eyes to "surf another pain-wave"—how insensitive Franklin always put it. When it was over, she looked at Mavy. "My son," she said, between trying to cough. "Doesn't have the guts."

"He loves you," Mavy said.

Mrs. Wells groaned, blanching again.

"I don't know if *you* wake up like that," Oprah said, "but my Steadman sure does." Close-ups of housewives cupping giggles.

"There's a son's love," Mrs. Wells said.

The nurse came with a carton labeled WELLS. It was dinner. They fed her with a tube. "You come back in a minute," the nurse told Mavy. She was young, pretty, gap toothed, lots of makeup. "I fix her then you come back in a minute," she said, rolling on a pair of rubber gloves.

Out in the hall cafeteria smells competed with bleach. A shrunken lady in a wheelchair pointed at Mavy and shrieked, "You never visit me!"

Last week the doctor, a tiny woman born in Hiroshima and educated at Harvard, put in a rare appearance. "Mrs. Wells doesn't look good." Even Franklin could see that. Franklin, born in Las Vegas, educated at El Camino Real College, had to decide whether to put a DNR on his mother. "That means, Do Not Resuscitate, in the event of cardiac arrest. Or respiratory failure."

"Yes," Mavy said. Mavy, born in Carmel, educated by tidepools, a goat, a mistaken marriage, photos on the fireplace mantel of her dead grandmother.

"Not over my dead body!" Franklin glared at his wife to keep himself from crying. "How could you?"

"She spelled it out in the living will."

"Living," Franklin had replied. "That's the point."

"Is okay," the nurse said, smiling. "You go back in now."

Franklin came every afternoon for a half hour, watched the news, then left. He thought the private room was care enough. He thought refusing to sign the order was care enough.

"After you learn to identify what having feelings feels like," said a woman onscreen, above a "Psychologist/Author" subtitle, "you must *practice* having them."

Mavy looked at her mother-in-law, and was heartbroken. Mrs. Wells already had a Goretex aorta, a Teflon hip, that bone grafted from a nineteen-year-old Korean girl raped and killed in a shootout at a Gift & Gas Plaza, an artificial eyeball, and now this.

"Uhhhh," she groaned, unable to cough. "Ohhhh." Mavy squeezed her hand. Suddenly, Mrs. Wells opened her good eye, and there was a peaceful look in it. "Lemme alone, all of yous."

Later, at home, Mavy told Franklin, "Be merciful."

Franklin paused, as if he'd never heard such an outlandish request. "Certainly." Mercy didn't come as easily as handing out tissues. Mercy was a contact sport.

As if to punish them both, Franklin's mother went on living forever.

Inside the cavernous red maple chest that was Mavy's inheritance, it smelled funky and sweet, vaguely orangey.

The Colt .45 six-shooter and its leather holster were in remarkable condition, a carton of bullets untouched.

Dr. Ghopal was her age or just a few years older. Twenty-seven or -eight. He had lots of bare skin between whiskers. Baby crow's feet. He had a long life ahead of him and lovely, lovely lashes.

Such a small thing, Mavy thought, rolling a single

bullet around in her palm. Small as the tip of my pinkie, but so heavy and cold. This bit of metal can tear through a heart, rip open a windpipe, mangle bone. She put the bullet into a chamber, then gave the barrel a spin.

Hopeful, Dr. Ghopal kept saying, kept looking at his watch. "Hopeful." Mavy wondered if he realized it almost rhymed with his name. But no, he wouldn't possibly. He was an oncologist. No kids of his own.

Not for Franklin would she have gone to the doctor. Not for herself. If in fact it was malignant, as Dr. Ghopal thought the tests may very well show, he'd like to start her on chemo and radiation ASAP. He declined to speculate on whether the cells had entered the bloodstream and "visited themselves" upon other organs.

"My grandmother died in my arms," she told him. It was a lie, but she felt the gist was true.

Dr. Ghopal said he was sorry. Hopeful.

She took the gun away from her temple and opened the chamber. Empty. Would've been lucky this time. She gave it another spin. The melodrama of what she was doing did not escape her, but "Hopeful"? Chemo and radiation? No guarantees. Brown rice and Chaplin movies. She just didn't have the energy.

"What's wrong?" Aaron said in a pant, having just turned the corner into her room. As usual he was clutching a half-eaten orange in one hand.

Mavy carefully placed the gun on top of her bureau. She had no intention of pulling the trigger. Just imagining it gave her a kind of relief.

"What?"

"Getting things in order." She turned toward the chest that Granny Franny had left her—that and a genetic predisposition to getting breast cancer. Inside the chest were the gun and bullets, ancient newspaper clippings, notes, land deeds, the daguerreotypes of her great-grand-parents, Eliza and Luther Tibbets, the bottle of petrified orange liqueur and the dog collar, and what appeared to be a baby coffin. It contained Eliza's wedding dress.

"Then why are you crying?" Aaron asked. She wasn't, but she wiped her eyes anyway. Aaron himself began to cry. Tears and drool.

She hugged him. "Remember I love you."

"Why would I forget?" he asked, inside the sobs.

But he was easy to settle down. Permission to eat a Popsicle sent him scurrying happily into the kitchen.

Unloading the gun, Mavy noticed this time she wouldn't have been so lucky.

Mavy became depressed. Franklin saw and worried and resented from afar. She slept more and more. She bathed less. Most days, she didn't bother getting dressed, but stayed in that tattered silk kimono. Food made her feel sick, yet she was always "a little hungry." She cut off her parents completely, never answering their calls, never responding to their letters.

She wouldn't tell him why.

Gloom was like another person in the house. If Franklin made her tea and showered her with kisses, Gloom grew darker, more severe. If he lost his temper with her, Gloom grew indignant and hostile.

Franklin missed the real Mavy terribly. Gloom's personality grew more pronounced as Mavy's receded. By turns, Franklin felt loving, exasperated, tender, spurned.

Eventually, he felt murderous.

Franklin sat in his office, bored stiff. Though it was well-appointed and expensively furnished, he hated being in his office. It made him feel captive. Already three o'clock, and the city manager still hadn't returned his call. The zoning permit dilemma was at issue. Franklin was sure to get the okay to . . . to *transform* the orange grove into houses.

His suite was on the eleventh floor of the mid-rise overlooking the intersections of I-10 and 215, a view of a fifty-pump gas station/truck stop/furniture warehouse outlet, of traffic jams, and of steel-skeletoned telecommunications cable support towers disappearing into smog.

As he poured himself another glass of The Glenlivet, the phone chirped.

"Yeah?" he said.

"Mr. Wells, Federal Express just left off a package," said the secretary.

"Yeah?" Franklin said. He always hired temps, partially because he spent so little time in his office, and partially because he liked having young pretty temps that wouldn't want advancement or, or whatever.

"It says 'urgent,' " she said.

But the problem with temps is that usually they didn't know tit from tat. "Okay, bring it right in."

The temp came in and handed Franklin the Federal Express envelope.

"Thank you," Franklin read the name on the signature line, "Jasmine."

She smiled bashfully. She was very long in the limbs, crazy haired, flat pink lipstick, bra seams showing through orange silk. Like Mavy in a temp costume.

Stunned, Franklin rubbed his eyes, but that did not change things. She was a leaner, sophisticated, southern California version of Mavy.

"College student?" he asked, tapping his fingers on the Federal Express envelope.

"Yes," she said, smiling again.

"What do you study?"

"Intelligence Protocol."

It surprised him that he had been expecting her to answer, "Tidepools."

She added, "With a minor in Industrial Anthro."

"Scotch?" he asked, tipping the bottle towards her. "Oh come on. The boss won't mind."

"Well, okay then," she said. "But just a little."

"Help yourself," he said, watching. She took the bottle by the neck and poured carelessly, splashing. The resemblance was remarkable.

Sometimes he wondered how things would be now, if only . . . Mavy hadn't decided to leave him. Sometimes he wondered if he was at fault. If he had driven her to it. But, of course he had. The way he had loved her was overbearing. He suffocated her with it. Still, that gave her no right—

"How many kids do you have?" she asked.

"Huh?" Franklin blinked. He had been openly staring.

She gestured toward the SUPERDAD plaque on his desk.

"Yeah," he said, fighting a sudden air conditioning

chill. "Two. My eldest, my son Aaron, gave me that for Father's Day." He beamed proudly. "He's a . . . my pride and joy."

"Allen?" She brought the glass to her lips, squinting as she sniffed. Her hair, her eyes. He *felt* he knew her.

"Aaron," he said. "His mother chose the name." Franklin sipped his scotch. "He takes after her. Not in looks so much, but in other ways."

She leaned against his desk, its edge setting off and making more pronounced her natural curves. It was as if she understood him.

"I hope he forgives me."

"For what?" The temp crossed her legs above the knee.

"Huh?" Franklin straightened. What on earth was he saying? And to whom? To this, this college girl, this temp. "For, uh, missing his soccer game." He stared down at the Federal Express envelope. Her frilly signature was not at all similar to Mavy's mannish slash and scrawl. "How old are you, Jennifer, if you don't mind me asking?"

"Jasmine." Her leg started swinging. "Nineteen."

Franklin let her feel the intent of his gaze, which focused on her collar, on her top button. "Protocol what?"

She raised her eyebrows in question.

"You study?"

"Intelligence Protocol." Her smile was still bashful, but somehow solicitous.

"Of course," he said. "Have some more scotch. The Glenlivet. Always say the 'The' if you want—"

The phone chirped.

Franklin picked it up, barked. "Smithers. Oh, Caroline. What's up? Out front? Here? Really? Well, that's a . . . surprise." With the back of his hand, he waved away the temp. "Jessica will be right with you."

"I got that kiss-ass a job," Franklin said, pacing and clapping the back of his hand. "And how does he pay me back? By not returning my phone calls."

"Aren't you going to open this?" Caroline asked, picking up the Federal Express envelope.

Franklin looked out the window. Smog was so thick now it was like fog. You could barely make out the truckstop across the twelve lanes of I-10. "Go ahead, doll. Open it for me."

Caroline ripped open the zip-strip. "It's . . . it's . . . something word-processed."

"Let me see that," Franklin said, grumpily. The temp had made him horny. Horny and grumpy, for him, was like unsalted potato chips, a petty version of hell. And, as everybody knew, hell was most hellish when petty.

Caroline was wearing jeans, Levi's 501s, shotgunned, and biodegradable sequins innerwear under a linen La Loma man's sport jacket. In any other stage of his life, Franklin would find her sexy. It mildly boggled him that he did not. But then, he had read somewhere that sexual passion only lasted a thousand days, and he and Caroline were fast approaching that ceiling.

"Assfuckinghole!" Franklin bellowed, after skimming the document. It was a Xerox of the county statute forbidding development of "live orange grove lands and/or territories," along with a personal note from the city manager, apologizing, unsigned (therefore inadmissible, investigative-journalistically speaking). "The mayor's got constituent-itis on this, I'm afraid." "I got that bootlicker a job."

"Oh, how sweet," Caroline said, lifting up the SUPER-DAD plaque. Another man would find her beautiful, Franklin saw. And he could respond to that. He was at the top of his league. But, just now, she was, to him, nothing more than a babysitter. A babysitter not doing her job.

"Aaron gave me that," he said, pausing a moment. "My eldest——"

"Okay, I'll agree to it," Franklin said. "We'll go to marriage counseling."

"It's too late for that." Mavy stood straight under the great weight of her backpack. Inside was enough food and equipment to last her five days. The straps cut into her shoulders, their edges slicing at her diseased breasts. It was not cancer, not at all, Dr. Ghopal said. Rather, an infection of the milk glands. "Didn't I tell you? It pays to be hopeful," he said, prescribing her antibiotics. But she wasn't hopeful. "This is what I want," Mavy said, nodding at the divorce papers on the bureau.

Franklin refused to even look at them. "Why can't we talk anymore?"

"You're not talking," she told her husband. "You're whining." As if he were one of her children, too. "I'm telling you, I'm going for a hike." He knew nothing about the blood, or Dr. Ghopal. As far as she could see, he knew nothing at all.

Aaron was at daycare, Billy inside sleeping.

"But you can't just leave us here, alone."

It's only five days! she wanted to thunder. Instead, very calmly, she said, "I am alone, Franklin. You are with three people."

"Kids aren't pe——," he began, but then said, "Ma! You look marvelous."

It was the astonishing truth. A second wind of youth had accompanied his mother's release from the hospital. She didn't talk much, but she looked fabulously renewed.

"I've got to get away," Mavy said, squinting at Mount San Gorogonio. Amazing. An hour's drive and a four-mile hike, she'd be in the wild. Bobcats, black bears, bighorn sheep. Columbines, gold, brook trout. Ponderosas, old plane crashes, mule deer, cyclamens, bald eagles. There the names made sense. Slushy Meadows, Dragon's Head Peak. There she had gone before to escape, well, here.

"You," Franklin shook his head. "Stubborn *chica.*" He was grinning, one of his few expressions she could almost respond to.

He tried to kiss her.

"Don't."

"Don't push me away!" he snapped.

"What do I have to do to get the message across?" she asked.

Franklin stomped across the room to the bureau, picked up the divorce papers, and, glaring at her, ripped them in half.

Mavy turned and left.

Franklin watched the battered old Toyota pickup truck go down the driveway. For five minutes he paced. Then he ran to his own car and sped after her.

"Aaron," Linda Delgado said.

"Yeah?" Aaron had his head buried in the maple chest. Newspaper clippings, photographs, old crate labels, and letters were scattered on the floor nearby, along with a "McKinley 1901" poster and a box of bullets, which fascinated Thumper. He couldn't stop licking it.

"Aaron," Linda Delgado said. "Who am I?"

He couldn't believe it. "You are so——," he said.

Eliza Tibbets's wedding dress fit her perfectly.

Now was the time to kiss her. Now. But he refused to let himself, as punishment for what he did to Prudey on his mother's grave.

Billybones used a computer scanner to get an image from the waves plying across the swimming pool.

"Where's Dad?" Aaron asked him.

"I saw him with Prudey," Billybones said. "Conjugating."

"Smartass."

And Caroline, "Can you please make that thing stop beeping?" She was lying in the sun, even though she knew it was cancerous.

"It can't read hydrolucent mediums," Billybones said, shaking the device. "Another piece of unapologetic American obsolescence."

"I've got to ask him something," Aaron said. "Where is he?"

"That's so sweet, that thing you guys got your dad for Father's Day," she said abruptly, bestowing upon him a sunny smile.

Aaron looked at her blankly.

"You know, for his office," she said, fanning herself with her hand. "That Superdad plaque."

"Oh that," Aaron said. Plaque? He had no idea what she was talking about. "That was nothing."

"Not to him it wasn't."

"Where is he?"

"Napping," Caroline said. "Before the party. He has a headache."

"Hey Dad!" Aaron didn't need to knock on the master bedroom door. He was armed, that's why, armed with his discovery, a birth certificate that said Luther Tibbets was both father and husband of Frances Tibbets. "Dad?"

Dad was naked, sprawled out on the king-size wrought-iron canopy bed. His eyes were shut, and he had a thin long erection.

Aaron stopped.

It was Prudey, standing there, in the dressing room doorway, in crotchless panties, cupless bra. Their eyes met and leapt away.

Aaron would picture her like this long after her death—and well into the twenty-first century—every time "Prudence Rises," Amazonas's healing anthem, would be performed at the opening ceremonies of the Olympics.

Aaron pulled the Colt .45 out of the slit in his mattress. He inserted six bullets.

"I'm a real jerk, all right? I'm the first to admit." Dad was bare-chested, wearing only trousers. "Jerk!" he barked, slapping himself on the forehead. "But it's not what you think. Prudence and I, wha!—" He saw the gun, pointed at him. "Sweetheart, Put That Thing Down."

"I said Don't Call Me That."

After a moment, his father raised his hands, stuck out his chest, and swaggered forward. "All right, it's *worse* than you think, Prudence and I— I'm a jerk. God, what a jerk! A jerk jerk jerk! So go ahead, big shot, shoot. C'mon. Shoot! Do it!"

"You killed Mom," Aaron whispered, gun barrel trembling.

Stunned, Dad halted. "Sweetheart."

"So I'll kill you."

Franklin Wells lowered himself to the floor, kneeling. "It just, *she* just went off," he said, trying to hug his son's waist. "She abandoned us."

Aaron put down the gun and tried to let himself be hugged.

Franklin sped up the mountain, finally catching up with her on the Fish Creek Trailhead dirt road.

Ahead of him, Mavy squealed to a stop and jumped out of the pickup truck.

Franklin tumbled out of the car and shouted, "Come

back!" Spires of dust collapsed on themselves. Every-where, pine trees were dying.

Mavy pointed the pistol at him. "Go away."

"I'm not going to let you leave," Franklin said.

The car motor ticked. A jay, very blue, streaked be-tween them, issuing a skull-rattling jabber.

"I said 'Go.' "

Franklin stopped, held up his hands. "I'm not going."

The gun popped, the bullet zinging off a rock at Frank-lin's feet. The smell of sage invaded his sinuses, lifting him, making him feel floaty.

"Go," Mavy said.

Franklin took a step toward her.

She pulled the trigger. The bullet flew somewhere over his shoulder.

"Mavy," he said.

"I'm aiming this time," she said.

"You'll have to." Franklin took another step.

"I," Mavy said. "You."

A shot rang out. Where the bullet went, Franklin couldn't say. "We made a commitment." He was now within ten feet of her. In the history of their marriage, he never wanted to touch her more. "Till death do us—"

"You're dead," she said, and fired again.

The bullet entered his thigh, tore through muscle, sparing the bone, and exited out the side into a little patch of yellow wildflowers. Franklin lunged forward, grabbing her around the knees, tackling her.

"Let go," Mavy croaked, like she was choking. Then she smashed at him with the handle, but it only glanced off his cheek.

He pinned her underneath him, and grabbed for the pistol. Suddenly, it was in his hand.

She clawed the bullet wound in his thigh, causing intense pain. It seemed to him a very cruel thing for her to do.

"How could you?" His eyes and nose ran from the pain. "Get off me."

He pointed the gun at her heart. "I love you."

"I can't understand what I ever saw in you." She tried to buck free. Because of her size and strength, he had to struggle hard.

The gun went off.

For a long time, they lay there. It was so quiet, except for the bluejay.

Finally, Franklin rolled off of her. He had lost a lot of blood. It made him light-headed and thirsty. After gulping the entire contents of her canteen, his head cleared. He felt exceedingly calm, purged clean by a series of strong emotions.

A few deep breaths, and he found himself strong enough to drag Mavy to his car. He stowed her gear in the back seat, and put her body in the trunk.

The bluejay cried and screeched, but it sounded like alto sax. The pine tree it was in had needles the color of rust. In fact, many of the pine trees here looked diseased. Franklin wondered if smog was the problem. Or could it be a forest plague, some new virus? That was probably it. Some new forest plague.

He kicked dirt over the blood-dampened soil, then used a tree branch to rake it back into a more natural appearance. Indian paintbrush swayed in a gentle breeze. High above, a 747 started its descent into LAX. Franklin drove away, leaving Mavy's white Toyota pickup for the investigators to ponder.

In Big Bear, he stopped at an ATM and withdrew $300

from his account, then he got cash advances on his American Express, Visa, and Mastercard, $300 each, giving him a total of $1,200. A security guard in the lobby pretended not to notice his tourniqueted, bloody leg. At the emergency room, he admitted himself under the TV doctor's name, and paid his bill on the spot, in twenties.

"It just went off," he told the triage nurse.

The wound, though briefly incapacitating, was clean, and left him with the barest hint of a scar to remember her by.

Dried juice sacs, also known as "pulp," powdered and mixed with water, produce a thick foam that is highly effective in fighting forest fires.

"Look!" Linda Delgado shouted, bouncing on the diving board. All the women looked in the direction she was pointing. All the men looked at *her*, except for Franklin, lifting training grenades out of the aluminum briefcase. Two years had passed since the last Fourth of July party, when Aaron had first caught his father staring at her bouncing on the board. Since the Prudey episode, Dad kept his eyes to himself. "Fire!"

"Smokey the friggin' Bear!" Uncle Brainy said.

Squat gobs of smoke rose over a hill, red flickers at their bases.

"Great seats," said Dr. Talkington, adjusting the brim of his Stetson. "But until CNN carries it, it ain't national."

Within minutes, a military jet rumbled above and emptied its belly of red powder.

"And you gotta get a friggafudgin' permit for a BBQ?" said Uncle Brainy, eating a third helping of steak, watching the ripples of smoke shoot skyward.

"I better go," said Mr. Delgado. "And hose down the roof."

"Whatchya getting' your doggies all riled for, Manny?" Dr. Talkington shook his head. "Santanas ain't blowin'. No prob."

"We should water the grove," Aaron said. He found adults pathetic whenever they started with their ain'ts and friggin's and no probs.

The sirens, air horns, and thunder of helicopter blades set off neighborhood car alarms, as if in a show of sympathetic grief. Car alarms were illegal, but that didn't stop automobile owners from using them. The noise was amazing, blunt, embraceable. It tripped the house's security system—red blinking spotlights and digitized barking—which had Thumper's hackles raised.

The Delgado family, all wearing swimsuits, stood on their roof, spraying hoses and dumping water buckets. The Wellses, meanwhile, along with the other party guests, sat in lawn chairs, or stood at the BBQ, and watched the canyon burn.

"Dad, we should water the grove," Aaron repeated.

If the firefighters didn't make a break soon, the fire

would reach the bottom of the arroyo. Flames would shoot up the near side, leaving only the grove between them and the house.

"Not necessary, Sweetheart." Dad licked a finger and held it up. An ash stuck to it. "No wind to speak of."

Ashes fell gently, at different speeds. No two alike, some white, fluffy, fully combusted, others sharp and black, like splinters. They began forming a skin on the surface of the swimming pool. Billybones, chin aloft, stuck out his tongue to catch them.

"Da-ad," Aaron said. "I really think we should water the grove."

"It's really not our concern, Sweetheart."

Dad wanted it to burn. Obviously. Groves all over town, why should it matter?

Aaron got a monkey wrench and slipped out the gate.

The coyotes had taken up howling, a heart and lungs chorus to the mechanized wailing. The fire began climbing the mountains on the far side of the canyon. A single eucalyptus tree exploded with the sound of a wave pounding and with an overpowering blast of menthol. The animals are all being medicated, Aaron thought.

The smoke had rolled up and flattened out into an enormous brown-black cloud. Fires glowed off its underbelly. The twilight was ocher and shadowless.

Aaron ran upslope, terrace after terrace, till he reached the top of the grove. There, a buck staggered out from under an orange tree. It blinked at Aaron, shook its antlers, snorted, licked its nostrils, then stumbled down onto its knees. When Aaron took a careful step forward, the deer rose and fled back into the burning hills.

Other animals spilled over the lip of the canyon. Lizards, rodents, insects. Surges of them. It was frightening. Owls were swooping down, picking off olivaceous kangaroo rats.

As Aaron cranked the irrigation spigot, he heard a rustle behind him. Linda Delgado lurched into a clearing.

"My feet itch," she said. Linda Delgado sat down and began scratching her feet. She was still in a bikini.

A skunk ran by, its fur burnt back, revealing a pink blistered tail. Judging by the smell, the creature had sprayed.

Good for you, Aaron thought, inhaling the charred odor. He admired the skunk's fuck-you attitude. The fire, impervious to stink, said "Fuck you," too, but without a soul to protect, it didn't need an attitude.

"Athlete's foot," Linda Delgado said. "Never really goes away."

"Help me," Aaron said. Together they pulled on the red-handled wrench. The pipe coughed. Spurts of rust gurgled out, boiling hot. It took a few minutes before the liquid ran clear, and even then it was steaming as it sluiced through the network of gravity-powered irrigation runnels.

The fire galloped towards them, gobbling the hillside. Smoke shot up, leaving a wake of superheated air that rippled like clear jelly above the flaming tumbleweeds.

"You have ashes on your eyelashes," Linda Delgado told Aaron. "Ashes, eyelashes," she said. "Asheseyelashes."

A helicopter thudded over, dropping retardant on the unburned brush. The grove was a shower of crimson. It tasted like saccharin in the back of the throat.

Linda Delgado sang, "Eyelashesashes."

Down in the arroyo, the dusted bushes caught sluggishly, then erupted. A blaze of flame trickled uphill, widening into a stream, a river of fire, branching off into forks, swirls, eddies, coursing around fenceposts, splashing against rocks.

Aaron grabbed Linda Delgado and kissed her.

Another eucalyptus tree burst in a flash. The blast of heat caught Aaron full on the face, singeing him. He waffled back, blinded.

Linda took his elbow and guided him back down a couple of terraces. It was like waltzing at cotillion, only this time, she led. "I don't believe you," she said, grabbing him and kissing back.

Aaron's eyes felt full of sand when he opened them. He saw shapes, yellow and red and blue. He *heard* shapes; they rattled like cellophane.

A propeller plane, some sort of antique, dropped a bellyful of white foam.

Linda Delgado cupped her hands into the runnel, splashed water onto his face. She was see-through, glowing. "I'm scared."

After the wash, Aaron's eyes instantly cooled. Still, nothing looked right. The whole orange grove seemed to exist in a state of advanced oxidation—crumbling at the edges, coppery green.

"Aren't you?" Linda Delgado asked, and Aaron saw she had a halo. "Scared?"

"I'm—" He hesitated, fear and desire indistinguishable.

They ran down the terraces, back toward the house. When they neared the backyard, an explosion knocked them flat.

"Aaron, Aaron, Aaron!" she was screaming.

"Okay," he said. "Shhhh." He put his arms around her,

and lay flat. Her hair was a mass of muddy knots that smelled like gunpowder and shaving cream.

"I hear, like, ringing," she said. "What's that ringing?"

Another blow shook them, cracking a tree. Branches sagged, leaves aflutter.

Grenades. Dad was throwing grenades.

"Stop!" Aaron shouted, jumping up.

"What?" Linda was curled into a tiny ball. "What did you say? I'm dizzy."

Jamming two fingers in his mouth, Aaron whistled, waved, whistled. He could see the colored lights reflecting off the pool. He could see the BBQ, and Dr. Talkington's cowboy hat. He could see Dad pulling another grenade out of his aluminum briefcase, handing it to Billybones, who was, oh shit, winding up to throw it.

"Why'd you sleep with Prudey?" Linda asked. "What do all you guys see in Prudey?"

"Hey!" Aaron shouted and waved his arms. Billybones stood there, shielding his eyes from the glare strobing off the clouds.

"Okay, we're safe," Aaron said. "Billy sees us."

They started down the path towards the house.

Linda sighed. "God, I'm so, so, what am I?"

"Bones!" Aaron hollered, as his brother began an exaggerated windup—rotating his shoulder, neck, lifting a knee. The windup, the pitch.

"Bones!"

Aaron hung on to Linda Delgado and they waited for it.

And waited. Behind them, fire crackled and spit.

"Look!" Linda Delgado said, exactly like she had on the diving board. It was Grandma Goretex! Grandma Goretex bearhugging Billybones.

Bless her polytetrafluoroethylene patched heart.

The next morning the world looked old, used, forgotten. The canyon was black, here and there a stand of charred toothpicks, glossed with a patina of red fire retardant and crisped foam. The cemetery had survived—appearing green and plump, obscenely so—but the orange grove had not. Destroyed. Gone. Only the Tibbets tree remained—along with a few in the row closest to the house—and even their leaves were badly scarred.

When Aaron blew his nose, black gunk came out.

Inches of ash flocked everything, the roof, cars, windowpanes. A scum had formed on the swimming pool, which was full of dead animals.

Aaron got busy with the skimmer net and by breakfast had removed two raccoons, a skunk, five toads, three lizards, a tortoise, a diamondback rattlesnake, a jackrabbit, a sparrow, a tarantula, and various insects. Thumper was too heavy, and after a couple of unsuccessful attempts, sank into the deep end.

Above, buzzards cruised, clinging with their wingtips to the thermals, buzzards by the thousands, looping this way and that, soaring as high as the eye could see, higher.

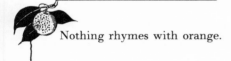

Nothing rhymes with orange.

Franklin hadn't used a shovel in a long time. Doing it made him realize how out of shape he had become, how weak-spined. And his palms had blisters. They looked very painful, but didn't hurt much. Actually, they felt like little pads, cushioning his grip on the handle. Nerves might account for that, and adrenaline. He'd been running on adrenaline for hours. Half a bottle of the Glenlivet had no effect.

The moon provided light enough to dig by. It gave off an antiseptic white light. NASA had men and women up there right now building plastic structures and performing family experiments. A complete lack of breeze held the orange trees very still, their leaves like blades.

At last, Franklin lowered Mavy's body into the grave. He had to drop down into it himself in order to properly lay her out.

Above, a rustle startled him.

"Ma!"

She stood over him, perfect posture, both her good eye and bad eye on him, the good one blinking.

"Where're the kids?" He jumped out of the grave and quickly scanned the shadows. No sign of them. It was the middle of the night; they would still be sleeping.

"Ma," Franklin said. "She was going to leave m——us. The kids and me." The assurance in his voice surprised even himself. He wasn't afraid of what his mother would do, or whom she would tell. He was no longer afraid of what she would think. Her mind was already more than half gone.

"The gun, she was trying, I was holding, the gun just went off."

Still, Ma wouldn't speak. Instead, she focused on the grave, her good eye twitching and watering.

"I had to," he said, not really knowing what he meant, but knowing there was no other choice.

Search and Rescue used teams of dogs to pore over the wilderness. A team of Marines from El Toro actually landed a helicopter near timberline at Tosh's Tarn where they set up camp—including the laying down of a thousand square feet of shag carpeting—for two weeks. But nobody ever found a trace. Mavy's white Toyota pickup revealed no mysterious fingerprints, no hint of foul play. Newspapers suggested bears, mountain lions, falls into crevasses. Franklin donated her backpack and tent to the Boys Club; later that year he would even include the receipt in his tax return as a write-off.

Detectives came around a few times to ask questions, once just after he had finished cleaning the Colt .45. He was wiping machine oil off his hands with a rag when their brown Ford sedan pulled up in the driveway. The pistol was on the kitchen counter the whole time they questioned him, next to the Mr. Coffee. And he had even offered them coffee. And they had even accepted.

It always surprised Franklin, the relative lack of suspicion. But then, he never behaved like a suspect. He was, in fact, deeply aggrieved. He didn't have to invent distraught feelings. Nor did he consider himself a criminal. If he was guilty, he was guilty of exalting and loving a girl who grew up.

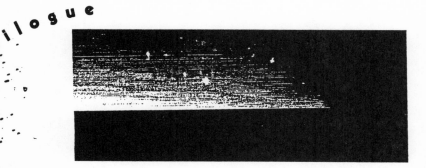

Days of rain had saturated the earth. A small rockslide
had blocked the concrete creekbed, backing the water up
into the cemetery, into the hills up behind the neighborhood. The canyon behind had turned liquid. Stones, roots,
soil, sand, and large boulders were held in a watery
suspension. The colloidal mass expanded, overflowing,
sending its goopy fingers along fall lines. Pressure built,
the dam burst. The resulting debris flow plucked up
anything in its way.

   The rescue helicopter circled the Wellses' house, its
searchlight waving like a single, frantic antenna. From
the sky, it appeared there were no survivors. The split-
level had piled into itself. Cement and timber mixed with
the slide's granite and silt, coffins and oranges and cars
smashed together with a crumpled satellite dish.

   Mavy's skeleton was set free when the last orange
tree—under which Franklin had buried her—was
uprooted. But Mavy's bones were fragmented and decom-

posed, like brown sticks, and went unnoticed.

Only the swimming pool had remained intact, though it had slid down the eroded hillside. Surface unrippled but slightly askew, the swimming pool was now perched next to a neighboring house.

Linda Delgado saw it just outside her bedroom window.

"You get back here, *mija!*" Manny Delgado boomed.

But Linda was already out the door, plunging up the mud to Aaron's.

Grandma Goretex giggled, then swung from the chandelier as if it were a trapeze. Giggling, she fell off. Giggling, she began to sink.

"Grandma!" Aaron stuck a hand through the grillework.

Grandma said something into her headset that sounded like, "Scaredy cat, scaredy cat, doesn't know where jackpot's at," before disappearing completely into the mud.

Franklin screamed, "Mom!"

Aaron rattled the cage of the bed. Next to him, Caroline whimpered, and Billybones stared.

The foam had grown thick and lathery, like a brown meringue. And, though outside the debris flow had exhausted itself, inside the foam was still rising.

Franklin wriggled, unable to slip out of the sweatshirt, which was knotted between his shoulder blades onto the TV arm. Arms spread, he coughed and gasped, facing the ceiling for air, his chin fringed with lather. Onscreen, Amazonas blinked in gorgeous high-definition slo-mo.

Linda Delgado, drenched and dripping mud, saw a tiny blue light like a drop of something shiny between two

Spanish tiles. She began digging with her bare hands, flinging aside splintered boards, ripping away chunks of adobe with her fingernails.

Manny Delgado approached and, panting, slapped her face.

Linda Delgado kept tunneling.

Manny looked down at the drop of blue light, then up at the sky. There was nothing left to do but join her.

Heaving himself from side to side, jumping on his knees, Aaron tried everything to wrack the bed loose. But three of the four poles were jammed hard into the ceiling; it wouldn't budge. Next, he kicked the wall, punching through gypsum board. A moccasin flew off, sinking in the foam. Linda Delgado had given him the moccasins. No chance now to wear them in. No chance now. He said, "Dad."

The foam fizzed and licked at the TV screen, swallowing it centimeter by centimeter. Amazonas blew a kiss. Franklin Wells writhed.

Aaron bit down on a loosened ceiling plank, clamping it in his molars, tugging and snarling like a dog, before a front tooth snapped. But the board came loose, allowing him passage. Now, he was free to help his father.

But he stayed put.

Up above, there were voices.

The foam covered Franklin's face. It tickled his eyelashes. What a funny thing to feel, Franklin thought. *This* is what it comes down to. What a funny little thing.

Aaron saw a slender brown arm poke through the ceiling, the hand searching, the loveliest hand. Aaron held it, and, blood dripping from his broken tooth onto the brackish lather, he watched his father vanish.